The Beauty of Truth

Bruno Bouchet was born in Spain of British and French parents. Having opted out of corporate climbing, he lives in Sydney and writes for a living.

'An audacious, rangy comedy that leaves few modern pieties intact, from self-improvement to pre-conjugal contracts. Bouchet's capacity to identify the absurd in every posturing executive is breathtaking. And I wish I had his eye for white goods.'

Serena Mackesy, bestselling author of *The Temp*

The Beauty of Truth

Bruno Bouchet

ARROW

Published in the United Kingdom in 2001 by
Arrow Books

1 3 5 7 9 10 8 6 4 2

Copyright © Bruno Bouchet 1999

This right of Bruno Bouchet to be identified as the author of
this work has been asserted by him in accordance with the
Copyright, Designs and Patents Act, 1988

This book is sold subject to the condition that it shall not,
by way of trade or otherwise, be lent, resold, hired out, or
otherwise circulated without the publisher's prior consent in
any form of binding or cover other than that in which it is
published and without a similar condition including this
condition being imposed on the subsequent purchaser

First published in Australia and New Zealand in 1999 by
Hodder Headline Australia Pty Limited
(A member of the Hodder Headline Group)

Arrow Books
The Random House Group Limited
20 Vauxhall Bridge Road, London SW1V 2SA

Random House Australia (Pty) Limited
20 Alfred Street, Milsons Point, Sydney
New South Wales 2061, Australia

Random House New Zealand Limited
18 Poland Road, Glenfield
Auckland 10, New Zealand

Random House (Pty) Limited
Endulini, 5a Jubilee Road, Parktown 2193, South Africa

The Random House Group Limited Reg. No. 954009

www.randomhouse.co.uk

A CIP catalogue record for this book
is available from the British Library

Papers used by Random House are natural, recyclable products
made from wood grown in sustainable forests. The manufacturing
processes conform to the environmental regulations
of the country of origin

Printed and bound in Great Britain by
Cox & Wyman Ltd, Reading, Berkshire

ISBN 0 09 941647 6

To Chris

Acknowledgments

Thank you to Chris Sims for his constant support and feedback; Lisa Highton, Andy Palmer and everyone at Hodder for their wonderful enthusiasm; Amanda O'Connell for her great editing; Marie-Laure Bouchet for storing the work in progress safely; David Coyne, David Eichman, Mark Hughes and Jeanne Walker for information and technical advice, and The Mavis's for supplying musical interludes.

'Beauty is truth, truth beauty,'—that is all
Ye know on earth, and all ye need to know.

John Keats, *Ode on a Grecian Urn*

'...*when I need advice on my Whipper, I'll ask someone* whose sales increase is more than a limp 2 per cent! What's wrong, sex life affecting your work performance?'

The recipient of this classic Monica tirade shuffled his papers, remembered an emergency phone call and asked to be excused from the meeting. There was a silent 14 to 3 vote that he was heading to the toilets for a good cry.

'I'd like it minuted that in real terms the Doughmatic, the largest item in our division, has had the biggest monthly sales increase.' Terry used the embarrassed pause to press home the success of his product, the fastest loaf-based breadmaker on the planet with additional bun attachments. Monica interrupted.

'Terry, you know as well as I do, that's an increase on a huge base which you inherited, not created. If there are going to be any minutes, I would like it noted the Whipper has had the biggest *percentage* growth for the fourth consecutive month.' Monica was Product Manager for the hand-held Whipper—it liquidised with a passion and could be wall mounted.

'It's totals that bring in the money,' Terry hit back.

'It's percentages that prove performance, yours are pretty limp too, you know. Any problems downstairs, Terry?' Monica tried her old tactic.

'Don't try your ball busting on me, missy. The only reason your percentages are up is a design fault means all the Whippers pack it in two months after the guarantee runs out.'

'Terry, Terry, Terry,' Monica used the most maternal tones she could muster, 'you sweet little boy, if you think that's a design fault, you're even more naive than I thought.'

'Stop pissing up the walls, the pair of you.' Greg Haddrick, Senior Brand Manager, Bench Top Appliances, was chairing the monthly bitchfest, otherwise known as the Divisional Brand Meeting. He knew this inter-product rivalry was a creative performance stimulator and generally encouraged it. However, it paid to make clear who was in control.

One person who had tried to assert his product but had not been heard was Mark Boyd. His baby, the Whoosh 550 turbo blender, had topped the *Woman* magazine survey as best food-processor for the second year in a row. It chopped, it beat, it whipped and it claimed to chip potatoes. Mark had tried the chipping plate several times at home but had only ever produced annoying potato scraps. He suspected many other Whoosh 550 owners had done the same.

The Doughmatic, Whipper and Whoosh 550 were all Vantex products. Vantex made domestic appliances for the Australian market. The monthly Divisional Brand Meeting was a key opportunity for the product managers to gain an advantage over their colleagues. This was where you flexed your muscles, pumped up your success and posed down hard for Greg Haddrick's attention. Mark never quite managed to out-posture Terry and Monica, the biggest, most assertive posers in the division.

'Bench Tops', so called because all the products sat on top of the kitchen bench, did not have the prestige of 'Stand Alones', responsible for fridges, washing machines, dishwashers and the like. At Vantex the bigger the appliance, the greater the clout. However, under the direction of Greg Haddrick, or Hard Dick as he was commonly known, Bench Tops had performed very competitively and was considered a training ground for Vantex stars of the future.

Greg brought the meeting to a close. He reminded his managers that the Vantex Ideas Conference, FutureVisions, was coming up in a few weeks time and he was expecting good things from his department. He would be making a submission and he expected all his brand managers to do so as well. They could present their concepts to him for feedback if they wished. A wry smile passed around the table. FutureVisions was the big chance for managers at Vantex. Every two years, all the company gathered at a conference venue where anyone was able to submit a concept for the advancement of Vantex, be it a new product, new accounting procedure, or new distribution system. The best ideas were selected by the Board for future use. Massive career advancements could be made. They all knew the conference meant they could leapfrog Greg on the management hierarchy. No-one in their right mind would share their concept with a man who would be their main competition.

◆

'It's complete and utter shit.'

Mark Boyd had presented his concept for FutureVisions to Greg and was receiving some constructive feedback.

'It would be a really smart career move never to mention it again.'

This was not the response Mark had been hoping for. He was convinced his idea was a winner and would finally get him noticed at Vantex. Colleagues would listen to him in meetings. People would say hello without him having to wave at them first. And all because he had the idea of placing great works of art on domestic appliances. Mark had a vision of beauty, of every household in Australia fitted with equipment that would foster the nation's interest in art, develop culture, reduce crime and bring a hearty satisfaction to the nation's meal preparers. 'Turn your kitchen into a gallery' with the Gauguin Toaster, the Van Gogh Breadmaker and the Monet Blender. He was disappointed with Greg's reaction. He wondered whether Greg was planning to steal the idea, but his contempt for it did seem genuine.

'Mark, son, you're doing a good job. The Whoosh 550's doing OK. It's due for a redesign in the next twelve to eighteen months, present some ideas on that—perhaps a chipping mechanism that actually works, that would be a world first in food-processors. But, and I say this as a friend, forget this wanky art shit the moment you walk through that door.' Making sure your rivals did not outshine you was one thing. Allowing them to present something so loopy reflected badly on him. 'Where are you going to be in five years time?' Greg hit Mark suddenly with the hard question.

'Well, I haven't really thought...'

'Exactly, you've no ambition. You've got an engine in your car, but where's the petrol? Just look at some of your colleagues. Terry on that bullshit breadmaker. He's presented me with one, two and five-year plans, personal and professional. Clear goals, clear objectives—he's going places.'

Mark shared an office with Terry. He had seen the plans. The five-year professional plan included the goal of becoming the most outstanding marketing manager in Vantex. (Terry planned to be MD within ten years.) The personal plan's greatest challenge was to be featured in *Business Review Weekly* and to meet Celine Dion.

'Yes,' replied Mark, 'Terry is very committed.'

'He's a back-stabbing bitch whose biggest objective in his two-year plan is to replace me, but at least he's going places.'

Mark agreed. He had seen Terry's real two-year plan. Monica, his other office sharer, would be mentioned next.

'Take Monica.'

Mark thought that no man could 'take Monica'. She was not the sort of woman to be taken.

'Her career time-line is a brilliant piece of life engineering. She's even scheduled in a baby to ensure a full and rounded life. Monica's thought of everything.'

Mark was well aware of Monica's pregnancy plans. Her ovulation cycle was pinned on the wall along with the critical milestones for her current baby, the Whipper. The human baby deadline was pretty tight. There were only ten months left for her to conceive, gestate and deliver and still meet her targets.

'She is committed to grasping career and life and I am prepared to do anything to help her.'

Mark shifted uneasily.

'Mark, you lack oomph. You're not committed to *you*. I've got a course I want you to go on. I think it will help. It's called *Assertion: the Path to the Head of the Herd*. It's a fantastic program. See that on the wall.'

Greg swivelled round in his arm-rest chair and waved at a photograph of himself looking like a Hollywood star. There was a warm glow around him and the large pores which were so noticeable on his real nose were completely smoothed over. The teeth, rather than their usual pale grey, were so brilliantly white that his father could have been an American orthodontist. The hair looked glossy, lustrous and considerably thicker than the live version in front of Mark. It was fascinating the way Greg's very ordinary features had been transformed into something almost attractive. It was like a different person had been modelled out of the same material. Rather than making him seem tougher (few things could make Hard Dick appear tougher), the photo revealed a hidden humanity, a soft sparkle in the eyes suggesting that perhaps there were things he loved more than himself. This was a startling revelation, particularly in view of the description below it:

I am the lion, a natural leader. I kill if I must.

'That,' declared Greg, 'is me. I spent twelve hours in a smoke-filled teepee to find out who I really am. Who are you, Mark?' Without waiting for the answer he declared that was why he was Senior Brand Manager (Bench Tops) while Mark was still piddling around with a fart-arse blender. Mark deserved the same opportunity as those sharks, Terry and Monica. If he failed to seize it and throttle it, that was his own fault.

'So Mark, are you on board? Does leadership beckon?'

Mark's attention snapped back to the real Greg in front of him and his eye was immediately drawn to the nasal hair and the uneven eyebrow as Greg squinted quizzically at him. Mark thought he too could have a glamour photo.

'It would be an excellent idea, but my schedule's pretty tight over the next few weeks. When does it next run?'

'Monday. The facilitator's a good friend. I can get you in. Reschedule your appointments, pick up a brochure from Linda on your way out and go slaughter a goat.'

Mark looked surprised.

'All will be revealed,' Greg announced with a knowing smile.

Once Mark left the office Greg acted quickly. One phone call to the *Assertion* facilitator had Mark booked for the middle of nowhere. Greg, on the other hand, was set for tropical paradise. As Mark was his fortieth nomination for the course, Greg was now eligible for his incentivisation prize: a weekend for two on Hayman Island. If he played his cards right, he might be able to persuade Monica to join him for a spot of semen donation at the height of her cycle—a sun-drenched fun-filled weekend that his wife would chalk up as yet another conference. Mark was the last person in Bench Tops to be sent on the path to the head of the herd. He had to go now if Monica's current window of fertility was to be fully utilised.

He asked Linda, his personal assistant, to summon Monica. He really did not want to take his wife, Jane. Greg's marriage had been successful but now was superfluous. Jane had been useful for corporate entertaining at home, but who did that nowadays. It was an insult to offer someone home cooking when a lavish array of restaurants with stunning wine lists and even a range of luxury cars on the menu continued to open. He and Jane did not have any children. They had never even discussed children and the chances of Jane getting pregnant now, by Greg anyway, were pretty slim. However, his time on *Assertion: the Path to the Head of the Herd* had revealed to Greg that children could be important.

As the lion he needed his pride, and as one of life's winners it was his genetic duty to reproduce. Luckily such duty could be carried out with the delightful, if forceful, Monica on a holiday paid for by the likes of Mark.

◆

'Here are the results from my tests—HIV, hep A, B, C, herpes. Look, have you ever seen a sperm count like that before? Christ, sit on a bus seat after me and you'd get pregnant.' Terry was pushing his claim to suitability for fathering Monica's scheduled baby.

'Terry, if I was to be inseminated by you, sitting on a bus seat would be the only way I'd consider it.' Monica was not impressed by his statistics.

'Call Sheila, call Yvette, speak to that girl that works over in Dishwashers about how memorable her Christmas party was. They'll tell you, getting banged up will never be more fun.'

'You're making me queasy and I'm not even pregnant yet. And besides, you've virtually come in your pants thinking about it. I'm off to see old Hard Dick—now there's a donor worth his salt.'

Monica jumped off the corner of Terry's desk where she had been tormenting him with her sheerly stockinged legs. She smoothed down the navy material stretched over her thighs which passed as a skirt. Backing towards the door as Mark entered she bumped into him.

'Mark, you really should look where I'm going, or at least stop padding around silently. Don't tell me you want to donate to the good cause too?'

'Kind of you to ask, Monica, and I really don't want to hurt your feelings, but no.'

Monica noticed the *Assertion* brochure in Mark's hand and an amused smirk smeared itself across her Mac Glam shade lipstick. 'Oh look, Terry, Mark's heading for the head of the herd.' She swept off to Hard Dick waiting for her in his office, suncream and air tickets at the ready.

It was becoming clear to Mark that he was one of the last to be sent on the path to the head of the herd. Although he could not imagine two people less likely to need assertiveness training than Terry and Monica, he tried to remember if at some stage in the past three years either of them had been miraculously transformed into the dynamic goal-focused marketers they now were. He failed. They had always been aggressive career bitches. Now he too could be one. This course might just give him the means of pushing his kitchen art concept over the line at the conference. He knew it was a great idea, but he lacked the presentation dynamism of Terry and Monica. Perhaps the view would be different from the head of the herd.

◆

In another office much higher up in the Vantex building the legendary David Mygrave was at his desk. He knew full well how the conference could affect a career. Although his office did not enjoy a terrace for cocktails and entertainment like the very top offices in the Vantex building, David could glimpse the harbour—an even greater achievement for the workplace than for the homestead, he thought. David Mygrave was an inspiration to Mark, Terry, Monica and the other bench top product managers. He too had been a lowly bench topper until he carved his niche in Vantex history with his conference presentation of the BF 2000—Australia's biggest domestic fridge. He had transformed the Australian fridge market. Suddenly everyone aspired to a two-door fridge–freezer with the capacity to feed Somalia for a week. Such was the size of the BF 2000 that people were forced to place the fridge in their living room or garage as the fridge space in fitted kitchens was just not big enough. Such was the demand for the product that, as new houses were built and old kitchens were ripped out and replaced, a bigger fridge space became standard. David Mygrave changed the layout of Australian kitchens. Competitors were forced to follow suit, but not until Vantex grabbed an extra 15 per cent of the fridge market. That was Vantex's moment of glory and nothing had eclipsed it since.

Legend had it that the 'BF' of BF 2000 stood for Big Fucker. Machine and man became one over time and David Mygrave, ascending to the dizzy heights of senior management, came to be known as Big Fucker to all who aspired to follow his exemplary lead.

Big Fucker did not have to go through the management hoops that the mere mortals of bench top appliances went through on a monthly basis. Life had been an easy ride for him since his rise. He had spent the last few years in a well-funded semi-retirement. From his harbour view office, he handed out advice and opinions whether the recipients wanted them or not. His god-like status had not been challenged for several years. Now, after being rested upon for so long, his laurels were looking distinctly limp. It was time for the next Big Fucker. Time to blitz them at the conference with another idea that would set the nation alight and propel him to the directorship he deserved. (More importantly, should the CEO resign, and fresh blood be appointed, the new leader might not be adequately immersed in corporate history. They might ask the question: What did he really do? and fail to get a satisfactory response.) He needed a coup at FutureVisions.

David 'Big Fucker' Mygrave was sitting at his desk because that was what he did. It was a gorgeous redwood desk. The grainy patterns of the large single sheet of timber swirled beautifully with depth and texture yet the varnished surface was never anything less than perfectly smooth. The knots in the wood looked like they might cause a slight hollow in the surface of the table but they did not. David had placed dollar coins on edge on the desk and they had not budged a millimetre. Even the ball bearing he had specially shipped over from the factory, spherical smoothness objectified, could not find an incline to roll down. He had cleared the desk of all objects and the ball had not moved. He smoothed his fingers over the scratchless gloss with his eyes closed trying to work out by touch where the knots in the wood were. He felt nothing but silky smoothness.

It was still not smooth enough for creative inspiration. In the last week his office had been cleared of every distraction. The painting, the awards, the photograph of himself at the Malaysian production line, even the BF 2000 prototype, had all been removed. The room contained nothing but the smooth desk, David Mygrave and his genius, which currently sat in a two-gram bag in his breast pocket. David needed all the genius he could get right now.

To get the creative juices flowing, some genius was chopped up on the pocket mirror with the corporate gold Amex—somehow coke always worked better with gold Amex. David snorted, and the coke smacked the back of his de-haired and blockage-free nose and worked its way down the back of his throat. He sat waiting for that numbness in his teeth. It arrived. He smiled. Now he was Big Fucker and he was going to fuck them bigger than ever. All he needed was an idea. Christ, the water on the harbour was bright…a water filter, dispenser, chiller? No. He really loved the smoothness of his desk. He leaned over and pushed his cheek along the blemish-free surface. Mmmm, a fridge with wooden sides so smooth? No. He pressed his lips to the lacquered perfection. A papier-mâché eggplant dispenser! Yes, environmentally friendly, keeps eggplant fresh, chops and salts them for you ready to cook whenever you want. Fantastic. Wall mounted, beautiful. That was it, the big one, the next Big Fucker. He came to his senses.

'It's wank. Come on, think, you've done it before, you can do it again.'

He looked at the desk, and its smooth allure.

'Fucking hell, this desk, it's distracting me every time. Jackie,' he called to his secretary, 'Jackie get this desk out of my office. How many times do I have to say, no distractions!'

◆

Sitting at his desk, Mark thought how drab it all was. He, Monica and Terry each had their own corner, expressing their personalities on their desks and the walls around them. The most frequently looked at item behind Monica's desk was her ovulatory cycle. The '10 reasons why I'm superior' illustrated chart ranked a poor second. Terry's Celine Dion calendar had the days when Monica was due for a period circled. On these days he scheduled meetings out of the office and generally steered clear. Mark thought this was too much bother and, in fact, Monica was at her most human on those days—mainly because Terry was out of the office. Terry surrounded himself with printed signs of his objectives and goals. These were not the same thing. Objectives were clearly achievable practices. Failing to achieve these needed intense examination. Goals were long-term objectives—something to aspire to. While not conceding defeat in advance, goals should not necessarily be easily achievable, hence Terry's stated wish to meet Celine Dion.

Mark's space did not reveal much of his personality. His lack of objectives had been made painfully clear by Greg. There was the odd amusing cartoon relating to the world of marketing and a postcard of 'Sunny Rwanda'.

Mark sat closest to the window, but as it neither opened nor let any sound through it may as well have been a computer simulation. The office was not high enough to have a view, but was too high to see what was happening on the street. There would have been a fine view into the windows opposite, but their tinted glass meant wild orgies of bottom photocopying could be going on all day and Mark would have no idea.

'What d'you reckon Monica's gonna pull for Future-Visions, then?' Mark was about to read his *Assertion* flier when Terry, fresh off the phone, interrupted him.

'No idea; it'll be hidden on her computer with a secret code that will result in instant testicle electrocution if you try to crack it.'

'What've you got going for the conference?'

'Oh, just some enhancement on the Whoosh 550, not really making a big effort,' Mark lied, unable to bring up his art scheme for more ridicule.

'Not the works of art then.'

'How did you know?'

'It's my business to know, got to keep up with what your competitors are doing to stay ahead.'

'I thought we were colleagues.'

'Not at FutureVisions, mate, it's dog eat dog there. Can't talk, got to review objectives.'

Terry reviewed his objectives at 5.15 pm every day. Each day had its designated objectives, graded 1 to 5 in importance. Importance was determined by degree of difficulty, career enhancement potential and personal challenge. At the end of the day the total score for the tasks done was compiled, then the total score for the tasks not done was subtracted from it. Terry had to reach a score of 30 to reward himself with leaving the office. He was one task short.

'Hard Dick wants me to go on——'

'Can't talk. On a deadline. If I don't make this call I can't complete the task. I won't reach my daily target and so I won't be able to leave the office. I'm supposed to be meeting Mike at the gym at six. I've made a commitment to him and a commitment to others is a promise to yourself. I don't want to let either of us down.'

He dialled the agency and bombed out, an after-hours message. He slammed a fist down on the desk.

'Damn, I hate letting myself down. This is shit, Terry boy, absolute shit. Those slack bastards, we pour thousands into their coffers every bloody month, just so they can sprint off at five and spend all the money before the shops close.'

'Give yourself a break, Terry, it's no big deal.' Mark was a little alarmed at the ferocity of Terry's reaction.

'Giving yourself a break isn't the way to become the next Big Fucker, Mark. I've set targets and I've made a commitment to myself to meet them. I'll have to cancel Mike and sit here all bloody night.'

'Don't you have a direct line? They might still be there.'

'No.'

'Dial the switchboard number and change the last three digits, you'll get through eventually.'

'Great, sit here all night and play guessing games. No thanks, Mark, I like to be a little more precise in my work.'

'Fine ... Tell me about this assertiveness course then. What am I in for—dancing naked round fires and making my own music?'

'When do you start?'

'Monday—I'm supposed to get there on Sunday night.'

'So you're going to let the softball team down. We've got a match on Tuesday—you made a commitment, Mark, that's something you'll learn about on the course.'

'I can't really learn about my softball commitment and keep it at the same time, can I? Besides, I'm hardly breaking a commitment considering the last team meeting.'

Terry remembered he had suggested to Mark that the biggest contribution he could make to the team was not turning up to the next game. Terry's pursuit of Vantex excellence included total commitment to catching balls, hitting hard and hurling abuse at the enemy in a friendly game designed to facilitate social interaction.

Mark realised he was not going to get anything from Terry about the course and decided to head home. As he walked out the door Terry shouted, 'Give my love to the goat!' and gave a rather too sinister laugh.

Once Mark was out of the room, Terry picked up the phone and dialled the advertising agency again, this time altering the last three digits of the number. On his third attempt the phone was answered.

'Lavinia, thank God someone's still there. Get me Nigel...

Nige, how you going, mate? Listen, my designs for the Doughmatic Soft Curve, when can I get a look? Tuesday? Great. Good night.'

With a dramatic swing of his chair and flourish of his pen, Terry ticked off his final objective. He had reached a total of 30. He just had time to write himself a congratulatory note for once again allowing his power to shine, and to read his identity statement, reaffirming who he was. Then he headed off to fulfil his commitment to Mike and himself.

◆

In an office somewhere above Mark's and somewhere below Big Fucker's, someone else was taking yet another look at the *Assertion: the Path to the Head of the Herd* brochure. Sitting at a desk that was distinctly secretarial size, Raelene Whyte believed the course would be her big break and really show the world her managerial credentials. As Frank Parkham's secretary she had plenty of practical experience of management. She averted crises, held forts and kept things ticking over as Frank drank through afternoons, bluffed through meetings and generally failed to earn his salary. She knew the organisation. She had done the courses and she had far more understanding of the work involved than the pimply graduates recruited as product managers. Sometimes she felt that trying to switch from secretary to manager was like trying to leap over the Grand Canyon and through the glass ceiling at the same time.

Frank had encouraged Raelene in her pursuit of managerial knowledge and to apply for promotions within Vantex. However, the 'quiet word' he had with the relevant departments when her interviews came up never quite seemed to 'do the trick'. Perhaps the rest of the organisation was not as ignorant of Frank's shortcomings as she had suspected, and a quiet word of recommendation from him was, in fact, the kiss of death.

Virtually all the managers who were progressing well through the company had done the *Assertion* course. It was obviously well respected. She had toyed with the idea of an MBA, but realised that so many educational establishments offered them you could virtually come out of kindergarten with one. She was paying for the course herself. Frank did have a quiet word with a mate who owed him a few favours in training and development, but regrettably he'd drawn a blank. There was no budget allocation to send secretaries on managerial courses and so approval would have to come from the very highest levels. Right now, additional funding requests were being knocked back left right and centre. This in no way diminished Vantex's or Frank's personal commitment to the principle of supporting and enhancing the careers of all employees regardless of their current status.

Rae looked at her reflection in the window as the evening sky grew dark between the buildings. At 27 she was trying to get a job most entrants got at 22. She was pretty, or so she had been told occasionally, but not too pretty. No-one had ever described her as a beauty. This was good for her career, she reasoned: beautiful women were assumed to be stupid. She looked at her clothes. Perhaps the pinstripe suit was just too needy. Perhaps it screamed her wish too loudly. None of the women in management at Vantex dressed as conservatively as she did. Monica from Bench Tops seemed to get away with skirts that no secretary would dare to wear for fear of inviting unwanted attention. Perhaps that was one of the perks of management, you did not have to dress for fear of anything.

If by trying so hard to look like a manager, she only persuaded everyone that she was not, then conservative suits were not the way to go. Perhaps outfits that expressed no fear, outfits that defied unwanted attention because you were too important, were the way to go. But then, would she be taken seriously? But then, was she now? But then…

She was interrupted by the phone. Without answering, she got up and went to the fridge. It would be Frank, wanting the semillon. David Mygrave was with him. Rae was convinced that Mygrave was the only reason Frank had got as far as he had. Frank had been sharing an office with David when the BF 2000 was first dreamed up. Being present at such a historic occasion vested Frank with a kudos far greater than his own abilities ever could.

Mygrave could prove a great ally for Rae. She knew his influence was waning but he still had clout and if he pulled off another coup at FutureVisions, as the rumours said he was planning, it might be wise to be hitched to his craggy star.

She swept into Frank's office, bottle and two glasses in hand, just in time to hear him shout, 'Where the hell is she?' He looked startled to see she had anticipated his request, despite the fact that whenever David came round at the end of the day he always called for a bottle of wine. He sometimes thought she must have his office bugged.

David smiled his successful smile at Rae and she smiled her 'I want to impress you so I'll pretend I'm impressed' smile.

'Rumour has it you're going to be wowing the whole of Vantex at the Ideas Conference,' she cooed.

'Well, I'm giving it a shot, but everyone's there on an equal footing. Anyone could come up with the next BF 2000, even you Rae, that's the beauty of this place.'

'I am hoping to go, but there's only one person can come up with another BF 2000.'

'Rae,' interrupted Frank, 'you're making me jealous. I might just have something special up my sleeve.'

Rae knew the only thing he had up his sleeve was an overly hirsute arm.

'So Rae, are you going to present at the conference?' Big Fucker cast a quick sideways glance at Frank. 'I think it might be a good move—it'll certainly put you in the managerial circle. That's if Frank lets you go.'

'It's a pretty busy time…'

'Oh don't be such an ugly sister, Frank, let Cinders here go to the ball.'

'Of course she's going, and she'll make a great impression. I'll lose her and next thing I know I'll be reporting to her.'

David shifted in his chair, adjusted his trousers. Rae let him catch her looking at his crotch. It always made men think you were interested in them.

'So what's your big idea, Rae? Maybe I can give you a few pointers, tidy a few aspects. After all, we're not really competing against each other—there's no limit on the number of ideas that are adopted.'

Rae hesitated for a moment. She knew competition was cut-throat and colleagues had come to blows over ownership of concepts before, but, as David said, her idea was hardly going to be in the same league as his and his help could be useful. If it were known he had some level of involvement in her concept it might just swing a bit of support.

'It's a development of your baby, David, the BF 2000. Research shows people don't really maximise the use of the freezer section. Plus I've noticed that we've really been losing out to the competition on the ice-cream maker front.

Generally people find it's too much trouble, freezing disks, inserting them in the machine and then struggling to get the ice-cream made before the disk defrosts. None of the ice-cream makers are really designed for our hot climate. So I thought...why not put it inside the freezer. Have a special ice-cream making shelf, with a specially made bowl, that can be used over and over again. It doesn't matter how long it takes to make your ice-cream because it's being made in the freezer, not with a disk, and you can make three different kinds all in a row. The blade motor would be in the ceiling of the freezer and the on–off switch on the outside.'

Rae was proud of her idea. It was simple but smart. Not a huge innovation, but an interesting development and a way of rejuvenating a tired fad market. David looked at her in silence for a very long second. Frank looked at David to see what reaction to have. David seemed frozen, then quickly snapped out of it. His smile returned but not quite effortlessly.

'You've certainly put a lot of thought into it, Rae, but really ice-cream makers are history. You're merging a bench top with a stand alone and that's too big a challenge for the corporate hierarchy. Your Stand Alone people won't like the idea of a bench top appliance trying to muscle in to their territory, and the Bench Tops will think it's a Stand Alone take over. Nice idea but it'll come a cropper on corporate politics.'

Rae kicked herself for not factoring in the rivalry between the various factions at Vantex. She smiled weakly.

'But it's still a good idea for you to come to the conference. Perhaps we'll do dinner and you can tell me what you think of mine...Idea that is.'

'Sure, I'd like that. I'll get off now Frank, if you don't need me for anything else. And don't forget I'm on my course next week.'

As she tidied her desk, her great plan in tatters, she determined more than ever to make the most of *Assertion* and force her way to the head of the herd. As she left she heard the unmistakable noise of the deep sniff and giggle as the boys passed over the wine and went straight for the real thing.

◆

Mark hated trying to get served at a crowded bar. Somehow he always found himself right in front of the taps, or by the sink, or on the line that marked the border between two bar workers' territory. Wherever he positioned himself and regardless of the copious tips from Terry, he always ended up standing exasperated as the thirst of all those around him was quenched before he could get past 'I'll ha...' Terry, of course, never failed to get served immediately. He caught an eye, held his note out and bourbon and cokes were his. Mark suspected that it was all based on looks. Good-looking people got served first at bars. Terry said it was an esteem thing, those with good self-esteem had a noticeable presence which bar staff picked up on. Mark thought this amounted to the same thing. Good-looking people obviously would have a lot of self-esteem. Mark redoubled his efforts and leaned as far over the bar as he could given his position between the taps, held out a fifty-dollar note and concentrated on the all-important eye contact. This time he was moderately successful and it only took three ignored cries of 'Two vo...' before he got the full sentence out. 'Two vodka and tonics, one schooner of VB and an orange juice please.'

The esteem thing must carry through into the general bar area, Mark reflected. Whenever Terry or some other self-esteem-rich person walked with a round precariously clutched between two hands, the crowd seemed to part, almost involuntarily, without turning or looking, as they swiftly and elegantly negotiated their easy way through. Mark faced a sea of backs and was forced into a long round of 'excuse me's repeated more and more loudly until whoever was blocking his path finally heard him and turned round. Mark would swiftly lean back as the person swung their shoulder right in the direction of the drinks to hear what was being muttered behind them. He was used to anticipating every move of every punter in his path.

He never did anything as spectacular as spilling the drinks over anyone. The round landed safely on the table.

'What took you?' asked Lucy. 'Honestly I reckon you must be leading a double life and having a drink with someone else while you go to the bar for us. They'll be sitting there now, thinking, what's taking him so long.' Lucy was Mark's girlfriend. They saw each other a few times a week, did not live together and neither had ever contemplated 'taking it to the next stage'. The relationship had just happened without any of the usual milestones. No 'where do we go from here' discussion after the third sex session. No meeting of parents. No 'there are things I want to say but I don't know how you feel' conversations.

They were out for drinks with Lucy's best friend from school, Janet, and her new man, Jerome. This was a regular occurrence as Janet introduced a string of new men to Lucy. Some people got into a rut of always going to the movies on Friday night; Lucy and Mark met Janet's new boyfriend. Usually Janet announced that this was the big one, and then phoned Lucy in tears on Monday. As Mark sat down, he took advantage of Jerome's absence in the toilets to ask if this one was 'it'. He met with a frosty 'who brought you' look from

Janet and the information that Jerome was purely for sex. They were both free agents who enjoyed each other's company: no strings, no commitments, no misguided attempts to get pregnant on the first date.

'So you and I could whip off round the back of the pub for a quick shag and it wouldn't matter?' Mark quizzed her. Janet replied she'd had better offers and didn't think Lucy was quite that liberated yet. Lucy had shrugged her shoulders, as if she didn't care either way as long as she had someone to talk to.

When Jerome returned he kissed Janet, his tongue penetrating her mouth before their lips even touched. It sent a nasty shiver down Mark's spine. The whole show was excessive, even if Jerome had been a long time in the toilets.

Lucy announced that she and Janet had been discussing sexual adventures and how far they were prepared to explore new territory. Mark wished that he had not been so quick at the bar. He preferred the dreary husband-hunting Janet to this newfound sexual predator.

'I'll explore new territory,' he quipped, 'I'll fly anywhere in the world to have sex.' Unfortunately this did not defuse the situation and the topic resumed.

'You're a handsome man, Mark, only you don't realise it.' Jerome believed in communicating first impressions immediately. Lucy tittered and Janet offered an explanation.

'Jerome is bisexual,' she announced proudly, 'and so am I.'

'I don't like being labelled like that, Janet.' Jerome smiled at his protégé. 'I prefer to say I make love to people, not genders.'

The evening was doomed. Lucy, who never usually discussed sex much, did not seem intimidated and was sharing a little too much in the impromptu workshop that seemed to be developing.

'Yes, it is very easy to get bored with sex: same thing day in, day out; same position; same person. Perhaps monogamy's not natural.'

'Thank you,' said Mark, 'that's me down as a lousy lay.'

Lucy tutted. 'That's not what I meant. Don't make this about the size of your dick, Mark. My sexual needs are not a reflection of your virility.'

Mark had heard this line before and realised it came from the latest issue of *Woman* magazine. Lucy was the editor's assistant. She spent half the day on the phone lining up freebies for everyone in the office and the rest of the time at photo shoots having a go at styling and ensuring all the right products were in the right shots. She took her work very seriously, went on every diet, explored every fad and continually redefined herself as required by the magazine as the modern woman of the nineties. This month's issue had explored sexual needs with a quiz on how adventurous you were in bed. Lucy had decided that a high score was the one to have.

'No, your sexual needs are a reflection of this month's *Woman*.' Mark knew even before he said it that the line would trigger a row. It was a deliberate sabotage of the evening. All sensible conversation was off and there would be no sex tonight, but at least there wouldn't be group discussion of Mark's genitals and how he used them.

'Here we go again. Does my job really threaten you so much? You just can't deal with women talking about sex and you can't deal with me declaring I have sexual appetites. If it was you and Jerome talking tits and bums in a strip club you'd be fine, but not an honest discussion about desire. You don't even know what desire is. Is there anything you've ever really wanted? You've got no passion, Mark, and you resent me finding mine.'

'Passion? You call wanting to come out top on the latest *Woman* quiz passion? Christ, you work for the magazine and yet you're the only woman in the world who doesn't realise it's a load of crap. Your sexual needs mean bugger all if there isn't product that can't be pushed with it.'

'Oh get fucked Mark. Go home and play with your little blender. Whip some cream and smear it on a cake because that's probably the most exciting thing you could think of doing with it.'

'Good idea. Jerome, good to meet you. Janet, have a happy bisexuality. I'm sure you can see Lucy safely home. That's if she's not too busy screwing the Brazilian soccer team while bungy jumping off the Harbour Bridge smeared with peanut butter and singing "Climb Every bloody Mountain".'

Mark stormed off. He had never done that before. Most of the disagreements he and Lucy shared were more sulking competition than actual row. This was real anger and he felt exhilarated and very horny as he headed back to the car. He wanted to go back to the bar, grab Lucy and make passion-ate love to her on the table while Jerome and Janet gasped in amazement. He could feel himself bulging and wished he could just go and have sex with anyone. Perhaps there'd be a woman in the carpark who had argued with her boyfriend and was storming to her car which just happened to be next to his. They would look at each other and be overcome with desire on the bonnet of his Festiva.

There was no fumingly passionate woman in the carpark. He would have to dig out those old magazines.

Inside, Lucy turned to Janet. 'See, I told you he couldn't deal with it. All that was just a show to get out of talking about sex.'

'Mmm,' said Jerome, looking thoughtfully at the space

where Mark had been standing. 'He's clearly got a lot of issues to work through, but he was quite forceful wasn't he?' Lucy looked puzzled until Janet drew her attention.

'So what is the most outrageous sexual desire you've ever had? Be honest.'

◆

The Hayman Island trip was not turning out as Greg had expected. His vision of lying by a sun-drenched pool, drinking, and shagging Monica in every conceivable place began crumbling on the flight up there.

He had ordered his usual gin and tonic, only to have it promptly changed by Monica to a mineral water. Greg was carrying a valuable cargo which had to be carefully handled. He thought his luck was in when she inquired about his underpants, but she only wanted to know their type. They were briefs, and two sizes too small to make his tackle stick out. Monica ordered him to the toilet to remove them and put on looser boxer shorts she thoughtfully provided. His underpants were damaging his sperm and every moment he spent in them was knocking points off her baby's IQ. The effects on the child of impregnation at high altitudes had not been researched, so Monica was not interested in Greg's suggestion she help him change.

Greg's removal to the toilet served an additional purpose. As he crashed and banged on the tiny cabin walls, she had time to go through his briefcase and search for information on his Ideas Conference presentation. Sensibly he trusted no-one at Vantex and had not left anything behind that might be accessed while he was away. Her expert fingers flipped over his documents at high speed, until at last she found a folder headed *Misc Notes To Be Filed*. She smiled at this pitiful disguise of his important work. It was the equivalent of a fake moustache. Opening it, she browsed the contents, glancing up every ten seconds to check if the toilet engaged sign had gone out. The proposal had merits. It wasn't a jump up and slap you across the face with a directorship idea, but she knew Greg would give it some zing when presenting.

Her mind did a lightning analysis as to whether it was a better proposal than hers and decided it probably was not. Still it was worth keeping up her sleeve in case her concept was 'pre-presented' by some other colleague. She memorised the key points just in time to see the engaged light go off and quickly returned the files to Greg's case.

◆

Sex had never been such work for Greg. It was timed to the second and linked precisely to Monica's body temperature. He did his best to hold back each ejaculation and then let rip as far inside Monica as he possibly could. He imagined his sperm flying bang into her fallopian tubes, traversing the uterus in a split second. He had plenty of time to contemplate its progress as he had to help Monica stand on her head for thirty minutes after each session. She did not share his confidence in the magnificent firing power of his pistol.

There was no alcohol, no smoking, no fatty food and no dessert. Any hint of additives and the meal was sent back to the kitchen. Greg was just a vessel carrying a cargo and Monica was ensuring it arrived in top shape; the vessel's feelings were as irrelevant as an oil tanker's.

In bed at night he lay awake thinking of his little sperm. He felt quite naughty, actually trying to get someone pregnant. It was different from the many times he had slept with other women. They were just fun. No feelings of guilt had ever entered his mind as he returned home and showered off the 'other woman' smell. Early in his marriage, Greg had made a habit of always showering as soon as he got home. That way, when he needed to, it was not suspicious. Here with Monica he was doing what he and Jane should have been doing all these years.

◆

It was their last night. Greg, exhausted and irritable, was beyond the sleeping threshold. His tired, half dreaming, half imagining mind had got to Monica giving birth. Instead of hearing the news over the phone in his office, proudly pulling at his pants at another job well executed, he was in the hospital overcome with emotion, biting through the umbilical cord.

The alarm rang, Monica woke and the confused thoughts of dawn, umbilical cords and Jane were thrown aside as Monica once again demanded his attention, coaxing his limp penis. After a night of challenging thoughts and very little sleep, the chief concern for Greg was being able to perform at all. This was the worst worry he could have. Nothing stopped a man performing like the fear of not being able to. He seized Monica's breasts in his hands and imagined milk squirting out into his mouth. He clamped his mouth onto one of them and sucked as if coaxing milk production. He imagined himself showered in warm white liquid as it gushed from her abundant breasts. The smell of mother's milk rose in his nostrils and he felt himself hardening. Monica sat astride him and he pulled her towards him.

'Back to work Daddy, it's your morning shift.'

That was as playful as she got.

As usual, Monica instructed him how to move, where to position himself, on the best angle for maximum penetration and how to stimulate her manually. Greg noted that she at least was determined to enjoy herself. According to *Woman* it was good for a child if the mother reached orgasm during conception.

As demanded he was holding her back with one hand, reaching down to stimulate her clitoris with the other, while still somehow finding the balance to maintain the rhythmic action required. It wasn't working. His feet lost their grip on the sheets and every time he tried to thrust, he slipped. Instead of showering him with imagined milk, Monica's breasts just banged on his head. Every time he gasped for breath, a breast got in his mouth or squashed his nostril. Monica began her steady chants of 'yes'. His back was sore, his face was sweaty and his thumb was getting cramped. Normally the powerful stimulation from his dick was enough to counter all this, but not this morning. He could feel himself growing flaccid as Monica's riding grew more desperate.

'Come on, give it to me,' she demanded, but he knew he could not. He had given her so much. He was a spent force. He had been impressed with his stamina over the last two days, but on this, the final day, he stumbled. They stopped. He fell back on the bed, happy to breathe easily again and relieved that it was over. Perhaps now he might get some time by the pool.

'You've done pretty well for a man your age,' Monica conceded. She realised some nice words were required. Greg was her boss after all. Not being able to perform would severely dent his ego and there was no knowing how he might react to failing a test of manhood. 'In fact the only reason I've driven you so hard is because you seemed so capable. I don't know any man who could have done as much. You're great in bed. It's fun making babies isn't it?'

'Fun.' That was all Greg could say. Old Hard Dick had failed. He knew she was being conciliatory. He was her boss after all. He could make life, if not his dick, very hard. They understood each other well.

◆

Mark was sitting on the Blue Mountains train with absolutely nothing apart from the clothes he was wearing. This was as instructed. The *Assertion: the Path to the Head of the Herd* brochure had said participants were not allowed to bring anything. All clothes and bathroom requirements would be provided. Those on essential medication were allowed to bring it, but medication did not include vitamin supplements. There were to be no reading materials: no books, newspapers or magazines. There was no explanation for the rules, but on the course, the brochure promised, they would 'travel through anger, frustration and disappointment to discover the true meaning of strength, leadership and determination'. The brochure's final words of wisdom were 'Expect nothing and gain everything.' Mark hoped they had not paid an agency too much for that copywriting gem. He was already travelling through anger and frustration on the train with nothing to do or read. All he could do was stare out the window.

The brochure had induced severe doubts about the course. Images of running naked through trees and finding the wild warrior within popped up with every paragraph. It did not help that *Assertion* was held in the Blue Mountains, the top drop-out destination for tired Sydney types. It was probably run by a former chief executive of a major corporation. He'd have had some life-altering experience: cancer, divorce, a drug habit or the near loss of a child, realised there was more to life and retired to the mountains to set up a more nurturing business.

Through the window the expanse of Sydney was a continual surprise. Mark hardly ever ventured beyond the edges of the inner city. Now the sprawl seemed to go on endlessly past his window. Indistinguishable suburbs had nothing to boast of other than the size of their Westfield Shopping Towns and the number of screens in their local Multiplex cinemas. The ascent to the Blue Mountains at least broke the monotony of the journey and gave an opportunity to view the urban area as a vast whole. Looking down on it from the train, Mark was daunted by the task that lay ahead of him. Standing out from all this was a tall order. The city was so big that any difference in a person could quickly be absorbed. From here, Hard Dick did not seem so special. His Hollywood portrait was probably one of hundreds hanging on office walls. How many Terrys were there totting up their day's achieved objectives in how many Vantexes?

Every time he and Lucy had tried to do 'something different', had gone to an open-air pool cinema or a ghost walk at the Quarantine Station, hundreds of others were all doing that same something different too, looking just the same as them. Sydney was a queenless hive where every drone thought they played a unique role, but really they were all doing the same thing. A jolt interrupted his miserable chain of thought. This no-reading lark was risky business when thoughts like those occurred. Did suicidal people read much, he wondered, and then wondered how many people had had the same thought.

◆

Staring out of the window of the next compartment was Rae. The suburbs were not a monotonous mass to her. She knew them well. Recognising many spots from her past, she was pleased not to be getting off anywhere near them. The train had passed the church where she had been supposed to get married, and like an automatic trigger it set off memories of that challenging time.

Rae had left school with pretty good qualifications but it had never occurred to her to study further. No-one had suggested it to her and she had grown accustomed to hearing Gary, her boyfriend, tell her how he was going to look after his 'little Lenny'—his pet name for her. Getting a secretarial job had seemed sensible. After a month she had learned everything she was going to in that position and discovered how much she enjoyed learning. At school learning things had happened without even thinking about it. She enjoyed understanding new ideas, finding things out, and had assumed this would happen throughout her life. After a month of reception and word-processing she knew this was not the case. You had to actively seek out learning.

She realised she had to change. This did not impress Gary. Serious questions in her work life might lead to serious questions elsewhere, like their engagement. Gary had proposed in an ambush so complete, she now marvelled at his ingenuity. In her favourite restaurant, he had arranged a tape of her favourite songs. Sitting in the blue tie she had bought him (and he had never worn before), he had gamely eaten a chicken liver entree and barramundi main course (the two things she loved and he hated). He even drank wine. With superb timing the ring appeared to the theme from *Beauty and the Beast* and she was lost. Tears, applause from the other diners, a nervous quiver in Gary's voice that suggested he might be unsure of her answer. She had no option.

Within seconds of telling her mother, *Woman in White* (the magazine's bridal supplement) was whipped out from under the armchair and material samples cascaded onto the sofa.

The speed with which the nuptials approached was terrifying. So were her dreams. She had dreamed she was sitting astride Gary in bed, about to have sex, when a giant scimitar shot out from between his legs and would have thrust right through her if she had not quickly moved a pillow into the way. Foiled in his attempt, Gary's smile turned to a scowl. When she woke up, she had already run into the bathroom. She gripped the sides of the basin, unable to believe the intensity of the terror she was feeling.

The terror subsided and was replaced with confusion when she told the dream to her mother and friends. She thought it was a huge, flashing 'Don't Do It' neon sign, embarrassing in its sledgehammer subtlety, but apparently not.

'It's perfectly normal,' said her mother. 'I had bad dreams before I married Dad.'

From there, reality became the nightmare. Rae, Gary and her parents sitting round the table shuffling bits of paper with names on them around various cups representing tables. Endless discussion about the shoulder straps for the bridesmaids' dresses. It was a lunacy that brought her to tears at work, at home, in the bridal shop. Every time she cried, someone said it was a good idea to get the tears out the way so she did not ruin her make-up on the big day.

Eventually, in the florist, as her mother was putting her foot down about peach blush roses for the bridesmaids' bouquets, Rae screamed. She screamed loud. The shop fell silent and then resounded with the slap of her mother's hand on her face.

'She's hysterical with excitement, she used to get like this before Christmas when she was a littlie.'

'Yes, Mother,' Rae spoke in steel. 'I am hysterical. Either you are all completely crazy or I am. I cannot marry Gary. It's not going to happen and I'm going to tell him right now.' She left the shop and did just that.

A new life was required. She left home, got a job with Vantex and started managerial courses. Course after course: marketing, accounting, corporate finance, environmental issues for management. Now, *Assertion*. This was make or break time, she thought, as the train pulled into Katoomba and she looked around automatically for the bag she did not have.

◆

Of the meagre Sunday afternoon crowd at the station, it was not difficult to spot the *Assertion* people. They were the only ones without bags, looking around sheepishly. From time to time they glanced at each other, but as the only thing they had in common was their need for more assertion, no-one made a move.

One man was hovering around the newsstand, flicking through a copy of *Business Review Weekly* as if looking for a feature on himself. Another stood near a bin clutching a bottle of contact lens solution, unsure if it constituted necessary medication, working it between his fingers and ready to discard it at a second's notice. A few wandered out of the station and looked up the road. One man stood leaning against the wall by the men's toilet with his arms folded. He was probably a pickpocket scoping the crowd.

As Mark contemplated the slowly milling group and wondered who would be the first to speak, he noticed a familiar face from Vantex. He could not place her exactly, but wondered what a secretary was doing on a course like *Assertion*. Then he remembered that Vantex, in theory at least, deliberately blurred managerial and support staff distinctions and she no doubt played a valuable role in the organisation. She looked at him and clearly recognised him too. Safe in the knowledge he was not making a complete fool of himself, he approached her. A wave of interest bristled through the group.

'You're from Vantex, aren't you?'

'Yes,' the woman replied. 'You're Mark Boyd, aren't you, product manager in Bench Tops. Sorry, can't remember which particular baby's yours.'

'I'm afraid I don't...' Mark was worried that she knew so much about him, and slightly put out that she did *not* know his baby was the Whoosh 550.

'Don't worry. I'm Raelene Whyte.'

'Of course. Hi, Raelene.'

'I make it my business to know the name and area of every manager at Vantex; it puts them at a disadvantage when we meet.'

'It certainly does, Raelene.' Mark smiled. 'So management thinks you need to be more assertive too?'

The word galvanised the crowd like breadcrumbs thrown at ducks. Before Rae could even answer, the *BRW* browser was between them getting a head start.

'So who's here for the assertion course? I think it's about time we did something or we'll be here all night.'

A visible relief broke on the assembled faces. Someone had spoken at last. A few people muttered phrases of muted discontent.

'Does anyone know who was supposed to meet us?' BRW continued. 'Really this time-wasting is not on.'

The general head-shaking indicated they had no idea. A few people started looking through the *Assertion* brochure they had pored over in the train, as if new information might magically appear on it.

'Perhaps there's been a delay,' came a hesitant voice from the back. It was the contact lens solution carrier. 'We could phone. I did bring a phone card.' The final line was delivered in a hushed confessional tone. There was no specific mention of phone cards in the rules.

'Good idea, make the call,' said BRW, 'or do I have to do everything?'

Rae looked at Mark. The course had not started and the group dynamics had already kicked in. 'If he gains much more assertion,' she murmured, 'we'll be invading Poland by Friday.'

They both burst into a fit of giggles.

'Is there a problem?' BRW looked at each of them in turn. 'Someone's got to take charge.'

'Don't mind us,' said Raelene, 'we're here to learn. Lead away.'

'You know your problem, don't you?' he hit back. 'You resent natural leadership in others. You're going to have to lose that if you're to get on here.'

'Great, I can just get the next train back. Two minutes in the station and my problem's been diagnosed and a solution found. Thanks, that's the quickest course I've been on.'

'You're not being very constructive, now are you. If it wasn't for me...'

'... we wouldn't be making fools of ourselves, would we?' finished Raelene.

'I think I might intervene now.' The man who had been

standing by the toilets moved to the centre of the group. He was not a pickpocket; he was a facilitator.

'My name is Brian and I'm one of your facilitators. Welcome to *Assertion: the Path to the Head of the Herd.* You have already begun your first exercise. The coach is waiting outside. We'll debrief on the way to the camp.'

Twenty-six forlorn participants boarded the bus. The relief of having been collected loosened tongues and the questions flowed.

'Shouldn't we do some sort of roll call? What if we've left someone behind?'

'Your collective spirit is commendable,' replied Brian, 'but this program is about initiative and commitment. Everyone who is really committed to doing the course is on this bus.'

'But what if someone missed the train, I nearly did,' offered Contact Lenses.

'As I said, anyone who is really committed is on this bus. You left home in time to ensure you got the train, they should have as well.'

'What if there are people here who shouldn't be?' BRW looked at Rae as if he knew a dark secret. She squirmed, thinking she was probably the only one who had to pay for herself. Perhaps she did not really belong here. Brian set her mind at rest.

'Well then, they should be congratulated for determination and initiative in finding out about the course, getting to the meeting place and climbing on the bus. They deserve to be here more than the person who could not catch the train. All I know is I have a group of people on a bus, determined to be leaders.'

They had done quite well in taking only ten minutes to reach the point of 'collective activity', Brian told them. One group had not even made it past the station. They had all got the next train back to Sydney without ever speaking to each other.

Brian outlined the rules for the course. There was to be no outside contact. No phones, radio or television, or reading of any kind. The only things they were allowed to read were what they wrote 'as a group'. Apparently reading reduced creative flow. They were there to bring things out of themselves, not put things in.

All participants would receive tracksuits to be worn throughout the course—a clean set each day. Watches were to be handed in. No-one would be able to use the trappings of everyday life to establish prestige. They were all there with clean slates.

Food would be provided at necessary times. Those on medication would be provided with it when needed. Everyone had to complete each course component, no matter how long it took. There were no time limits. The course was open-ended and it was made clear to employers that the participants might take longer than the estimated week to complete it.

'This is a challenging course,' Brian was finishing off, 'you'll face things about yourself perhaps you don't want to. We are deliberately removing all the external prompts that tell you who you are or what you should be doing. It's only then you can discover the real you. It's bloody hard but giving 100 per cent is the easiest way of doing the course, believe me. When you hand in the trappings of your normal life, hand in your inhibitions too.'

Mark gulped. Talk of inhibitions nearly always led to parading around naked. Not a thought he relished. His body was not great. He went to the gym, but not with Terry's single-minded purpose. Perhaps the course would give him the determination to achieve the body he wanted. Feeling good about your body gave you inner confidence. He had read that often enough. Good-looking people got away with so much more. He too could have a set of physical development goals along with career and lifestyle goals, just like Terry. Yet he did not really want to be like Terry. He was on this course to grasp something, but what? If only he knew what it was, then his potential would be unlimited. He would have the drive to make his kitchen art the greatest idea in the history of appliances.

The coach plunged on into the evening. As night fell, it seemed to journey into a black void. With nothing to see out of the window it was difficult to tell whether the coach was moving at all, or just jigging on the spot.

◆

The first full day of the course started with ripping up sheets of cardboard. This was supposed to alleviate tension and teach them not to be afraid of destroying things. Apparently one of the things that inhibited unassertive people was fear of the negative impact of their actions.

After the cardboard they moved into the canteen to start on the crockery. Brian, the facilitator, casually dropped a cup on the hard linoleum floor, while explaining the importance of releasing anger in safe ways. Soon they were all releasing anger safely by smashing plates, cups and saucers.

Mark and Rae smashed a few items and enjoyed the child-ish glee of feeling naughty yet realising they were not going to get told off. Contact Lenses managed a cup, a side plate and a dinner plate that was already chipped. Everyone had smashed their fill and was surveying the sea of broken white except for BRW who refused to stop until every piece of crockery in the room was destroyed.

The facilitator for the next exercise was Lorraine. A trained psychiatrist from the UK, she had turned her back on conventional therapy and focused on helping people through role-play activities.

'I want everyone standing in a circle,' she declared in her identikit Northern English accent. A circle formed of uniform grey tracksuits. 'Is everyone here?' asked Lorraine.

They all looked at each other, as if they could remember all the faces. A few shouted yes. Lorraine declared everyone had to take responsibility for the decision and asked each person individually if everyone was there. She came to Maureen, an executive with an improvable sales record. She had smashed a respectable four plates and had carefully counted all the people present.

'I think there's supposed to be twenty-six of us but I only count twenty-five.'

'So who's missing?' Everyone looked around, but without the aid of individual dress it was difficult.

'Is Mike here?' asked BRW. Mike answered yes from two places up.

'The guy with the contact lenses, he's missing,' said Mark. No-one seemed to hear him, apart from BRW.

'It's that guy with the contact lenses,' said BRW, as if the mystery had now been solved.

'So what are we going to do about it?' asked Lorraine.

'Nothing. Let's move on.' BRW asserted himself again.

'But the rule is, everyone has to complete all parts of the course.'

Mark decided to intervene before it got painful.

'Let's go and look for him,' he practically shouted to

ensure he was heard. They divided up the areas and set off to search. Mark had been given the toilets and was not surprised to find Contact Lenses there.

'Hi, I'm Mark, sorry I can't remember your name, but we're looking for you. We can't do the exercise without you.'

'It's Ian and I've lost a contact lens. It was hurting my eye so I had to take it out but then I got a shiver down my spine and dropped it somewhere down here.' He indicated the expanse of the tiled floor.

'You'll never find it now. Have you got a spare?'

'No, we weren't supposed to bring anything.'

Ian did not have glasses either, in a very strict interpretation of the no-luggage rule.

'Come back to the group. We can sort something out.'

There were a few cheers as Mark and Ian walked into the meeting room. Mark explained the situation to the group. Ian tried to focus through his one lensed eye by closing the other. It was giving him a headache and he suspected it did not look very assertive.

'Does anyone have any suggestions for Ian?' asked Lorraine.

'Yes, go home,' shot BRW.

'That's not very constructive,' Lorraine replied. 'Ian's problem is everyone's problem.'

It was getting frustrating. A few tuts and sighs were heard. In the absence of suggestions, Lorraine asked Ian why he wore contact lenses. He was short-sighted and needed them for television and reading at a distance. Lorraine pointed out there was no television on the course and limited reading opportunities.

'But I can't just wear one lens, it's giving me a headache,' Ian complained.

'So?' said Lorraine. There was a pointed silence and Lorraine willed him to make the right conclusion with wide open eyes and a nodding head.

'So...I could take this one out and just make do.'

'Yes,' shouted Lorraine, jumping up and clapping her hands, 'that's fab. You don't need contact lenses here. Free yourself. Glasses and contact lenses can become a prop, a barrier to protect us, or hold us back. They are tools to help us and when we don't need tools we should put them down. You don't carry a hammer with you all the time just in case you might want to bang in a few nails, do you?'

Everyone was thrilled. Ian joyfully removed the offending lens and tossed it away to the cheers of the group.

'And lo the blind shall see,' thought Mark. By the end of the week, he suspected they might all be friends with Jesus. The hammer story had the terrifyingly simple logic that some Christians used to justify castrating themselves and jumping on a spaceship.

'Right. Are we all here?' Lorraine asked again. Everyone shouted a gleeful 'Yes'.

'This next role-play is called Spaceship.'

Spaceship, Lorraine explained, was a really smashing role-play for challenging how they viewed themselves. The whole group was aboard a spaceship, flying through the universe to start a new life on a new planet. However, the ship was malfunctioning and they had lost almost all their oxygen. The emergency capsule had to be launched but there was only room for six people. They had to decide who was to get on the capsule. That was it. Lorraine stepped back. Silence descended.

Seven hours later an exhausted group of weary space travellers were having dinner. They were eating off paper plates as BRW's zealous participation in the plate-smashing exercise had tested the limits of the camp's crockery supply. More would arrive the following day.

Mark and Rae were sitting at a table with Ian and the facilitator, Lorraine. She was drained. Spaceship had been a bloodbath. The arguing started with Ian volunteering to stay behind because of his sight problem and raged long and hard. Screaming, tears and four ballots had proved inconclusive. There was a two-hour debate on whether you could vote for yourself, one hour on whether those volunteering to stay behind were allowed to vote. Should there be gender parity or if they were populating a new planet should there be a majority of women? Could all the people on the capsule guarantee their fertility? Should they select names out of a hat?

They had tried each casting six votes. Each person was to keep a tally of how many votes they received. With twenty-six people there should have been 156 votes. Somehow 156 votes were cast and 345 votes received. The honour system had cracked under the pressure for survival in outer space. Lorraine was forced to monitor every person's voting to ensure fair play. Just as the ballot winners (including Rae, who was secretly thrilled, but not Mark, who had correctly assumed no-one would notice him) were getting into the capsule, BRW called a recount and seized the opportunity to stage a coup, occupying the capsule with his supporters and claiming to have blasted off. Lorraine burst into tears and had to seek counselling from the other facilitators to deal with strong feelings of inadequacy. Brian came in and closed the exercise with an overworked analogy. It had made sense at the time, but at dinner Mark could only remember that it involved carrying parcels on your back and putting chairs upside down on the floor.

Lorraine, suitably counselled, now felt able to discuss the exercise. Mark had made valid contributions but had not been properly heard, she said.

'That seems to be my problem. I come up with ideas which are OK, but no-one seems to hear them or take them seriously.'

'Do you take them seriously?'

'I suppose so. I never feel very passionate about them. I don't think, this is it, I've got the right answer and no-one else has.'

'What do you feel passionate about?' asked Rae. To her, Mark lacked determination. She wanted to be a manager so badly, it sometimes made her clench her fists. She could not imagine Mark clenching his fists. Yet there was something about him. All he needed was to discover what he really wanted to be.

'I know we're all supposed to be passionate about something,' said Mark, 'but nothing really seems worth it. Whatever you do, you know someone's doing the same thing or doing it better. I'd like to be the best something in the world.'

'The best what, Mark?' asked Lorraine, 'Tell me straight-away, without thinking, the best what.'

'The best-looking man there is.' Mark fired the answer off. It seemed to come from nowhere, or from a long-forgotten hiding place. He smiled, trying to make it sound like a joke, but no-one laughed. They just looked at him, startled not by the answer but by the truth of it.

By the time they were on dandelion coffee (caffeine was a stimulatory distraction), Mark and Rae were alone. Lorraine had a facilitators' meeting and Ian was asserting himself at other tables.

'It's weird,' said Rae, 'getting into management is all I want. Yet you're there and it seems nothing to you.'

'It's no big deal.'

'It is when you've typed all the memos and made all the coffee that I have. You're making a difference, making decisions. It's a chance to get right to the top. I'm not going to be content with just junior management. Are you presenting at FutureVisions?'

'I've got a concept but Greg says it's a load of crap.'

'What is it?'

'How do I know you won't steal it?'

'I've got my own concept, but David Mygrave kind of shot it down.'

'Big Fucker? You told him your idea? Big mistake. He's desperate. Had all the furniture cleared out of his office because it's cluttering his mind.'

'There's only one thing cluttering his mind.' Rae rubbed a finger across her nostrils and sniffed heavily.

'I'd heard that. Well, OK, I guess I can trust you. I want to transform the kitchen into a place of beauty. I want every household to reconnect with great works of art and really appreciate beautiful things so I'm going to put art on bench top appliances. The Degas Toaster, the Monet Breadmaker. Incredible quality reproduction on machines designed to enhance the beauty of the art. Turn your kitchen into a gallery! What do you think?'

Rae stared at him in disbelief.

'It's brilliant, absolutely brilliant. They're always white, except for that chrome phase. Colours go out of fashion, but art...they'll love it.'

'Hard Dick thought it was a pile of piss.'

'You probably didn't pitch it very hard. It's great, I can

see it now. The Mona Lisa staring up at you from the bottom of a processor bowl. It makes mine seem really stupid.'

'Go on, I've told you mine, tell me yours.'

'It's daft really. I thought we could combine the ice-cream maker and the BF 2000. Actually have a compartment in the freezer where you can blend your ice-cream, so you don't have to use those frozen disks which never last long enough in summer.'

'It's good.'

'I thought so, but Big Fucker pointed out it would never get through because of the old Bench Tops and Stand Alones rivalry. Neither side will support it.'

'But if it goes well at the conference, they won't have a choice. The board isn't aligned either way. Go for it.'

'I sort of gave up on it after I spoke to BF. It needs work.'

'I'll help you, if you'll give me advice on mine. We can work together.'

'What? You mean not stab each other in the back and trample the corpse underfoot on our way to the top?'

'That *is* tempting, but I won't if you won't.'

'It's a deal!'

They shook hands. The dining room was empty. They got up to go back to the sleeping quarters.

'You know what you said before about being the most beautiful man, or whatever?'

'Don't remind me,' he groaned.

'I actually think you could do it.' Mark stared at her as she walked off with a surprisingly cheeky smile. He shrugged his shoulders. It was just what had come from the top of his head. He had not meant anything by it, or so he thought.

◆

In the Vantex building, Terry had the office to himself. Mark was off slaughtering goats and Monica had not made it back from her mysterious weekend away. The timing was perfect for a little espionage. He knew Mark's proposal for the conference and did not need to concern himself with it. Monica could come up with something good, though, and she had been particularly tight-lipped lately. This was his year for pitching the concept of a career. Nothing was going to get in his way, especially not a rival colleague who had refused a free sample of his potent sperm. He would show her the winning genes she was missing out on.

Sitting at her computer he tried to access the files containing her project. Scanning through her desk diary and notebooks, he found a few possible clues to her password. They led nowhere. He went through all the names in her computer database, all the objects on her desk and everything he knew about her personal life, which, apart from her pregnancy wish, was not much. He had gone through every baby, insemination and pregnancy term he could think of, with no success. This was his last chance. It was his most urgent task for the day. He needed to crack this code to reach his daily objectives total.

He sat in her chair. 'Right, I am Monica...I want to protect my files...Who am I protecting my files from? Terry... What do I think of him? I underestimate him...I pick a word I'm sure he doesn't even know, being a puny man, and so I choose...V.U.L.V.A.!'

Terry cracked the code.

'Brilliant,' he said aloud and settled down to copy Monica's proposal onto a disk, happy to have met his daily objectives target once again.

◆

The group spent the next morning discussing the importance of setting objectives and reaching them. Mark had heard all the talk from Terry, but here it made sense. They all had to set an objective for the day, involving some level of personal difficulty or, as Brian put it, comfort zone stretch. BRW's objective was to establish a good talking relationship with every person in the 'team' (as he now termed the group) so he would be able to speak about each member after dinner. Ian's was to avoid breaking anything or knocking anything over. Rae had determined to fast for twenty-four hours. Mark could not think of much to do within the confines of the course. He opted to complete the five-kilometre voluntary run that was organised every evening. He hated running.

After the high drama of Spaceship, the day was relatively quiet: information interspersed with energy-building games and exercises to reinforce points. Mark and Rae had tried to do most things together, but the rules stated that you had to pick new partners for exercises. They got together at meal and herbal drink breaks. Rae was a remarkable person, Mark decided, and hardly in need of the course. He had no doubt she would end up heading some great corporation. He was a little dismissive of her view that management was nirvana, but he envied her belief in it, in anything. So far the course had not given him the kick start he needed. There were plenty of useful tools and he was learning that his ideas and suggestions were generally some of the best, but nothing gave him 'oomph'.

Rae sat through dinner, stoically sipping her water with a dash of lemon juice and honey. Ian walked slowly and carefully between the buffet table and his seat, focusing on the plate in his hands. Unfortunately, not everyone else was focused on him. Just as he was walking past the final table, someone pushed their chair back and leaped up, knocking Ian's elbow. His tight grip meant the plate stayed in place, but the food was sent flying. He did his best to catch it as it began to fall, but his face did a better job than the plate.

There were embarrassed giggles from the tables around him. His assailant apologised profusely and attempted to help wipe up the mess. Taking all the blame, he tried to reassure Ian that he had not failed in his objective. Ian smiled through the ratatouille, but knew that no-one else suffered such accidents. It may not have been his fault, but *somehow* he had caused it. His lack of presence meant that no-one was aware of him as he walked past their chairs with a plate of food. To reinforce the point he heard the unmistakable voice of BRW. 'What a loser.'

After dinner, BRW made everyone stay in their places. He had picked the most showy objective, determined to have a bigger comfort zone stretch than anyone else. He'd spent the day striking up conversations with all the people he had hitherto ignored and asking them what they knew about the others on the course. This way he could surprise everyone with what he had discovered. Going through his mates first, to warm up, he told stories about each of them involving beer, women and embarrassing moments. Josh had once puked in El Alamein fountain in Kings Cross; Mikey had kissed a drag queen, thinking she was a real woman until he went for the 'tit-squeeze'; Col was a triathlete whose swimmers had once come off.

Rae was glad she had not eaten, as she was ready to be sick by now. It made her realise that for all his faults Gary, her ex-fiancé, was no different from other blokes. It did not matter how well educated they were, all they were interested in was beer and dicks. They might talk about tits and women but what really fascinated them were their own genitals. She was pleased to catch Mark rolling his eyes. She thought he might be different, and then realised it was pathetically unlikely. This was promptly followed by the inevitable 'I hope he's not gay' reaction. She was feeling doubly predictable when BRW announced her name.

'And over there we have our very own anorexic, Rae, or Raelene to be precise. Raelene is a secretary hoping to break into management. Not only that, but she's the only person here who is self-funding. Her company isn't coughing up the dough.'

Rae could not believe what she was hearing. How did he find out? She had not told him. He was looking at her with a smug raised eyebrow. 'I think we should all give her a round of applause for trying so hard. Don't you?' He led the clapping.

'Give it a rest,' she shouted, stung and embarrassed. 'Your gossip isn't interesting anyone, you know.'

'I'm only trying to achieve my objective. We're supposed to help each other on this exercise.'

'Your objective seems to be putting everyone down. I don't think I want to help in that.'

'Really Rae, you know there's no "I" in teamwork.'

She could not believe he had rolled out such a pathetic old maxim. She paused, then looked at him directly with a pleasant smile. 'No, but there's a double you in wanker.'

The room cracked up. Mark clapped and whooped,

joined by several others. BRW looked furious. The remainder of his presentation was a low-key affair, the minimum needed to achieve his objective. He sat down, and mentally elevated Rae from irritation to enemy. A frustrating adjustment to have to make.

Mark turned to Rae and apologised. 'I'm so sorry, it was me who told him. I really admire the fact you're so determined and that you're not here because someone else said you should be. I had no idea he'd use it like that.'

The success of having turned the tables on BRW meant Rae did not feel angry any more. She accepted the compliment.

◆

Lucy picked up the phone in her living room. Mark's number was on speed dial. That would have to change, she thought as his phone rang. As expected, she got his answering machine.

'Hi Mark, it's Luce here. Look, I know you're on your course hugging trees or whatever but I've got to say this now. I can't put my life on hold for you any longer. The other night with Janet made me realise just how much you're limiting me. I need so much more than what you can offer. So it's over. OK...Sorry...Bye.'

That had been easier than she thought. She adjusted her dressing-gown, feeling it rub against her naked breasts. Her skin felt like silk. Her thighs rubbed lightly together as she walked seductively into the hall of her apartment. Looking in the mirror, she thought she had never been sexier. Dumping a loser boyfriend obviously agreed with her. She was a siren, a sex goddess. She had wild and exotic tastes which Mark had kept locked away. She envisaged herself in a leather corset, six-inch heels and a whip. Dominatrix of the World. Then she noticed the coffee stain on her dressing-gown lapel. The terry towelling would have to go, she decided, as she made her sultry way to the bedroom.

Pausing at the doorway, allure oozing from her every pore, she looked towards her bed. Janet was lying there naked, sighing gently to herself and trying to wipe away the hair stuck to her face with chocolate body paint. Jerome, still in his leopard-print G-string, was astride her on his knees. He had a joint in his mouth and was banging a thin white object on the palm of his hand.

'Got any batteries, love? The vibrator's dead.'

◆

Had Mark known that the next day's activity would be running around in the bush he would never have set a five-kilometre run as his objective. He had completed it without too many problems and had even been quite impressed with his aerobic fitness. But the following morning, as he showered and climbed into his clean tracksuit for the day, he was stiff. His thighs ached and he felt he was walking like a geriatric waiting for a hip replacement.

The group assembled outside. On the far side of the courtyard the rainforest began. A few paths led through it. The run on the previous evening had taken them down one of these paths, but in the daylight Mark could not tell which one.

Brian came out to address them.

'For many people this is the most challenging part of the course. Few of you will be exactly the same person tonight as you are now. We are stripping away layers of civilisation, of learned behaviour, and we are getting down to the raw materials that really make us who we are. The most basic thing that humans do, and what we still do every day of our lives, is gather food. Every day as managers and leaders you are hunting. Seeking out your deals, competing for your clients, winning the struggle with the economic elements that rule in the urban jungle. Today we take away the pretence. Today we take our jobs back to their purest, most primeval form. You are going on a hunt.'

At this word, Lorraine and the other facilitators burst from one of the storage sheds carrying spears and knives. The participants were given one of each. The sound of comfort zones being stretched to breaking point was deafening. Eyes widened and stared. Who were they going to hunt?

'In this forest,' continued Brian, 'live feral goats. They escaped from a farm several years ago and are now a nuisance. We want you to hunt a goat. You can work in teams, pairs, alone, however you want. We will also be in the forest to check on your progress and give assistance. Along with your spear and knife you will receive a whistle. If you need assistance of any kind, blow it and we will come to your aid. The forest is extensive but has a perimeter fence. Do not go beyond the fence, or we may not be able to find you. Any questions?'

Rae was incredulous. 'Are you actually expecting us to kill something?'

'That is entirely your decision. There are no expectations in this exercise. You are hunting goats in order to learn about yourselves.'

'Are we supposed to drag the carcasses back here when we're done?' Another question from the bemused group.

'When you feel you have completed the exercise, stay put and blow your whistle. We will come to you.'

Like forlorn extras from a low-budget remake of *Lord of the Flies*, the hunters moved off into the rainforest. BRW had gone bounding ahead with a whoop, only to get his spear caught on some undergrowth, winding himself on the shaft. Mark, Rae and Ian set off together. The rest of the group could be heard far and wide asserting themselves through the trees. Any feral goats in the vicinity would have sprinted for cover immediately and would be busy eliminating native flora in some undisturbed part of the forest. It was a hopeless task, thought Mark.

It seemed like they had been trekking along paths for several hours without so much as a sighting. Apart from a few birds calling from the safety of the tree tops, the journey had been devoid of other living creatures. They had heard a few charges and screams from their co-coursers earlier, but even those had died out. They were alone. Mark was increasingly sore after the triumph of meeting yesterday's objective. Rae was feeling weak having only just broken her 24-hour fast. Ian was quietly processing the food spill of the previous day. He had almost workshopped himself to the point of believing it was not his fault when he tripped on a tree root and had to begin again.

Coming to a clearing in the forest where a tree had fallen, they decided to take a rest and perhaps plan some other strategy. It was a warm day with the forest canopy protecting them from the harshness of the sun. The forest smelled fresh. Once the sounds of their own movement had stopped there was a stillness which they all sensed and enjoyed. After three days of constantly asserting, challenging themselves and stretching their comfort zones, a few minutes in the tranquil wood was a welcome break.

'Let's stay here and wait for the goats to come to us,'

suggested Mark. He sat on the ground, leaning against the fallen tree trunk, but only after he had checked for redbacks and bull ants. The others agreed. They laid down their weapons.

'D'you really think we're supposed to kill these goats?' asked Ian. Although not a vegetarian it seemed pretty barbaric to him.

'If all the people on every course killed a goat,' Rae did some statistics, 'they'd get through hundreds of goats a year. They'd have to ship them in.'

'It's probably some big test: we all unleash our killer instincts just to prove we have them, then at the last moment we realise there are limits to how far we'll go. Then we get a talk on the importance of finding our own ethics and limitations.'

'That's a very complete analysis, Mark. Perhaps we should just blow our whistles and say we've finished.'

'I'm rather enjoying this, Rae,' he replied. 'Let's just relax for a while and commune with nature.'

They fell into silence, each taking time to enjoy the location. Mark looked up and saw the blue sky through the canopy of gum trees. It was a sight he loved—the strong pure colours. It was Australia, it was warmth, it was nature at its most pure. It put life into perspective and made the world seem so permanent. There would always be blue sky through gum trees. His eyes closed.

There was a noise in the forest. Something moved through the undergrowth. Ian's head snapped up.

'Rae, Mark, I think we're being watched. I'm sure I heard some movement.' They looked up. All was still, but then there was another sound, unmistakable this time, something working its way through the undergrowth.

'Look.' Mark pointed to their right. Just through the clearing something was nosing around the forest floor, digging here and there in the soft earth and then sniffing the air. It was a goat.

'Oh my God,' whispered Rae. 'There actually is one. What are we going to do?'

'I can't see it,' said Ian, looking in the wrong direction. Rae grabbed his head and turned it to face directly towards the goat, just as it emerged into the clearing.

'Shouldn't we hunt it, somehow?' asked Ian, who could now make out a moving blur.

'If we moved for our weapons, it'd run off,' answered Mark. 'Let's just watch and see how close it'll come to us.'

'I've got an apple left over from breakfast,' said Rae. 'We could lure it.' With a quiet stealth she reached into her pocket and removed the apple. At the rustle of her track pants the goat looked up. They froze; it continued. Rae handed the apple to Mark, who reached forward and placed it as far in front of them as he could without moving anything but his arm. The goat was slowly making its way toward them. A move, a pause, a move. It had seen them, but as they did not change position it carried on its way. Glancing at the apple, it abandoned caution and trotted a couple of steps. Rae smiled, realising they had all been holding their breath. The goat reached the apple and started eating. The three of them relaxed. Mark crawled forward, showed his hand to the goat and started to pat it. The goat seemed indifferent. They smiled with innocent glee.

Suddenly, a spear whistled past their shoulders from behind the fallen log. Ian saw the shaft in clear focus as it flew within ten centimetres of his head. The goat started and scrambled back in the direction it had come. As it moved, a figure leaped into the clearing and threw its weight on top of the goat, pinning it to the ground. It kicked and bleated but BRW had it covered. He manoeuvred himself to grip the goat firmly between his legs, holding its head in one hand and his knife in the other.

Mark, Rae and Ian sprang up. Behind them was a bank of six hunters. Another two emerged from where BRW had been hiding. They stood watching as BRW raised his knife and shouted, 'This one's mine!'

Horrified at the impending slaughter and the role her apple had played, Rae blew her whistle hard. Everyone turned to her and BRW paused.

'You can't kill it,' she shouted, 'let it go. The game is over.'

Brian and Lorraine emerged from behind another bush.

'Everyone stay calm,' Brian said. 'What are you going to do? You are in control.' He was addressing the knife-wielding maniac. Mark looked at BRW and saw the knife quivering in his upstretched hand.

'Kill it,' said Mark.

Rae looked at him in disgust. 'How can you say that?'

'He's got the beast. He did the hunt. Let him kill it...if he wants to.'

BRW was looking nervous. Everyone's attention was focused on him. This was his opportunity to prove once and for all that he had what it takes, that he was a hunter. He felt the goat struggle to move its head and heard a clicking sound as it tried to bleat. Gripping the knife harder he pushed his resolve, determined to draw blood, but it was no good. He did not have it in him. His hand and legs relaxed, the goat seized its chance and bounded into the undergrowth, leaving all the players standing in silence.

'OK, let's sit down and debrief, shall we?' said Brian. 'You all worked very well as a team and as individuals. Mark, Rae and Ian, you realised that calmness and stillness were required to lure the goat. Rae, bringing the apple was great foresight. Well done. The rest of you moved quietly and swiftly. For people who have never hunted before you all did remarkably. You have all fulfilled a basic human function. If we were on a desert island, we would survive. You should all look inside yourselves and note the skills you drew out today. How much came to you instinctively? Remember what that instinct feels like. If you can recognise your real instincts, as opposed to mere hunches, then you've got a clear competitive advantage.'

Lorraine took up the talk.

'You all did fab. Let's look at what happened with the goat. We came to the crunch where we knew we had accomplished our aim. The point had been proved. We had captured the goat. What's so fantastic about this exercise, and it make me dead proud to be a human being, is the way everyone co-operates almost without knowing it; that's brill, and it's fab how no-one actually kills the goat. We're not savages, we know a kill is not needed and would serve no purpose. Remember that in your work jungles. You don't have to kill every time. Remember what is appropriate and do that. There is part of you that knows what is right and does it. We've all shown that today.'

There was in fact only one goat and every month for the past few years it had got the fright of its life as some marketing whiz held a blade to its neck and then released it. The clearing was specifically designed to facilitate the climax to the exercise. Brian and Lorraine had a hidden vantage point from which they were able to see everything.

As they walked back to the camp buildings, a sense of satisfaction spread over the group. The exercise, which had seemed at first a wild goose chase, had made them bond and brought them to some powerful realisations. Mark, Rae and Ian were not quite as enthused as the others, feeling they had deceived the group, but Lorraine assuaged their doubts with words of wisdom.

'It was crucial for you three to be relaxed and calm, to rid yourselves of the hunter aura for the goat to feel safe to come out. Without your fab relaxation, the exercise could not have been completed.'

They all felt empowered, except BRW who could not get the image from his mind of the goat's back hooves as it leaped out of the clearing.

'Has anyone ever killed a goat?' he asked Brian.

'We aren't supposed to discuss the other groups, but without giving too much away, yes. A couple of years ago a particularly determined young man leaped on the goat and stabbed it repeatedly. Everyone was horrified. We had to bring in grief and trauma counsellors and hold a funeral. Lorraine has blocked the experience from her memory and has no recollection. Don't know what he's doing now, but God help the people who work with him!'

Over dinner the participants debated whether they had now completed the course. As they had been given no timetable of events there was no way of knowing for sure. But something had gelled with them all. There was a keenness to get back into the real world and start moving to the head of the herd. Several of them were itching to set themselves daily objectives and meet their targets. Ian had even devised a points system. It sounded very familiar as he proudly detailed it to Mark.

◆

The hunt was not the end of the course, they discovered the following day. The group was led to a different part of the forest where a large teepee had been erected. There was smoke coming out of the top, but the rest of it seemed to be airtight. This was to be the climax to the course. No tricks, no hidden lessons to learn. They were going into the smoke teepee and would come out when they knew who they were. It was an exercise based on an ancient Native American ritual in which warriors got in touch with their ancestors and sought truth.

'This is the most challenging thing you will ever do,' said Brian at his most sombre. 'The smoke is uncomfortable. The fire's a special blend of barks and herbs—nothing illegal, but the experience may have some strange effects. You may see people, you may hear voices, you may not like what you see. Participants have emerged from this and completely changed their lives. Only you can tell when you are ready to emerge. When you come out you will be asked, "Who are you?" and you will answer immediately. That's all you have to do.'

Mark flashed back to Greg's photo and could see him emerging as 'the lion'.

'You may be in there an hour, you may be in there a day. You will probably have no idea. Do not come out until you are ready. We will be taking shifts in there with you to ensure everything is OK. If anyone looks to be in any medical danger, we will remove you. You do not have to think of anything but who you are.'

With that, the flap entrance to the teepee was raised. Smoke billowed out. It had a rich thick smell that was immediately heady. They all walked in. It was virtually impossible to see as the heavy smoke stung their eyes and caused them to wince. There was coughing, choking, groans. The facilitators guided them to spaces where they sat cross-legged or lay down. Mark opted for lying down, thinking the smoke might not be so thick near the ground. Once they were settled, a drum beat commenced. Slow regular beats every two seconds. Then the facilitators started a chant. It was the incantation used by the tribe which had developed the ritual, or at least it was a close approximation, as its usage had died out for many years until revived by self-development gurus relying on the none too accurate memories of an 80-year-old grandson of the last tribe member to use the chant. The words were meaningless to Mark, but focusing on them took his mind off the stinging in his eyes and the panic in his lungs as they desperately searched for oxygen in the smoke. Those of the group who smoked were for once at a distinct advantage.

After ten minutes of gulping and thinking, 'I know who I am, I am a complete fool for doing this,' Mark began to calm down. The incantation continued; he could almost make out words as opposed to strange noises. His breathing became normal. His eyes, which had been shut so tightly it had given him a headache, began to relax. Part of him worried that he was suffocating and the relaxation was death coming on. It might be like drowning which, once you gave in to it, was supposed to be quite pleasant. Minutes seemed to pass; he was still breathing. The sound of coughing which initially had echoed round had died out. Perhaps he was the only one left alive. He could still hear the incantation; someone else had survived. The sound took over, rolling in his mind like an aural tumble dryer on a perpetual slow cycle. There was a task in hand. The sooner he completed it, the sooner it would all be over and the course would be finished. But then, he thought, he would only have to wait for everyone else and he would be kicking his heels outside with not even a watch to read. He tried to focus his mind. Who am I?

Suddenly a clear vision of Greg appeared before him. It was the Greg of the glamour photo, crouching with dazzling teeth on his desk reciting his identity, 'I am the lion, a natural leader, I kill if I must.' His mouth opened wide, his teeth grew large incisors and his voice turned into a roar, his hair streaming out like a mane. He leaped naked over Mark's head, displaying his vast genitals. Mark turned to see him land on Monica who immediately flipped him over. The two wrestled and growled on the floor, each trying to dominate the other. Fighting like this they did not see the giant BF 2000 descending from the sky. It hurtled down, casting its shadow larger over Greg and Monica and then bang...it crushed them into the ground. The fridge door opened to reveal David Mygrave, Big Fucker himself. He looked directly at Mark. 'I'd invite you inside, but you'd take up too much room.'

Then BF blinked, and looked at Mark anew in complete awe. He fell to his knees still inside the fridge and sobbed, 'I love you.' The fridge slammed shut. Monica had pulled and squeezed herself out from underneath and kicked the door to. She stood beside it, smoking a cigarette in a holder so long it had to be held up by Greg. 'I want your seed,' she purred, looking directly at Mark. Terry appeared, pushing the fridge over on top of Monica and Greg again, and then stretched out on top of it. He was wearing red gym shorts, his body as honed as he had always bragged it was.

'Look in the mirror you idiot.' He spoke to Mark in his usual offhand manner.

Terry jumped off the fridge and pushed it around to reveal the reverse was a gilt-framed mirror. Mark looked into it. He saw himself, but his face took his breath away. It was the most beautiful face he had ever seen. If ever a man could fall in love with himself, Mark did so at that moment. He traced his finger over his cheek feeling the fine definition. Soon both hands were feeling this remarkable face. This face could achieve anything. This face had the power to change the world. Greg, Terry and Monica had all walked round and were also looking at Mark's face in the mirror, sighing contentedly. I am the most beautiful man in the world, Mark thought. It's true. He smiled, it had been pretty easy really. He knew who he was. He was that reflection. The world would adore him, hang on his every word. It did not matter what he said or did, he would triumph with that face. Mark laughed. Mission accomplished.

Suddenly a pair of hands appeared on either side of the mirror. The hands lifted the mirror to reveal a body standing behind it. As the body stood up, the hands hurled the mirror to the floor and smashed it. It was Brian.

'Sorry Mark, but it's just not that easy.'

Lorraine stepped out from behind Brian. 'But you're doing brill, honestly.'

Greg, Terry and Monica all screamed in horror and vanished. Mark was alone in the dark once again, but in his mind was the memory of his face in the mirror. The pain of loss cracked through him and he clung to the memorised image, determined not to lose this one moment of pure truth. He screwed his eyes shut, focusing on his beautiful self. Rae's voice came to him.

'Mark, you are the most beautiful man in the world, you just have to show it.'

He opened his eyes and there was Rae. She gave him a clay bust of himself. 'Here, do it yourself.'

It was just like his face. The skin, the eyes, the lips, they all had a real texture and colour, yet were solid, like clay. With the vision in his mind, he started to mould the face. It was tough, not like the clay he had moulded at school that you could squeeze through your fingers and burst between your knuckles. This was hard work. Each attempt to move some of the face met with resistance. It would not budge or if it did, it gradually moved back. In desperation Mark worked at it feverishly, pushing over and again with his fingers. As he worked, he realised just how little it took to make a face perfect. He just had to shift an eyebrow here, bend the nose slightly, work the chin a little. He thought of the train ride and how awful it felt that everyone was so similar, but now it was a relief. The difference between the ugliest and most beautiful face in the world was virtually nothing. As he brushed over and over again with his fingers, he made progress. The changes were sticking. It was happening, he was moulding his face.

This work was the most important thing he had ever done. He had to recreate that heart-squeezing image. As he toiled, he was aware of people around him watching. Terry, Greg and Monica all seemed to be pacing about, curious to see what he was doing but pretending not to be interested. Rae flashed by occasionally with words of encouragement. He thought Lucy really should make an appearance, she was supposed to be important, but there was nothing of her there.

He felt exhausted and stopped to rest. The work was not quite finished. The face was very close but did not match exactly what he remembered. Something was not quite right but he could not figure it out. It was like being a child again, trying to draw a face, knowing what a face looked like but not being able to recreate it. It had infuriated him when he was young. He could not understand why he could not draw what he saw. His hands had felt like big clumsy papier-mâché balloons, blundering their way with the pencil. That feeling returned now. Something still had to be done. He searched the face pore by pore, checking it against the vision in his mind. Everything was exactly the same except...

He sat back, reeling with exhaustion and trying to get some perspective. The work was pretty good, he had to admit, the finest thing he had ever created, but that was not enough. It was not perfect. It had to be perfect.

He gazed into his own eyes and saw something was missing from them. The shade of blue was deep and strong, the irises were cleared of the debris iridologists read so much into, but there was nothing there. That was it, he was missing from his own eyes. He picked up the face and brought it up to his own. He was distracted. Seeing his lips so close, he realised it would be his only chance to experience kissing Mark. There was no-one to see, it would not mean anything, it was just an experiment...so he kissed his own lips. They were delicious. He was the greatest kisser he had ever shared lips with. He felt a tongue move into his mouth and reeled from the guilty pleasure that swirled through his body. Suddenly the tongue grew stronger, gripped his own and pulled back hard, taking Mark with it. He felt his entire body being dragged by the tongue into the mouth he had created. He plunged into the mouth which consumed him and left him in darkness. He lay in the pitch black wondering, waiting for something to happen, not daring to assume again that it was all over. He felt weak. Awareness of his body crept back over him. It began to ache. He could feel the hard stony floor underneath him. Suddenly the acrid smell of the smoke switched back on. He coughed and opened his eyes. The smoke teepee was empty save for Lorraine who was sitting cross-legged beside him. He looked over at her. She smiled and without a word stood up and helped him to his feet. He stumbled. His head spun as she held him for a few minutes and then moved him towards the flap.

The light outside was blinding. He shaded his eyes and could just hear Brian's voice ask, 'Who are you?'

'The most beautiful man in the world,' he answered.

There was silence. No laughter, no cheers, no applause. Lorraine guided him to the shade of a tree, his eyes growing accustomed to the daylight. He turned to look around and saw most of the group standing nearby, others were running fast towards him. As the faces came into focus, he saw a sea of wonderment. Jaws were literally hanging open and he heard a whispered, 'My God, just look at him.'

He saw Rae and she smiled, 'You did it Mark, you did it.'

He was confused, the dreams from the smoke tent were still with him but retreating fast into a hazy memory.

'I think,' said Brian, 'on this occasion we can bend the rules slightly. You should look in this mirror, Mark.'

Brian held up the mirror and the vision brought the memory of the smoke tent back to a terrifying reality. He saw his face, the one he had created, and the eyes, along with the rest of him, were absolutely perfect.

Greg sat at his desk, exhausted. He had been back at work for three days after the Hayman Island marathon, but there had been no respite. Monica, not wanting to miss any opportunity while her window of fertility was even slightly ajar, had insisted on three private meetings in his office every day that week. In the past, Greg had fantasised about shoving all the items off his desk with a woman's backside but when it happened three times a day and, each time, she swept out leaving him to pick up everything and put it back, the glamorous allure faded. His papers were in constant disarray. The urgent, semi-urgent and non-urgent trays had been combined on his office floor so many times and his brain was so scrambled from continually having to drop everything including his pants, he may as well have stayed on Hayman Island for all the effective work he was doing. Monica's fertile period seemed to have lasted forever.

He looked up to find Terry sitting opposite him: fresh, fit and with that revolting smile he had perfected. Greg hated him.

'So, how's Monica's baby objective going?'

'That's a confidential matter Terry, I shan't discuss it with anyone.'

'So you gonna be ready for FutureVisions next month? Got your concept mapped out?'

'Of course, everything's on schedule. If you want to run your idea by me, as Monica and Mark already have, I'd be happy to give you my assessment.'

'Nice try, Greg.'

'I thought Monica's idea was excellent, didn't you?'

Terry took the cue and spilled everything he knew about Monica's proposal. Greg managed a smile through his disarray. He may be exhausted and have the emptiest balls in Australia, but he was still the lion, a natural leader. He'd had no idea what Monica was planning, but Terry rectified that. As for Terry's plan, he had been fully briefed by the ad agency which was secretly helping Terry out.

Linda, his personal assistant, buzzed through. She sounded dazed.

'Greg... Mark is back from his course, and he'd, er, like to see you.'

'Send him in. This should be interesting,' he added to Terry, 'apparently he was four days in the teepee, played havoc with everyone's schedule and made quite a...'

Greg's voice trailed off as the door opened and Mark entered. It was the first time he had entered that office: before he had just walked in. Noticing the sudden change in Greg's face Terry turned round. The winning smile collapsed like broken knicker elastic, his jaw dropped and then his face squeezed into a tight wrinkle-enhancing scowl. It was not that

either of them could have said what was different. Taken sep-
arately, every part of Mark's face was just the same as before,
but somehow they now added up to this remarkable visage
before them. It was as if the pieces had always been there,
only someone had taken them apart and reassembled them
in the right order.

'Mark,' Greg finally spoke, 'seems the course agreed
with you.'

'I just came to thank you. I've found direction and focus.
I think I can make a real contribution to Vantex now.'

With this, Mark smiled. Greg and Terry automatically
smiled back. His charm was so complete there was no other
response.

'That's great, Mark. We'll have lunch together, you can tell
me all about it.'

'Great Greg, love to. Hi Terry, been meeting your objectives while I've been away?'

'You know me, committed and focused.'

Mark left his colleagues to look at each other in amazement. They speculated on what could have happened on the
course and tried to work out what was different.

'He's had surgery,' said Terry.

'In one week? Besides, he's exactly the same!'

'But he's, he's…'

'He's a complete spunk. The bastard's bloody gorgeous. I
practically wanted to kiss the fucker when he smiled… That's
you knocked off your perch.'

'What d'you mean?' Terry looked angry.

'Sorry mate, you've been wiped out. You're not the Vantex
heartthrob anymore.'

'Yeah, but what about his work. That's what really counts,
he'll never be as good as me on that.'

The phone rang again.

'Sorry Greg, Monica's here to see you. Says you have an appointment.'

Greg looked at his watch; it was her scheduled time. He looked at the neat tidy desk and dreaded the thought of her thrashing around all over his papers yet again. It was only the thought of holding that little baby in his arms that kept him going.

'Look, I've been called up to the top floor, tell her we'll have to reschedule.'

Terry raised the second most attractive eyebrow in Vantex and gave a smug smile.

'Want me to wait till she's gone?'

Greg grinned weakly.

◆

Mark's first day back at work reinforced the strange feelings he had experienced since leaving the smoke teepee. As each participant emerged, they were taken immediately to the temporary 'glamour studio' for their power photo session. Stylists, make-up artists, lighting and camera people were on hand to make everyone look their most assertively attractive. The best print for each trainee was framed with their answer to the question, 'Who are you?' printed beneath the photo.

By staying so long in the teepee, Mark had single-handedly quadrupled the cost of that component of the course. The stylists, photographer and lighting crew were kept on each day—and night—in case he emerged. When he did, their services were mostly not required. Dishevelled and dirty, he had insisted that the photograph be taken immediately, without so much as a drop of moisturiser touching his face. The lighting technician had set up a simple harsh light and bang, the photo was taken. Just one shot and there was 'the most beautiful man in the world'. It was a stunning photo that spoke the truth. No tricks of the trade to con Mark into thinking he was something he was not. Instinctively he had known the photo would be perfect and everyone had followed his lead. There had been no argument, no suggestion of alternatives, no looking at it from a different angle.

The train ride home was his first opportunity for reflection. It was evening and the vastness of Sydney was just a blur of dotted lights behind the magnificent image of Mark's reflection. It was difficult not to touch his face or to keep from sneaking glances. Most of the course participants travelled back together. Spirits were not quite as high as for other groups returning from the course. They all had their own achievements, they all had a photograph of who they really were, but they were in awe of Mark. Ian was 'a man of grace and determination' set to impress his colleagues with a newfound inner calm which stopped accidents happening around him. Rae was 'a leader of men' whose time in the teepee had made her realise that Frank, her boss, was the one person who had impeded her progress most. The next part of her journey up the Vantex ladder was going to be considerably easier once she brushed him aside. After his experience with the goat, BRW had decided the business world was not for him. If he could not kill the beast, he would not eat the meat. He was now 'a gentle soul seeking harmony'. His portrait featured him in saffron robes, reunited with the goat which had visited him so powerfully in the teepee.

Walking into Vantex the next day, Mark had never been greeted so many times. Some people looked bewildered. Others said 'Hi' and smiled as if it was what they had always done. The number of cups of coffee he was offered would have caused a less assertive person to suspect a plot of caffeine poisoning. Mark bided his time. He knew everything had fallen into place for him, but was not quite sure what that place was. Although he got a kick out of all the attention, he was shocked by the change his new looks generated. He was suddenly good-looking, but rather than being told that, his every word was taken as an utterance of genius. In one day he was credited with more good ideas than in his previous entire career at Vantex. Beauty, it seemed, was truth. That was all they knew at Vantex, and all they needed to know. He was surprised that beauty could lead to such a complete re-evaluation of his other qualities. He had expected some improvement in his standing, but thought he might have to prove something first.

Late that afternoon, Terry and Monica were discussing the day's remarkable news in their office. Mark was in Project Development, casting his eye and giving his opinion. No bench top product manager had ever been invited there before.

'You have to admit, Terry, there is something there that wasn't before. He's just so much more, more…'

'Not you too. Half the female staff are suddenly swooning. Besides, aren't you using Greg to achieve your personal goals?'

'He's straining under the pressure. I don't know if he has what it takes.'

'I told you Monica, I'm always prepared to give generously to your appeal.'

Monica rolled her eyes. 'Thanks, if I ever get desperate… How committed do you think Mark is to that girlfriend of his?'

'Lucy? They're practically married. He won't do it. Forget it.'

'There's no harm in trying.'

'Two weeks ago you didn't even contemplate Mark. He could be in here hours before you even noticed him. Now he's Supersperm. What's wrong with me, for Chrissake? I've been a spunk a lot longer than he has. Two weeks time, he could be nothing again.'

Mark came into the office. Even though he did not make any noise, they both turned to look at him. Terry realised he never used to do that and cursed under his breath. Mark knew he had caught Terry out.

'Please, don't let me disturb you guys.'

'You didn't. I was just leaving.' Terry grabbed the nearest file on his desk and walked out.

'What's wrong with him?' Mark looked at Monica, knowing full well.

'Oh, I turned down his sperm...again!'

'You're terribly cruel, couldn't you just accept some in a Vegemite jar and pretend you'd used it?'

'And miss out on all the fun?'

'Greg told me about the fun over lunch, he's an exhausted man.'

'Perhaps I should go for someone younger, more virile.'

Monica got up from her desk and casually paced about. Equally casually she shut the office door.

'I might still be ovulating, you know. There's still a chance.'

Mark blinked. Things were moving too fast. Lucy's answering machine message ran through his mind. The insult still smarted—dumping him when he was not even there. If only she could see what she had tossed aside. On the other hand, he was now a free agent. There was no doubting

Monica's sexual allure as she looked at him and turned the lock on the door. It had been she who insisted it be put on, and he now knew why. She sat on the edge of her desk and kicked her shoes off. The elegant black pumps settled together on the floor, their very position suggesting seduction.

'Are you going to get me pregnant just by looking at me?' Mark could not move. He stared at Monica's shoes until they were covered by her blouse. He looked up just in time to catch her shimmying out of her skirt. Whatever was going to happen it would have to happen quickly. The door may be locked but that would not stop people from knocking or phoning. Everyone knew that sex took place from time to time at work, but a table-top tussle in the afternoon was not something you could linger over. Monica's bra descended to the floor.

'Am I going to have to do everything myself?' He still could not move, trying to pretend a thousand things were running through his mind, but they were not, there was just one.

'OK, if that's what it takes, I'm begging you for it. Fuck me, please.'

Mark was paralysed by her naked gorgeousness. The fine body which her work clothes always suggested now offered itself. Her breasts hung full and he imagined the feel of them in his hands. For the first time in his life, he was being presented with sex on a plate. He felt the pressure in his pants and saliva in this throat. She was looking directly at him. She had exposed herself completely. The mighty Monica had been reduced to a desperate woman and he had not even tried. He really had no choice but be swept along by his own power. He walked over to her, taking off his tie and unbuttoning his shirt.

One hand went immediately for her breast as he kissed her. The relief softened her whole body into his arms. Afraid that he would change his mind, her expert hands quickly undid his trousers. They fell to the ground. He shoved his underpants out of the way. Monica leaned back. Moving her legs around his body she pointed her toes to the ceiling and lifted her bottom from the desk. He removed her panties and threw them behind him. They landed on Terry's desk. Mark moved in. Monica was surprised to find no thoughts ran through her head. She just stared into Mark's eyes and was worked to an orgasm without having to give any instruction. Mark, whose thought processes had finally kicked into gear, could not believe the pleasure he was giving. He was just doing what he always did, which he thought was nothing special, but somehow it was driving this woman wild. Her orgasm was so intense, he came too just at the thought of the effect he was having. This was real power. She was going crazy, refusing to let him go. He bent over and kissed her gently on her neck until her convulsions died down. Her body relaxed, giving way to goosebumps as he pulled out.

They looked in amazement at each other, both stunned by how much she had enjoyed the experience. Monica's phone rang and they sprang to attention. She answered while hitching her skirt back on. She couldn't see her knickers and decided to get them later. Mark suddenly felt guilty about what he had done. He had screwed her because she was available and wanted it. It was totally unprofessional. What if she became pregnant! He did not want a relationship with her. He certainly did not want a child. He took advantage of the phone call to unlock the door and slip out of the room. He made his way to the men's toilet, where he could collect his thoughts.

Monica watched him leave. He was so cool. Most men got really flustered after such an encounter. They panicked, felt guilty, gushed about being sorry and rushed off to hide in the toilets. Not Mark, he really had it. She felt sure of his sperm inside her. This was the batch to hatch her egg. She dispensed with the phone call and hurried to the women's to stand on her head for a few minutes. She did not want Greg's sperm to have any advantage over Mark's.

Terry walked back into the office, relieved to find neither Monica nor the new improved Mark there. This had been a shit day. He could not even bring himself to total his objectives score. He knew the results would be lousy. Sitting at his desk, he saw Monica's knickers on his mouse pad. The bitch had fucked him. He grabbed the underwear, silky and soft, just as he'd imagined it would be. He thought of posting it back to Monica in a badly sealed envelope via the internal mail with a strongly worded memo on the sanctity of the work place. Then he sniffed it, got caught in the lovely warm woman smell and decided to take it home instead. He totalled his points for the day, achieved one more objective, said an affirmation and left for home.

Mark's encounter with Monica and subsequent processing session in the toilets left him late for his after-work drink with Rae. They had agreed to meet so they could debrief on their first day as the new them.

Rae was just finishing her first drink so Mark went to the bar to get a fresh round. The bar was busy. It was the classic after-work haunt. In an hour's time it would be deserted but for those celebrating promotions or commiserating sackings. At the bar Mark found his way to the front quite easily. Removing a twenty-dollar note from his wallet he got ready for the wait, but before he could even begin to focus on attracting the bartender's attention, she looked at him, pointed at him with her index finger and raised her eyebrow. He returned through the crowded bar with ease. Without even looking, people seemed to move out of his way.

'So, tell me about your day.'

Rae's first day of the new her had not been an unqualified success. Having realised that her boss, Frank, was the single biggest obstacle to her advancement, the man now irked her at every turn. Everything he did, from clicking the top of his pen to saying, 'if you get a moment,' when he asked her to run ridiculous personal errands, grated on her. Every tut and sigh was evidence of his vile duplicity.

'I decided the only way to really know what's happening is to keep the intercom on line. He's got no idea how the phone operates so it's quite easy. I read through the manual and discovered I can program his phone so not only is the intercom on all the time, I can listen in on all of his calls. It's designed so management can spy on the workforce. It's very handy. I can monitor everything he does which, believe me, isn't much.'

'Did you learn anything useful?'

'Nothing until Big Fucker came down for the usual afternoon time-waste. He grinned at me as he flounced into Frank's office and shut the door. That's when I nearly blew it. I had to sit at my desk and rip paper for ten minutes to calm down. The bastard's stolen my idea. He's planning the new advanced Big Fucker with ice-cream maker inside. Idiot wants to make the stupid fridge even bigger. Like it's not a complete nightmare to shift already. But with my ice-cream maker, after he looked me in the eye and told me it was rubbish! I can't believe it.'

'What are you going to do?'

'At first I felt like screaming and walking out there and then, but after the paper ripping I decided to take him on.

Beat Big Fucker at his own game. All I need is to get to the conference, visit a friend to get some supplies and I'm all set.'

'Taking on BF, you realise what you're doing? It could be a disaster.'

'And sitting around doing Frank's job for him and saving his backside ten times a day isn't? It's time to take some risks and stake my claim. Cheers!'

Rae downed her drink with relish. She was firing on all guns.

'So what about your day? Did anyone notice anything different?'

'I don't know if I can take much more of it. In twenty-four hours, Lucy dumped me via the answering machine, Greg took me to lunch, I was invited up to Product Development for my input, Monica insisted I screw her on her desk and I had eight cups of coffee made for me.'

Rae had been chewing on an ice cube while Mark finished his drink, but immediately lost it.

'You screwed Monica?'

'I shouldn't have done it.'

'Christ, you're just like all the others. Here you are, you've been given extraordinary power and what do you use it for, a quick shag with the nearest woman. No wonder this world's fucked.'

'Look, I know it was a mistake.'

'Mistake! Oh no, you'll get away with it. You're good-looking, you've got a winning smile, charm, charisma. Everyone will think you did the poor bitch a favour, got to spread yourself round now, can't be selfish with those looks.'

Rae was overreacting, thought Mark. It was not that simple. Being berated for his good looks was a strange experience.

'Rae, no woman has ever thrown herself at me before. Any

sex I've had I've always felt grateful. It was a wild fantasy moment at the end of a very weird day, the type of moment men buy dirty mags to experience. I couldn't not do it, it would have been like letting the team down. Boys will be boys.'

For the first time, he flashed a smile deliberately, trying for a winning forgive-me-because-I'm-cute effect. It worked and he immediately felt guilty. She was the one person he should never have used it on.

'So are you and Monica an item then?' Rae asked sulkily.

'No, she just wanted my sperm. She's got having a baby down as one of this year's objectives, she's only got ten months left so she's pretty desperate.'

'She'd have to be. So apart from that how's the day been?'

'It's so strange. You have no idea how people respond to good looks. It's like everyone's hearing's increased tenfold—they pay attention to everything I say and suddenly I'm this genius whose opinion is absolute gold. People kept saying hello to me all day. Before, I could walk through a room and no-one would know. Now I can't even go to the toilet without a major meet and greet happening.'

'Didn't take you long, did it?' They were interrupted by Lucy suddenly appearing behind Mark. He was supposed to be desolate, a pathetic heap but here he was with another woman. As he turned round, she saw that being single had transformed him. He was looking fantastic. He was gorgeous. How could she have even contemplated dumping him?

'Rae, this is Lucy. Lucy, Rae.' Mark resigned himself to the day's challenges not being over. Rae saw it was an awkward moment. Having just heard about Mark having sex with another woman, she did not want to cop the flak for something she had not even done. She picked up her bag.

'It's time for me to go. There's a Lean Cuisine with my name on it at home. Bye Lucy, nice meeting you.'

'Sorry, Rae, we'll talk tomorrow. Thanks.'

Lucy sat in Rae's warm seat.

'So who's she?'

'A friend...a colleague from Vantex. I met her on the course. What do you want, Luce? The message on the answering machine was clear enough.'

'Well I saw you here and I couldn't just ignore you.'

'So you thought you'd come over. Then you saw something was different and you thought perhaps you'd made a mistake and I had something after all.'

Mark smiled. Lucy was the one person he could use it all on and not feel guilty.

'And you wondered why you'd got these feelings about me you never had before, and in your mind you're seeing my eyes staring at you as my head rests on your pillow. You're looking at my lips as I speak, just dying to brush them with yours, thinking perhaps if I move my hand like this onto yours, you'll feel a surge that says every part of your body has to be wrapped around me.'

Lucy was breathless, giddy with the thrill of having her mind and body read out to her. Mark was intoxicating.

'Something like that. Mark, I've——'

'Forget it Luce,' Mark snatched his hand away, 'it's over, you finished it.' Her stricken face revealed just how powerful his new looks were. Lucy had been transfixed...and was now utterly crushed.

'But Mark——'

'Hi guys, good to see you getting on. Shall we join you?' It was Janet and Jerome, the self-confessed bisexuals.

'We saw you over here with that woman, Mark, so we

thought it was a good idea to send Luce over so you two could talk things out. It looked to be going pretty well, so we decided to join you. Mark, you're looking great.'

'Luce, have you told Mark what you've been up to?' Janet giggled. Lucy looked straight at Mark.

'I've been sleeping with Janet and Jerome. They've been helping me explore my sexual boundaries. I'm a changed woman, Mark, and I think you're a changed man.'

'I must say Lucy has blossomed quite remarkably,' said Jerome.

Janet giggled again like the oldest schoolgirl in Sydney.

'Why don't you all come back to my place for some dinner. Are you hungry, Mark?' Jerome spoke with an innocence so fake a soap actor would have been ashamed, and pierced Mark with a purposeful look.

Mark's heart sank. He was going to have to accept that his appeal was universal, but of all the men he could stand cracking on to him, Jerome was not one, particularly if exploring Janet and Lucy's sexual boundaries was also involved. He downed his drink and stood up.

'Sorry Jerome, I don't think you'd be serving anything I'd like. Goodbye Lucy—happy exploring.'

◆

At seven o'clock Monica was alone in the office. The sound of the lift door opening echoed round the empty floor. Looking up she saw it was a courier and paid no further attention, continuing to work on her version of Greg's conference presentation and trying not to think of Mark.

'I'm looking for someone called Monica. Can't read the surname.' The delivery was for her. He was a bicycle courier.

She liked them best, you could see their bodies better than the motorcycle couriers and the exercise was great for their legs. As for the van-based couriers, she did not want to see them at all.

'That's me. Working late aren't you?'

'It's my last delivery.'

Monica looked up. The muscled legs, rock solid, brought back the memory of her earlier encounter with Mark. Everything brought that memory back. She wanted more, she wanted Mark again, but in his absence this courier might be persuaded. Every little bit helped after all.

'Perhaps there's one more thing you could deliver for me,' she said, pacing around to the door and locking it for the second time that day.

◆

Mark sat at home having a drink and evaluating his day. It was not straightforward being beautiful. He had thought that underneath it all he would be the same person, but that simply was not possible. How could you be the same person when everyone treated you differently, and made new demands of you?

Swilling the chunks of ice around his empty vodka glass, he thought of his art in the kitchen vision. FutureVisions was a month away. That was when Vantex would get a true sense of his potential. By then he figured he might be used to the attention. He would have lived with his new face, shaved round that smile and brushed those teeth many times over. He would take the company with a charm offensive. He smiled and then laughed louder and louder until he was help-less. Tears came into his eyes and he held his arms around his stomach and shook as the laughs convulsed through him. There was just one thought in his perfect head.

It was going to be so easy.

◆

'OK, another ten, mate, rep it out.' Mark pushed himself through another ten bench presses. His chest had gone beyond the burning stage, now it just wasn't there. Every muscle but his chest was pushing up the bar.

'Good work, mate, stand up.'

The trainer took Mark's arms and pulled them behind his back for the ideal chest stretch.

'You're making real progress. Never seen anyone get so much definition and maturity in a month. Sure you're not on the gear, mate?'

Mark, who had no idea what 'the gear' was, said no.

'Hey Freddo, come over here. Take your singlet off, Mark.'

Mark was almost embarrassed. After a month of the new him he was used to attention and happily addicted to the ego-booster shots he received throughout the day. However, standing in the middle of a gym half-naked with a personal trainer and his mate looking on was a bit much. Freddo lumbered over, his huge thighs looking even bigger in the diagonal stripes of his skin-tight pants. He grunted several times. These, it seemed, were a form of communication, because Mick, the trainer, grunted a reply.

Mark had always been half-hearted about going to the gym, but the new him had found it easier to put in the hours required to hone his body to perfection. He had invested in Mick's services for a couple of months. After two sessions, Mick had negotiated a deal whereby Mark gave him advice on marketing his gym business in return for workouts. Mick had seen the other guys at the gym eagerly asking Mark for advice and asking him out for protein shakes after their workouts. He realised he was onto a winner. When people saw that Mark had chosen Mick as his personal trainer, Mick's standing at the gym went up. Since starting with Mark, he'd gained at least six new clients and was charging them ten dollars an hour more than before. The free sessions were the most cost-effective advertising he had ever done.

'OK mate, we've had our fix for today,' Mick smiled. The gym virtually stopped when Mark took his singlet off. Even Mick had to admit he was impossibly good-looking. Mick was absolutely straight and had a girlfriend to prove it, but as a fitness professional he was used to looking at men's bodies and assessing them objectively. He could enjoy the curve of a man's muscles or the clear-cut shape of his pecs without being aroused. His protégé interrupted his reverie.

'I won't be able to make it for the next session. We've got our Ideas Conference next week and I'll be making a big presentation there.'

'Oh, OK.' Mick felt a pang of disappointment. 'Don't think you can slack off just because you've made good progress.'

As Mark left, Mick started some very heavy, very fast dumbbell curls, repping it out to feel the pain that brought the gain. Mark wondered if Mick's professional pride in his body went a little too far, but stopped himself. He did not want to get big-headed.

At Vantex, the air was thick with intrigue, mistrust and suspicion. Monica and Terry each refused to leave the other alone in the office. Both knew the other would ransack their rival's desk for information on their FutureVisions presentation the moment they stepped out. Greg was cloistered in his office. Occasionally he emerged guarded by Linda, his personal assistant, to use the photocopier.

As Mark arrived in the office fresh from his workout, Terry was trying to call the ad agency which had mocked up his designs. He planned to collect them after work, but was determined not to let Monica know. He had taken advantage of an alleged afternoon bout of morning sickness that had seen Monica sprinting to the toilets, presentation folder in hand, to make the call. As the door opened he slammed the phone down, but seeing it was Mark, he just rolled his eyes.

'It's you, pretty boy. I thought Monica was sneaking back in. Forget you heard anything you're about to hear.'

Despite his new status as golden boy, Mark was not an immediate threat. Even after he had come back from the course so 'refreshed', they had laughed over his ludicrous art in the kitchen scheme. Apparently he still wanted to present it, but he did not seem sufficiently competitive to worry about. Terry assumed that Mark realised the conference after this one would be his for the taking and so was not bothering too hard now.

Completing his secret call, Terry rushed out of the office. He wanted to take advantage of Monica's extended infirmity to get some photocopying done. Arriving at the machines, he found Monica hard at work, operating a copier with her right hand while holding her left hand out, keeping everyone at a distance of at least two metres and shouting, 'Face the other way,' every other moment. So much for late morning sickness.

'Should stay away from the photocopier,' warned Terry, 'you've a child to consider now. Glad it's not mine.'

'It's the mere thought of having your baby that gives me morning sickness. Now stand back.'

When she finished, Monica counted and gathered all her

documents, checked the scanner bed to make sure nothing
had been left and opened the automatic document feeder to
ensure it was clear. As she moved away from the machine,
Terry moved towards it, both of them keeping two metres
apart and facing each other. Once Monica had scurried off,
Terry loaded his document and screamed at the machine to
hurry. Every second that Monica was alone in the office was
an opportunity for exposure.

◆

It would have made sense for Terry, Monica and Mark to
travel to the conference venue in Terrigal together, but there
were too many risks involved. Monica, already annoyed at
getting morning sickness earlier and more virulently than 'the
average mother', did not like the idea of Terry sniggering
through emergency stops while she emptied her stomach.
Also, she did not want Terry to discover she had prepared a
complete presentation based on his concept and, in addition,
an emergency presentation on the concept she had found in
Greg's notes. She guessed that Terry would have seen her
proposal, but she did not want him knowing that she was prepared for every eventuality.

Monica decided her best option was to travel with Greg.
He was too concerned with the baby to worry that she might
be about to carve him out of his last chance for the top floor.
He had been Senior Brand Manager for eight years. He only
had a couple of years left to make the big break to vice-
presidential level before it would be generally considered he
had missed the boat. Monica almost felt sorry for him. In one
weekend he might find out her baby was not his and be
robbed of his big idea. She felt sure in her bones that Greg

was not the father. It had to be Mark. She did not even briefly consider that the courier with the legs might have made the grade and forced his sperm past the combined forces of Hard Dick and Pretty Boy.

◆

Terry went up to Terrigal alone. His last port of call on Friday had been the ad agency to pick up the presentation boards. It had cost him plenty: dinners, drinks, and approving a couple of ludicrous invoices he had been questioning. At the agency, his parcelled up winning ticket was waiting in reception. Nigel, his contact, was in a meeting. Downing martinis more likely, thought Terry. He noticed there was a similar package waiting for Greg. Sly dog, he thought, using company funds to draw up his presentation. He felt vindicated that he was operating at the same level as Greg, and smug that he knew Greg was cheating, but Greg did not know it of him.

He set off immediately for Terrigal. It was the classic conference venue for Sydney businesses. Far enough away to be out of town; close enough to dash back for emergencies. The beachfront hotel had everything: great location, several meeting rooms, a gym and a relaxation centre. Everyone else was arriving for the introductory social on Sunday night. Terry wanted to be there early to hide his presentation in his room and completely familiarise himself with the venue. Every possible advantage counted.

This was to be *the* conference for Terry. Everything was riding on it. Monica had been his only real competition. But for all the company's equal opportunity policy, he knew the impending kid would be a deadweight. The new improved

Mark was a problem. He was heading for the top. Terry knew his best option was to get there first. He needed to get his concept accepted this year or any advantage he held over Mark would be lost.

Terry's blood boiled. He gripped his steering wheel, floored the accelerator and ignored the superb scenery as he made his way up the freeway. That bastard was stealing what should rightfully be his. He had been a nobody and suddenly he was everyone's favourite. The latest game at Vantex was proving who had been friends with Mark the longest. Terry even got a date with a girl because he shared an office with Mark, not because he himself was a spunk, but because his desk was in landing range when Mark ripped the knickers off his prey. Terry slammed the horn at the car in front. He flashed his lights and virtually hit the bumper.

'Shift it Grandma, the loser lane's to the left.'

◆

Mark and Rae travelled up together on the Sunday. There was not much conversation in the car. Through her simple but effective monitoring of Frank's office, Rae knew all the details of BF's plan to present her idea. BF was very excited; for that Rae read nervous. Everything was riding on this if he was to maintain his reputation at Vantex. It was just as crucial for her. If she failed to steal her idea back, she would be out of Vantex quicker than she could scream 'glass ceiling.' BF, on the other hand, would be finished if her plan succeeded. It was about time the company knew exactly what was in BF's head.

'I'm meeting Big Fucker for a drink tonight,' she announced.

'Really, should I be jealous?' The teasing tone irked Rae. Mark did not care who she saw.

A strong element of flirting was involved in Rae's plan. She had to persuade BF of her total commitment to his cause. Flirting was not something she was particularly good at, especially when it meant bailing out at the right time but still leaving a good enough impression for her to be at BF's side just before his presentation. Determined as she was to succeed at the conference, the thought of making the ultimate sacrifice with BF was not a pleasant one. Several years ago, at the time of his success, it might have been possible, but too much nose candy and corporate wining and dining had taken a toll. He could still have been appealing in a faded sort of way if he had not been so obnoxious. He was like a ruined building, attractive—because you could see the splendour that it once was—until you realised it had housed an abattoir.

She looked at Mark and imagined what he would look like after several years of inevitable success. She suspected he would age beautifully—good bones did it every time.

'Are you nervous about your presentation?' she asked.

'Sort of, more excited really. I know everything's going to change at this conference. This is where it's all going to start. Don't you feel that?'

'I suppose so. I'm sure there's some *Assertion* thing we should be doing to motivate ourselves; perhaps we could stop and slaughter a goat.'

'You know Brian told me someone once killed the goat.'

'Anyone we know?'

'Perhaps it was Greg—"I kill if I must."' Mark quoted Greg's affirmation.

'No, I've seen his type, his corporate tiger stuff's all bluster. Deep down he's a big softie, even if he doesn't know it.'

'And there he is overtaking us.'

Rae froze as if she'd been caught impersonating the headmaster. Mark beeped the horn and waved. Greg was looking harried but turned at the sound and immediately smiled at Mark. Noticing Rae he raised a knowing eyebrow. Monica just had time to smile condescendingly before Greg's BMW surged forward and was lost in the traffic.

Inside the BMW, conversation was not flowing freely. Both Greg and Monica knew how important this FutureVisions was for the two of them, but Monica was feeling it more keenly. Now that she was pregnant and on target to meet her baby objective, her plan did not seem so brilliant. After her turn on the *Assertion* course, she had experienced a surging of need to fulfil herself as a woman as well as a business executive. At the same time she had read in *Woman* magazine that women who incorporated child-bearing with their career won greater respect, advanced further in their organisation and performed better than their childless sisters due to their sense of complete fulfilment, free from the pangs of procreative regret. The baby had seemed like a stroke of genius and certainly the Vantex senior management had been impressed. Now, she was scared.

How was she going to manage her career and her baby without support? Could she afford to take six months off and resume where she had left off without being at a disadvantage? She imagined the schemes Terry would set in place while she was away, not to mention all the other young guns eager to advance. Currently she was a favourite for promotion. She was one of the toughest, most determined operators at Vantex. Junior guys did not contradict her in meetings. They might savage each other's proposals, but they held off Monica. This was not out of some outmoded concept of respect for women, it was fear. Monica was the top 'tear-jerker' in management. She had sent more men scurrying from meetings, desperately trying to stave off the collapse of bravado, than anybody else.

Now it was her turn to feel weak and emotional. No tears yet, but she knew an onslaught of weeping could hit any time. Career-wise, she needed to make her move now, get past Terry and be in a good position to benefit from Mark's inevitable charge for the top. She had realised during their intimate encounter what a powerful force he was.

Perhaps if she pulled the old-fashioned girl routine, Mark would do the right thing by her. It would do no harm having a formal alliance with him and she would not have to weather the whole baby thing alone. The fact that marriage would bring regular sex on a par with his previous performance was a significant ancillary benefit. She would still have to put in a good performance at the conference to prove she was not riding on his coat-tails, of course. She would need to establish her senior management credentials before the baby arrived and before she became too identified with Mark.

'Are you going to answer me or not?' Monica was pulled from her options review by Greg demanding an answer to the question he had asked her several days before. Would she marry him?

'I'm not going to think about anything except this conference until it's over.'

'I've already told Jane. We're getting divorced.'

'What!' screamed Monica. 'You idiot, you don't even know if it's yours for God's sake. You're not the only donor. I made that clear.'

'The baby's mine. You can't make love like we did, right at peak fertility, and not get a result. It's mine.'

'Actually it's mine, Greg, whoever the father is.'

'I want to be a father to my child. I want to be there at the birth. I want to hear it gurgle; I want that milky smell where it's sick on my shoulder.'

'You're being revolting; no baby of mine will be sick on any shoulder.'

'Just try and stop it,' Greg smiled. 'A baby is the most powerful thing in the world. Do you think you can stop it doing what comes naturally?'

'Spare me the parenthood empowerment. You must have been on another touchy feely course.'

'No, but I have changed. This baby is the most important thing in the world to me... and you of course. Marry me, Monica. You need some support. You can't do this career thing on your own. Suppose you don't come out tops at the conference, you're going to have to work extra hard, right when you physically can't. Terry's pitching hard, and then there's Mark...'

'Stop it now, Greg... Christ, I can't believe you're getting divorced.'

'It was over anyway. She was relieved more than anything. We've got on better than ever since I told her. I think we're going to be friends.'

'Just wait till the divorce settlement.'

'Jane's not like that.'

'Neither was Ivana Trump till it happened.'

Much as it irked Monica to know someone could match her thinking, she had to admit Greg had a point. Mark was the preferred co-parenting option, but she might have to keep Greg sweet as a back-up plan.

'So you really want to marry me?'

'Of course.'

'That's so sweet. I didn't know you had it in you.'

'Neither did I. For the first time in my life I want to be a father, and a real husband.'

Monica relaxed slightly for the first time on the journey. 'It's good to know you're there to fall back on.'

Greg spurted on another ten kilometres per hour.

◆

Anyone standing on the beach looking up at the conference hotel in Terrigal would have seen the makings of a great photo. Row upon row of hotel windows with the lights on and the curtains drawn back revealed nervous junior managers pacing their bedroom floor, presenting their bids for management stardom to the night sky. Doors were locked, friends banished and top-secret documents were lying on beds in rehearsal for the big competition. Occasionally the less sure of the window lecturers would dash away to the bathroom, expressing their nerves in whatever way their body saw fit.

FutureVisions had been designed to foster creativity, planning and corporate enthusiasm. In reality, it was a viciously competitive bloodbath that created a few stars and destroyed many others. To go ill prepared, to go unaware of the total lack of rules or thinking that cheating got you nowhere, was to invite disaster. It was the gladiatorial combat of the modern age.

One aspiring presenter was not pacing nervously in his room, but sitting relaxed and happy in the bar, enjoying a few scotches. BF knew that tomorrow would be his triumph. He would reinforce his position in the company and be on target for the top job when the MD finally realised that the thing he did best was taking chunks out of the greens on the golf course.

'It's in the bag,' he told Frank.

Frank had been too busy playing the faithful retainer to tell BF that he too would be presenting at the conference. It was time for him to step out of the shadows and show what a smart operator and creative manager he really was. He'd worked up his plan in secret at home. No-one knew a thing about it, not even Rae. He had one strong card up his sleeve that would get everyone's attention pretty soon. In the meantime, he made his usual noises to BF.

'Now careful mate, I'm behind you one hundred per cent, but please, lay off the coke tonight. You need a clear head. Don't take anything for granted.'

'Yes, Mother. I'll need a snort just to get in top form for the presentation on the day, but I promise I'll go careful tonight.'

'Perhaps you should go careful on the whisky?'

'Anything else?'

'Get a good night's sleep.'

'Fine, I'll do that. Now leave me alone...I want to run through the presentation.'

'I'll see you tomorrow. Good night.'

◆

BF had spotted Rae coming into the bar. She had seen him with Frank and had gone to sit behind some potted palms, making sure Frank did not see her. BF read the message. She did not want her boss knowing about their meeting. It was understandable. He had been through this sort of meeting enough times to know that most secretaries were more worried about being unfaithful to their bosses than to their husbands. Once Frank was safely out of the way, Rae came up to BF with two drinks. It looked like a vodka and tonic for her and a double Scotch for him.

'I thought I'd get you drunk and take advantage of you,' she smiled as he took the Scotch and hastily downed his previous one.

'Isn't that what *I'm* supposed to do?'

'Yes, but I didn't want to take any chances.'

'You'll go far my girl, I can tell.'

'That's what I'm hoping. Are you all set for your presentation tomorrow?'

BF smiled tentatively, unsure how much she knew about it. She was bright, he knew that.

'I know you're doing the in-freezer ice-cream maker.'

'It's more than that.' BF grew nervous. This woman could make trouble for him.

'Oh I know, you've transformed it. It's a great concept now.'

'How do——'

'I've been monitoring your meetings with Frank through the intercom. I'm honoured that you thought my idea was good enough for developing. I think you'll be able to take it so much further than I could.'

'Well, that's a refreshing attitude in our company, very impressive. Let me get you another drink.'

'I'll get them, or Frank'll get them, I should say. They're coming out of his expense account.'

Rae went to the bar to replace BF's large whisky and her vodka-free drink. So far the plan was working well. She returned with the drinks and turned the conversation to polite flirtation—how much she admired his work, how impressively he maintained his physique despite the corporate life. The drinks flowed, the conversation ran. BF got drunk.

'There's just one thing I want in return for you using my idea.' Rae leaned forward and patted BF on the knee. 'Just one tiny weeny request.'

'What might that be?' BF lurched closer. They were at the 'move off to my room' point, he could tell.

'I want to be part of your team. You'll be able to pick who you want to work with you. I want you to pick me.'

On the words 'you' and 'me' she tapped BF's chest and then her breast.

'I think we'd make a great team.' BF was doing some serious slurring. 'But first I'd like to show you my appreciation for your input...in my room. Some real team work. Just you and me, working through some concepts, thrashing about... out the presentation.'

'I think I'd get a lot out of that.'

'Lesss go.'

BF stood up suddenly—and remarkably well. He appeared completely sober. They walked normally out of the bar, BF waving to a couple of people. Rae panicked. Perhaps she had misjudged. He had been knocking the Scotches back, but perhaps he was pretending to be more drunk than he was. If he was not legless, she could be in serious trouble. She braced herself nervously as the lift door shut on the two of them.

'Fooled you, didn't I,' BF said as the lift moved off. Rae desperately thought of how to salvage the situation. There was no way she could have sex with this oaf, but that was clearly what he expected. It was going horribly wrong and the lift seemed to take forever.

'What do you mean?' She could think of no other response.

'I fool 'em all, the patent Big Fucker exit-the-room looking completely sober when really you're as pissed as piss
can piss...piss. I fooled you...didn't I. Only lasts three
minutes...it's all you've got till you start...starting again.'

Rae laughed with relief.

'Yes, you certainly had me fooled. I hope you're not *too*
drunk now, are you?'

'Never, never too drunk to discuss negotiations, con-
ceptsssstrategies. Oops here we are.'

BF straightened as the lift doors opened. Stepping out
smartly he looked round to check no-one was in the corridor, then slumped again.

'Sis way.'

They staggered into his room. BF immediately went to the
bathroom to relieve himself. Rae could hear it thundering into
the bowl and then onto the seat. BF grunted and the water
on water noise returned.

'Ssbetter.'

Rae fixed another drink from the mini-bar.

'Here,' she said, 'sit on the bed and I'll show you some
ideas I had.'

BF downed the drink and sat on the bed.

'Issshowtime!'

'I've just got to get ready.' Rae ducked into the bathroom
to wait for BF to fall asleep. She heard another drink being
poured, then his shoes hitting the floor and a sigh. She waited
longer. Deciding not to waste any time, she looked through
his toiletries bag for his stash. It contained the usual dull male
stuff, although the hair tweezers were interesting. The after-
shave was Polo Sport—boringly predictable. Would he have
passed out by now? There had been absolutely no noise. She
had to risk it.

She had not closed the bathroom door, so that opening it again would not make any unnecessary noise. Gingerly peeking round the door she saw BF sprawled on the bed, holding his glass on his chest. The Scotch had poured out onto his shirt leaving a big brown patch as if he had been shot. Perfect.

She removed the glass and then his clothes. He mumbled a few incomprehensible words as she gently moved him around. Co-operating unconsciously, this was not a novel experience for him. He lay still in his off-white underpants— a ruin of what once had been a good mind and body. If he was to believe they'd had sex, he would have to be naked. She removed the underpants, realising his penis was definitely not the source of his nickname. She eased him into bed, scrunching the sheets and the two sets of pillows. She lay down next to him and wriggled around as much as she dared to make the sheets look well used. Satisfied, she turned to BF. She could not resist a quick kiss on his Scotch-soaked lips.

'Thanks, it was great.'

Getting up, she set to on the real work. First, she had to find his cocaine stash. She guessed he would keep it with him at all times. She went through his suit pockets, but found nothing. His briefcase held the presentation she would have to read, but not his inspiration.

This was a major stumbling block. The whole plan would fail if she did not find the coke. Then her eyes landed on BF's keys on the bedside table. The key ring had a large metal bullet attached to it. She picked up the keys and carefully unscrewed the bullet. The top came off to reveal a small bottle hidden inside. In the bottle, white powder. Sealing the bottle, a lid with a little spoon attached.

How very convenient, Rae thought. In the bathroom she tipped the coke down the basin. She had no idea of its value, but the bottle was full: fresh supplies for the weekend.

Reaching into her pocket, she pulled out a little plastic sachet also containing a white powder and tipped the contents into the bottle. She filled it to the same level, replaced the lid, rescrewed the bullet and rearranged the keys precisely on the bedside table. The powder had been supplied by a party animal friend, known to always have the best Katamine (otherwise known as Special K) in Sydney. As a vet he had a ready supply and was happy, if surprised, to furnish Rae with some.

'Be very careful,' he had said. 'Only take it in tiny doses. It feels great but have one grain too many and bang, you're in the K hole. It's like you're cut off from the whole world. You can't speak, you can't move, you just have to sit it out. Believe me, you don't want to be in the K hole.'

Rae had no intention of visiting the K hole, but she thought BF might rather enjoy it.

Next she went through his presentation. The notes were sloppy and brief and not much help. She already knew his amendments to her proposal and knew that most of them added nothing. There was no way that she would recommend a ridiculously large fridge-freezer be made even bigger.

Before leaving the room, she took a condom out of her bag, unwrapped it and, building up enough saliva, spat inside it a couple of times. It looked realistic enough, especially in the state that BF would wake up in. She threw it onto the floor and then wrote a note on the hotel stationery.

'I know why they call you Big Fucker now and not a fridge in sight! Thought it best to leave early so no-one catches us out. Look forward to giving you a pep talk before the presentation tomorrow.

Love, Rae.'

She slipped out and made her way to her own room. She needed all the sleep she could get if the rest of Operation Fuck Big Fucker was to go as planned.

◆

At the breakfast buffet, it was easy to tell who was making a presentation that morning. As everyone else was busy piling on the hash browns, scrambled eggs and breakfast sausages in the usual free for all, presenters nervously played with bran muffins and downed multiple cups of coffee.

The order in which the hopefuls presented over the three days of the conference was determined by a strict 'names out of a hat' routine. On the Sunday evening, all those with a concept to present put their names in a ballot box in the hotel reception area. The CEO's secretary, Francine, pulled the names out at random and set the order down. This was done in the privacy of her room to ensure no-one attempted to seek an unfair advantage.

That was the official description of the procedure. The reality was different. Even before the box had been placed in reception, Francine had been wined, dined, lobbied, bribed, seduced, presented with several exceptional gifts and had held an auction for the best spots in the running order. She loved FutureVisions. It made her feel like a beautiful, wealthy, eternally young heiress besieged by suitors. She blushed at compliments, she giggled girlishly over dinner, she feigned surprise at the lavish gifts and succumbed coyly to irresistible charms, all with an expert grace perfected over the twenty years she had been involved with the company. As long as there was an Ideas Conference, Francine knew she would be desired and courted.

Over the years, she had never devoted herself to just one man, aware that a married woman could not score as many spoils of combat as a single girl. Although she would never admit to being anything less than fragrant and lovely, Francine was no fool. She knew her greatest asset, natural or otherwise, had always been this ballot and she played it harder each year as her physical attributes, never a strong suit, faded towards old age. Without it she was just another grey-haired fifty-something never admitting to more than 49, bleaching her hair and giving full vent to the 17-year-old virgin within. Rumour had it that the bribes accumulated over the years had paid for her weekender at Pearl Beach, scene of the deflowering of several ambitious junior managers.

It was considered that the first and the last days of the conference were the best days to present; the middle day sagged too much. Mornings were optimal, late afternoons were duds. The last spot on the middle day was the dead zone. It was allocated to idiots who believed the ballot was fair and unbiased or given to those who had failed to pay the correct tribute to Francine.

BF and Francine went way back. As a desirable young man, on the eve of presenting his fridge sensations, he had initially baulked at the idea of what Francine was demanding from him. She had asked the ultimate sacrifice. Over dinner BF had drunk even more than she had, and managed to push himself through the seduction. He had been given the first spot on the final day, the greatest compliment Francine could pay a man. After his astonishing success, he had never bothered to pay her much court as he rarely presented anything. This year he'd had the foresight to look up her date of birth in the records and send her flowers. She had been touched. She told him he was the only one who had bothered. Thus, when the conference allocation came around, he got away with a lavish dinner and a rather beautiful brooch. This time she didn't demand the ultimate price, not when there were less time-damaged executives keen to further their careers. BF was rewarded with mid-morning on the first day. A good spot, but not her finest.

Everyone was keen to discover who had the top spot. The rumour mill nominated Mark. Everyone knew that Francine would demand nothing less of him than the sacrifice—and probably several times. They almost pitied him. However, when the list went up, competitors were shocked to find, not Mark's name, but that of Frank Parkham, Rae's boss, in the prime spot. This was his trump card, and what a card. The shock revelation threw the game wide open. Over breakfast, the allocation of the top spot was discussed in detail. The consensus was it must have cost a fortune: an annual stipend for at least five years they reckoned. Given Frank's sex appeal, it was a toss-up whether the ultimate sacrifice would be his or Francine's.

Debate over Frank's payment was swiftly followed by the news of Mark's placement—3 pm on the middle day, the dead zone. He was sunk. Those unaware of his loopy great art idea were relieved that their strongest competition had been dealt a death blow. Those who had paid an additional tribute to ensure Mark did not get a good spot considered their money, time or virtue well spent.

While most people expected Mark to be devastated, it came as no surprise to him. He had deliberately not wooed Francine. He knew what she would demand and in the week leading up to the conference had made a point of walking frequently past her desk, leaning over her on occasion. Just as she started to get flustered, he would smile and disappear.

There was a danger that she might give him the top spot regardless, so he made a point of brusquely rebuffing her suggestion of lunch at her Pearl Beach retreat. That had sealed his fate, the dead zone was his.

Now Mark had to make sure people were in the room for his presentation. He was banking on the lure of seeing him crash and burn being enough to pack the hall. Monica and Terry would have got the word out on how bad his idea was, sparking ghoulish fascination in his demise. That was what he needed. A triumph in the dead zone would give him twice the authority of success in the top spot. No-one could then say he owed it all to good timing and Saturday lunch with Francine.

Greg, Terry and Monica were all presenting on the first day and directly after one another. They had done what was necessary. Greg had sent flowers on Francine's birthday every year. She was always so grateful. She said he was the only one who remembered. A voucher for a full day's luxury treatment at Sydney's top beauty salon had sealed his deal. Monica, immune from the ultimate sacrifice, had discovered Francine's favourite perfume, made a cash donation, and used her pregnancy to solicit sisterly feelings. Terry had planned ahead. Earlier in the year he had sent Francine Belgian chocolates on her birthday. He was the only one kind enough to remember, she said. She had been charmed and so taken with Terry that she invited him to Saturday lunch. At Pearl Beach Terry had made the ultimate sacrifice. He reckoned his athletic performance and genuine orgasm was worthy of the top spot, but was not so foolish as to let his manly pride block the best possible deal: a good spot for him and Mark in the dead zone. Francine had been as good as her word.

While most of the managers discussed the coming

competition over breakfast, Rae was nervously playing with her smart executive briefcase in the hotel lobby. It held her version of BF's presentation notes. She had to meet BF before he took his place in the meeting room to ensure she was by his side every step of the way. Whenever the lift doors pinged, she turned to see who was arriving. The room was filling up, but there was no sign of BF. Rae was getting very anxious. The lift pinged again, and Mark stepped out.

'How were your drinks with BF? Did you get what you want?'

Not knowing what Rae was up to annoyed him. He had come to think of her as a confidante. She knew all his plans and had been very supportive. He could have tried using his infallible charm on her, but it would not have felt right. He congratulated himself for developing a fine sense of its appropriate use.

'It went according to plan, thanks, but you're going to have to move on. He'll be down any minute.'

'Am I ever going to find out what's going on?'

'If you don't, it means it hasn't worked. Please Mark, you'll know everything, just go.'

Mark shrugged his shoulders and wandered off. Moving into the conference hall, he was greeted by waving hands and cheery smiles. Mark recognised the self-satisfied grins. Everyone had made a mental note to get a good spot for the three o'clock session on the middle day—it would be dull as anything but someone had to witness the wonder boy's demise.

Beginning to despair that her plan was going to fail, Rae decided to go up to BF's room, risking missing him in the lobby if they passed in the lift. She knocked on his door. There was no answer. She knocked harder and then tried the door. It was unlocked. She went in. BF was still asleep. She toyed with the idea of leaving him there, and simply presenting the concept herself, but there was no guarantee he would not wake up and get down in time. Anyway, she needed him to fail miserably and publicly. She shook the carcass on the bed and eventually he stirred. Slapping his face she brought him to.

'You idiot, the conference is about to start and you're not even up, come on!'

Rae turned on the shower and, dragging the groggy genius naked from his crumpled bed, she pushed him in. The cold water did not even register, he just groaned. Holding him under the spray, Rae soaked his whole body.

'What the hell...what time...I'm naked...' BF was slowly waking.

'The conference has started, you've overslept, you've got half an hour to get ready and down there for your presentation. Get a move on.'

Now BF was fully awake.

'Shit, why the hell didn't you wake me?'

'I just did.'

'Pass me my washbag, then get out.'

Rae waited in the bedroom. There was some fumbling and crashing, then she heard the deep sniffs of BF preparing for his presentation. He shouted for his clothes, specifying the shirt, tie and suit. Twenty minutes later he emerged. Rae had to admit the transformation was impressive. He looked immaculate—hair perfect, eyes shining, clean-shaven and spotlessly dressed. This was a man well used to pulling his shit together in a few moments. He'd taken just the right amount of the K (or coke as he thought it to be) to perk himself up.

He beamed, ready to triumph, and kissed her on the lips. He smelled of stale Scotch and toothpaste.

'Let's go make history...again.'

In the lift, Rae knew she had to get him to snort more of his inspiration. She gambled on the fact that as smooth and collected as he appeared, somewhere in the midst of his drug-induced confidence he was shitting himself.

'God, I am so nervous. You've got your notes, haven't you?'

'Yes,' he replied breezily, 'not that I need them!'

'But what if you stumble, you haven't eaten, you're hung over, you didn't rehearse last night. Everyone says this year's going to be the toughest competition yet. There are three people before you; if they make good presentations you could be sunk.'

'That bitch Francine. I should be on the last day. Who'd she give the top spot to?'

'Frank.'

'What? The backstabbing little bastard. The last decent idea he had was to stop pissing in his pants, and that was when he was twelve. What the hell is going on?'

'Something's up, I know it, I'm really worried. You are going to be all right, aren't you...aren't you?' Rae tried to sound hysterical.

'Yes of course.' The lift reached the lobby and BF strode out confidently.'I just need to go to the men's.'

Rae breathed a sigh of relief. He was going for a second helping. One more blast just before his pitch and she reckoned it would be perfect. He emerged from the toilets rubbing his nose.

They stood at the back of the hall. Rae waited nervously, BF beamed confidently and railed against the inordinate amount of time the presentations before his were taking.

Overhead projections, video presentations, computer-generated graphics, clear voices, smart clothes, readable sheets with just the right amount of absorbable information, the odd joke and lashings of impressive statistics. Every trick from every management presentation manual was being employed. Everyone was settling down for a marathon contest. The first presenter was usually lucky enough to have everyone present and paying attention. After that, attention drifted; people wandered in and out. Plots began to hatch and deals were made. Although the winning presentations were selected by members of the board, audience response could not help but sway them. It was in no-one's interest to show support for anyone else, but being seen not to applaud colleagues was bad form and would lead to reciprocal silence. Terry was feverishly getting as many colleagues as possible to agree to cheer and clap loudly in return for his support of their efforts. He was doing well with allies strategically placed throughout the auditorium.

He looked at BF, assessing whether it was worth approaching him for a deal. It would mean a lot if others saw BF supporting him, but an approach right now would seem too obvious. The groundwork should have been done weeks ago. Besides, Mark's little pet was hovering around him. She must have taken a look at the running order and jumped ship when she had seen Mark was dead in the water.

'When the hell is this idiot going to finish? They should set a time limit for God's sake. Shift it sonny and let a real pro show you how it's done.' BF was getting anxious five minutes into the presentation before his own.

'Sshh.' He was just a bit too loud. Rae did not want him boiling over before he got onto the stage. 'Christ, you must be going through hell,' she whispered to play on his nerves.

'My stomach's one giant knot. You do know it all backwards, don't you?'

'Stop it, you're making me nervous. Come on, let's have something to calm us down.'

BF grabbed Rae's arm and pulled her into the lobby and over to the women's toilet. He pushed her inside and into a cubicle. Out came the novelty key ring.

'One last blast for me and a quick one for you to stop you vomiting on my shoes.'

He dug out a spoonful of white powder and with expert precision held it to his nose and breathed deeply. He scooped out some for Rae and handed it to her. He closed his eyes as he blocked the unused nostril and jiggled his cheek to get the full force of his snort. Rae quickly emptied the spoon onto the floor and made a snorting sound. BF took the tiny spoon back and began screwing the lid back onto the vial.

'Hang on,' said Rae, 'you can't do one nostril, it's bad luck and you might lose your balance.' She giggled. He laughed and took another healthy snort, not realising he had used the same nostril again.

They made it back to the auditorium just as the previous speaker was receiving the muted applause of his colleagues and a few enthusiastic claps from those he had made reciprocal arrangements with. BF and Rae made their way to the front and stood at the edge of the stage. The CEO introduced their presentation.

'It is one the great things about this company and this conference that everyone competes on even ground. Everyone has a chance to alter the course of Vantex's future. Our next presentation is from a man who is living proof of that. What have you got for us this time, David?'

The CEO led the applause and made way for BF who was finding the entire procedure hilarious.

He had started giggling the minute the CEO said the words 'even ground' and was helpless with laughter as he staggered onto the stage, leaving his presentation on the floor next to Rae. The audience was in silence. The deals being brokered at the back suddenly stopped. Here was a giant of Vantex in hysterics in front of the entire managerial staff and the board. It had to be a ploy for attention, but the laughter seemed genuine. He did not seem to be able to stop.

Reaching centre stage, he turned and faced the audience, held his arms out, then bent over, holding his nose and shaking. A few titters started in the audience. This was brilliant, everyone decided. Their attention was undivided. It was bold and imaginative. It almost did not matter what he came up with, they were all hooked. The titters grew to laughter and spread. Soon the entire hall was laughing, roaring, cheering. It was fantastic. BF stopped and stood up straight. Like a laugh track being switched off the hall fell silent. He stared out, not moving, just looking towards the audience in a weird way as if he could not see anyone, as if he himself was not really there. Again he had thrown the audience. A few people shook their heads, some in grudging admiration, others annoyed that such obvious theatrics were having so good an effect. The staring continued, even longer than the laughing. There were a few coughs. The situation was getting uncomfortable. Big Fucker had made his point, he was the best, now where was the presentation? Someone shouted, 'Get on with it, mate!'

BF's head moved slightly as if he realised someone had addressed him.

'Is... is this carpet?' he managed, 'what... standing on... it's... I can see... no...'

It was obvious that this was no presentation gimmick. BF had lost it completely. The man was finished. A few people rubbed their noses in a knowing way.

Sensing that it was now or never, Rae stepped onto the stage and walked over to BF. Taking him by the hand, she led him to a chair at the edge of the stage and right in the middle of the K hole.

'I am a Russian statue,' he declared as he was pushed down onto the seat. She had no idea how long the effects of the drug would last and so her presentation had to be quick. Everyone was so taken aback by BF's behaviour that no-one moved to stop her.

'My name is Raelene Whyte. David Mygrave was going to present a concept which he stole from me. I have a concept outline signed and dated by a JP which pre-dates any of David's work on this idea. I also have tape-recordings of his conversations with Frank Parkham clearly showing he knew the concept was mine.'

Rae was surrounded by a sea of open mouths, like a choir frozen mid-note. The audience was stunned. She had everyone's attention. A bloody secretary had just shot down the company's biggest star. Scary stuff for every manager who trusted their support staff implicitly. It was taking the level playing field way too far.

'It is only natural that in our hot Australian climate, ice-cream is a popular sweet. Delicious, cooling, and a fond memory of happy childhood. No wonder home ice-cream makers came in with such a bang. Our market was flooded with overseas designs. However, figures from both Vantex and our competitors show that the market was never as big here as overseas. Why? We have a sweeter tooth than most countries, we have warmer weather than most countries, we love our kitchen gadgets more than most countries. The answer is simple. Most ice-cream makers were designed for cooler climates. In our summer, the cooling disk which is the core part of the ice-cream maker cannot last long enough to chill the mixture effectively. If more of our managers had tried to make ice-cream at home in 35 degrees of heat, we might have discovered this earlier.'

A few nervous titters acknowledged this truth, but no-one guessed where the ice-cream thing was going. Ice-cream makers were history, replaced by breadmakers as the kitchen appliance of fashion.

'Ice-cream makers with their own cooler are too bulky and often still not powerful enough for our climate. If only, said one homemaker, I could put my ice-cream maker in the freezer, I'd have no problems.'

A murmur went up; the smarter managers knew where she was heading and it was good.

'So why not give the homemaker what she, or he, wants. The BF 2000 family of fridges without doubt has the size.' She looked over at BF, staring vacantly from his chair, and raised her eyebrows in a contemptuously dramatic gesture. Her audience loved it. 'The top shelf could easily house the pot and stirring mechanism. The ice-cream could be made in an energy-efficient, climate-friendly way. That's my concept— put the ice-cream maker in the freezer! We could revive one moribund market and give our leading white good a significant competitive advantage in another. I have all the back-up information and figures in these hand-outs.'

Rae marched over to BF, stood him up and walked him off stage to the sound of considerable applause. It was without doubt the most dramatic presentation in the history of the company and the concept was so simple, so basic, it could not fail. It would not launch a whole new era for Vantex but it would certainly milk more money out of the current one. The board members were busy writing notes and looking at each other inquiringly. Why had this formidable woman been held back as a secretary?

Mark's applause was the longest and hardest. He was filled with a combination of admiration and relief. Rae had scored a knockout blow—one which no-one else would have dared to attempt. He put his relief down to the fact she was his friend and not his enemy. He dismissed the fleeting notion that it was because she had not succumbed to Big Fucker's ageing charms.

BF managed to hear the applause, dropping out of the K Hole as quickly as he had dropped in.

'It worked then,' he said to Rae, 'it fucking worked.'

'Yes,' replied Rae, allowing herself a self-congratulatory smile, 'for once you are absolutely right.'

For most of the conference attendees, the rest of the day passed without incident. Frank, still basking in the glory of his curious top placement in the competition order, had whisked BF as quickly as possible up to his room. He did not want to risk being seen in public with the company's latest and most spectacular loser. As gently as an overshadowed sidekick could, Frank explained in gruesome detail exactly what had gone on, including a joyfully accurate impersonation of the 'silent stage'. BF was torn between snorting everything that might possibly fit up his nose or washing it all down the toilet. He decided, on careful balance, that both options were too extreme and settled for the mini-bar instead.

Rae was the hot talking point at the coffee break, the lunch break and well into the afternoon. Everyone wanted to be seen with her—she was destined for success. Several members of the board had approached her with questions on the detail of her proposal and had all been seen nodding approvingly at her responses. She was a shoo-in.

Greg, presenting first in the afternoon, decided that drastic action was needed. It was a safe assumption that after the dramatic events of the morning, anyone presenting later in the day was doomed. His own concept was stronger than Terry's, but he realised he had no chance of a triumph. With parenthood strongly on his mind, he did not have the hunger necessary for a serious push. The lion had a different agenda. Monica, however, needed all the help she could get. If he could stuff Terry, Monica might have a better chance of being noticed by the board. So with the proud thought of sacrificing himself for the mother of his future pride, he strode onto the stage with a duplicate set of brilliantly designed boards and presented Terry's concept. It was a new machine for grinding flour at home: maximum freshness and nutritional impact.

Terry had been too busy talking during the first five minutes of Greg's presentation—trying to divert as much attention away from him as possible—to notice he was being carved. Glancing at the stage he glimpsed the presentation boards he had guarded so carefully. His mind flashed to the second parcel waiting in reception at the advertising agency. They must have been exactly the same boards waiting to go to Greg. Some bastard at the agency obviously reckoned there was more to be gained in helping Greg rather than him. He had been shafted by the agency, fucked by Greg and now Monica was grinning at him nastily. Managing a quick 'Shouldn't you be vomiting somewhere?' he stormed past her.

His high hopes of advancement had first been dealt a blow by Mark's bitch and now, thanks to Greg, he would be struggling to maintain ground. Knowing full well just how much longer there was of his own presentation, he shot up to his room to get his notes for Plan B. He had about five minutes to refresh his memory. Breathing deeply he recited his mantra: plan, control, achieve, triumph. With this, he could do anything. He could emerge with a miracle. He would award himself ten points for the day just for having a back-up plan.

Back in the auditorium, he strode past Monica, smiled and waved Plan B at her. If he was going down, the bitch was going with him. He made it to the stage just as he was being announced. The applause for Greg had been fairly muted. Grinding your own flour had not been such a great idea after all. Terry walked confidently out to centre stage and bluffed his way through Monica's presentation. It was a combined breadmaker, slicer and toaster. Terry thought they might have really had something if it had been presented with his grinder. Terry got away with the presentation and, more to the point, he had blocked her advantage.

This time it was Monica's turn to storm off to her room. Thank God for her notes on Greg's unused presentation. All she could do now was put forward a fairly decent proposal to save her face, even if it was not as good as her own, currently being butchered by that wanker. She made it through her presentation without vomiting or emotional fluctuation. She threw everything she had into it and persuaded herself and the audience that a stand alone unit to house all Vantex bench top appliances was the future of kitchens. For a conference hall already satiated with drama she received a good response. At another time it might have been a triumph, but at this conference it was a pass mark with no gold stars. Greg watched with mixed emotions. She had double-crossed him and was prepared to destroy his career to further her own. It was magnificent. The half of his heart that was not furious swelled with admiration.

◆

The first night cocktail party was usually a dull post-mortem of the day's proceedings, but with so much drama on the first day, conversation was loud and excited. The topic of Rae and BF was peppered with speculation by those who had seen them in the bar the previous night and, thanks to the rival who had paid a cleaner to hand over the contents of BF's bin, reports of a used condom.

News of Greg and Co's presentation merry-go-round was the joke of the day. All three, in the end, had performed competently, but not made any real advance. Monica glowered over her pineapple juice as Greg once again espoused the virtues of marriage. Terry hovered around the bar with mates from free-standing appliances. He could enjoy the rest of the conference, but not until he had denounced Greg for back-stabbing and favouritism. He stormed over and let rip. In retaliation, Monica complained loudly that she did not mind him using her presentation, as long as next time he learned how to pronounce 'actualisation' properly. She threw the rest of her pineapple juice at him with the words, 'and it's not the hormones.'

BF had staggered down to the bar for the cocktail party, ready to denounce Rae for her treachery in the time-honoured tradition: calling her a filthy slut and letting everyone know he had slept with her. Unfortunately he only made it to the doorway. The high-speed lift triggered his alcohol-filled stomach and he was forced to empty it into the nearest potted palm and retire. This worked in his favour as it confirmed the story that Frank had circulated suggesting a particularly virulent bout of food-poisoning as the cause of his strange behaviour.

For everyone bitterly disappointed with their day's results, there was one consolation on which to pin their hopes. The one moment they could all look forward to enjoying: Mr Perfect Smile suffering a long, slow, agonising death in the dead zone. That was something no-one wanted to miss.

◆

By three o'clock on the middle day the drowsy boredom which normally descended on the conference was not apparent. True, the novelty had worn off. The morning's presentations had been dull, taken up mainly by accountants and IT bores. The behind-the-scene fighting had difficulty living up to the previous day's spectacle, yet there was still an expectant hum. The auditorium was as full as it had been for the opening session. There was talking, laughter and lots of movement. It was an audience hungry for a spectacle not seen since Christians were put into an arena with lions.

Mark had kept a low profile throughout the day, rehearsing his laptop graphics again and again, checking his hair and smiling his smile. As he looked into the mirror he was worried. In his reflected eyes he recognised his old self. For the first time since the course he understood that he was still the same person, and not a witness lodged in the mind of a completely different man. For all the recent attention, the sex and the beauty, he could see the Mark who had sat at product meetings trying to make himself heard. He cursed his confidence in taking this risky route. It had taken all his reserves of charm not to succumb to the slight smiles and cheery shoulder shrugs of yesterday. For his colleagues to smell blood was one thing; it would be fatal if he smelled it on himself. He reminded himself who he really was in true *Assertion* style: 'I am the most beautiful man in the world.' He could do it, he would do it and even if he did not do it, he still had a job...and incredible good looks.

He phoned the hotel's highly qualified audio-visual professional support. Justin was not available as he was still laying the tables for afternoon tea. Mark had to trust that Justin clearly understood his lighting instructions and was committed to following his script. He needed exactly the right spots to highlight his hair, bring out his eyes and project that dazzling smile. Justin was a local boy hoping to make it big in theatre. He seemed totally committed to Mark's goals and had come up to his room the previous evening with a complimentary bottle of champagne to wish him luck.

Mark looked at his watch; it was time to go down to the conference room. He breathed deeply, searched inside himself for a silent moment and asked himself if he really wanted to do it. The answer was a resounding yes. Armed with this sure knowledge he headed for the lift.

After the event, few people could describe what had actually happened during Mark's presentation. Everyone present would boast later that they were there, but no-one could give a blow by blow account. Most could remember the loud and boisterous reception Mark received as he walked onto the stage. Wolf whistles, cheers, cries of 'You go girl!' in best Oprah-guest accents. Terry remembered a sudden sense of doom as he realised, even before Mark had started, that this was no dead zone. The energy level was through the roof. The crowd wanted a show. If Mark gave them one, even the kitchen art scheme could take off. Perhaps it was not such a stupid idea after all. He was about to get up to walk out, refusing to witness a triumph, when Mark stepped into a spotlight. His face filled the auditorium and there was simply nothing else to look at and nothing else to do.

Everyone could remember Mark's first words: 'The problem with kitchens is they're just plain boring.' Beyond that, it was like a dream as they stared at Mark and words without meaning made perfect sense, logical connections emerged and pointed to the future of the company. Some people remembered seeing great works of art suddenly morphing into kitchen appliances on the screen behind Mark. The *Mona Lisa* wrapped herself around a food-processor, Picasso's *Guernica* was transformed into the most perfectly stylised breadmaker imaginable, a Henry Moore became an iron to seduce any man into a lifetime of pressing. It was a vision of a kitchen as a gallery. Art became function became job security for everyone at Vantex. Others swore there was just the power of Mark's words creating the images: no graphics, no projections, just Mark.

When Monica came to, she was wiping a tear from her eye, standing, cheering and praying Mark was the baby's father. BF, who had stumbled into the back of the hall just as Mark started, felt a wonderful warmness spreading over him. Only the sound of cheering made him realise it was spreading from his underpants. Terry had leapt to his feet along with the others, but soon snapped out of the hypnotic state and sat down, only to be dragged to his feet again by those next to him who slapped him on the back and said how proud he must be. Rae alone had not been transfixed. She saw a great concept and a wonderful man, but she saw the nerves and the eyes which had recognised themselves that afternoon. She had been doubled over with anxiety and now cheered from relief and joy. She watched as Mark took his plaudits with a comfortable ease that knew they were his due.

The triumph was absolute. Mark had taken the dead zone and in one fell swoop knocked BF off the company legend perch, crushed the power of Francine and cleared his path to the head of the herd.

That night was party night. Everyone knew the next day did not matter. The conference was as good as over. In the bar Mark sat with Greg, Monica and Rae as one by one all the Vantex managers came to pay homage.

'It's fucking remarkable, I knew you had it in you. I'm proud of you, son, and I hope you're not going to forget those who encouraged you.' Greg was venting his paternal feelings.

'I believe your words were, "It's complete and utter shit",' said Mark, remembering Greg's initial dismissal.

'Yes, but would you have been so determined to succeed if I hadn't said that?'

Monica rolled her eyes. 'Get me another orange juice, before you totally demean yourself. You're supposed to be our superior, remember.'

As Greg left for the bar, Monica slid close to Mark.

'I've been meaning to have a chat, Mark.' Her thigh pressed hard against his and her mouth clamped to his ear. 'About our little get-together.'

'Monica, I'm sorry, it was unforgivable and it won't happen again. I value and respect you as a co-worker.'

'Cut the crap. You know I'm pregnant. You're the father. Marry me or get sued.'

. Mark could see his crystal tower shatter. One stupid moment and everything teetered on collapse.

'But you didn't want a co-parent, you only wanted the baby,' he whispered back.

'Well you and your secretary pal just fucked my climb up the career ladder. I need a partner to help raise the child. I'll lose too much ground if I have to take time off.' Mark caught the note of panic in her voice.

'Monica, I'm...what can I say...how do you know it's not Greg's?'

'It has to be yours.' She was determined. Greg returned with the orange juice, putting an end to the conversation.

This was not what Mark wanted to think about. He did not want marriage, not now that he was beginning to reap the harvest of his good looks with women. Now was not the time to be tied down. He felt cheated. Monica had changed the rules after the game and declared him the loser. He decided: no marriage. He would pay alimony, he would be generous, but he would need proof the child was his. He wanted blood tests.

Rae watched from the other side of the table. Monica had freaked Mark out. Perhaps it was something to do with their little encounter...and her being seven months away from a happy event. Poor silly Mark, she thought, the gift of incredible beauty and he messed it up on his first day.

◆

Several people were not at the celebrations. Big Fucker, having wet himself in Mark's presentation, had left Terrigal that afternoon. It was time for immediate rehab. He never wanted to touch any powder again.

Frank Parkham, who had been given the top spot—the first session on the final day—was sitting crushed in his room. The first days of the conference had been hard for him. He had realised his concept was ridiculous. Who the hell would want fridges with photographic landscape views on them? Besides which, after Mark's show, no-one would believe it was not a transparent attempt to jump on his bandwagon. The only relief was that after this day's huge success, virtually no-one would be in the conference room when he withdrew.

He stared despondently at the empty bottles from the mini-bar, but he was not alone. His fragrant and lovely new wife was with him. The day before the conference started they had been married in a secret ceremony and now Francine, the eternal Vantex virgin, was Mrs Frank Parkham. He had paid a price greater than anyone had ever paid for that top spot and it was all for nothing. He had wanted to outshine Big Fucker and prove he was not just a pathetic sidekick. He had been going to show the young guns how it was done and now all he had to show them was a tired old bitch who had just destroyed her greatest asset in marrying him.

Terry, too, had not joined in the celebrations. He wanted to dismiss Mark as a weak bastard. He wanted him to still be the twerp who was the last to get sent on *Assertion*. But he was not. Mark had surpassed him. Mark had him beaten on every front. It was unbearable. Terry repeated his identity over and again. Anger and frustration seethed in his veins as it seemed Mark could rob him even of the deep-seated knowledge of who he was. There was only one thing that could calm him. One thing that could make him refocus on his goals and remind him of his ability to achieve anything. He pulled out his precious hunting knife. He caressed it and brushed its razor-sharp blade against his cheek. This was his power. This knife had taught him who he was and showed him he had what it takes. It was the knife he had used to kill the goat.

six months later

Mark and Rae's concepts were adopted, along with a dull new accounting procedure, set to save the company $1.5 million a year. As Mark's concept was a fresh direction in need of its own identity, a discrete Strategic Business Unit was created within Vantex, with Mark as its president. He was allowed to pick his own staff.

Everyone made their pitch. Greg emphasised his seminal role in fostering Mark's brilliance—and Mark would need an experienced guiding hand to support him in the exciting journey ahead. Monica patted her stomach and suggested how important it was for them all to work together. Terry, loath to ingratiate himself with the Golden Boy, bit down his resentment and reminded Mark of the importance of having people around him he could trust. Terry had realised there was no point railing against fate. Mark had gazumped them all and the quickest way of advancing at Vantex was to be in the division that everyone wanted to be part of.

Mark decided to take his colleagues with him up to the floor newly dedicated to KitchenArt, one level below the CEO's offices. He knew what Greg, Monica and Terry were capable of and how their minds worked. In the absence of people he could trust, people he knew were the next best thing.

Within six months, the product designs were complete, the rights to use the works of art had been bought and everything was on track for the launch of the most exciting new range of kitchen appliances in the world. The prototypes had been sent under great secrecy to an ad agency for focus testing and strategic promotional concept development. The agency people were hard at work developing the criteria by which their own campaign concepts would be assessed.

The initial hard slog behind him, Mark decided the recently refurbished floor which was home to KitchenArt needed decoration. He persuaded the CEO, to whom he reported directly on first name terms, that art was the answer: the division had to be seen to be supporting the arts, and Australian artists in particular. The CEO 'liked his thinking' and agreed to an initial $200,000 budget. It was only proper to approach Oxman Studios, the largest and most prestigious contemporary art gallery in Sydney, to help with the establishment of the Vantex collection.

Mark sipped a glass of particularly fine semillon on the viewing deck of Oxman Studios. The deck overlooked the sculpture garden, a stark, gravelled courtyard with a pile of rubble taken from the recently demolished Women's Hospital in the middle.

'It's a very powerful statement. I find it difficult to look at it for too long. An intensely emotional work.' JayJo Bonnet (pronounced Bon-nay) was the director of Oxman Studios.

She was unable to stand close to Mark because of the wire hoop that held out the bottom of her black dress. The moment Mark walked into the gallery she had cursed herself for having worn the garment. She wanted to feel his breath on her face. She wanted to examine his skin to see if there was a single imperfection. He was a living work of art. She would have paid any sum to have him in her private collection.

Mark looked at the rubble. Bent and rusted iron rods stuck out of broken concrete. He tried to imagine what it would look like reproduced on the curve of a rice-steamer. JayJo continued the hard sell.

'I was born in that work of art. I took my first breath within the walls that now form themselves anew before us. If you stand in the far side of the sculpture garden on that ladder, you can see the sky, which used to be blocked out by the hospital. It's a marvellous juxtaposition. The joy you feel in the azure heavens, slashed with the guilt of our collective responsibility for removing the hospital—it's very challenging. I haven't yet made it past the third rung.'

'I think it might lose some of its potency if it were moved to our office. We're looking for paintings really.'

'What a pity. I can tell you're moved.'

Inside the gallery JayJo showed Mark a series of works from the finest artists currently working in Australia. They all happened to show at Oxman Studios. He assessed them with an eye to the future, looking for colour, movement and clearly recognisable images that would fit on the motor housing of a food-processor. JayJo was in raptures.

'You really do respond beautifully to art, Mark,' she said, leaning as far she dared over the edge of her dress. 'You have an intuitive understanding. It's quite uplifting.'

Mark had confined his responses to a simple 'yes' or 'no'

as to whether the works should be included on his short list. He must have been engaging with them on a much deeper level than he realised.

Together they compiled a list of works for further consideration, but they both knew that given the size of Mark's budget, much more wooing had to be done. This was no disappointment to JayJo. She would take Mark to the Contemporary Benefactors Event at the Museum of Contemporary Art. She planned to wear a much more approachable outfit.

◆

Raelene had not been given the same free rein as Mark. Because her concept was an advancement on an existing product—the BF 2000—it could not be completely handed over to her. She had to work within the existing department. Rae did not mind. She had broken through to management. She was making decisions, being consulted, attending meetings with colleagues and making a difference.

It could not be said that she was welcomed with open arms. Anyone who had packed David Mygrave off to rehab was a force to be reckoned with. She had done some serious leapfrogging and office space had to be made for her; little empires were made even smaller. As most managers had paid no attention to her when she worked for Frank Parkham, few knew what she was like.

Rae discovered this was a great starting place. It was assumed she had a ruthless temper and was not to be provoked. A slight show of annoyance was all that was needed to get her way on most issues. Despite this, most of her new colleagues did not take long to discover she was not the queen of darkness but a committed and honest worker, even if a little too determined to succeed. The project went well. The design of the in-freezer ice-cream maker proved trouble-free. The focus testing produced positive results. At the six-month mark, the machine tools had been made and were ready for production. Everyone admitted that Rae had managed the project brilliantly. Any hitches had been dealt with quickly. She was imaginative and positive, and the machine-makers worshipped the ground she walked on. She listened to them and had even adopted some of their suggestions.

It was time to begin work on the promotion of the BF 2010 (Ice-Cream Unlimited). Rae was called into the CEO's office. He was effusive in his praise.

'Rae, you've done a wonderful job so far. You've been carefully watched and we've all been very impressed. This next stage is the hardest part of all. We've got to sell the damn thing. The marketing has to be spot on, otherwise everything could be lost. It's an area where experience is everything.'

'I know I can handle it. I'm aware of my limitations and I've made a point of seeking advice from experts and taking on board their views.'

'That's why I'm sure you'll be pleased we're bringing in someone who has tremendous experience in the marketing of Vantex fridge–freezers. He is a bit of a maverick but he does know the product. He should do, he invented our best seller.'

The CEO buzzed Francine, the office door opened and David Mygrave walked in.

'This can't be serious.' Rae let it slip before she could stop herself.

'Rae, we understand your concern but we feel David deserves a second chance. He is completely rehabilitated. He's lived clean for six months and we think this is the ideal opportunity to get him back in the swing of things, and, I might add, to make amends to you.'

Rae was aghast. The man she had battled to the death at the conference stood before her, the image of pious sobriety. The glaze had disappeared from his eyes, he had lost some weight and he projected an aura of calm. He spoke.

'Rae, it's taken me a long way to get here. First I want to thank you. If it weren't for you I would not be clean now. You triggered a crisis that needed to happen. You saved me.'

He was right, but she had never thought of herself as doing him a favour. It was typical of him to turn a public humiliation to his advantage. He fixed her with a sincere eye.

'It's very important for me to help you with your concept. Yes Rae, it *is* your concept. I want to be part of *your* team.'

Rae was trapped. If she said no she would appear vindictive and be overruled anyway. It was the marriage proposal all over again. Men were so good at ambush. She swallowed hard and put out her hand.

'It's good to see you've got yourself together. I'm sure you'll make a great contribution.' As she spoke, relief burst into the room like overcharged champagne.

'That's settled then. David will be driving the marketing and promotion,' the CEO declared. 'Now I'm sure you've both got a lot to catch up on. I'm expecting great results.' He manoeuvred them out of the room before either could change their mind.

Outside the office, David turned to Rae. 'I think we should do dinner to discuss how we're going to go, don't you?'

'No, David. All our meetings will take place between the hours of nine and five, at the office, with other people present. Got that?'

'Yes. I'm sorry.' He pinned her again with his sincere look. 'I have to earn your trust. I'm prepared to do that.'

She groaned. The lack of anger made her suspicious. She had shafted him good and proper. No amount of rehab workshops, psycho-play or 'process through drama' could change him so completely. At Vantex the people you trusted least were those who refused to expose their bitterness.

◆

Monica's belly continued to grow. It was not a 'Princess Di' blooming pregnancy, but she had got over the morning sickness. She was determined to work until the last moment and would have had the child under her desk if Greg had not booked and pre-paid the natural birthing centre. At first she refused point-blank to go there, but at last consented to an inspection. After a guided tour of the painkillers available and receiving a guarantee that within five minutes she could be transferred from a paddling pool featuring underwater whale sounds to a high-tech operating theatre with epidurals on demand, she agreed to at least think about it.

Greg continued the marriage pressure; Monica resisted. In turn, she pressured Mark who demanded proof of paternity beyond her 'I just know'. Two months out from the due date, she realised she would have to put up or shut up before the baby came. Either Mark or Greg would see her through this, preferably Mark.

Both were keen to undergo blood tests and both hoped for exactly the same outcome.

Her maternal hormones still had not kicked in. She did not wander round her spare room at home kissing booties. If she had wanted to touch any objects of infancy she would have had to go to Greg's. His divorce was final and he was living alone in a pleasant terrace house, building up a ridiculously well-stocked nursery, fully confident that his child and the mother of his child would be moving in soon. Monica had reiterated he was not the only sperm donor, but had refused to reveal the names of the others. It was a confidentiality issue, she said. His confidence was unshaken.

The results took a week. Monica sat in the doctor's surgery receiving counselling before the doctor would tell her the outcome.

'Look,' she exploded, 'it's not a bloody HIV test. Give me the results.' The one thing she liked about visiting the doctor was that she did not have to play the caring mother role. It amazed her that just because her stomach was protruding, she was supposed to become some kind of earth goddess. Suddenly everyone was shocked if she used the word 'fuck' or walked past a shop window full of baby clothes without crying.

The doctor sighed. All those directives about making patients feel human, keeping them informed and comfortable, and this was the reaction she got.

'We effectively run two separate tests, one for each potential father. It's quite complicated. I'll explain it if you want, but basically you'll see at the bottom of each report whether the subject could in fact be the father. If there is a match, it's not conclusive proof, but if there is not a match, then that's definite—he can't be the father. Not sure if it's the result you want, but there you go.'

Monica looked at the bottom of Mark's test result and then at Greg's. The results were certainly not what she was expecting and far more conclusive than the doctor thought. Folding both results, she put them in her briefcase and walked out.

She went straight from the doctor's surgery to Greg's new home. She had promised to go there. He was pacing nervously in the nursery, tidying the baby's clothes once again to the tune of the soft-cornered musical merry-go-round he had bought that lunchtime.

'I'm not listening to that drivel for the next four years. I'll tell you that now.'

Greg turned round, thrilled that for the first time Monica had let herself in. She had always refused to use the key he had given her, insisting his house was not her home. This could only mean one thing.

'I told you.'

'Yes, you did.' Monica tried to look pleased.

'Let me see the result. I want to frame it. I want the baby to see it.'

'I don't have it. The doctor just told me.'

'So will you marry me?'

'I'm not giving up work. I'm not going to be a housewife. I'm keeping my name and at work you're just another competitor cluttering up my career path.'

Greg squeezed the booties he had been holding when Monica came in.

'It's a deal, and I've got a plan to clear some of the obstacles in your career path.'

This piqued Monica's interest. Perhaps there was still a spark of 'Kill if I Must' Hard Dick left; it would be great to be the beneficiary. Greg refused to divulge his plan. There were details to lock into place first.

◆

Lucy discovered that Mark had a new and more important job at Vantex when she tried ringing his old work number. A strange voice answered and she was politely transferred to switchboard, then to his assistant. Something was definitely up. First there had been his amazing looks, now he had an assistant.

The assistant, Constanza, put the call through to Mark. 'She says she's your girlfriend, but that could be any one of dozens of women, couldn't it?'

Mark grimaced. Fortunately, what Constanza lacked in deference she made up for in astonishing efficiency.

Assuming it could be any of the beautiful women he had been dating over the last few months, Mark flicked on his humorous charm. 'Hello, Mark here, so you want to be my girlfriend. I'll have my secretary send out the necessary forms and we'll take it from there.'

'It's Lucy.'

Mark flicked off the humorous charm. 'So, why've you called, outgrown Janet and Jerome?'

'Don't talk to me about them. I'm very disappointed in Janet. After all we've been through, after the endless stream of Mr Rights turning into Mr Disaster Zones—she says *I* have problems with relationships.'

Janet and Jerome were now exploring monogamy. Lucy described the break-up of the threesome in gruesome detail.

'Lucy, this is fascinating, but I am busy. Why did you call?'

'Well, I arranged to meet them for dinner and I said I would bring along someone and I really want to show her I can maintain a relationship so I was wondering if you ... well, you owe me that much at least.'

'I owe you nothing. You dumped me.'

'But I tried to get back together that time and you were horrible. It's only dinner.'

There was an extended cajoling and refusing. Mark had

not thought of Lucy in months and had assumed she had not thought of him. He was wrong. His persistent refusals were now making her angry.

'You'll regret this, Mark. You can't get through life being a user, you know. You used me till things took off for you and then I was dropped because I didn't fit in with your glamorous new life. I'm warning you, Mark, don't curdle my love for you because it'll leave a very sour taste.'

She slammed down the phone. Mark was perplexed, then realised that her parting line was from the *Woman* 'When Love Goes Wrong' feature. It was the first time either of them had used the word 'love', and it was months after she had broken up with him.

Lucy's strange phone call was followed by a visit from another would-be partner, Monica. She told him the news about Greg and herself. Smiling ruefully in resignation, she continued, 'Greg is going to be a horribly good father.'

'And what about you, Monica? Maternal feelings started yet?'

'I'm pre-paying a therapist now. It'll save a fortune when the kid's sixteen, sitting on the couch and detailing what a bitch his mother was. And if you can't breastfeed over the phone while you're at work, then I'm not doing it.'

'You can have time off.' Mark had never felt so warmly towards Monica as he did now. She was in *the* department to be in at Vantex, the baby was due within her time-plan, her objectives were all being met and yet an air of regret seeped through her make-up. The generous offer snapped her back into Monica mode.

'Get fucked!' Her baby was not to be interpreted as an inability to cope with the demands of her new work role.

As if on cue, a call came through from a sobbing media

buyer who had been in a meeting with Monica earlier that day. Mark put him on speaker-phone to facilitate a reconciliation. Monica had been on the verge of apologising until he foolishly used the word 'hormones'. She informed him that if her baby cried as much as he did, she would strangle it. She left the office to return to her schedule.

Mark took another call. It was Nigel from the ad agency. He had quickly assessed the changed dynamics at Vantex. Greg Haddrick had always been the one to be mates with; now it was Mark. Not that Nigel resented taking Mark out on expenses, introducing him to the models the agency used and generally schmoozing him. It did his reputation no harm to be seen with the highest flier in marketing or to hang out at the bar with a guy women cricked their necks to get a second look at. The reflected glory enhanced his own features.

'Mate, heard you were out with Nathalia again last night.'

'Who from?'

'My spies are everywhere, mate. So, d'you find out?'

'Oh yeah.'

Nigel unleashed the dirty laugh he had perfected in the early years of high school and not changed since. Nathalia was the new hostess on 'Million Dollar Babes', a quiz show giving ordinary people the chance to win a fortune if they were under thirty, beautiful and prepared to answer questions in a swimsuit. There was on-going debate at the agency whether Nathalia's breasts had received surgical help.

'So was it silicon valley?'

Mark laughed as he remembered the previous night's events. They had eaten dinner at a refurbished and almost chic revolving restaurant, at Nathalia's insistence. However great the food and elegantly understated the decor, there was no escaping the kitsch humour of the rotation and never quite knowing which direction the toilet would be as you spun slowly above the city. Nathalia had chosen the restaurant so she could point out every skyscraper in the CBD, name the company that owned it and quote the company's current share price. Whenever they passed the building of a company she had shares in, she proudly pointed to the results in her portfolio statement which sat between them on the table. She had made $590 that day alone.

Nathalia knew that even with surgery and the fine role models of Adriana and Vanna, she only had a few years of game show hosting ahead of her. Breaking into serious television would be hard. She had decided early on that wise investments were essential. Once she had the name and money she wanted to launch her own range of designer carpets. Clothes, underwear, swimwear and restaurants had been done to death by models. Carpets were totally new. 'Get Laid by Nathalia.' Nigel had suggested the slogan, free of charge, and she had enthusiastically adopted it.

Nigel had briefed Mark on how to tell if the breasts had implants. 'Mate, it's the Egg Test. When she's lying down without clothes on, if the boobs sag to the side like poached eggs, they're real, if they stay sitting upright like ten minutes hard-boiled, they're fake.'

Nigel was now on tenterhooks. He had two hundred dollars riding on Nathalia's breasts.

'Come on mate, poached or boiled?'

'You won't believe it.'

'Spill, mate, spill.'

'One of each.'

There was silence on the other end and then an explosion.

'You are having me on.'

'No. You *cannot* tell anyone. She swore me to secrecy. She

had surgery when she was seventeen because one breast developed more than the other.'

'She told you!'

The hysterical amusement on the other end of the phone made Mark uncomfortable. Nathalia had been a truly remarkable date and he felt guilty about spilling all to Nigel, not the man most likely to keep a secret.

'So you Got Layed by Nathalia.'

'Sorry Nige, gotta go, CEO's on the other line. When are we seeing the results of the focus testing?'

'Friday mate, you'll love it. And I expect a full account of Nathalia.'

The CEO was not on the line, but Mark did not want to reveal the previous evening's activities. He and Nathalia had made love. She had been overwhelmed and, as usual, Mark got off on the pleasure he was giving. It seemed that everywhere he touched became an automatic erogenous zone. Her skin, so soft and smooth, became so sensitive that the slightest caress became unbearably intense. After she had reached orgasm, he could not touch her for ten minutes; her postcoital pleasure was just too great. He lay beside her, breathing gently onto her skin, watching it tense and listening to her gentle moans. He loved this moment. Nathalia, like the other women he had dated in the past few months, lay blissfully cocooned in pleasure.

Unfortunately, Nathalia took his pensiveness as evidence of a deeper interest. Not leaping out of bed immediately or snapping out of the post-coital mood in seconds was interpreted as a sign of emotional commitment. Nathalia bared her soul and poured out her life story over the next four hours, including full details of the surgery.

The life story left little room for sleep. Exhausted in the

morning, Mark was at a loss for words when Nathalia, even before she called her broker, went to her chest of drawers, pulled the second one right out and tipped its contents onto the floor.

'This one's for you.'

He smiled and pretended he was late for an early meeting. He would have to call her and arrange to meet for coffee at Cafe Bilbao. A window table was perfect for 'the talk'. The cafe was noisy enough for him not to be overheard and the window tables looking onto one of Sydney's trendiest streets meant the recipient of 'the talk' could not make a scene without the whole world knowing. Especially if she was conscious of being a role model to today's impressionable youth.

◆

Word of David Mygrave's return from the clinic swept round Vantex faster than the latest vacuum cleaner. It was a major comeback. The last time people had seen him was in the K hole. Now he looked better than ever and had wangled his way onto the project he had so very nearly stolen. He still had a touch of his old magic.

Terry was particularly interested in his return: the enemy of the friend of his rival was his potential ally. He did not believe the 'it's an important part of David's rehabilitation to help Rae with her project' line. All reports from that division suggested David was being supportive to the point of sycophancy and that the in-freezer ice-cream maker project was going well, but there was a chemistry seething underneath the surface visible only to those who shared the frustration of blocked plans. It was time he and David Mygrave got together for a little chat. He decided to strike while his anger was hot.

'David, it's Terry here from KitchenArt.'

'Good to talk to you, Terry. It must be wonderful working on such a great project.'

'Yes, Mark is quite outstanding. I was pleased to hear you were back and working with Rae. That's marvellous.'

'Yes, I'm determined to see she gets all the success this project deserves.'

'Just how I feel with Mark. I'm behind him all the way.'

'Marvellous.'

'We need to get together. Meet me at Grainger's Bar at six tonight.'

'I'll be there.' Mygrave put the phone down and smiled. Kindred spirits were always useful.

Terry worked rapidly through his daily objectives to reach his target in time for the meeting. At six he was sitting in Grainger's Bar with a full set of completed tasks and a couple of self-affirmations under his belt. FutureVisions was not the end of everything, but the start of a new campaign, he mused. He really ought to thank Mark for creating a large and dynamic new department in which he could assert himself.

Grainger's Bar was tucked away on a street several blocks from Vantex. It was the chosen venue for secret work-based affairs. Mygrave turned up, bought himself a mineral water and sat down with Terry.

'So you were the Vantex golden boy until Boyd launched KitchenArt and flashed his smile and now you need revenge. You've seen I'm working with his little friend, who you believe totally fucked my career, and you think I'll be a valuable ally.'

'It's obvious we understand each other.' Terry held up his drink as if to confirm the alliance. Mygrave did not respond in kind.

'I don't think so. I am a reformed man. I'm not going to revenge myself on a woman who saved my life.'

Terry choked on his drink, more in surprise that David thought this line would work than in belief it was genuine.

David continued. 'I won't have anyone hear me say a word against Raelene or our project.'

'But surely…'

'But nothing. I'm giving it my complete support. If, for example, one of the tooling engineers on the new freezer suggested a last minute change that I secretly knew contained a serious design fault, I would argue most strongly against it. If Rae's personal prejudice against me ensured she adopted that change because I opposed it, well that's entirely her issue. I will have done my best for her and the project.'

Terry understood. There was no point openly tearing down the company stars. It was better to facilitate their self-destruction. Terry cooed at the subtlety of Mygrave's plan, and for the first time since the conference felt a gurgling of delight in his throat. His mind was racing for possible ways to help Mark to his own downfall.

◆

'You're a wonderful, exciting, intelligent person.' Mark was giving Nathalia 'the talk' in the window of Cafe Bilbao, just as the waiter was setting down one decaf long black with soy lite milk on the side and a flat white. The waiter rolled his eyes. How many times had that line been used in that window? The long black would be sent flying any moment, he thought, as he turned to fetch a cloth in readiness.

'Thank you Mark, I know you mean that.'

The waiter did a double take; this guy was seriously smooth if he got that reaction.

Mark had carefully not used the word 'beautiful'. Non-physical compliments would make her feel less of a sex object. He continued, 'It's not you, it's me. I just don't have time for a relationship right now. Mentally, spiritually, I'm just not ready. I could go along for the ride, but I'm not prepared to do that to you. I don't want to hurt you and I know for a fact you'll do just fine without me.'

Nathalia smiled and jokingly pulled a face. 'You got that right.' They both smiled soulfully and sipped their coffees.

'I appreciate your honesty, Mark. We're both really going somewhere, but perhaps it's not the same place.'

The waiter, cloth still in hand, started to wipe the table behind them.

'Wherever it is that we go, it's important to me that we still be friends.'

'Yes, Mark, I'd like that very much.'

The waiter's jaw dropped. She had actually fallen for the 'we can still be friends' line. He left the spotless and rather damp table to fill in his co-worker by the espresso machine.

'I made $2125 today.' Nathalia indicated that 'the talk' was over by revealing her investment profits. Her mobile rang. It was her friend Lianna. Nathalia, after getting the summons to Cafe Bilbao, had realised what was in store. It was Sydney's premier dumping ground, after all, and so she had arranged for Lianna to call her to facilitate a quick getaway. She had expected to be storming away furiously by now, but somehow she was not angry with Mark. She looked into his eyes and saw a real regret. She did not feel used. The memory of how her skin felt as he had made love to her was by itself worth 'the talk'. It would see her through many a lonely night.

'That was my broker. There're some papers I have to sign urgently.'

'That's OK.'

'Please, Mark, stay in touch. We'll do lunch.'

'I'd love that.'

Nathalia gave one more smile and left as her phone rang again. It *was* her broker. There had been a late swing, she had lost $23 on the day.

Once she had gone, the waiter printed the bill and took it over to Mark.

'If you want to leave a tip, just let me know how you got away with all those lines. Any other guy saying them would result in me mopping down the window and him heading for the dry-cleaners.'

'The truth is, it's just the way you say it.' Mark flashed him a smile to reinforce his point.

'Coffee's on me,' the waiter said, hurrying back to the espresso machine to recover from the dizzy turn that suddenly came over him.

◆

ANBB&D was in chaos. The clients from Vantex were due any moment for the KitchenArt presentation and the visuals were still being finalised. Somehow, every presentation or bid seemed to end in chaos. Regardless of how many planning meetings were held and critical milestones adhered to, something always caused panic and tantrums at the last moment. Nigel had spent the previous day screaming from his glass office down to the main creative floor. The office, with glass floor, walls and ceiling, was in a corner of the building and designed to keep him in constant touch with the world he sought to influence. It was accessed via a runway suspended from the roof. There was a fireman's pole exit straight down to the creative floor. Nigel's inner child kept his work fresh, vibrant and relevant.

The KitchenArt campaign had started well. Progress had been well ahead of schedule. Focus testing revealed that people were excited by the products and that many wanted complete sets for their kitchens. Seventy per cent of people who expressed an interest in one product, expressed strong interest in buying more than one. The agency had tried various faces to represent the product as Nigel was committed to the human touch for all machinery promotion. The celebrity faces tested all gained similar results—good, but no greater than the products on their own. There had not been a single face that screamed 'KitchenArt, buy it now' above the others. Nevertheless, the campaign had been developed and the computer presentation completed three days early. Just as the account managers and art directors were congratulating themselves with particularly fine espresso from the agency's Gaggia, Nigel stormed back from lunch.

'Sweetheart, I want totally new focus testing organised now!'

Everyone knew what the word 'sweetheart' meant. It was addressed to whomever he saw first on entering the creative floor and it meant big changes to be carried out immediately—and a late night for all.

'I know the face for KitchenArt, it's brilliant. We're gonna knock 'em dead...Look, I don't care if they all live in the middle of nowhere, I want the focus groups in here NOW... Sweetheart, we need new roughs. Look at this, it's shite. We've got a fucking brilliant product here and we're treating it like some crap new cheap range that's gonna fall apart when you switch it on. Come on guys, let's get creative about this.'

Nigel had come to Sydney in the 1980s advertising invasion. A cockney barrow boy made good, he may have dumped the red-rimmed glasses and the ponytail, but for Nigel the eighties had never really ended. Life was still a series of fucking brilliant campaigns, shite products and clients who couldn't market their way out of an arsehole if a turd was pushing them along'

KitchenArt was the exception. This time he had something decent to work with and he was not going to let slack bastards sipping poncy Italian coffee let the product struggle to sell itself.

'Come on guys, don't you want to be the best? I want Carolyn, Nick, John, Andy in the boardroom in ten minutes... I don't care if Carolyn's on leave, get her in. This is important.'

In three days the agency completely redeveloped the campaign that had taken three weeks to get to that stage. Carolyn, Nick, John, Andy all agreed that the worst thing about Nigel's last-minute hunches and changes of direction was that they usually proved right. This one was no exception. The new face of KitchenArt had scored through the roof. Respondents were 60 per cent more likely to buy the products if presented with the new face.

The team worked constantly under the never-ending encouragement of Nigel, usually encapsulated in the lines 'That's shite, start again' or 'I fucking told you to use the teal. I don't care if there's none in Australia, get some in.' Social engagements were bypassed, homes abandoned and lives cancelled until the presentation.

Nigel was finally persuaded that the computer presentation was not shite—at three o'clock on the morning of the big day. He took the rest of the morning off to focus himself and prepare for the pitch of his life, leaving the sweethearts to finish off. When the clients arrived, Nigel still was not there. He was round the corner, honing his presentation in the bar. Carolyn called him, leaving a message on his mobile, and finally sent the receptionist round to drag him in to the cry of 'Sweetheart, why the fuck didn't anyone call me? It's just not on.'

Mark, Monica, Terry and Greg were sitting in the ANBB&D boardroom trying to get comfortable. Monica, well aware of the agony that more than thirty minutes on the ANBB&D steel chairs provoked, had brought a cushion. Even without the weight of a baby the seats gave everyone a dimpled bum pattern for the first three hours after getting up. ANBB&D made up a chair for every client, with its logo marked out in raised bumps. Mark, Terry and Greg chose their seats carefully, aware that whichever company they sat on, they would be promoting it on their backsides for the rest of the afternoon. They looked longingly at Monica's cushion, but even Terry couldn't think of a valid reason why he should take it from her.

'What wankers,' Terry fumed, still angry at Nigel's betrayal at FutureVisions. 'We've paid for these damn chairs, you know. I'm sitting on Jedcorp. If you hear a farting noise, it'll be me passing comment on their new campaign.'

'We'll probably assume you're trying to say something intelligent and ignore it.' With her cushion, Monica knew she had the upper hand in the meeting. If it came to arguing till the bitter end, she would win.

Without announcement or the appearance of any ANBB&D staff, the room went dark. The Vantex logo appeared on a screen. The theme from *2001: A Space Odyssey* started and domestic appliances rotated in an expanse of universe, form-ing a star system round the sun of Vantex. A meteor hurtled across the galaxy with the word 'Welcome' emblazoned in its tail. The lights went up and Nigel was standing in front of them. He did not do friendly chit-chat at the start of meetings. The more intimidating, the more theatrical the presentation, the harder it was for clients to alter or reject anything. He launched into his pitch, honed, primed and refreshed. Carolyn, Nick, John, Andy, all exhausted and at snapping point, remained hidden in the control booth ensuring the pre-sentation went according to Nigel's specifications.

He presented the initial focus test results. 'It seems that KitchenArt will sell itself,' explained Nigel, 'or that's what any other agency would tell you. But not here at ANBB&D. Here we go a step further. If the products will sell well with any old person fronting the campaign, how much better will they sell with the right person? Ladies, gents, we have that person. We did a second set of focus tests with a new face, a fresh face, a face no-one out there in the real world has seen before. The face says, "I tell the truth" and people believe it. Once in a generation we get this perfect synergy of man and machine, person and product.' As Nigel spoke a fanfare of music gradually built up until he was almost shouting his final words. The room grew dark, a single spot lit Nigel's face.

'My clients, I present to you the face of Vantex KitchenArt.' With those words his face disappeared, the music reached its dramatic climax and a dazzlingly bright image burst from the screen behind him. They gasped and then, in the darkness as the face faded, they all leaned forward, as if scared of losing the image. The presentation had gone perfectly. The face on the screen was Mark's.

In the black silence that followed, the clients took a

moment to adjust. Somebody slammed a fist onto the table. Then Mark spoke. 'I think we could do with some light now.'

The lights came on and Nigel was sitting at the table with them grinning. Carolyn, Nick, John, Andy came in to join the meeting and discuss details. No-one knew where to begin. Using real managers to promote products was a minefield: identification with a person who could leave the company and join the opposition; ego inflation; time away from the serious issue of management. Greg spoke first. He was used to dealing with the agency and had seen more Nigel productions than performances at Sydney Opera House.

'Well, you practically drowned your sausage in sizzle this time.'

'I think Mark should abstain from any discussion on this seeing as it concerns him directly.' Terry, not sure how to play the meeting, decided it best to downgrade Mark's role in the decision-making.

'I'm head of the department. Whoever we use to promote the campaign, it's my decision.' Mark slapped him down.

'So how do we play this?' asked Monica. No-one wanted to start a discussion on Mark's physical attributes with him in the room.

'First, we're going to register our dissatisfaction that additional focus testing was carried out without consulting Vantex. We will not be paying for it.' Mark shifted in his chair, aware that the large 'V' of Vantex was now burned into his right buttock. 'However, the results, if as conclusive as Nigel says, cannot be ignored. We will discuss the proposal as if that was not me, but a model for hire, albeit a very intelligent one. We will decide whether that model is right for the campaign. If the answer is yes, then we at Vantex have a private discussion as to whether it is appropriate for me to play that role.'

It was calm, clear, logical.

'You knew about this, didn't you,' Terry flashed at Mark.

'No, he didn't,' Nigel broke in. 'This is an ANBB&D initiative. Unconventional, I know, but that's what gets results.'

'You can cut the sales talk.' Monica, despite her comfy cushion, was getting impatient to leave. 'We need the layouts for ads, storyboards for TVCs, POS material and the breakdown of your figures.'

'Monica's right,' Greg agreed as Terry raised his eyebrows. Greg always agreed with Monica nowadays. 'These focus test results are the strongest I've ever seen. It's now up to us to decide whether it's worth the risks. Mark?'

'I agree. There're some major decisions to take but we're not doing it while our backsides are branded with logos.'

Carolyn, Nick, John, Andy distributed copies of the layouts and test results, having said nothing in the meeting. Nigel, having completed his show, went into mate mode as they left the boardroom.

'So Mark, Nathalia was on the phone. Don't know how you get away with it.'

Mark flashed a brief smile. He did not want to discuss his private life in front of his colleagues.

'I get it, mate. But, honestly, one of each, you gotta be having me on.'

'We'll get back to you. Very impressive presentation—you'll win an Oscar yet.'

◆

Crammed into one cab, the Vantex team headed to the Harbour Bridge, and their southside territory. Once out of earshot of the agency they had started talking.

'So Mark, what are you going to do?' Greg kicked the discussion off.

'I don't know, it's as much a personal decision as a professional one.'

'I think it's a bad move. The results of the previous tests were good enough to run a viable campaign. If you become the public figure, you'll have no time to run the division. You'll be touring shopping malls, getting your photo taken and kissing fat housewives.' Monica did not make it sound like an attractive proposition.

'I disagree.' They looked at Terry in shock. If one person was going to slam a whole advertising campaign based on Mark's good looks, surely it was him.

'It's too great an opportunity to miss. Mark's loyalty to the product is solid, he won't run off and endorse the opposition when it's his concept. And let's face it, he's got a winning smile. We all know that, don't we?' The last comment was addressed directly at Monica.

'Yes, we know he's pretty, but he's needed at the office. I don't like management getting caught up in the whole advertising PR thing—it leads to disaster.'

Mark interrupted the discussion on himself.

'I'll have to consult the CEO. Greg, you haven't said what you think.'

'I was wondering if you could see Ascham from the Harbour Bridge.'

That killed the conversation. Ascham was an exclusive girls' school with phenomenal harbour views. Greg's mind was not on the matter in hand but on which school his baby should be put down for. Monica groaned. There was no forgetting the large lump on her stomach, Greg brought it up

at every available opportunity. That reminded her of the weekend event that had been organised.

'While I remember, we're getting married this Saturday.
The two of you should come round to Greg's house at 2 pm.'

'That's fantastic, congratulations. Why are you only just
telling us now?' Mark was relieved.

'Don't get excited,' Monica interrupted his well-wishing,
'it's low-key—keeping the baby legit, that's the only reason.'

'Monica doesn't want a song and dance. We can't really
have a big do, not——'

'When the bride's banged up and sticking out like a camel.'
Terry finished the sentence for him.

The cab driver cursed the bank of traffic they had run
into. These had to be the weirdest passengers in weeks. First
this model guy doing a prima donna routine over some ad
campaign. The other young guy obviously had a crush on
him and then the other two suddenly announce they're getting married as if it's a pop in for coffee if you're not busy
event. He thought of his own wedding, the twelve months to
organise and the four years to pay for it—perhaps this lot
had the right idea after all.

◆

Back at the office they went their separate ways to plan their
personal strategies. Monica had genuinely thought it was a
bad idea, but also did not like to think of Mark completely
taking over the identity of the products. It could be a brilliant career move for him. If the products sold and he became
a household name, any demands could be made. He would
be so far ahead of her, there would be no catching up. She
sat down on her ergonomic chair. Her back ached, she was

exhausted and once again she felt the game slipping away from her. She knew the birth would be painful, every mother she had met since getting pregnant had told her so. Still, she looked forward to being relieved of the burden. Greg and she had still not discussed their arrangements for child-rearing. This worried her. He said that he was sorting it all out, but she did not like uncertainty. If it involved her taking any more than two weeks off work, it was not on.

Terry was worried that he had been too obvious. The sight of Mark's face in the presentation had sent rigid spasms through his body. The man could take over the whole company. He tried to focus on a plan to maximise the situation for himself. That such a campaign would put Mark in an incredibly strong position was good. He would be a threat to the CEO and the board. By endorsing the campaign, he would get their backs up and mobilise forces against him. This might just be the rope by which Mark would hang himself—and his vanity would tie the knot. He called Mygrave to get his opinion. Mygrave thought he had done the right thing and added a piece of advice: 'If you've got any staff stock options outstanding, take them all up now...today.'

Terry dialled his broker.

As Mark looked at his own face on the screen at the agency, another piece of his life had fallen into place. It was inevitable. No-one could sell the product like he could. He knew that the CEO would take some persuading, because of the threat that Mark would pose to his authority. He needed to make clear he was not angling for greater power. He would offer to sign a five-year contract, terminable at any stage by Vantex. He would not be able to resign without the company's consent, but he could be fired at any stage. Five years would give Vantex time to develop a second wave of the products and a supplementary promotional strategy, one not focused on him. It would be his own head on a plate. One thing he knew for certain, being the visible face of KitchenArt was inevitable. Whatever price had to be paid, would be paid.

◆

For the first time since the conference, Rae was not enjoying her work. Mygrave scrutinised her every move seeking his own advantage. His rehabilitation at Vantex was complete. Everyone had warmed to his new humility. He made herbal infusions for colleagues, blending specific herbs to help with their stress, their exhaustion, their colds. Rae felt that for a company full of career-focused, backstabbing, ruthless operators they were incredibly naïve to fall for the reconstructed, drug-free, harmony-loving David Mygrave. Once again Rae found herself at odds with her world—either they were mad or she was.

What she needed was a talk with Mark, but their days of regular get-togethers seemed to be over. They had played telephone tag for weeks. Whenever she phoned him, Constanza smugly informed her he was at a photo shoot, filming a commercial or being interviewed. As the face of KitchenArt his time was no longer his own. She missed his company and the sense of having him on her side. She needed his advice. She needed to know what he thought of the new Mygrave and, if she were honest, she needed his smile and the warm comfort of having him look directly into her eyes.

The issue she really wanted to discuss was a modification to the ice-cream blade motor housing that one of the toolmakers had suggested. Any change at this late stage would have to be rushed through to meet launch deadlines, but this promised to deliver far greater efficiency and reduce the amount of heat generated by the motor. This would reduce the energy spent cooling the freezer. It sounded like a good idea, but one that might be kept over for the next model so as not to delay production. She decided to raise the issue at her team's next planning meeting. Virtually before she had finished detailing the amendment and its implications, Mygrave vehemently opposed it. He made it ridiculously clear that he thought it was a bad idea.

If he opposed it so strongly, her knee-jerk reaction was to support it. Was he counting on this, she wondered. Or perhaps he wanted to provoke her into rejecting it, so she could look stupid later on. She needed Mark. He would be able to clarify the issue. But a decision needed to be made straightaway if the amendment was to go ahead and production to remain on schedule. Rae decided to eliminate Mygrave from her decision. What would she do if he had not come back on the scene? The tooler had suggested an amendment; it sounded like a good idea; it put some pressure on their time-lines, but the energy saving would be a considerable asset. She reread the full report. It raised the slight possibility of moisture encroachment from the freezer weakening the casing in the long term. It read as if the toolers were dredging up anything negative to make the report look more balanced. She decided. They would go ahead with the change. Although it was a relief to have the issue sorted out, Mygrave remained in the back of her mind. She could not be confident of anything she thought he might have a hand in.

As if to confirm her doubts, the minute her decision had been communicated, a memo, copied to virtually the entire company, landed on her desk, restating David Mygrave's opposition. He was brewing something, and it was not a herbal infusion.

◆

The publicity campaign for KitchenArt was going to be huge, the biggest in Vantex's history. The industry buzz was reaching fever pitch even before the product was sighted by the general public. Only one of each item in the KitchenArt range had been allowed out of the security warehouse. Mark had to be aware, at all times, of their whereabouts. At present they were in his sight at the studio hired to film the television commercials. As he gazed at them under the studio lights, Mark had to admit they were beautiful. The quality and clarity of the printing on the plastics was finer than anything he had seen before. The colour reproduction matched that printed on paper. Their shapes, the gentle curves that in Mark's opinion enhanced the beauty of the art, were revolutionary in the world of bench top appliances. He was rightly proud of his creations.

It was the end of a long day of filming. The director was thrilled with Mark's performance. Trained actors had never needed as little preparation as he did. With the minimum of make-up, scant attention to his hair and wearing a black shirt with just enough buttons undone to reveal a hint of the glorious body underneath, Mark had to stand holding a food-processor and saying, 'You want it in your kitchen don't you?'

It was a simple shot: no camera movement, one line from Mark and no other action. If it had been down to Mark alone it would have required just one take, not fifteen. He delivered his line with sincere suggestive perfection, then flashed a seductive smile. It was the smile that caused the problem. On the first take, everyone had been so transfixed they simply stood gaping. The director forgot to shout cut. The second take caused a production assistant to faint. On the third take the mike operator dropped the boom, narrowly missing Mark's head. Each time something went wrong: somebody was overcome; someone had to take a break. No-one had experienced a shoot like it. The crew would have happily given up their working lives and spent their days in a kitchen with a food-processor, waiting for Mark to come home and give it to them.

Nigel was thrilled, even if the shoot was costing a fortune. He called for the set to be cleared of non-essential people and the take finally worked. Unfortunately the day's filming was not over. The tricky shot of the commercial involved the camera sweeping down from a crane on high, passing through a window and closing in on the food-processor like a heavenly muse drawn irresistibly to art in its most perfect form, or so the director described it.

Each time the director was satisfied with the shot, Nigel would yell, 'Shite, mate, shite.' Each time Nigel thought it was 'triffic,' the director found a technical objection. So it went through twelve takes.

'Sweetheart, we're not slapping together a bloody porn film, this is supposed to be art,' Nigel snarled.

Grabbing a reflector shield the director smashed its soft fabric over Nigel's head. Mark intervened.

'As the person who is paying for this artistic tiff, I think we'll call it a day. You've enough takes to get a decent shot. The two of you can argue in your own time over which one to use.'

Both men looked sheepish, feeling they had let Mark

down. The director pushed the reflector down Nigel's body so he could step out of it. Mark turned his attention to another person who had been watching the filming with delight, Felicity from Vantex's PR firm, Attention! She had been taken on specifically to monitor and enhance Mark's public image. It was a dream job. She had started by organising a set of publicity stills of Mark. From there it was easy. Setting up media interviews, television guest spots or personality profiles was a simple matter of sending off the pics and waiting for the call. No begging, cajoling or persuading required. Mark was hot and she had arranged to make him the best known face in Australia by the date of the product launch.

Mark was Felicity's big break. The bigger she made him, the bigger she made herself. No-one was aware quite how grand her plans were. Everyone believed Mark was promoting the products. Felicity knew Mark *was* the product. She had already arranged for him to get into the final selection for *Woman*'s most eligible bachelor feature and had turned down an offer of $5000 from the Men As Art calendar for him to pose nude. She planned to put out a press release two weeks after the launch informing the world he had turned down $20 000 for it.

Her brief from Vantex for the product launch was to organise a low-key industry and media affair. Felicity reckoned she could do better than that. She had persuaded Nigel to give her a few shots of Mark and some commercial footage in advance to leak to television and print media. A bit of pre-publicity never did any harm. She wanted to ensure the night was huge. If she did it right she could be running her own PR firm within six months—with Mark as her principal client. He interrupted her forward projections by requesting a briefing on launch preparations.

. 'It's going to be a very exclusive, very limited affair,' she lied, getting as close to Mark's ear as she dared. 'We don't want GP there. TV commercials, in-store displays, that's for them. I've found some gorgeous fabrics for the reveals. Now, location. I'm putting my foot down, it has to be the Museum of Contemporary Art, because that's what it's all about, isn't it. You can check out the space this evening, you're going to the Benefactors do there, aren't you?'

Mark was surprised she knew of his date with JayJo, but let it pass. He asked her about the product assessments organised for the print media.

'Great news on that front, my love, I've persuaded *Honest Opinion* to give each product the top marks in its category in the next Household Appliances issue.'

Mark, who had always referred to *Honest Opinion* for its impartial recommendations when buying anything, protested, 'But they haven't even had samples yet, how can they know what they're like?'

'Darling, we don't waste samples on them! No, I've already proofed their reviews and made a few changes. I'll send publicity shots of the gear when the media embargo's lifted.'

Felicity had everything under control, thought Mark. She survived on the oxygen of publicity and could probably spot a fabulous PR opportunity while scuba diving in custard. He left to meet JayJo.

Their work together in assembling the Vantex collection was complete. JayJo had been moved to tears by Mark's final selection. 'They're exactly the selection my late husband made,' she remarked. Mark found it odd that a dead man could select artworks created after his demise, and a little worrying that he would choose the same himself. Nathaniel Oxman had bankrolled JayJo's gallery and been one of

Sydney's leading art patrons, but only after his death. He had left an impressively large portfolio of a different but more lucrative kind to the grieving JayJo. A devoted businessman who loved corporate takeovers, he had literally died of excitement when floating a small telecommunications business in which he was a majority shareholder. As the shares hit four times the launch price on the first morning of trading, he leaped down a set of steps at the stock exchange only to concuss himself on a drop in the ceiling, causing internal bleeding on his brain. He died before trading closed, leaving JayJo in serious need of a hobby to fill the void that was his absence. Thus Oxman Studios was created. Nathaniel lived on in JayJo's heart and through her expressed his opinions on art. Somehow he always seemed to like works that increased rapidly in value.

Mark picked up JayJo in a taxi at her gallery. She had carefully chosen a dress that would not prevent intimate contact which she initiated immediately, getting into the back of the car and sliding next to him as if another three people had yet to squeeze in. From a distance her dress appeared to be made of a coarse sack-like material badly fitted over a none too thin body. Closer to, it was revealed as pure silk so tightly pleated it could have stretched to fit the additional people Mark thought would be getting into the taxi.

The MCA American Express Hall was packed with the cream of Sydney's art society: buyers, artists, critics and those whose only participation in the art world was attending such functions. JayJo clamped her hand onto Mark's arm as they entered, determined that no-one would whisk him away from her that evening. There were some important artists she was keen for him to meet. All from her own gallery.

'Mark, I want you to meet Jeff Tourner, he created that gorgeous piece you were so taken with.'

Mark had no idea which piece she meant, but before he could find anything suitable to say, Jeff grasped his hand.

'I don't allow just anyone to take my work. I have to know it will be nurtured.' Mark smiled in an attempt to get Jeff to release his hand. He failed.

'My works grow, you know. They mature. In the wrong hands they are transformed to a point where I do not recognise them. They are no longer my paintings. But with you, my work will be in safe hands—you have a remarkable nose.'

Jeff finally let go of Mark's hand only to grasp his chin, moving it round to see the way the light played on his features.

'I think the nose is everything. The nose I could work with.'

'Blinded by superficial beauty as ever, Jeff.' They had been joined by another of JayJo's artists, Lucia Knox. 'Can't you see it's that forehead that anchors the entire face in history?' She placed the heel of her hand on Mark's forehead while Jeff held fast to his chin. JayJo remained firmly attached to his arm. 'That forehead has conquered nations, ridden bareback across the Steppes. It has a magnificent slope. I could do an entire show...'

'It's the eyes.' Both Jeff and Lucia grimaced as Mike Carnell, a realist whose work they despised, clambered between them to gaze deep into Mark's eyes. 'I would do the eyes.'

Mark had to forcibly remove himself from their attention.

'Perhaps if all your artists worked together, JayJo, they might manage the whole of my face.'

JayJo burst into delighted applause and the artists snapped out of their reverie. JayJo manoeuvred Mark away just as

Lucia began to wonder aloud what had happened to the payment for the most recent sale of her work.

As they worked their way through the crowd Mark noticed more people, presumably artists, staring at him intently: at his hair, his mouth, his shoulders, even his shoes. No-one seemed concerned with the whole Mark, just the component which most appealed to their artistic sensibility.

Mark had no idea where he was being taken. The thick crowd meant he had little sense of his whereabouts in the room. After some thirty minutes of thinking he was bound for somewhere, Mark realised he was being paraded around in a circle like a prize bull, his only destination the following day's gossip columns.

'JayJo, could we take a rest somewhere a little less crowded.' Mark decided to put an end to the display. JayJo smiled with surprised delight and immediately led him to a terrace overlooking the harbour. The vision of the Opera House and the expanse of the water, its waves tipped in light reflected from the city, provoked the inevitable response of anyone who lived in Sydney—the sigh of satisfaction that this calming view was theirs for the taking whenever they wanted it.

'It doesn't matter how familiar it becomes, it's always remarkable, isn't it?' Mark commented.

JayJo, staring at his profile, agreed. 'I could look at it forever.'

Mark turned and saw what JayJo was admiring. She was not the slightest bit embarrassed. Sitting on the wall with her back to the view, she invited Mark to join her. She placed his arm on hers and it immediately disappeared in the mass of silken pleats on the arm of her dress.

'You're wasted on domestic appliances, Mark. I could put you at the head of any corporation in the city.'

'JayJo, I'm very excited by my project. It may not be high finance, but I'm creating something.'

'And you'll be a huge success...You know there has been no-one since Nathaniel. Several have tried but he always said no. He knows who will be right for me...He said yes to you.'

Mark had not expected her to get to the point so quickly. He had hoped to hint his way out of it before ever it was reached.

'I'm not an unattractive woman, Mark, and I could make you one of the leading figures in this town. I think you should consider it. I don't fool myself that you could love me with the passion of Nathaniel, but you could love me with honesty.'

'JayJo, you *are* attractive but I can't. I need to do all this myself.'

'I understand. You are a beautiful man, Mark.' She spoke with the resonance of a fairy godmother and kissed him gently on the forehead. 'Nathaniel said that would be your answer. If it hadn't been, I don't think he would have recommended you. Now, if I can't have you, can I at least set some tongues wagging?'

They both smiled, stood up and walked back to the event. It was not until they were three metres from the wall that JayJo felt a tug. A thread had caught on the wall but the expansive nature of her pleats stretched her dress out behind her, like an extra sail on the Opera House.

◆

Rae was sitting in Mark's office. It was 7.30 in the morning. The telephone tag had gone on too long. It was over four weeks since they'd had a conversation together. Her product with the modified motor housing would be hitting the shops that week. Mygrave had been suspiciously happy. Even if she couldn't have a long talk with him, Rae wanted to speak to Mark, hear his voice and see him smile. She would not let another day pass without seeing him. If she had to wait in his office for him she would. She heard voices outside the door. It was Mark, but he was not alone. The door burst open.

'How the hell did this happen?' Mark stormed in followed by Terry, Monica and Felicity.

'Get me Nigel, perhaps he can throw some light.'

Rae felt like a schoolgirl hanging out by the seniors room, hoping to meet the head boy she had a crush on.

'Rae, what are you doing here?'

'I was hoping to have a word.'

'Absolute crisis, but stay—I want your input.'

'Can't, I've a couple of fires to put out myself.'

She headed for the door and Mark followed her out of the office.

'Is everything OK?'

'I don't know. I was just fed up with message banks. Can we get together?'

Mark was glad to see her. He knew this day was going to be a killer and he suddenly felt an aching need for her calm support and the fun of the debriefs they used to enjoy.

'Tonight, 6 pm, usual bar.'

'Great.' Rae felt another girlie crush-rush. He had seemed pleased to see her. Perhaps he had missed her as much as she missed him. Then she shook her head in disbelief—what next, writing his name on her briefcase in secret code?

◆

Mark had a crisis indeed. *Woman* magazine had hit the streets with one of the ad agency shots of Mark on the cover with the shotline, 'Who is this man and why we'd buy a box of smog from him if he hand-delivered it.' Inside was an 'exclusive interview' with the man who was going to transform the nation's kitchens, plus a sneak preview of some of the products. Not only that, but *Woman*'s sister program on Channel 8 had broadcast one of the commercials, causing a station switchboard meltdown. The media launch was not for another week; the products were not due in the shops until the week after that. Riots could break out before then.

The Vantex night-time emergency line had been jammed from the moment the magazine hit the newsstands with homemakers demanding the new product or claiming they were Mark's mother/sister/brother/wife/boyfriend and had to speak to him. No-one was able to make calls out of the office. Vantex would be at a standstill all day. Already eager shoppers were on the street waiting for the building to open, wondering if the products were available. Department stores had faxed through urgent requests, unable to get on the phone.

There had been a serious leak. Felicity was over the moon.

'I don't know who did it, but it's a stroke of genius. I've drafted a press release, unprecedented response, blah blah, *Woman* sold out in four hours, blah blah, reprinting, media launch forced forward.'

'What?' Monica did not like it. It smacked of lack of control and private agendas other than her own. Her stomach was now vast. Every day she rose from her futile attempt at sleeping to find that her belly had doubled in size. She was going through a jar of vitamin E cream daily, and almost crying at the distance her poor skin was stretching. Her contributions in the meeting were reduced to carefully chosen monosyllables.

'I think we should bring the media launch forward, bow to public pressure, get everything into the shops early. We'll have every TV network in the country covering it. It's brilliant. We couldn't hope for better.' Felicity had it all planned.

Terry was fuming but focused on the seeds of doom which the chaos was sowing.

'It's a travesty. We can't possibly bring the stuff forward. The expectations are far too high. When they find out it's just another bloody food-processor, another boring breadmaker, they'll be furious. It's too much hype, totally out of proportion. Mark, you're responsible.'

'Thank you, Terry, I'm well aware of that. I want you to put the heavies on Nigel to find out where this leak came from. Get on the phone to *Woman*, find out what you can. Felicity, we want statements from everyone at Attention! This leak must be plugged now.'

'But.' Monica's chosen word focused on handling the more immediate crisis.

'Thanks Monica,' Mark continued. 'Felicity, how ready are you to bring the launch forward to Friday?'

'I can fax all guests with the press release, phone the crucial attendees, emphasise the top-secret nature of the venue and time.' Felicity had the material ready to go. She had banked on an early launch.

'Monica, can we get the goods in the shops to go on sale on Saturday?'

'Yes.'

'What about point of sale material, signage, display stands?'

'No.'

'We don't need them. If we had them ready it would look like this was planned deliberately. OK Felicity, leave the press release with me. I'll contact you in an hour.'

'Mark, darling. I think we need you on TV appealing for calm. I've got "Frontline" waiting for a call and also the ABC news—low ratings but prestige value. You can announce the products will be in the shops on Saturday.'

'I'll do it. Let me know times. I better get onto the CEO to tell him the change of plans. I think we can pull this off. OK, let's go...Felicity, stay, I want a word.'

Terry sprang into action and Monica waddled out as authoritatively as she could.

'As Monica pointed out,' Mark turned to Felicity, 'the immediate crisis is not who did this. Frankly I'm not too worried about finding out where the leak came from. However, if another leak occurs without me knowing in advance and being able to plan for it...' Felicity understood, she squirmed with satisfaction.

'It's going to be bloody marvellous. I promise you.'

By evening, the police, too, had insisted Mark appear on television to appeal for calm. It was the day's top news item. Crowds were protesting outside department stores. Vantex reception was under guard. Twelve arrests had been made across the country. The public was demanding access to KitchenArt—it was their right, and Vantex had no business holding it back.

In a live studio debate Mark was confronted with footage of the public camping outside stores and then with New South Wales's top consumer advocate angrily demanding how long the project had been under wraps and who was responsible for deliberately keeping it secret.

Mark smiled. The viewers may have thought he was smiling at their advocate, but he was smiling directly at them. Looking straight down the camera lens, he released a slow, understanding, grateful smile that no-one in a room with a television tuned to that channel (62.6 per cent of viewers) could avoid. He explained that the release of the products had been brought forward. They would be available on Saturday and not before so as not to disadvantage those working during the week. Orders at the factory had doubled and there was to be no stockpiling, all production would go directly to the shops.

'I would just like to finish,' said Mark, coming to the end of the longest uninterrupted speech on 'Frontline' ever, 'by saying I have been humbled by this experience. I thought I was marketing kitchen products. But it seems they are far more than that. They are a significant part of our lives and it is an honour to have brought this to Australia's attention and to have given these important cultural artefacts the respect that the public demands. I can only apologise for the leaking of information which caused this unrest. I hope everyone will understand there is no need for panic, just a little patience. As yet nobody, I repeat nobody, has any of the KitchenArt appliances. The first person to have one in their home will be the first person back from the shops this Saturday.'

The consumer advocate beamed and got in the last word. 'Can I just say that it is indeed refreshing to see a representative of one of our corporations finally putting the needs of the country before profit. Consumers have long demanded the respect lacking from so many retailers. I would like to thank Mark for giving us all that respect.' The studio audience burst into applause, barely needing to look at the large card with 'Applause' written on which Felicity had sneaked in.

Before leaving the studio Mark had a briefing with security. There was a car waiting for him at the back door. A decoy car would be sent out shortly, and he could then leave the station in safety. There was already a large crowd outside his apartment block. They recommended he did not go there. Was there somewhere he could stay?

The 'Frontline' producer, the host, the head of security and Felicity simultaneously suggested he stay with them, then, embarrassed, fell silent, though they were all longing to shout 'I asked him first.' Mark thought a large house surrounded by walled gardens was probably his best option for peace and privacy. The only person he knew with accommodation like that was JayJo. As he made arrangements Felicity interrupted.

'The PM wants a briefing,' she shrieked, forgetting to move the mobile phone away from her mouth and deafening her caller. 'We'll have to get the Opposition Leader in too— you could do it in JayJo's lounge, one local crew, one photographer and CNN, of course. It'll be marvellous, shall I greenlight?'

'No Felicity—I think you've PR'd me to death today. That's it for tonight.'

'But I think there's still a few ounces to squeeze, I honestly——'

'No.'

'I'd be failing in my duty if I didn't get maximum exposure,' she cried, but he had already set off down the corridor.

He needed time to think. He had been going non-stop since that morning when he walked in to find Rae.... Rae, their dinner catch-up. It seemed like a week ago. Everything that had been planned to take weeks had hit at once like a tornado. Suddenly, he was a household name responsible for people crying in the streets, for arrests, for national hysteria and for Matilda Hughes of Glen Innes driving her ute through the window of Thom's Retravision. It was breathtaking.

Once in the relative safety of the car, he gave the driver directions to JayJo's then called Rae's mobile.

'So when are they making you president?'

'I've got that scheduled for Monday; want to sit with me at the inauguration?'

'And incur the hatred of every woman in Australia? No thanks.'

Mark felt an emotional welling in his throat, his eyes moistening with gratitude at her voice, reassuring and without a hint of anger.

'Rae, I'm sorry. Did you wait long?'

'I didn't even go. No-one at Vantex managed any work today. All phones were jammed, reception was a no-go zone and we could only get to the carpark under escort. I figured our date was off.'

There was silence on the phone, then a muffled thank you.

'Mark, are you OK?'

A toneless 'yes' came back. Mark hung up. He had controlled everything on the run all day, but the quiet humour of Rae had flicked his 'let go' switch and his eyes, throat and lungs blocked with relief, gratitude, affection, any and every emotion. Eventually it gave way to tears. Not joy, sadness or regret, just tears. He sat back and allowed them to roll as he reviewed every step he had taken that day. Felicity had been right. This so-called crisis was the marketing coup of the millennium. People were demanding his products and demanding him. He'd shivered at his own power when he'd looked into the camera during the debate. He had convinced a nation he was telling the truth—because he was beautiful.

He could have said anything. He could have called a national strike.

The tears stopped, the emotion cut out and he got back to work. He called Constanza. He wanted letters of apology to everyone in his apartment block and a bottle of whisky for the caretaker. He called Monica to confirm delivery of supplies. Greg answered because she was doing breathing exercises. They seemed to consist of her trying to grab the phone while screaming 'You do the bloody breathing' at the devoted father-to-be.

He called Terry who did not answer. Terry had spent the evening in front of his television flicking it off and on again. He watched Mark with fascinated revulsion. This was that geek, this was the guy who could spend twenty minutes in a room before anyone noticed he was there—and now he had a nation screaming for the right to buy a food-processor. Terry had to admit his life had been transformed by Mark. He had risen to a hot spot in *the* Vantex department, but he had to thank that bastard gazing sincerely from the screen.

Terry switched the television off. His only satisfaction was knowing this success had to precipitate a fall. It was all too fast, too uncontrolled. The best Terry could do was make Mark go faster and faster until it all fell apart. Success was the way to destroy Mark, Terry's mind knew that, but all his fingers would do was dig his nails into the palms of his hands so hard he made himself bleed.

◆

The media frenzy abated slightly in the following days, or rather everyone got used to living with it. There would be no rest until the launch on Friday and the opening of store doors on Saturday. Eager customers were already camping in front of the stores. A live internet site had been set up webcasting from the main entrance to Grace Brothers' City Store. Eager shoppers discussed their expectations and answered quizzes about Mark. The questions (and answers) had been supplied by Felicity. By Thursday there were four websites claiming to have nude pictures of Mark. Felicity checked them out—all cut and paste jobs, the same photo of Mark's head on four different bodies: three male, one female. None of them, from the little she had seen, were a patch on the real thing.

JayJo had welcomed Mark to her home with open arms. The gates and high walls protected him from the media which had taken twelve hours to find his hiding place. It would have been sooner if they had thought to contact Felicity who had her mobile at the ready to let slip the information as soon as Mark left the studio.

Security at the MCA for the launch was tight. Tickets were barcoded, guest lists checked and photo ID required. There was a 100 per cent response rate. Those who had initially declined the invitation suddenly changed their mind after Mark appeared on television. Arriving at this launch would be the smartest career move of the year, whatever the career.

Greg and Monica were planning to go to the launch as their last appearance before the happy event. As they were getting ready, Monica felt her first contraction. Greg hyperventilated for five minutes, then found the prepacked case and bolted for the car. Sitting in it with the engine running, he panicked as Monica failed to appear. She must have collapsed. Her waters might have broken. Leaving the engine running, he rushed back into the house, calling desperately when he could not find her in the hall or the living room.

Looking up the stairs he gasped. There she stood in a

black evening dress, her swollen belly sculptured in the lush fabric, a vision of alluring fecundity. She was trying to put on an earring.

'For God's sake, Monica, what are you doing, we've got to get to the birthing centre.'

'Didn't you read those turgid pain-free birth books you brought home? That was the *first* contraction—it could be hours yet. We'll pop along after the launch.'

'You do *not* pop along to have a baby. We can't do the launch.'

'I have to be there.'

'You have to be at the centre.'

'Why? Are the whales booked to sing live?' Monica grabbed the banister and inhaled sharply. It was the second contraction, just twenty minutes after the first.

'Damn.' Monica stomped back to the bedroom, removing the one earring she had installed, then called to Greg.

'Are you going to help me out of this dress or do I have to do everything myself?'

A glowing Greg leaped up the stairs and was in the bedroom in seconds. His years of experience in removing female clothing came to the fore and he quickly unclasped the fastenings. The dress fell to the floor in a small pool of black that could not possibly have covered Monica's body. She stood completely naked. He looked up and met her eyes in the mirror, shocked, bewildered and then turned on. His nine-months pregnant wife had been going to the launch without any underwear.

'It ruined the lines of the dress and the fabric felt great.'

Greg looked at Monica's milk-heavy breasts with their vast nipples and thrilled at the thought of her moving them through a huge crowd with just a thin sheath of black silk covering them. He put his hands to them and cupped them. He imagined the milk in his hands, then moved them down to the massive belly. The skin was taut yet soft and iridescent. He kissed Monica's neck. She had never looked more stunning.

A sharp tightening sensation beneath his hands and a cry from Monica brought him back to the reality of the situation: his wife's contractions were coming alarmingly fast and he was getting a hard on.

'I think we should hurry—that was only about ten minutes. Christ, it hurt. What the fuck am I doing? Help me.'

Greg saw complete panic in Monica's eyes. He had never heard her ask for help before. The control queen was losing control of her own body.

'It's like an alien movie, it's not *my* body anymore. I want it back, I want my body back.'

'Shush, you'll get it back,' Greg soothed her. 'It won't be long, you're going to have the fastest birth ever. You'll be able to go the launch afterwards. Look, I'm taking the dress just in case.'

Monica smiled briefly, relieved she was not alone.

'It'll be too loose by then. Let's go.'

The car was still running with the door wide open. Greg helped Monica in, raced round to the driver's seat and careered down the road at top speed.

'For God's sake slow down. Do an emergency stop now and the baby'll shoot out onto the dashboard.' He slowed down briefly and phoned the birthing centre on the car phone to alert them of their impending arrival.

◆

Guests were late arriving at the launch. Mark paced nervously round the hall. Long drapes hung at regular intervals around the room. To him it was obvious they were concealing something. He contemplated running and hiding when Rae finally broke through the security.

'You didn't tell me the queen was launching the goods. Only she would need this much security.'

'Is it chaos?'

'Yes and it's all your fault.'

Mark looked alarmed.

'Well, not entirely. It's your fault there are thousands of people out there thinking this is Hollywood, but it's not your fault a truck overturned on George Street and traffic is a nightmare. The whole CBD is gridlocked. I had to get out and walk.'

'It's a disaster.'

'I figure most people are close enough. I'm sure Felicity is thrilled.'

'She probably overturned the truck...Listen, thanks for the other night. It was so good to hear your voice. I needed it.'

'That's want friends are for...I got you a present.' Rae pulled out a T-shirt that had been crammed into her bag.

'Now you know you've made it. They're selling like hotcakes on the street.'

On the T-shirt was a picture of Mark—the same one that had been pasted onto the mismatched bodies on the internet. The words 'A real piece of art' were printed underneath.

'It's official: you're an industry with your own black market. Congratulations.'

More guests were beginning to get through security and filling up the vast hall. Mark was the preferred destination; everyone approached him as if they were his closest friend.

He did not recognise most of them, but one he certainly did. Turning in response to a tap on his shoulder, he met with a pair of heavily coated lips and a camera flash.

'Darling, I forgive you, let's never argue again!'

It was Lucy, affecting a touching reunion in front of the *Woman* photographer. Before Mark could recover from the first flash, Lucy had snuggled into his arms and a second shot had been taken. She clasped his hand in hers and was not going to let go.

'I'm just so proud of him,' she beamed to the crowd gathered around Mark. He realised he had to act quickly before it was officially established that Lucy was his girlfriend.

'I have a lot to thank this woman for. If she hadn't broken off our relationship I would never have had the determination to make a success of KitchenArt. Now, we're great friends. It's good to know your ex can be so supportive. Thank you, Lucy.'

Lucy fumed. She had persuaded her editor to send her to the launch with the promise of exclusive pics of her and Mark, but she had not thought beyond the moment of ambush. She had no back-up plan in the event Mark tried to extradite himself. She would have some serious explaining to do.

Mark had known success would be his, she thought, even before she had finished with him. He had trapped her. He had deliberately provoked a row in order to be free to pursue his career—and other women. By rights she should be by his side, sharing the limelight, starring in photo spreads of their gracious home. She had put up with him when he was a dull nobody, and now that everything she had ever wanted was dripping off him like sweat during sex he did not want to know her. He had humiliated her in front of those she wished were her peers. She grabbed a glass of champagne and skulked to a quieter corner of the hall. Gripping the stem tightly, she dreamt of crushing it in her hand and hurling it at the first domestic appliance to appear.

The hall filled. The noise grew louder. Everyone raised their voices to make themselves heard. Finally, there was a call for attention. The speeches began.

The CEO spoke first, praising Mark, espousing the virtues of the company. He was not a great public speaker. Most guests continued their conversations. Terry was standing with Mygrave. He saw a slight firming of Mygrave's jaw every time Mark's name was mentioned. A kindred spirit indeed.

'It's hard to believe this man is the public face of Vantex; it's an embarrassment,' Terry commented as the CEO droned on about Mark.

'Not for long,' replied Mygrave. It was Terry's turn to firm his jaw. Would Mark take over the whole company?

'Not him.' Mygrave read his mind. 'Look over there, the two guys talking even more secretively than we are.' Terry spotted them.

'They're from Glocorp.'

Glocorp was a massive American appliance conglomerate against which Vantex fought a never-ending battle for the kitchens of Australia.

'Surely they're not spying. They can't launch a similar range, we've got water-tight copyright. Vantex owns it lock stock and barrel across the globe.'

Mygrave smiled. Terry was pleased he was an ally. Since his spectacular debacle at the conference, he was sharp. He was hungry.

Terry decided to take a gamble.

'Perhaps we should have a private celebration.' He rubbed his nose and sniffed.

Mygrave looked at him hard. Either he was seriously living clean and sober or their professional relationship would go to the next stage, figured Terry. Mygrave did not respond.

'I think you deserve a little something. You've pulled yourself together, you're sharper than ever, you've got everyone's respect and trust. Time you gave yourself a break.'

They headed for the toilets—empty while everyone was being bored by the CEO. Terry pulled out a little bag, dug out some of the reward with the end of his key and held it up to Mygrave. Mygrave stared at the tiny mound; it looked pathetic, harmless. Slowly he lowered his nostril over the key, steadying Terry's hand with his own. He paused, then inhaled so sharply Terry feared the key would disappear. Mygrave groaned with pleasure and relief. They exited to thunderous applause as Mark took the stage. One by one, the curtains around the room fell, revealing giant prints—stunning photographs of each of the appliances. The crowd was in raptures and did not notice the glass of champagne which smashed against the wall near the Gauguin Breadmaker. Each revelation was greeted with applause like bursts of fireworks. Terry and Mygrave oohed and aahed louder than anyone.

◆

Greg and Monica were stuck in the gridlocked traffic. Greg had turned a corner at such high speed he had missed the last possible exit before joining the bank of traffic. Other cars backed up behind them. Nothing was moving. Horns blew, people left their vehicles to walk. It was a carpark situation.

'Shit.' Monica's contractions were thick and fast, each one more intense than the last.

'OH FUCK.' Her seat was soaking. 'It's coming, it's coming now. Do something, Greg.'

Greg started his controlled breathing, trying to think. He phoned the birthing centre and put them on the speaker phone.

'We're stuck in traffic, nothing's moving, the waters have broken. Help!'

Dr Toscani came on the phone and told Greg he would have to deliver the baby himself. They had sent out an ambulance, but it probably would not arrive in time.

'Now listen to me, Monica.' Toscani's calm timbre filled the car. 'This is going to be a beautiful experience for you and something that will bond the two of you forever. There is nothing more powerful than a couple creating and delivering their baby.'

'It's not beautiful right now, it's fucking painful.'

'That's good Monica, release it all, don't hold back. Greg, push her seat back as far as you can. Then tilt it back slightly.'

Greg got out of the car, rushed round to the other side, adjusted Monica's seat and continued to follow the doctor's instructions, listening carefully above Monica's screams.

The doctor paused and Monica stopped screaming. Greg was as ready as he would ever be. Gradually, the car filled with a new sound, harmonious, peaceful, soothing. It was the whales calling, playing over the speaker phone.

'Monica, listen to the music of nature,' intoned Toscani. 'In your mind you are with them, swimming joyfully, creating a new life. On the next contraction, I want you to push. Push with the power of the whale, she is huge, she is force and she gives you her power.'

'I want her fucking drugs, not her power.' Monica let out her most piercing scream as car horns suddenly drowned out the whales. The traffic had cleared. They were blocking the road. An irate motorist coming forward to see what the problem was, saw and ran back with the news. The horns fell silent. Everything was quiet; there were only the whales calling on the phone.

Monica screamed. Greg shouted.

'It's out, it's out...he's out. A boy!'

The doctor came back on the line.

'Clear his throat, hang him upside down if necessary. I want to hear a scream.'

The baby screamed on cue.

'The cord, what do I do about the cord?' yelled Greg.

'Bite it,' said the good doctor, 'bite it and give your son independence. You are so lucky.'

As caught as he was in the moment, Greg did not feel lucky as he put the umbilical cord in his mouth and bit down hard. It severed. It tasted revolting but there was nothing to rinse his mouth with. He tied the two ends, grabbed the dress that Monica had worn and wrapped the baby in it.

'Look, Monica, look.' There was no answer. Monica's head rolled back on the headrest. Greg realised he had been so engrossed with the baby, he had paid Monica no attention.

'She's dead, oh my God!'

Dr Toscani calmly told Greg to check for a pulse on her throat. Greg stabbed wildly at it with one hand, holding the baby with the other. There did not seem to be anything. The doctor told him to slow down, press gently and give his fingers time to feel the pulse. Greg calmed his breathing and tried again. He found the pulse. Monica was not dead, she had just passed out.

'She's alive!' There was a burst of applause from the street. Greg stood up and held his baby before the gathering crowd.

The front seat of the car was like a crash zone: blood, dirt, stink—and a placenta. The pain-free birth books had not mentioned how smelly birth was.

The ambulance arrived and Monica was moved onto a stretcher. A quick check from the paramedic revealed she was fine, and just coming to. The baby was placed in her arms and the ambulance rushed off. A stranger gave Greg a cigar and he leapt into his stinking car to follow the ambulance. He decided he would have the seat removed and set in bronze. This was the greatest launch of all and now he savoured the foul taste in his mouth. He never wanted to forget it was he, Greg Haddrick, the lion, who had delivered their son and made him a whole human being.

In the ambulance, an exhausted Monica looked at her baby. His bald wrinkled head made her think of the CEO. She hoped he had not droned on too long at the launch.

◆

In the Sydney suburb of Kogarah, Anita Bennett was furiously preparing for her stepson's fifth birthday party. She had some serious wooing to do. This was her first children's party and it had to be a success. Only her third attempt at a cake had been deemed good enough, and now Harrison wanted ice-cream, lots of it, 'every flavour in the world'. Thank goodness for her BF 2010! Anita was determined that every child would go home from the party and tell their mother that Harrison's new mum had made twenty different flavours of ice-cream herself. Her new Vantex fridge–freezer with the built-in ice-cream maker churned and churned, never grew warm and produced perfect ice-cream after perfect ice-cream. At least one part of her preparations was going well. As she broke up the Crunchie pieces into the honey ice-cream mix, the timer rang. The banana mocha fudge was ready.

Opening the freezer, she breathed deeply waiting for the rich sweet scent of fresh ice-cream—and was rewarded with a face full of ice-cold sludge. A crack in the motor casing had caused a leak, leading to a short circuit, prompting the blending arm to go crazy and fling ice-cream mixture in all directions. The compartment was coated, Anita's face received a second dollop, the blender went faster and faster until it finally emitted a loud bang and the waft of banana mocha fudge was suddenly infused with burnt wiring. The blending arm flew out over Anita's shoulder.

She was outraged. The entire fridge–freezer had now short-circuited, the ice-creams would melt, the drinks would be warm. The party would be a disaster, Harrison would hate her even more, her marriage would be strained, her psoriasis would come back and it would all be Vantex's fault. She reached for the phone. There would be hell to pay.

The call came through while Rae was at lunch. In the event of serious malfunction, it was Vantex policy for the head of the department to personally reassure the client and offer all manner of replacement goods. In Rae's absence, David Mygrave took the call. He was horrified, soothing, conciliatory and thrilled. He set off in a company van with a replacement model, a complete set of KitchenArt and an indemnity contract. He spent the afternoon installing the new fridge–freezer, rescuing the ice-creams in the nick of time and providing the kind of personalised service that makes shoppers moist with delight. Anita wept with gratitude and hugged Mygrave. His body felt hard and reassuring, he must have been a fine athlete once. She let herself go limp in his arms as he stroked her head and gently laughed. As his hand reached around her back, she felt it brush briefly against her breast. It was an accident, she assumed. She smiled. Vantex really knew how to correct their mistakes, that was for sure.

◆

Rae sat dumbfounded. A top-level meeting with the CEO and all involved in the new BF 2010 (Ice-cream Unlimited) project was under way. There had been another three cases of cracked motor casings creating chaos.

Rae knew she was doomed the moment the CEO had opened with, 'We're not here to apportion blame.' She knew exactly what that meant, and if she did not, Mygrave's barely concealed glee said it all. She knew that in the folder he had so ostentatiously placed in front of him was the memo he had sent to all and sundry opposing the change to the casing. No doubt he would have a copy of her signed authorisation. He probably had a draft resignation ready for her to sign too.

It was agreed that all models should be recalled immediately. The original casing would recommence production—if research suggested the product could recover from flinging ice-cream at Australia's homemakers.

'I think it can,' announced Mygrave, 'and I've just the person to do it—Anita Bennett, the first victim of the machine. I personally resolved her situation with a temporary replacement item. We'll be sending her a non ice-cream making fridge today after her son's party. She understands it's a temporary fault and—thanks to a little persuasion from me—she's prepared to endorse the new product nationally on television. Consumers love us admitting our mistakes and generously correcting them. I think we might just pull through.'

Rae squirmed. She had been on a late lunch only because Mygrave had kept her waiting for a meeting. Thus he took Anita Bennett's call and the credit for salvaging the situation. It was as if he'd known all along this would happen and had been ready to pounce.

The meeting ended. Mygrave had not needed to produce his memo; everyone was aware of it. It was all the worse for not being raised. Everyone knew she had fucked up in triplicate. Mygrave did not even gloat, he just revelled in her silent shame.

The CEO kept Rae and Mygrave back. Crunchtime. Mygrave was almost trembling with delight as he spoke first. 'It should be said Raelene has done a marvellous job, all things considered, particularly in view of how fresh she is to management. I support her 100 per cent.'

'Absolutely,' concurred the CEO. 'Everyone has admired how you have handled this project, Rae, myself included. However...'

There it was, the inevitable however.

'However, perhaps you're a victim of your own success. You've been so competent everyone thought there was no end to the amount you could handle, but we all have our limitations. Perhaps we gave you too much responsibility too soon. Sadly, the public will demand that heads roll. We have to put a fresh person in charge to resolve this situation. David is in an ideal position to do so.'

'I'll clear my desk.'

'I hope not. You're still a valued member of the Vantex team, but you will be reporting to David now. I'm sure you'll both continue to work well together.' So she was not going to be executed, just subjected to torture for the foreseeable future.

Mygrave was generous in victory. 'Raelene, we all have setbacks, I know that more than anyone, but if you've got what it takes, you come back. Look at me. Now, I've got a great raspberry and sage combination tisane which I think you'll enjoy.'

'Thanks.'

Rae wished to God he would just do a victory dance on the table and cry revenge. Instead she got his revolting support and a vile-tasting brew.

◆

KitchenArt was a triumph. As Rae came to terms with reporting to Mygrave, Mark was touring the country. His in-store appearances drew screaming crowds. Women swooned as he demonstrated the chipping plate on the Monet food-processor—it actually worked. Within a month of the launch Mark was one of the most familiar faces in Australia, with an 89 per cent recognition level. *Woman* had declared him Bachelor of the Year, and, thanks to Felicity's machinations, Hot News, the 24-hour Cable Gossip Channel, had broken the story that he had turned down $30 000 to pose nude. *Barf* magazine (for blokes) had asked famous men whom, if they had to do a bloke to save their lives, they would choose. Fifty per cent nominated Mark.

Lucy had begged her bosses at *Woman* to run an exclusive on how Mark had cast her aside once success came his way: his depression, his mood swings, his attempt to make her participate in group sex. But, as her editor pointed out, that was not what the public wanted to hear. Rubbishing Mark Boyd would be circulation poison.

'Honey, you could have photos of him screwing ten-year-olds and murdering their grannies and the public wouldn't believe it. Besides, he's just so nice, we couldn't hurt him like that.'

Lucy was amazed. This was from the editor who had run a feature titled 'Mother Teresa: Bitch from Hell Goes Back' the week of her funeral. Mark had the entire country under his spell. He could do anything and get away with it. The world might be charmed, but she knew what he was really like. They might love him now, but as soon as the novelty wore off they would be screaming for his seamy side and she would serve it up.

He may have been able to get away with anything, but all Mark could actually do in the evening was sit in his hotel room flicking channels, trying to avoid looking at himself. The free and easy social life he had begun to enjoy vanished the day of the launch. He was boxed in by his own celebrity. Every encounter was a potential headline. Every model, actor and TV presenter wishing to further their own career flung themselves at him, then offered exclusives on 'My night of passion with Mark Boyd'. There could be no casual sex now, no more Nathalias. She had been offered a considerable sum to reveal all, but in view of what he knew about her breasts she felt it best to remain quiet. Besides, she was above that sort of cheap publicity.

Mark was consumed by the possible repercussions of everything he did. His public image had snatched away his private life, ably assisted by Felicity. As the homemakers' dream, he had to be more wholesome than the combined cast of 'The Waltons'. He had to wear Australian designers, support local businesses and never be seen drinking. Each evening he and Felicity ran through every word he had said during the day to ensure nothing could be misconstrued. No wonder so many celebrities uttered such banalities, anything else could lead to disaster. All it would take was one person bingeing themselves to hospital because Mark had said there was no harm in eating a chocolate, and personal ruin and plummeting sales would follow. He was relieved not to have had a life before all this started. He did not even have a closet, never mind skeletons.

He looked at his reflection in the hotel room window, and the illuminated dots of Melbourne beyond the glass. Every dot represented a person who knew him, who had an opinion on him, while he knew nothing about them. People could say, 'Hi Mark,' as if he was their best friend and he would be thrown into a panic about whether he had met and should remember them. He had perfected a smile of recognition which he shot out whenever it happened. It seemed to work. A flush of pleasure would appear on the person's face as if they realised they really were special to Mark.

The frenzy had to end soon. You could only be the man of the moment for a minute. He hoped a more stable life of celebrity marketing would set in. Sales of KitchenArt were going so well, plans for the second wave of designs had to be brought forward. The market saturation point Vantex had estimated would be reached within three years had been achieved already, yet sales were still going strong. In another week one in four households would be graced by at least one KitchenArt product.

◆

Within a week of her son being born, Monica was back in her tiny skirts and back at work with greater relish than ever.

She caused five sets of tears on her first day. Life was good. She had done it. She had a baby and her career was sky-rocketing. As Mark focused on promoting KitchenArt around the country, she and Terry ran the department. She had made senior management. KitchenArt was virtually an independent company. The CEO popped down occasionally, usually with congratulations, for the sales figures were unbelievable. Everyone was expecting the peak to come soon, but it did not. Mark phoned in every day, but neither she nor Terry suggested he was needed at the office. They were coping fine without him.

Her immediate ambitions achieved, there was yet another prize up for grabs. The position of Senior Vice-President KitchenArt was vacant and Monica wanted it. She deserved it; after all, it had been her husband's post. Greg had opened the door for her by negotiating a generous early retirement for himself. Monica was thrilled and felt genuine warmth towards him. Greg had turned out to be the perfect choice. He dedicated his life to their son while she focused on her career.

Greg was filled with the importance of his new life's work. His ruthless determination to succeed in business had morphed into an equal determination to rear the most magnificent human being on the planet—their son, George. He had been named after the street that caused the gridlock which meant he was born in the car. (The car had actually been stranded on Elizabeth Street, but they did not think it an appropriate name for a boy.) Nothing would stand in the way of George's development, Greg vowed. Every opportunity would be his.

Monica's main rival for the position of Senior Vice-President was Terry, but he did not seem concerned. His indifference worried her, so she grilled Mark over the phone.

'If he's got it I'll scream discrimination. What do you know, Mark?'

'Nothing, no decision has been made. It's down to the CEO, but based on my recommendation.'

'Who are you recommending?'

'I've submitted a short list...of two.'

'Shit.' If it was down to buttering up the CEO, Terry was better at withstanding his stultifyingly boring conversation.

Monica decided to confront her rival. Now they weren't sharing an office, he was harder to find. She stormed to his room, but he was not there. She caught him coming out of the men's toilets and firmly pushed him back in.

'Want to make another baby already? OK, if you insist,' he teased.

'Don't mess with me. It was the mother in *Aliens* who was the real bitch. The VP spot—what do you know about it?'

'I know I've been running this place single-handed while you've been dropping babies in the street and pretty boy's been seducing housewives around the country.'

'Bullshit. I took one week off and achieved more from my hospital bed that you ever did.'

'I've no doubt they'll choose the best man, sorry *person*, for the job.'

'So why aren't you doing your usual suck-off-the-CEO-if-I-have-to routine?'

'Perhaps I don't want to be vice-president?'

Terry realised he was in danger of saying too much. Monica was good at arguing things out of him, especially when she had him pinned against the hand-dryer with hot air pouring down his back. He pushed her aside and walked out.

'I've a meeting at the agency. I'll just get on with the job while you focus on your career.'

Monica knew something was up. She went back to Terry's office to search for clues. A secretary got as far as holding up a hand and saying 'Excu——' before Monica was in with the door locked. The computer revealed nothing so she moved on to his voicemail. The messages were bland and irrelevant until she heard one from his broker.

'Terry, shares purchased, that's all your employee options plus the additional $10 000 you got. Nick of time too, you've already made a tidy profit. Whatever you've heard I don't want to know, but someone out there's buying up even bigger than you.'

Monica knew Vantex shares were on the rise, but that was only to be expected with the phenomenal success of KitchenArt. Perhaps there was more to it. Figures on KitchenArt sales had not been released. The market, in theory, should not know quite how astounding the success was. If someone was buying up big, they did not simply want a profit—they wanted Vantex. It was a takeover bid and Terry knew it.

◆

Mygrave continued to be revoltingly supportive to Rae, and insisted on checking her every move, supervising her every decision and knocking back, in a very positive way, her every suggestion. It was all in her own interest, he repeated. 'You're far too valuable to this firm to leave yourself open to that kind of exposure again.'

Mark, as usual, was unavailable, touring shopping centres in Western Australia, blending, chopping and toasting his way into the hearts of the daytime masses. Unable to speak to him since Anita Bennett got her faceful of ice-cream, Rae had endured her humiliation alone.

Rae heard the takeover gossip. The share price had soared, but no buyer had revealed their hand as yet. Staff members were debating long and hard whether it was time to cash in share options or if there were further profits to be made. Suddenly everyone was a financial analyst: Vantex was overvalued; Vantex was undervalued; KitchenArt had changed everything; the ice-cream debacle could still wipe millions. Every time ice-cream was mentioned a glance would be cast at Rae, as if she had snatched bread from the mouths of starving children. The E-trade website was up on every computer and internal e-mails ran hot with tips, news and queries.

As speculation—on the stock market and in the office— reached fever pitch, the CEO mysteriously became unavailable. Francine, thrilled to be in demand once again, teased the whole company, desperate for information, like the gorgeous coquette she was. The CEO had been in conference with the board the whole of the previous day, she announced to one of the distribution heads after a magnificent bouquet appeared on her desk. The board was still meeting at an undisclosed venue in the city, she revealed to Terry after her favourite chocolates arrived through the internal mail system.

The only pleasant note for Rae this rumour-laden day was that Mygrave was not in. He had phoned her in the morning confiding he would be at an all-day Living Clean and Sober seminar.

Terry and Monica turned up in Rae's office, seeking information.

'Has pretty boy called you? What does he know?' Terry decided to play the innocent.

'I've heard nothing,' Rae replied with a slightly crisp bitterness.

'Had a row?'

'Did Mark give any indication of what he knew before he went to Perth?' Monica chimed in.

'Honestly, I haven't seen or heard from him in ages. You two have probably had more contact with him than me.'

They all drew blanks and sat silently as if the truth would descend on them if they listened hard enough. Terry broke the silence.

'What is going on?'

Monica pulled a face. This *faux naïveté* was the least convincing of his many acts.

'Drop the innocence, Terry, you're like a whore swearing she's a virgin. I know you've been buying up shares.' Terry looked appalled.

'What makes you think——?'

'Your voicemail makes me think it...you should turn the volume down when you're playing back messages from your broker.' Monica might have been provoked into revealing what she knew, but certainly was not going to reveal her modus operandi.

'So there is a takeover bid on. But who?' Rae was finally getting into the discussion. Deciding there was no harm in releasing some limited information, Terry glanced over his shoulder and whispered, 'The Americans.'

'Glocorp?' whispered Monica in reply.

Terry nodded sagely.

'Are they getting inside help?'

'Possibly...it's not me.' Terry was thrilled to have these two women hanging on his every word. 'But I'm not at liberty to say who.'

'Mygrave,' said Rae, and suddenly everything fell into place. She had seen him and Terry together. He had been smug, over and above the ice-cream fiasco. His ship was coming in. He would be making a fortune from the takeover. His share options over the years would have accrued substantially and he was probably spending all the money he used to blow on coke on shares. Perhaps he was going to retire on a happy high, in the knowledge he had sold out one of Australia's few remaining locally owned large businesses.

Terry's surprise at Rae's correct guess gave him away. He hastily looked about him as if Mygrave himself would pop up to denounce his betrayal.

'Don't worry, he's off living clean and sober today, you're safe,' Rae reassured him. Terry found this amusing.

'I guess we'll be pretty safe in KitchenArt. They'd be mad to meddle with such a winner.' Monica was assessing her situation.

'Besides, none of us is really senior enough to be ousted with the board. The CEO may be in trouble but they won't bother with us.' Rae reminded them that, for once, their lack of real importance would work in their favour. It was an unflattering comfort.

'Mark'll be safe too. He's the one who made Vantex such an attractive proposition.'

'Don't be so sure.' All three started at the voice from the doorway. It was Mark. They leaped up, but before they could ask their questions he spoke again.

'I got an emergency call from Francine telling me to get the next flight back and call her on my arrival. She told me I'm to go straight up there and speak to no-one... except for you, Rae. You're to come with me.'

Although it was common knowledge they were friends,

professionally Mark and Rae had little to do with each other. It was strange that they should be summoned together. Terry and Monica were suspicious that there were further intrigues of which they were not aware. Something else was going on. Mark and Rae went to the top floor.

Outside the CEO's office, Francine was waiting at her flower-festooned desk with a significant smile on her face. She was very pleased.

'How nice to see you, Mark, Raelene. I'll let the CEO know you're here.' She placed a peculiar emphasis on 'CEO'. Rae put this down to a smug revelation that he was in the building after all.

'You're to go right in,' she beamed from behind an especially vibrant strelitzia.

When they entered, the high-back chair at the desk was turned melodramatically away from the door, facing the harbour view. The CEO was hiding, but he began to speak.

'As you'll no doubt have realised, there's been a hostile takeover bid. Successful. The coup's been clean and quick. Obviously the new majority shareholders—yes, it's Glocorp—are keen for everything to continue with as little disruption as possible. However, changes at the top are inevitable—too closely aligned with the old board and all that. So I have been appointed the new CEO.'

The chair swung round. Mark and Rae stared aghast.

'Aren't you going to congratulate me?' David Mygrave asked, drinking in the stunned faces that appeared before him. He did not wait for a response. 'Yes, I'm Big Fucker again and bigger than ever. It'll come as no surprise to either of you that you're fired. You'll get a very generous three months pay in lieu of notice. Hand in your ID tags to Francine on your way out.'

'You can't!' gasped Rae. 'Me, OK, you've got your revenge, but Mark? He's the very reason the company's worth taking over. They won't let you sack him.'

Big Fucker rolled his eyes and smiled in an absurd caricature of the role he had played with Rae over the last few months.

'Only halfway there, as ever, Raelene. You really are going to have to learn to think things through more thoroughly. Naturally, being able to fire you was one of the conditions on which I accepted this... onerous position, but I haven't fired Mark. It's Glocorp—*they* insisted that he go. Of course I argued, but what could I do? My hands are tied. You can go.'

They turned to leave, still too taken aback to produce any meaningful words. As they reached the door, Mygrave spoke again.

'Just one more thing for both of you to remember, but especially you, Raelene... Never, never NEVER FUCK WITH THE BIG FUCKER!' He bawled out the last words, venting all the accumulated rage he had strategically held in check for so long. As the door shut, he gleamed with satisfaction and caressed his new desk. It was so smooth, a wonderful surface. So perfect, he had to press his cheek against it.

◆

There was only one thing to do when they left the building. Without consulting each other Mark and Rae headed to the nearest bar. It took three vodka shots each before they could say anything. Realising it was not yet lunchtime and a long session was in order, they slackened the pace and ordered tonic with the next round.

'I can't believe it. What the fuck are they going to do with-out you? You *are* the bloody product.'

'It can still sell without me. The research showed——'

'Fuck the research, that was before half the population started putting their hands in their pants whenever they thought of you. It doesn't make sense.'

'It's not part of the plan.'

'Plan? Don't tell me you've been keeping a secret objec-tives and goals tally like Terry? Brian would be proud of you.'

'No. I don't know what the plan is, I just know that every time something happens it's part of it. But I can't believe *this* was supposed to happen. What about you, Rae? That was just personal revenge; surely you can sue or something?'

'Ice-cream.'

'Oh…yeah, I forgot. Pity it wasn't Big Fucker who opened the fridge.'

As the drinks took effect, the morning's events became hilarious. Terry's whispering, Francine's smirking and Mygrave's dramatic chair swing. They started whirling round on their bar chairs.

'So, Meester Bond, I am firink you, F.U.C.K. ees now een control.' Mark reckoned it was very James Bond.

'No, no it's this.'

Rae swung round on her chair, crossed her legs with dra-matic flourish and knocked over a stool. 'Denver-Vantex is mine, Blake, do you hear? Mine and I want you out of my office. You're finished or my name isn't David Morell Car-rington Colby Dexter Rowan Big Fuck.'

It was the funniest thing they had ever heard. Once again they were silent, unable to speak as they helplessly flayed their arms and struggled for breath.

'I'm glad you find it all so amusing.' Monica had appeared.

'Monica, sit down, how did you find us?'

'I left the Vantex building and followed the sound of shrieking. Waiter! Double Scotch on the rocks...quickly.'

'I guess you heard the news.' Mark favoured her with a boyish pout.

'Yes, you fucking bastard,' Monica replied. Her drink came, she drained the glass and handed it back to the waiter for another.

'Why am I a bastard?'

'Thanks to you I've developed some goddamn principles and I don't fucking like it.'

'What do you mean?'

'I resigned.' She drained the second drink and looked meaningfully at the waiter who went to fetch the next.

'For God's sake, you of all people falling on your sword to support a colleague! There was no need.'

'Yes there bloody was. Straight after you two, Terry and I were summoned to the CEO's office. He did this pathetic routine facing the window then swinging round like he was fucking JR Ewing or someone.'

'Meester Bond...'

'I want you out of my life forever, Blake!'

'Whatever. Anyway, I get told I've got Greg's job, the KitchenArt Vice-President. "Woop di do," I thought. Then he drops the bombshell that you've been sent packing and Terry's got your job. That pathetic little jealous wannabe. It was disgusting. He and Mygrave grinned like they'd staged a takeover of the whole fucking schoolyard. So I let rip.'

'What d'you say?'

'Well,' she smiled—the third Scotch was working—'I suppose you might call it classic Monica.'

'Come on, we want the full re-enactment.'

Monica shook her head in disbelief but stood up.

'Wait,' shrieked Rae, 'let's do it properly. I'll be Mygrave.' She swung round on her chair again, snorted a vast imaginary line of coke off the table, then shouted, 'You're fired d'you hear me, fired.'

'The two of you are pathetic!' Monica re-enacted her tirade for all it was worth. 'You've probably got hard ons, only your dicks are too small to show it. Congratulations Terry, I suppose taking someone's job and imagining you are them is the next best thing if you can't get them to fuck you. But if you think I'm sticking around to watch you jerk off over Mark's desk, forget it. As for you, Tiny Fucker, I suppose the only innovation you'll come up with is a coke snorter with a picture of the *Mona Lisa* on the side. Good luck boys, you'll need it.'

Furious applause burst forth. Monica took her bow and shouted for another drink. Sadly the manager appeared instead, suggesting they go elsewhere.

By ten o'clock, Greg had arrived with George in his front-loader baby sling and taken Monica home. Mark and Rae continued the same conversation—over and over—yet felt they were gaining fresh and astounding insights into the human condition.

'It's amazing, you think you're there, you're on the top, the right path, the head of the herd and suddenly the herd kicks you in the shins and tramples you underfoot.' Mark was entering the melancholic stage. 'I've got these looks, I could seduce anyone in this bar right now, the nation's screaming over me and it's nothing. I couldn't go out, I couldn't meet anyone, because this face is a barrier, it's a curse, people can't see behind it.'

'Some people can.'

'Who?'

'Me, I knew you before, I knew what you were like and I know you're still the same and that person is really really...'

Rae trailed off.

'Really what?'

'Special. You're amazing and you always were.'

'That's the nicest thing anyone has ever——'

'Yeah, let's go.'

Mark insisted on seeing Rae home. In the cab, the driver looked in the mirror and said, 'Hey, aren't you——'

'I was,' answered Mark.

The cabbie ignored the comment and stopped the car. Getting out, he went to the boot and brought out the Gauguin Breadmaker, still in its box.

'I got this for the wife's birthday. Could you sign the box? It'd make her day. It'd make her bloody life, mate.'

Mark shrugged his shoulders, managed a smile and signed 'To Kimberley on her birthday—the very last KitchenArt I'll ever sell and it's yours. All the best, Mark Boyd.'

The driver looked puzzled.

'Read the papers tomorrow, mate, you've got a collector's item there.'

At Rae's place Mark got out too. Using his final Vantex cab-charge docket, he gave the driver a hundred-dollar tip. At the apartment door, Mark put his arms around Rae and gave her a big hug.

'Thanks for everything, you're the one person I can really trust. You know me, Rae.' He was mumbling into Rae's hair and getting strands caught in his mouth. He pulled away. Rae was beginning to cry.

'I can't believe it's all over, I can't go back to typing and coffee, I couldn't stand it.'

'Sshh.' Mark wiped the tears from Rae's eyes, then kissed them.

'Whatever happens now, there's no going back,' she whispered.

He held her chin in his hand and gently put his lips to hers. Rae felt the beautiful warmth, their lips parted and they stopped being friends.

◆

They went straight to the bedroom, scattering clothes on the way. Neither said a word. Any speech, and it would all stop. In the bedroom, Rae turned on the light. Mark switched it off. He did not want Rae to be able to see him. Within minutes, they experienced the delicious thrill of two naked bodies pressed together for the first time, the tickly delight of pubic hair gently knotting together. Rae sighed at the strength of his body over hers. In the pitch dark she felt his body and cupped her hands on his deliciously smooth buttocks. He was soon inside her, and licking her breasts, and with each lick eliminating the final vestiges of thought she had begun to shed with her clothes. There were no consequences, no repercussions, there was just Mark's penis inside her, waves and waves, and the intensity of her skin as her entire body clenched.

◆

With the morning came the awakening to uncertainty, the hoary breath and the terror of being seen by anyone in such a state. The sex might have been a wild, passionate, thoughtless act, but sleeping together, sharing moments of intimate unconsciousness, was a decision that could not be ignored.

Consciousness was raised by a loud endless buzzing. Looking at each other, Mark and Rae realised they had both heard it; it could not be inside their heads. Someone was at the door. They did not move, not having spoken to each other, let alone had the 'Where to from here' conversation.

Still without speaking, Rae got up, put on a dressing-gown and went to the doorphone. By the time she returned, Mark had also risen and was making the bed in a blind panic.

Rae's words did nothing to allay his anxiety.

'Get in the shower, wear whatever you can. The President of Glocorp is on his way up to see you.'

'Big Fucker?'

'No, the worldwide president, the top dog...the bloody American.'

Mark ran for the bathroom, wondering how he had been tracked to Rae's place and what on earth they wanted from him. His warped morning logic deduced they had the press with them so they could take a photo of him looking absolutely wrecked and publish it as the reason for his dismissal. 'I've got to look hot,' he decided. He had two minutes to remove all traces of last night's binge from his face. If they thought they could catch him unawares, he would foil their plans and look magnificent. He decided to do some press-ups, get his blood circulating and flushing through his skin. Rae, poking her head round the bathroom door a minute later, screamed. Mark was naked, lying on his back with his toes touching the floor behind his head. It was probably his least attractive side.

'They're here you idiot, come on.'

'Hold them off, I'll be through in a minute.'

Rae glanced in the mirror on her way to the door, noting her pillow hair and slit eyes. Her chance of making a good first impression was to be sacrificed to Mark's. She shrugged her shoulders and opened the door.

There were three men in business suits. The one in the middle raised his eyebrow, but made no other comment on her appearance.

'Good morning, I'm Bob Jervis, president of Glocorp. This is Hank Rustin, VP Marketing, and Tom Petrillo, our contracts consultant.'

'Lawyer,' he explained as he shook Rae's hand.

'I'm sorry to disturb you, ma'am,' the president continued, 'but it is imperative we liaise with Mr Boyd. He's been unavailable for some time.'

Bob Jervis spoke as if dictating a memo.

'Sorry, it was a traditional Australian celebration,' responded Rae.

'Really? We were unaware...which one?' Tom Petrillo was puzzled.

'Getting rat-arsed when you're fired. It was a joint celebration, but I guess you know that.'

She turned, not interested in their reply. There was absolutely no chance of her making a good impression, so she took the unique opportunity of letting rip her frustration on the top guy.

'Do you always visit people you've fired while they're in their dressing-gowns? Is that the latest American management technique?' She led them to her clothes-strewn living room.

'Glocorp acknowledges your external relocation distress.'

'Excuse me?'

'You're pissed at being fired,' explained Petrillo, obviously used to Jervis's memos.

'Not as pissed off as you'll be unleashing Mygrave on your

profits—hope you've got some good connections in Colombia, otherwise it'll be pretty expensive.'

'Glocorp is aware of the current CEO's limitations and does not envisage a long-term tenure. Where is Mr Boyd?'

'I'm here.'

Mark posed in the doorway ready for the cameras and watched as jaws dropped and eyes swept over his body. He had a towel round his hips and was nonchalantly drying his hair with another. He looked fresh, pumped, relaxed and slightly surprised.

'Well,' said Jervis, 'our reports certainly did not undervalue your marketable potential.'

'Not good enough to employ though, huh?' Rae was impatient with the polite formality. She adjusted her dressing-gown so her boobs would not fall out completely.

Tom intervened. 'I think I'd better cut to the chase. First I want to apologise for yesterday; it must have been unpleasant, but it was necessary.'

Rae was about to set to, but Jervis raised his hand and took over. 'Ms Whyte, your being made free to pursue other avenues was not part of Glocorp strategy, but inevitably in such events there is collateral damage. Glocorp will give you two years salary, along with an excellent reference.'

Rae shrugged her shoulders and determined not to get too close to these men. Her morning breath might melt their faces before they could hand over the cheque.

'Mr Boyd. We require some confidential negotiations.' Jervis looked at Rae.

'It's OK, I'd tell her anyway.'

'Very well. There has been an unavoidable element of deliberate misinformation in the takeover of Vantex.'

Tom explained: 'We're not really interested in Vantex. It's a good little company, sure, but not a global competitor.'

'However, reports reached Glocorp on your particular operation,' said the president. 'Our research evinced the certainty that you and your concept will be equally, if not more, impactful on the American market.'

'We wanted your KitchenArt and we wanted you,' Tom translated once more. 'As a lawyer, I must say your patent on the products is real impressive. To get the concept we had to get the company. Then your contract with Vantex didn't allow you to leave for several years, but it did allow the company to fire you. You were *very* accommodating.'

'We forced a redundancy scenario in order to recruit you for the transformation of our domestic market.'

'Our projections suggest you'll sell more product in California in one day than you do in the whole of Australia in a week.'

An entire company had been bought and left in the hands of a barely reformed coke-snorting egomaniac, just to get Mark to the States. It was the scariest compliment he had ever been paid.

'Put simply,' continued Tom, 'we want you to head up KitchenArt America. Your products and your face will be in every household across our great country. Whaddaya say?'

two years later

There was stalemate in the Inspiration Centre of Del Rio Studios. The air-conditioning was off because its hum was being picked up by the microphones on the shoot on the back lot. Three men and two women sat exhausted round the table, stifling in the heat and unable to open a window for fear they too would be picked up. The plate of Olestra-based, fruit-sweetened, gluten-free cookies had been devoured out of sheer frustration. They had consumed their fill of chilled herbal infusions. It was time for desperate measures. Bart D'Elgaro, executive producer and team leader of this vision session, buzzed the support staff.

'Unlock the safe and bring out the coffee—with caffeine— and get some cookies with goddamm sugar in them... yes, everyone here has signed Del Rio Studio's health indemnity clause and is aware of potential long-term effects. Get the goods.'

The others looked down at the well-worn film treatment on the table in front of them.

'OK, let's go…again.' Bart was ready to resume the brainstorming.

'Wait!' Sheronda interrupted. 'I think we should first do some energising breathing exercises.'

'Christ, here we go. Why don't we meditate a script out of our fannies?'

'I'm sensing some unconstructive negativity here.' Sheronda, the facilitator, was struggling to keep a cohesive team. 'We've not proceeded as rapidly as we would have liked, but let's acknowledge the achievements we have made and open our minds to new paths to resolution.'

'OK Sheronda.' Bart submitted. They had been meeting for four hours already to finalise the treatment for *The Mark Boyd Story*. Initially it had seemed a fantastic idea. The most popular guy in America, a brilliant success story, and an Australian angle which could bring in lots of wacky characters. The studio had negotiated the rights with Boyd to do a film of his life and then sent a researcher to get the facts. There were not many. He was a loser, he had done some hippie course, become beautiful, sold kitchen appliances and made homemakers scream. That was his whole life. They had been hoping for a little more—some child abuse, some deprivation—but there was nothing. Bart and his vision team had to come up with a treatment for the scriptwriters to work on. They had to give Mark's life a plot.

Along with everyone else Bart moved his chair to a different space in the room then kneeled in front of it, taking sudden deep breaths and bringing his arms from above his head to his stomach in a non-violent stabbing motion as he exhaled. He knew the routine, he had done it before and, though he would never admit the fact, it usually worked.

They returned to their chairs and resumed the discussion, looking at the problem from a different angle.

'OK, let's recap the good points.' Sheronda was keen to pick up on the vibe her exercise was beginning to restore. 'We like the funny life-changing experience in the tent thing. Lots of special effect possibilities, some special guest appearances. So that's staying. The Jesus issue is still on the table. Should he be appearing in this vision?'

'That depends on the whole coke-snorting, gambling, sex scenario beforehand,' Dirkon, one of the scriptwriters, interceded. 'If we're having some sort of spiritual turnaround in the tent, we need the bad boy bit at the start.'

'But I thought we'd agreed on the Nutty Professor scenario,' Colin, his potential co-writer interrupted. 'Funny loser becomes hero. Jim Carrey could carry it off: he's got the loser, we can computer enhance the looks.'

'Colin, we did not agree anything of the kind.'

'What if we combine these: loser becomes stud, leads a wild life of women, drugs et cetera, then turns to Jesus and transforms the world with food-processors.' Sheronda was the patron saint of compromise.

'Good, good,' Bart could see something coming here, 'but we need motivation for him to turning to God.'

'AIDS. He could share a needle, have unsafe sex.'

'Oh please...can we have something people care about.'

'AIDS still kills...'

'Put your red ribbon away, Colin. We all know the facts, we're talking about audience-impacting drama here.' Bart did not want reality creeping into this important discussion.

'What's with this girl, this...Raelene? What kind of a name is that?'

'Apparently it's quite Australian,' Dirkon said. 'Could give a bit of Aussie colour, start a new name trend. I think we should keep it.'

'Whatever, but what's the story? She's there. They're friends. He screws her and runs off to the States. No-one's gonna like that.'

'I think we've got a potential best-friend-in-love-with-him-but-he-doesn't-realise-until-last-minute scenario. We could bring the character over for a happy reunion...'

'Get real, everyone knows Pergone's Mark's girlfriend; he's got to finish up with a model.'

'Kill her off.'

'Colin, I said drop the AIDS stuff. Does no-one have sex in your scripts and live?'

'Go with me on this one,' Colin pressed his point, 'do the best friend in love thing. She gets *cancer*. He realises he loves her. They make love and she dies. Tears and halfway low point from which he has to climb up to happy ending.'

Everyone burst into applause. That was the first real breakthrough. Strong emotional love story.

'And sex with cancer victim: confronting, great publicity angle, we'll get all the right support groups on side.'

'OK, so that's a Raelene with cancer scenario, all agreed?' Everyone nodded their assent to Sheronda. 'Super, let move on.'

'A kid, we need a kid,' Dirkon shrieked out a brainwave. 'I've got it. Boyd, ugly loser, no-one pays attention. Goes on this course, gets pretty. Meets this Raelene, best friend in love scenario kicks in. He becomes hot stud, has business success, drugs, women, perhaps even some kinky stuff, full frontal sex scene for the male audience. He gets fired, implicated in corruption, perhaps even blackmailed...'

'Where's the kid?' shouted Bart, the caffeine working double after such a long absence.

'Don't block me, I'm creating here...blackmailed. Low ebb. This Raewhatsername picks him up off the street. Takes him in—he falls in love, we get a tasteful love scene for the female audience. Redemption, happiness. Then she gets pregnant AND discovers cancer. Ethical dilemma: baby or not. Opts for baby. Tear-soaked controversial final love scene. Publicity hook, sex while pregnant and with cancer. Child born, she holds it, then dies. Mark raising kid alone, needs to start all over again. Does the whole KitchenArt thing to keep himself busy and give kid a future——'

'Australia won't back his appliance concept,' Bart took up the ball and ran, 'he comes to America—land of opportunity. We believe in him. Success...'

Jubilee, who was there to take the notes, was desperately trying to keep up. She hated it when coffee and sugar were brought in, it was like taking minutes at a speed users' conference.

'He finds a new love, but the daughter resents her...Situation resolved by, by...' Dirkon was struggling in the final half-hour of the film.

'LEUKEMIA!' Colin triumphantly announced yet more disease. 'Rewind a moment. Raylon or whatever has leukemia. They deliberately have the baby to provide a transplant 'cause she's a rare blood type. Baby born, but Raything's too weak and dies before donation possible. Fast forward, daughter gets same thing and MIRACLE, Mark's new love is right blood type—she donates, saves daughter, bond as family.'

'All travel to Australia, visit Raymonda or whatever's grave, film ends where it started. Full circle, tears all round and Oscars for all.'

The room whooped with glee and the director on the back lot yelled cut. Glory was poised above their heads like balloons at a New Year's Eve party. They silently revised their, as yet unused, Oscar acceptance speeches.

'Right. Got all that down, Jubilee?' She nodded as she hastily scribbled 'Full circle' and beamed at her achievement in capturing the magic.

'Good. Dirkon, Colin, I want the prelim script in three weeks. Focus tests on the outline by Friday. We need this film out fast while Boyd's still hot. Jubilee, get those notes to these guys by the end of today and get me Giovanni from casting. We're gonna have to pull someone special to play Boyd—he's gotta be even better-looking.'

Jubilee smirked. She'd seen Boyd when he'd been in for the contract signing—it would be a tall order.

◆

Mark stared into the mirror in his bathroom. The bright circle of electric light surrounding it would have been enough to send the average person scurrying into the darkest cupboard in the house, but Mark confronted its harsh scrutiny with pride. His eyes were a little worse for wear, slightly off-white with three little red veins in the left and two in the right. They would be gone by the end of breakfast, they did not concern him. However, he noticed a minor change in the deep blue of his irises; the one on the right had developed a slight bloom. He would have to get his iridologist to check it out. He pulled away from the mirror so his face was at least 10 centimetres from its surface. An objective bystander would say his eyes had their usual clarity. He grimaced, stretching his mouth as wide as he could, then suddenly snapping it back to its normal position. He was pleased to see the surrounding skin spring back too; there was no time-lag wrinkle.

He turned his attention to his forehead. Perhaps there was the beginning of a permanent line there. He smiled and the skin wrinkled just at the point he thought he had seen the line. Relaxing his face, he moved closer to the mirror, tilting it upwards for a better look. He could not be sure. He closed his eyes and smoothed his finger over the site of the potential crease. He could feel nothing and deftly transformed the examination into a soothing finger massage as recommended by LA's latest facelift without surgery guru.

'Honey,' he shouted through to the bedroom. The woman lying on the bed, twirled in a sheet in an attempt to cover her naked body, stirred. Mark walked into the bedroom, threw open the blinds and let the Californian sunshine crash into the room.

'Honey, can you see a wrinkle on my brow?' He bent over her.

'I can't see anything but light.' She screwed up her eyes, producing more wrinkles than Mark would have been able to deal with.

'No honey, you're fine: fine today, fine yesterday, fine tomorrow.'

Pergone's wrinkles were not serious. Her skin matched Mark's for consistency, clarity and smoothness. It was considered by the people who knew that Pergone was the only woman who came close to matching Mark in the beauty stakes. Together they formed the most glamorous couple outside the film industry. For six months they had been seeing each other regularly and denying the constant marriage rumours placed by their publicist.

Their 'poor' appearance this morning was due to the

heady celebrations of the previous night. At 6 pm, Pergone had completed work on her record-breaking commercial. She had received the highest amount ever paid to a model. She arrived at the shoot at 1 pm. Dressers, make-up artists and stylists fussed for three hours, she meditated in her outfit for one hour to assume the correct persona, walked onto the set, looked at the camera and pronounced, 'Just breathe.' Three takes later she was getting undressed, having her make-up removed and hoping the limo was waiting for her. She'd just earned $15 million.

The deal had caused some controversy, not because of her minimal role for maximum return but because the contract stipulated she could not work for a whole year after the shoot. No promotions, no fashion shoots, no favours for Tom Ford. Attendance at charity events and television interviews were permitted, but absolutely no other endorsements.

Pergone's peers challenged the wisdom of the agreement. They all claimed to have turned down the offer because of its restrictions and the impossibility of calculating the long-term costs of reduced exposure. But the kudos could not be denied. In any case, Felicity from Attention to US!, Pergone's personal publicist, had produced a busy schedule of exclusive profile-enhancing, contract-permitted happenings, one of which would be a wedding to Mark.

Pergone looked up at his perfect face. She knew that just being with Mark was a profile in itself. He was America's most famous marketer, a face on billboards across the country. The engineer and promoter of the most successful marketing campaign in history, one of the most desired men on record and soon to be the subject of a major Hollywood film. His profile was so strong, Pergone had to tread a careful line: to reap the benefits of being seen with him she ran the risk of being seen as part of him.

No-one would ever control Pergone or her image, that much she promised herself. It was the second most important thing she had learned. The first had been that her astonishing looks, however she used them, were the easiest path out of the hell of her Carolina childhood. Her first object lesson in controlling her career came from her first attempt at bulimia. At sixteen, she had tried making herself throw up because all her friends were doing it and, according to Tracey-May, bosom friend and mentor in senior high, it was impossible to become a model unless you were doing it. All the top agencies checked you could be sick on demand before they would even look at your portfolio, so Tracey-May insisted. Her sister had met this model who knew these things.

The young Pergone had tried for nearly a week, but never managed to make herself sick, regardless of how many fingers and vomit-inducing chemicals (prescribed by Tracey-May) she stuck down her throat. Tracey-May reckoned a bottle of creme de menthe after dinner would set Pergone on the path to empty stomach happiness, but it all stayed down and charged for her bloodstream instead of her toilet. This got Pergone rushed to hospital, causing the admiration of her starving peers, but it was to have her stomach pumped rather than to be injected with life-saving nutrients. From that point, her control had to be absolute.

It was the reason she had done as well as she had. She left nothing to chance, trusted no-one with her personal advancement. It was the only way she could operate. Bile churned in her stomach at the thought of not being in control of her life. It was the only thing that could make her sick.

Prior to her record-breaking deal, Pergone had stipulated

that Mark could attend no more than sixty per cent of her public appearances. Their contract of non-financial commitment further provided that all his comments to media at those events must concern her. To mention KitchenArt would constitute a breach of contract. Now that Pergone had forgone official public engagements, the contract, which formed the rock-solid legal basis of their relationship, would have to be renegotiated.

'Do we really need yet another contract?' Mark was weary. The renegotiated contract would only be an interim measure until their pre-nuptial, currently under exhaustive legal discussion, came into force. But life without a contract was too uncertain for Pergone.

'Yes we do, hon. Besides, it's romantic,' she argued. 'I don't want any petty matters to niggle at the perfection of our relationship. It is perfect, isn't it?'

Mark could find no fault that would stand up in court.

'In my profession, so many relationships fall on that treacherous ground of personal profile and financial jealousy,' Pergone continued. 'I don't want that to happen to us.' There was a logic to it all, which Mark might not have seen when he'd first arrived in LA. The rules were different here. The clear definition of roles, responsibilities and limitations in mutual career support, and strict boundaries on financial meshing were the only way to keep these issues out of the magic that was true love.

Mark took himself to the shower wondering how he had found himself in this relationship. Things seemed to happen in LA without him doing anything. When Felicity had suggested he go on a date with Pergone, he'd accepted. She was incredibly beautiful and—a novelty in his experience of models—sexy. There was nothing fragile about her. Her body did not look as if it would break if she drove over a speed hump. Best of all, she ate and digested three meals a day—a healthy rich variety of foods. For an Australian in California, meeting someone with a fully functioning digestive system was virtually a cure for homesickness. One date with Pergone had led to another, to a mutual discretion agreement, to sex and the contract of non-financial commitment.

Mark's work for Glocorp had proceeded in a similar way. The products developed for the Australian market required very little altering for America. A couple of photo shoots, the odd commercial and the stampede began on cue. The largest crowd ever assembled in Mall of America brought traffic chaos. The queue of cars full of homemakers demanding the products had stopped the trucks from the warehouse reaching the mall to deliver the goods. The resulting stand-off had lasted two days. Customers were not prepared to move out of the traffic queue and risk losing their chance to buy the first American product release of KitchenArt. Only an appearance by the Vice-President of the United States in a helicopter laden with a batch of KitchenArt had defused the situation and allowed some customers to grab the products and move on. The President himself would have made an appearance, but his advisers considered it too risky for him to be seen next to Mark Boyd, who may well have commanded a greater level of respect, support and sheer public stature. The President could not be seen to be the number two in any situation—that was the Vice-President's job.

The management of KitchenArt seemed to take care of itself. Glocorp had set up an independent company with a generous profit-related share option scheme for Mark. The scheme would give him 25 per cent of the KitchenArt company if triple the highly speculative projected sales figures was achieved. That milestone passed, Mark's stock was capped at 30 per cent. He attended the important senior management meetings, made suggestions, gave directions, made appointments. His management position was not a token one, but compared with the hard work he had put in at Vantex, there was not much for him to do, other than be seen at the right places with the right people.

He was America's first megamarketer. The term had come to Felicity on her way from Sydney to LA. She had wanted to put Mark on a par with supermodels and superstars. The obvious word would have been supermarketer but anyone who did their shopping at Safeway could claim to be that.

Felicity had made the switch to the States with Mark. She offered to do his publicity free for two years if Glocorp sponsored her green card. Within a year her range of clients—attracted through Mark—made her the hot publicity agent in LA. Within another, a New York office of Attention to US! had been opened. It was all part of the New Aussie Invasion (NAI)—another Felicity-coined term. Crocodile Dundee, Priscilla and the pig were finally laid to rest. The new Aussies were beautiful, smart and taking care of business.

Mark and Felicity had been in the States for two years now. It had been a remarkably easy ride. After his sacking, the Australian public had expressed shocked outrage that their favourite son could be used so cruelly. A few windows had been broken, a few nasty letters sent, but there were no reports of people destroying their KitchenArt.

The outrage had lasted a week until *Woman* magazine exclusively revealed Mark had been recruited for the States. Our true blue Aussie hero was back on top and set to conquer the world. Good luck messages, jars of Vegemite, cuddly koalas and boomerangs inscribed 'don't forget to come back' flooded into Terry's office at Vantex in a weak attempt to find Mark. They failed; he had already gone.

As he felt the power shower pulsating on his stress-free neck, Mark had to admit he was leading a very pleasant life. Actually, he was not leading it at all. It was gently easing him along. LA was a completely different reality from Sydney. It was difficult to believe that both could exist. He had sat in a restaurant with a woman who had been paid $15 million to do nothing for a year, and caused a sensation at the other tables, not to mention panic in the kitchen, by asking to see a dessert menu. This was a different dimension from that of the occupant of his old office at Vantex—arguing component flaws with a plant manager in Malaysia while a vendor wandered through with a basket of mid-morning muffins.

Mark had not been back to Sydney. It was hard to believe it was still there: full of people he knew leading their lives, plotting their careers without him. At first the dream-like existence of LA had seemed just that, a dream from which he would awaken. As time had passed the coddled easiness of LA had become the stronger reality. Now the knockabout existence of Sydney was the dream. He had little direct contact with the everyday world. There was always a publicist, a vice-president, a trainer or an assistant standing in the way. He glimpsed it occasionally—at a service station or if he was forced into a supermarket—but it seemed like a quaint fairground attraction.

The increasingly prune-like consistency of his fingers brought Mark's reverie to a close. The coming evening would provide his first contact with his previous life. Monica was in LA and they were doing dinner. Monica had been keen on a very public get-together. Being seen out with Mark would be a huge boost for her. However, Pergone's personal assistant had highlighted a problem when she and Mark's PA were doing the monthly diary mesh. Pergone had no objection to Mark catching up with an old friend, in private. A public dinner for two could be construed as him seeing someone behind her back. There was no way that Pergone was going to let herself be seen as someone spurned for another woman. The dinner would have to be private.

Mark was irked. He wanted to help Monica and did not want the choice of dinner venue dictated by Pergone's zealous PA. Negotiations over venue and media presence raged back and forth. Felicity was drawn in. She attempted to mediate a settlement between her two top clients, but was unable to come up with a concept that did not involve flash bulbs going off. She was physically incapable of not seizing a photo op.

Monica sat on the sidelines, amazed that a simple catch-up dinner could be so complex. Her last two years had been successful. After leaving Vantex, she had been recruited by a local cosmetics firm, Pout. Founded in the early nineties by a young dynamic woman, its sensational shades of lipstick had enjoyed instant success both in Australia and overseas. However, expansion had led to problems, and to being copied and outpriced by the big firms. Dramatic steps were needed for survival. Monica had been brought in by Pout's new investors; they could see she was a tough woman who'd had a key role in one of the greatest ever Australian marketing triumphs. She succeeded, paring back the operation ruthlessly, establishing core lines and constantly innovating. She introduced an unwritten law—no product was to be available for more than two years. Currently, the women of Australia were devastated as their latest favourite shades of lipstick were disappearing fast. Panic buying had doubled the total sales of each product.

The new shades, good enough to make them forget their panic stocks of old shades, would soon be snapped up.

Monica had an infallible eye for shades. Presented with fifty lipsticks, she could take them home at night and in the morning return with the three or four which would sell phenomenally well. She had a golden touch.

The new investors had decided to launch Pout on the American market in a joint venture with one of the local majors. Better to share with one ally than take on all the big girls at once. Monica was in LA to finalise negotiations. Being seen with Mark, she realised, would increase her bargaining power. A photo of the two of them would mean she had influence. She wanted that publicity, as well as wanting to see Mark himself. If she had to settle for a private dinner she would, but Monica was not a woman to back down. If she could have spoken directly to Pergone, the matter would have soon been resolved. Pergone may be one of the most famous women in the world, but she was just a model and Monica had soon got the knack of handling them at Pout. Admittedly they were tougher nuts to crack than the men of Vantex. Tears were not a humiliation for women and so other tools of intimidation were required.

Because people who were anyone did not speak directly to each other in LA, Monica had to suggest a compromise to Felicity: she and Mark would have dinner and Pergone would join them later for cocktails. That way Monica got her publicity, she and Mark got to catch up and Pergone would emerge as warm, trusting and as beautiful inside as out.

Felicity loved it. The PAs conferred, the lawyers approved and affirmative recommendations were submitted to Pergone and Mark who both gave consent. Everyone was happy. Monica could not believe she had not only snared publicity with Mark but would also be seen out with the model who had just been paid a fortune to not promote anything. Not bad for an Aussie cosmetics exec hoping to impress big business. She toyed with the idea of a Pout gift basket, whipped out from under the table and presented to a flash-blinded Pergone before she could scream 'breach of contract', but that would have been pushing it, even for Monica.

Monica made sure she met Mark at his Laurel Canyon house so they could arrive at the restaurant together. That would give her even greater exposure. She was surprised when Mark, and not some butler, answered the door. He looked as devastatingly beautiful as ever. Physically he had not changed, but there was a more relaxed air to him. The jawline she had once held in her hand was somehow softer. As he gave her a guided tour of his pale wood floors and soullessly elegant vases shaped like lakes, she tried to look into his eyes. Rather than capture her gaze as he used to, feeding from her admiration, he looked away, turning to highlight a coolly elegant Finnish side table or pointing to a tree that was actually located in Neve Campbell's garden. It was frustrating and bewildering. If there was one joy that Mark had always given everyone, it was the chance to be drawn into his eyes.

Talk was polite. There was so much catching up to do in such a short space of time it was impossible to start—until panic that it would never happen set in. Mark drove to Lucques, the selected restaurant.

'The decor is stunning,' Mark assured her on the way, triggering memories of his charmless corner of their shared office. Launching a range of appliances had obviously broadened his interest in design. As the valet took the car away, the photographers moved in. Not a paparazzi scrum, just a couple of reliables Felicity had thoughtfully tipped off.

'Stepping out on Pergone, Mark?'

He smiled and rewarded the journalist with a direct look. Monica felt a pang of jealousy.

'Now Dave, you know better than that. This is Monica Haddrick, MD of Pout, a friend and the next wave of the New Aussie Invasion. Pergone's joining us later after we've had our top-secret discussions about taking over America.'

Everyone laughed, the cameras clicked and Monica smiled like she was about to enter the Academy Awards. It broke the ice between them.

'Well, you launched me good and proper; I feel like the QE2,' Monica whispered as they were ushered to a very visible table.

'God bless you and all who——'

'Stop right there...I'm not going to be intimidated by you or your new surroundings.'

'You're doing fine.'

'So are you by the looks of it. If the maître d' fawns any more, he'll come in the water glass.'

'Not lost your touch then. So, how are George and Greg?' Mark finally flashed her a look and a smile.

'It's George, Greg and the twins now.'

'You got pregnant again!'

'Ugh please, I've got a bronze-coated car seat in my living room to remind me of that particular brand of hell. No, Greg adopted some Kosovar things that were on "Frontline" or something.'

'Their names?'

'The twins...I'm not sure if they're even sisters, but all babies look the same to me. Anyway, they're all fine. Greg is as ruthless at being a good parent as he was in the office.'

'And George?'

'Actually, he's proving to be a bit of a genius.'

'Oh you doting mother, you.'

'No, he really is.' Monica looked round to check no-one could overhear her and revealed the secret of her infallible lipstick selection. When she had first taken the job at Pout, she had to familiarise herself with all the products and so had taken samples of all the lipsticks home. She had been a dedicated Mac girl and was not familiar with the Pout range. She'd wanted to test the products as a woman—as a consumer—without knowing which were the best sellers. Monica knew she herself was the perfect target market. If Pout was to climb its way back to the top, Mac women like her would have to be wooed.

It had been her moment for 'quality George time', which usually meant Greg was in the kitchen weighing the correct proportions of the development-enhancing, child-nurturing nutrients which passed for dinner. George sat on the floor in front of Monica as she looked through the lipsticks, tried each on the back of her hand, then lined them up on the floor so all the colours showed in a row. She put the ones she liked to one side. George, in the absence of loving maternal attention, started playing with the lipsticks. He was supposedly too young for crayons, but no-one had told him that. Following his mother's example, he played with the fat tubes of colour. Toying with Monica's selection, he drew on himself, then tossed them aside. Next he went through her rejects, pushing some around and picking up others. He found three colours which clearly he felt matched his complexion. He was soon covered in them, as were the carpet and Monica's notepaper. Eventually Monica noticed the devastation that was being wreaked on her samples, her house and her baby.

'George, stop it.' At the sound of a raised voice, Greg came running.

'Monica, we agreed, no shouting.'

'Look,' was her simple reply as George smeared Riot Red up Monica's calf.

'That's marvellous.' Greg was thrilled. Picking up George, he kissed him several times, proving that Pout smears genuinely were kiss-proof.

'He's not supposed to have colour cognition for at least another six months. Wait till I tell the encounter group.' Greg took his little genius off to get clean for bedtime. Monica reassembled her lipsticks and noted the ones she had selected as the probable best sellers.

The next day in the office she discovered she did not have winning judgement. Her selections sold reasonably well in the 30–40-year-old category, but overall were not favourites. When her marketing manager took the tops off the three runaway top sellers, the sticks were severely damaged.

'What did you do to these Monica, smear them on elephant lips?'

Monica experienced a frisson of excitement. Perhaps Greg was right about their little genius. George's three favourites were the top sellers. The next night she tried the eye-shadows and George once again came up trumps. From that time on, George was the secret of her success. It was he who selected the core colours for the new Pout ranges and he who put the business back on a winning track. Of course Monica harnessed his talent and backed it up with smart marketing and killer advertising, so she could rightly take some credit, but Pout's most fundamental business decisions were taken by a baby whose greatest delight was making wee-wee water fountains when he had a bath.

Mark burst into laughter. Monica's story had that classic earthy Australian quality which was becoming alien to him. It made him realise how much he missed being involved in his work. He could not remember the last time he had used a piece of KitchenArt. He even thought fondly of the BF 2010 spewing ice-cream into the faces of Australia's home-makers. Perhaps he needed a faceful of ice-cream.

It did not take him long to fill Monica in on what had been happening in his life. *Woman* magazine had kept her updated on his public life, and as for his private life, there was not much beyond what *Woman* reported.

As they talked, Monica glanced round, taking note of the stars dining at the restaurant and trying not to be impressed when Mark nodded to some of them. One man stood out in particular. It was Brett Josco. He had been one of the stars of the *Vanity Fair* new faces in Hollywood cover story a few years before, and had begun to fulfil his promise. His films had done well, and the critics had not completely panned his acting. He was hot, but not yet at his absolute earning peak. One big budget blockbuster and he'd be in the $30 million plus category. The magazines loved him. He was the most beautiful man in films at the moment. His face, Monica could see, had a delicacy with its manliness. He was not boyish but there was something slightly vulnerable about him. The golden hair which in the past had flopped blondly to one side was short and tousled. The lips seemed to be on a tremble frozen in time, as if waiting for the kiss of his life.

'I guess you have a bit more competition in this town.' Monica indicated Brett. She noticed that he seemed a lot more interested in Mark than vice versa. She wanted to meet him. 'Are you going to say hello or not?'

'Probably not.' Mark steadfastly refused to look in Brett's direction.

'You know, if you weren't you and he wasn't him and this was a gay bar, I'd say he was interested. Is he, do you know?'

'He's supposed to be seeing that woman from his last film.'

'Aren't they always.'

'He'll be observing me. Actors do that, study people. Ignore it.' Mark concentrated on his food in silence as if trying not to say something. He gave up.

'So who's better looking—him or me?'

'You vain thing. You're having a beauty stand-off.'

'So, your answer?'

'He's the sexiest thing I've ever seen on film...and you're the hottest thing I've had sex with, but I've not seen you on film and——'

'Cop out...Actually the nation is deciding. *Mega* magazine is doing a most beautiful man in the world today story. They reckon it's gonna be down to the two of us.'

'How convenient for *Mega* that out of God knows how many million men across the planet, the two most beautiful are living in LA. Oops, he's getting up.'

Monica smiled at Brett and he returned the compliment. She had banked on him wanting to score points with Mark's date. He approached the table. Mark smirked quietly to himself. The approach meant he had won the stand-off.

'Brett, didn't see you there! I'd like to introduce a friend, Monica.'

'Hi, Monica. I'll have to get you to tell me everything you know about this guy. He's a tough nut to crack.'

'I'm sure you'll do just fine,' Mark intervened, 'you're the best there is.'

'Don't make me blush. Good to meet you, Monica. Have a great dinner.'

He swept off as Monica finally allowed her jaw to drop.

'Tough nut... best there is? What is going on? You guys were flirting fit to put a ten-dollar hooker to shame.'

Mark was saved from replying by a new arrival at the table.

'Did you see Brett? He just left. Hi, you must be Monica, I'm Pergone.' With utter charm Pergone kissed Monica on the cheek. Monica discreetly checked for a lipstick smear as she saw a camera approaching. The goodwill shot was taken: Monica in between her two great friends.

Monica, determined to find out what was happening, asked Pergone if she and Mark were close to Brett.

'Brett and Mark close? Honey, Brett's gonna *be* Mark—he's got the lead in *The Mark Boyd Story*. It's the hot project in town. Mark, shame on you for not telling Monica.'

'*The Mark Boyd Story*?' Monica roared with laughter. 'What's to tell! He got pretty and made a fortune. Are you for real?'

This was exactly the reaction Mark had expected and had hoped to avoid. Monica turned serious.

'Oh my God, who's playing me?'

'Woody Allen... It's not so much my life exactly, but a story suggested by my life so far.'

'So I'm not in it.'

'You may be, honey.' Pergone tried to sound reassuring. 'I read the first draft, it's very exciting. Now obviously you're not the girl who dies, 'cause you're still here, that was a weird name, Raymonda, Ray——'

'Raelene... Rae dies! She'll be thrilled to hear that... and she's doing fine in case you were wondering.'

'Raething is alive!' Pergone joined in the wide-eyed shock and glared at Mark, one eyebrow forming an almost perfect semi-circle. Mark had intended to tell Pergone about Rae, but had never found the right moment. He was going to wait for the legal disclosure of all previous partners session which would form part of their marriage contract. Now he was stuck with two women waiting for some serious answers.

He grinned and hoped someone else would break the embarrassed silence. Monica, still reeling with delight and amazement, obliged.

'So, pretty boy, why aren't you playing yourself?'

'Well...er, it was raised, but at Glocorp we felt it would diminish my status as a professional business person, while to have someone else playing me would raise it.'

'Not forgetting the terms of our pre-nup expressly forbid Mark to enter the entertainment and fashion industries as those are allocated to me.' Pergone came in with a powerful conclusive argument.

After a little more polite chat, Pergone felt obliged to say 'hey' to some friends at other tables. As she moved off grace-fully, Mark took advantage of her absence to mention the tricky subject.

'How is Rae?'

'What, apart from dead?'

'Be serious, we haven't been in touch really.'

'She's doing OK. She got a good job with one of the big duty-free firms. Her career's going great.'

'And?'

'Are you really interested?'

'Is she happy?'

'For God's sake, she's in love with you and always has been. You do the old best-friend-I-can-confide-in-and-torment-with-my-sexploits routine, then you fuck her because you got fired and disappear off to the States when a big fat cheque is waved in your face. Now I'm not sentimental about relationships, you know that, but even I'd say you'd done her over.'

'So I'm a bastard.'

'Yes, but as per, that's a turn on and all you'd need to do is click your fingers.'

'I've got Pergone now.'

'I can see. I hope the sex is good—or haven't your lawyers let you get that far?'

'Guys, I think it's time to go. We don't want to be the last ones here.' Pergone returned from her tour of duty, much to Mark's relief.

◆

Bart D'Elgaro was sitting in his office after a day of hell on the set. The new director for *The Mark Boyd Story* had insisted on script changes. A drug dealer sub-plot had to be written because the director, fresh from a high-profile tree-hugging Warrior Within course, thought that male-appeal was being neglected. Mark's daughter was now being kidnapped and brought to the States, a consequence of his former bad days. The film's spiritual adviser was also keen on this plot as she felt Mark had not been punished sufficiently for his days of debauchery by his lover dying of leukemia. Brett Josco had objected he was not an action player. Extra stunt doubles had to be brought in. Brett was moody, sulky and his every other sentence was, 'But Mark's not like that, Mark wouldn't do that,' until finally Bart had screamed, 'If we wanted Mark fucking Boyd, we'd have got him, not you.' Brett had stormed off the set and refused to return that day.

On top of that, the actor playing Raelene or whatever was insisting on having leukemia patients on set with her at all times to 'keep her reality churning'. They needed special minders, nurses and practically a whole field hospital. It was all costing.

Bart did his relaxation exercises as prescribed by Sheronda. 'Every film goes through this,' was his mantra for the day. He looked at the old still from *Titanic* signed by James Cameron and thought of all the hellish stories about that production— no-one remembered those once the film started making money. This film would be a winner too. It had emotion, sex, tears, a happy ending and now an action plot too. Bart tried to drain his head of thoughts, pulling out the mental bath plug and imagining his worries draining away.

The bath filled up again. Brett Josco was the only real problem. He was being so precious. Everyone had said he was a dream to work with—got on with the job, no pretensions to artistic integrity. He knew he was there to look good and that's what he did. All of a sudden he was Orson Welles, obsessed with getting everything right, demanding retakes because his Aussie vowel wasn't right, questioning the script changes. He had never been so concerned with getting into a character. His sudden interest in acting was making filming really difficult.

Bart took some deep breaths and tried draining the bath again. It would all be OK. Mark Boyd was still hot, people would go to the movie just because it was about him. As long as Boyd did not cock up...A quick car ride with a transsexual hooker and they would be finished. They were setting up Boyd as Mr Perfect in this film; any hint that he was not and it would collapse. He *did* seem totally genuine in that cute way people not from LA could be. Bart relaxed, the bath was almost empty and then the phone rang.

It was the editor of *Mega*. She needed a decision as to who was going to be the most beautiful man in the world, Mark or Brett. As the magazine and the studio were owned by the same company, it was only sensible that the winner should be the one who would maximise interest in the film. Bart's first thought was for Mark. The magazine would raise interest in the film's subject. Then he remembered the golden rule: Hollywood had to be better than reality, otherwise why would anyone go to the cinema? The screen Mark had to be an improvement on the real Mark.

'Go with Brett,' he told the editor.

◆

When he heard the news, the real Mark was not happy. The readers' poll, the panel of experts' judgement, and the psychic handwriting analysis had combined to declare Brett Josco the most beautiful man in the world. It was said to be the most comprehensive, tamper- and fad-proof selection system ever devised. There was no doubting the result. He had lost and was crestfallen. Like the school swimming champion who'd never lost a race until he went to the state titles, Mark was confronted with the hard evidence that he was not the most beautiful man in the world. Before, logic and good sense would have dictated that someone in the world might be better looking, but no-one had proved it. Now *Mega* had. He wanted to pout and allowed himself a minute of bottom lip drooping in front of the bathroom mirror. It helped, but not much.

To compound matters, an appearance by Brett and himself at the KitchenArt offices had been scheduled for the day of the announcement. It would show there were no hard feelings, whoever won, and prove that Brett was researching his role thoroughly. Even though filming was nearly complete, it was good for the public to see research happening. As he drove to work, Mark perfected hiding his disappointment in the rear-view mirror and wondered why Brett was so interested in researching the role. Brett had played himself in every one of his films so far, why should this one be any different?

Mark was to meet Brett in the lobby of the building for a brief chat to the press, then they would spend some time in Mark's office. Mark had gone through the journalist's questions with Felicity in advance. He would appear magnanimous and friendly, and use the occasion to push his business side rather than play up his glamour and personality. If he could not beat this bastard with beauty, he would do it with gravitas and long syllables.

His personal disappointment and niggling bitterness had to be completely smoothed over. He looked into his office mirror and practised a smile bursting with healthy male warmth, but somewhere in the recesses of his mind he could hear Rae tutting. He was being petty and childish, but this was the first time the new Mark had lost a contest he had set out to win. He was only just finding out how competitive he was.

◆

As Mark entered the lobby from the lift doors, Brett walked through the street entrance. It was a miracle of time engineering, masterminded by Felicity and Brett's publicist in constant mobile phone contact.

They both burst into publicity smiles, moved quickly to

each other, shook hands and then hugged in a manly sort of way. Mark felt an extra little squeeze, a lingering on Brett's part for a split second longer than necessary. It was doubtless a tactic to unsettle him.

Mark brandished a copy of *Mega* and insisted that Brett sign it. The cameras loved it and the press corps practically squealed at the ultimate double date guys getting on so well. The KitchenArt receptionist, who had sat at her console all through her coffee break, determined no-one would steal her prime spot, gripped the desk tightly as her mind grew woozy. Seeing them together, smiling and touching, drove her mind immediately to the image of herself right in the middle of the hug. She clenched her thighs and breathed deeply as she felt herself go moist. She would have to remain seated for a very long time.

'Mark, how do you feel about losing out to Brett?'

Mark wished that just once he would get a question for which he had not rehearsed the answer.

'I'm furious,' he laughed and the world laughed with him. 'No, really. It was obviously going to be Brett. Just look at him, he's gorgeous.'

Brett blushed modestly, and laughed as if it was all so unimportant.

'Let's not forget looking good is my job, I have to work at it. This guy's the most brilliant marketer at work in America today. For God's sake, he's got a real job and still he's one of the handsomest men on the planet... without even trying.'

'Mark, have you set a date for the wedding yet?' It was the gossip reporter from *Newsbreak*.

'Jane,' he smiled, 'you tell me, you seem to know what's happening in my life before I do!' Jane blushed with delight.

Soon Brett and Mark were sitting alone in Mark's office

enjoying a chamomile tea to calm them after the excitement of the press conference. No crowd to play to, no publicity briefings—just Mark and the one man in the world who was better-looking than him.

Mark could not resist looking at the face in front of him. He was used to assessing men's beauty, comparing it with his own and coming off best. Now he was searching this perfect face for the reason he had been beaten. The eyes were a remarkable blue, not deep oceans of blue, but a light clear brightness that reminded him of the smog-free Australian sky. You were not pulled deep into the eyes, but lifted into their heights.

He realised he had been staring, blinked with embarrassment, then noticed Brett had been staring back.

'I really thought you were going to win.' Brett broke the silence. 'No-one could fix it. I know, my agent tried. I've never won anything that hasn't been fixed before. It's kinda cool.'

'It was deserved, but really we both know just how important it is.'

'It's an extra million per film for me.'

They talked. Mark discovered Brett was charming and not as self-absorbed as most actors he had met. He genuinely seemed interested in Mark, which was always a plus. He asked about Australia, about what Mark's life had been like before the *Assertion* course. Mark was happy to talk about himself. He was flattered, a feeling he had almost forgotten. It reminded him of when he'd first started receiving attention. It was refreshing to feel it once again, and slightly alarming to realise he had taken people's interest in him so much for granted. He had not even felt this way when Pergone had made her intentions clear. Perhaps that was because her approach had been made through an agent.

Mark began to relax; maybe there was nothing to dread here. He had believed that because Brett was better looking, he would be immune to Mark's charm, but perhaps for all his perfect stubble and the symmetry of his jawline, this man was as susceptible as anyone else.

It was a beauty war and smiles, warmth and laughing were the weapons. Each player knew that Brett's *Mega* win was just the start of the battle. One had to be completely charmed by the other, gunned down and beaten by friendly fire.

Mark had not risked his big smile yet, the one that conquered the world. Brett's *Mega* victory had made him a little unsure of himself, and to have his most powerful weapon land a dud would be too much.

As Brett chatted Mark began to formulate a plan, a way of proving *Mega* wrong and putting himself back on top. If the most beautiful man in the world fell in love with him, it would prove that he, Mark Boyd, was better looking when it came down to serious business.

Mark had no idea of Brett's sexual preference. He knew he had been seen out with a collection of women, but that meant nothing in LA. He decided to consult William, his PA. If there was a gay mafia, William was its Robert de Niro. He had the dirt on all the stars. Mark was suddenly excited—this was a competition he was going to win and something he could do himself, not delegate or outsource. With the company running itself and his relationship in the hands of publicists and lawyers, he had little to occupy his mind. Now he had a serious project.

Brett was mid-sentence, practising his Australian accent, when Mark smiled the smile and stopped Brett dead.

'Fuck...' Brett was bowled over by the force of his rival.

He recovered his composure and feigned professional interest. 'How do you do that, man?'

'Do what?'

'That smile.'

'I'm sorry, it was your accent. Can you do "A dingo stole my baby"?'

They laughed.

'Actually, can we take a quick break here? My PA is your biggest fan. I'm afraid he's totally in love and the entire company will have hell to pay if he doesn't get to meet you. You OK with that stuff?'

'Sure, bring him in.' Brett flicked into superstar mode as Mark called in William.

William walked into the office like the confident, competent executive he was. Only a slight flaring of the nostrils revealed he was blown away.

Brett stretched his hand out and introduced himself. William gave him a firm long shake, looked him in the eyes and said what an honour it was.

'William, the enhanced production schedule I mentioned last week, I've still not had the report. Can you chase it up?'

'Sure thing, Mark, on your desk when you get back from lunch.'

'No, come in and see me, I'll want you to run me through it.'

'Absolutely.' He stood still.

'Great to meet you William.' Brett tried to end the encounter but William did not move.

'You can go now if there's nothing else,' Mark suggested. William came to, smiled and left.

'Listen, Brett. I'm actually going to have to do some work today, but why don't we do dinner this week. We can work on your Aussie accent if it's not too late. Perhaps you should come to my place, then you can see how I live. I warn you, it's not very exciting.'

'No worries, mate.'

Mark cringed and smiled again. 'I'll have William tee up a time that fits in with your schedule.'

◆

Brett was puzzled by his meeting with Mark. He had expected to hate the guy. He hated other beautiful men as a matter of course—it made life in Hollywood easier. If you started liking or, God forbid, falling in love with any of your rivals, it made life really difficult. His career depended on being the hottest guy around. To Brett, loving another guy would mean believing someone was more beautiful than himself. If Brett believed that, he could no longer believe in his own physical supremacy. And if that was the case, he could not play the hottest guy in Hollywood convincingly. Not falling in love was a vital career stance.

Brett accepted that he was into other men, and he accepted the rules of Hollywood. In a couple of years he would get married. Sadly, the available pool of closet lesbian partners was dwindling now that they kept coming out. It annoyed him; they were betraying the team and making marriage a lot more expensive. He could offer excellent exposure for any woman trying to establish herself in Hollywood. Usually the lesbians wanted no more than that: career exposure and private-life cover. If he was forced to marry a straight woman, it would cost big time and there was always the threat of exposure, no matter how watertight the pre-nup.

When it came to sex, Brett took no risks. He had to have

regular sex to avoid frustration and the dangers that led to. He had casual sex with reliable, pliable men and made sure there was something about them that turned him off: a mole, a habit, a bit of flab. Gorgeous men were an emotional security risk, he didn't allow himself the luxury of them.

Mark was gorgeous. The smile he'd flashed was spectacular. Receiving it, Brett felt an incredible rush as if for that moment he was the most important person in the world. The glow was quickly replaced by insecurity. His own killer smile did not have that power. His enemy had revealed a secret weapon and he was not sure his defences would hold. This charm war was going to be tricky, but at least he had a worthy opponent. The very real threat of losing made it all the more exciting.

◆

Terry sat in the MD's office at Vantex, looking out at his harbour view. It should have given him immense satisfaction, and it almost did. His stated ten-year career goal had been achieved in five—he was MD of Vantex, the youngest ever MD in the history of the company. He'd had the most meteoric rise. He was the most ruthless operator. The superlatives and records flowed for him, but came to an abrupt end with the words 'Mark Boyd'. That name stopped the flow with phrases like, 'Of course, you have to exclude Boyd from the field,' or, 'But he hasn't really made it in the States, like Boyd.' No matter how hard Terry vaunted his own achievements, Mark Boyd clipped the edges of any satisfaction. The one thing he could not admit, the one thing a senior vice-president had been fired for saying, was that Terry owed it all to Mark Boyd.

His final leap to the top of Vantex had been made totally

independently of Mark. Big Fucker, after the touching reunion with his old friend cocaine, had re-established a regular and loving relationship, determinedly making up for lost time. He had believed that Glocorp, having taken over the company and whisked Mark away to the States, would no longer take any interest in Vantex. New products would come from the glorious Mark Boyd design studio in the States. An Australian flag and a picture of the pretty boy on the packaging and they were away. Nothing to it.

He was wrong. All corners of the Glocorp empire were carefully monitored. Targets had to be set, increased by head office and then achieved. There was constant pressure for increased profit, increased productivity, streamlining, downsizing, core expansion, skills enhancement. The phrases came in a steady stream of e-mails from LA. It had been so long since Mygrave had been involved in real management issues, he was quickly out of his depth. Only one thing made him feel he could cope and that got snorted off a pristine, smooth, clear desk.

Getting rid of Mygrave had been easy. Given his record, there was a strict living-clean clause in his employment contract, with six-monthly drug tests. Naturally, Mygrave arranged for false tests to be sent off. Terry allowed the first false result to go, but decided after a year that he could easily handle the top job. He ensured genuine test results were submitted to Glocorp.

To be on the safe side, Terry arranged a back-up plan. An old school mate rising fast through the police force after making a big impression at the Kings Cross station happened to walk into the men's toilet at Grand Pacific Blue Room just at the right time. Mygrave was caught, cut-off Tiffany silver straw in nose, with enough coke to face a prison sentence.

Big Fucker was fired and facing trial before he could work out that Terry had done him over. He had even called Rae at her new job and hurled abuse. Sadly, his rage did not permit him to notice he was screaming at her message bank and thus leaving a record of death threats which did not help at his trial. The courts, keen to be seen as tough on the rich rather than on poor streetkids, decided to make an example of him. He went down for three years.

Terry assumed the top job, and the running of Vantex was never tighter. Every manager was required to set professional targets. Terry's points system was adopted across the whole organisation. While no-one would be compelled to stay late if they had not met their daily objectives target, Terry instigated a culture that made sure they did. Inevitably the 'manager of the month' had stayed overnight at some stage to ensure a target was met. At 4:50 every day the offices rang to the merry sound of calculators totting up scores, and at 4:58 the switchboard would be jammed as the slackers furiously made those final calls to get them over the line.

Terry lobbied hard for the adoption of the system across Glocorp globally. He felt sure he and his innovative practices would soon feature in *Business Review Weekly*. The whiz-kid transforming the face of Australian management.

Terry had done very well financially out of the Glocorp takeover. He wasted no time off-loading his overpriced Vantex stock before the takeover became public. He had made what analysts describe as a killing. That killing had been ploughed back into dirt-cheap internet shares which had since quadrupled in value and been sold again. Terry was rich.

His lifestyle did not reflect his wealth. He had all the trappings that someone in his position should, but they were not a fraction of what he could afford. His wealth was a war chest, dedicated to the primary purpose. His new key objective—to be achieved within the next three years—was the ruin of Mark Boyd.

Thinking of his primary objective reminded him to call Rae Whyte. He had decided that maintaining contact with her would be a useful move. After Boyd had disappeared, she was a potential ally. She had to be bitter after what had happened—and what better final insult for Boyd, when the glorious moment came, than finding his best friend on Terry's arm. Even if Rae was not bitter, she would surely be a valuable source of information, Terry had reasoned.

Rae did not understand why Terry kept in touch with her. They had both worked for Vantex, but they had hardly been colleagues, and as Mark's co-conspirator, she was Terry's natural enemy. However, since Mark had left for the States, Terry had called her regularly, met her for a drink occasionally, and even attempted to headhunt her back to Vantex. He was not the most exciting company, but any date who could talk and hold a knife and fork was better than no date at all.

Their encounters were perplexing. Neither of them mentioned the one topic that brought them together. They had polite conversations about work. Terry asked her advice. She gave it. He was quite pleasant in a try-hard sort of way. She assumed he wanted news of Mark, inside information on what he was doing. She did not have anything to give him that was not from the cover of *Woman*.

Terry phoned her to confirm a dinner that night. 'I'll meet you there at eight.'

'Sure you'll have met your objectives by then?'

'Dinner is my last objective. If you cancel I will have to reschedule some of tomorrow's tasks to today.'

'I'd hate that, I'll see you there.' Rae hung up. Terry was OK, but he could do with being able to spot a joke.

He had chosen one of the more established restaurants in Sydney. The food was not innovative and no longer caught the attention of the reviewers, but it was good and the place had a quiet privacy that more fashionable restaurants could not offer.

They talked shop. Rae was a sucker for good management-strategy discussions. They spoke of Vantex and Rae's workplace, Destination Duty Free, the difference in their markets, new developments and strategic alliances.

'I was thinking a range of Australian souvenir appliances might go well in your shops.' Terry was nothing if not persistent in ideas management. 'You know, small stuff, Opera House electric can-openers, manufactured to the different world voltage standards, duty-free price on electricals, perfect presents. What d'you think?'

'We could toss in one of those cuddly kookaburras in a tin as a gift with purchase.'

'Brilliant. I'll get some figures to you. We could be in business.'

Rae had been joking, but the scary thing about the duty-free industry had been the huge success of laughable concepts.

Rae did not go out much. After her Vantex experience, she kept very much to herself in her new job. Her evenings usually involved the television and an early night. She had not dated anyone since Mark, and tried to pretend it was because she was too busy. For all his backstabbing career objectives, Terry felt safe. There was no question of her falling for him, or being taken advantage of. She had nothing to lose.

Rae emptied her wine glass and the waiter refilled it.

Tonight she was ready to relax. Having company was good, eating off a table and not her knee was great, no television was wonderful. Where was the harm, what could she give away? The number of kangaroo scrotum purses sold that year? Besides, she did not have any quarrel with Terry. It was not as if he had ousted her from Vantex; that was pure Mygrave, and with her 'external relocation adjustment allowance' she had done pretty well out of it. She was not going to trust Terry with her life, but there was no danger in enjoying herself.

Terry read the signs and smiled to himself. Tonight could be the night he would score those advanced points.

◆

Terry took Rae home. At the door to her block, they stopped to say goodnight. There was that awkward moment of hesitant eye contact as Terry leaned in and tilted his head slightly to the side. His lips touched Rae's and then stopped. Rae did not move, answering the question his lips had asked. Terry kissed her again, parting her lips and pushing his tongue into her mouth. It was surprisingly tender. He was a good kisser, she thought, he must have read all those magazine articles on how to impress with a kiss. Technically very accomplished. Not that she had much to compare, she had hardly done a pashing survey of Australia.

Rae realised that too many thoughts were going through her head for it to be a genuinely great kiss. She brought her lips closer together to bring it to an end. Terry did not get the hint and she had to push his tongue out of her mouth. His eyes were shining and searching hers. He waited, but she said nothing.

'So?' he asked. The look in his eyes was almost maniacal.

She realised he was not asking to come in, he was asking for a comparison. She felt repulsed by the thought that his saliva was in her mouth. Had she really believed anything positive could have come of this liaison? She shivered, wanting to run inside and cry, but she could not let the likes of Terry get the better of her.

'You want to know who the better kisser is?...You bad boy!' She smiled playfully and prodded him on the chest. 'You know it's not polite to kiss and tell.'

'I think we're beyond polite, we know what's going on.'

'You're right, we do. Truth is I couldn't tell you. When Mark did that I could only remember the first two seconds, after that I just passed out into the most incredible bliss I've ever experienced. Goodnight Terry.'

She slipped inside the building as Terry's rage boiled over and he kicked the door. Rae suspected he would not respect her in the morning.

◆

Rae showered thoroughly that night. As she loofahed her skin, she shivered at her close escape. Part of her felt satisfied that she had not betrayed Mark. Then she shook her head in disbelief, wondering why she had been so loyal. Several people had told her he had done a 'fuck and chuck'. They'd had sex once, then, next thing, he was off to the States. They had tried to talk about it, but the constant interruptions as he prepared for departure, the awkwardness of the situation and, she believed, the magnitude of their feelings all conspired to silence. He *had* to go the States, it was his next step. She could not drop everything to cleave to his side like a dutiful wife on the strength of one drunken night. There were her own career goals (she shivered at the image of Terry those words evoked) for one thing.

She applied more shower gel to the loofah. She resented the assumption that Mark had done her wrong. There had been no tricks, no lies, no promises. Why did people always assume a one-night stand was the man's choice and that the woman naturally wanted four kids and a BF 2010?

Silence had been easier than rationalising their solitary decisions to one another. Despite the low cost of international phone calls, they could not share their lives as they had previously. As she finally decided she was clean and got out of the shower, Rae admitted to herself that she missed him. Perhaps an e-mail, she thought, and spent the next four hours mentally composing a three-line hello.

◆

The dinner at Mark's house for Brett had gone well. Mark had given him the tour. Brett had admired his vases. They talked, relaxed and laughed. Brett brought over a video of his out-takes with scenes that would never make it onto television. Mark could not help but roar with laughter when Brett, supposedly moving in on the female lead to kiss her with intense passion, tripped and landed with his face between her breasts. 'She threatened to sue because I bruised her,' Brett added.

Mark could not determine Brett's motives for bringing the tape, though he noted that half the out-takes involved Brett's clothes coming off. Brett sneaked a glance at Mark every time he appeared naked. Mark always managed to catch him looking.

The dinner was followed by regular get-togethers. Brett introduced Mark to the joys of baseball. Mark organised a taste-testing of Australian beers. They became 'Hollywood's real-life buddy movie' according to Jane from *Newsbreak*. They were seen at dinners, at charity events and Mark even negotiated a double date with Pergone and one of her colleagues. They hurled their friendliest gestures at each other, complimented each other, and had fun. Mark had never had a real male friend before and Brett was great company.

Mark's car rolled up to the gates of Brett's house for their latest get-together, a swim-training session. Brett's house was a palace which made Mark's Laurel Canyon home look like the maid's quarters. The inevitable palms lined the driveway, with some serious topiary happening at the lower level. Bushes were carefully clipped to resemble men in various poses. When he first saw them, they had seemed a bit of a giveaway. William had confirmed that Brett was 'Absolutely, definitely, no-holds-barred gay...a friend of mine was at an audition with this guy who used to work for an escort agency, just on reception mind, which used to send guys out to a house on Brett Josco's street and the invoice would go to a Steve Manson...Yep, you guessed it, the first name of Brett's character in *Woozy Angels* and the second name from his part in *Conflict of Ages*.' Proof positive.

Having since seen all of Brett's movies, Mark had realised that the topiary specimens were not objects of desire but images of Brett himself from his various films. Brett had explained that the bushes were not just a major ego-indulgence, but an important security measure. 'Weirdos who hate me can take it out on these instead of killing me. Cool, huh?' As his car reached the end of the driveway, Mark noticed a new bush was being planted. He struggled to identify which scene from his life the bush had been clipped to represent.

Brett greeted him at the door, dressed in a robe and ready for some serious laps. They walked round to the 25-metre lap pool. Brett had wanted fifty metres, to make his the biggest pool in the street, but the far end could have been photographed from the hills, so the security analysts had vetoed it. Mark saw that it was not going to be a one on one session.

'Mark, I'd like you to meet my swimming coach, Jane Bradley. Jane won gold at Barcelona. She's the best.'

Mark went to change in the poolside cabana that looked more like a themed honeymoon hotel than a changing-room. There was a serious abundance of red velvet and someone had run riot with a home gilding kit. Mark looked for a heart-shaped bed, but there was only a crescent moon chaise lounge. He wondered if this was where Steve Manson did his entertaining. When he returned to the poolside, Brett was swimming slowly up and down while Jane sat at a computer. She was monitoring his water displacement and energy efficiency. Brett's body appeared on the computer screen in a net of green lines while the water swirled around him in a profusion of red. He was over-displacing, Jane pointed out.

'Your turn,' she said, and asked Mark to sign an indemnity clause acknowledging she was not a professional lifesaver and had no legal obligation to rescue him should he get into difficulties. As Mark completed his first lap, he heard Jane's voice under the water, like a sea goddess booming out over her watery domain. It was the underwater speaker system, he realised.

'Mark you need to slow down. We're monitoring, not

racing. Follow the camera mounted on the track on the side wall of the pool.'

'Move yer butt, Fatso.' Brett had got out of the pool, grabbed the microphone from Jane and was giving a pep talk.

Mark's laps completed to her satisfaction, Jane switched on an inspirational CD and told him he was a dolphin gracefully exploring the oceans.

◆

Brett and Mark sat in the shade on the terrace, surveying the gardens and finishing their post-exercise high-protein low-glycemic zone lunch of sashimi and four leaves of mesclun.

'You really love this place, don't you?' said Mark.

'No, I love what it means. Status. You still don't know what it's like here, do you? Everything you have or do says something about you. You can't get something just because you like it. I never get what I really want.'

'What *do* you really want?'

'I think, right now, I want our charm war to stop...we both know we're doing it. It's what we both do best and we both want to be the best, but this is my home and I wanna relax here. Truce?'

Mark had underestimated Brett's understanding of the situation and was impressed by his bravery in waving a white flag. Unless, of course, this was a bold new tactic.

'You mean, be real friends instead of pretending?' He joked away the possible embarrassment of a truthful moment.

'Don't tell my agent.'

They talked as friends all afternoon, about their lives, the pressure of beauty, the search for visible signs of ageing every morning. The trauma of not knowing if people liked you for yourself, and the fear that perhaps you did not care. They spent an hour on moisturisers. Mark asked Brett about the movie business.

'It's crazy, man. I could never work again and live in luxury for the rest of my life. I only went into this because it was the fastest way to earn big bucks. After I was discovered, I figured I'd make a couple of films, then get out, live off investments, have no-one telling me what to do. But you get sucked in. You have to keep climbing, you have to earn more and more. You're trapped. Just the thought of the words "has-been", "peaked" or "faded" bring me out in a cold sweat. To give up, allow those words to be used is too big a jump. I don't have the guts to do it. I wish I had.'

He looked at Mark as if he were looking through a window at the free life he really wanted. 'You know I'm gay, don't you?'

'Yes.'

'It's not easy in this industry.'

'I guess not.' Mark did not feel comfortable going beyond essential monosyllables. This was an unexpectedly frank turn.

'There was this guy once. I was doing daytime TV, "Children and Friends". He played my sister's fiancé, who was my daughter's hypnotherapist, telling her subconscious mind to kill me because I'd caused his young brother to have an accident ten years before. They kept putting us in all these conflict situations, usually at a gym or a sauna, anywhere we would be bare-chested. There was this thing between us, and it sizzled on camera, this brooding hatred. Off screen we got on great. I think we really liked each other, but we were both new, we didn't dare say or do anything, it would have been career death.'

'So what happened?'

'He developed a brain tumour, confessed everything and died begging my forgiveness.'

'That's awful.' Mark was moved.

'We're talking soap here, not life. He left the program, we spent his entire leaving party together not saying anything, and I never saw him again.'

'You should have said something.'

'Yeah I know that, I swore I'd never make the same mistake again...but I haven't really thought about it much since then.'

The confidence was interrupted by the arrival of Brett's agent. Brett looked searchingly into Mark's eyes as the footsteps of his inescapable career imperatives made their way through the house. The truth Brett had never dared admit unleashed itself. It was liberating, the possibilities were mindblowing. As his agent said hello, they put their smiles back on.

A couple of days later, Mark was having a rare busy time at work: four meetings and only half an hour for lunch. This was capped by a meeting with Pergone and her lawyers to discuss the pre-nuptial agreement. There were a couple of sticking points. Pergone was concerned that Mark's celebrity status might lead to invitations for him to guest spots on television programmes. This could breach the entertainment/fashion industries anti-intrusion clause. However, as the official public face of KitchenArt Mark could not avoid promotional work. Pergone's lawyer was attempting to define the difference between promotions and pure celebrity appearances. It was tricky, given Mark's close personal association with KitchenArt. The lawyers relished the hours they spent and charged on this issue.

When the meeting ended, Mark and Pergone did not leave together. Pergone believed, after legal meetings, that it was best to avoid any suggestions of either exerting undue influence on the other to change position. They always went to their separate homes alone and met up the following day. That way it was all clear-cut and neat.

Mark was not unhappy with this. It would have been great to have sex with Pergone, it always was, but the next day was the premier of *The Mark Boyd Story*. It was a big event and he needed some rest. On Brett's insistence, he had not seen the film. Brett wanted Mark to see it as a member of the general public and be blown away. Mark was not looking forward to the next day, in fact the whole idea made his stomach churn. Perhaps too much of Pergone was rubbing off. There was a lack of control in this situation that he did not like. The film's release would have a major impact on his life, and hopefully on KitchenArt—but he was just a bystander. He had agreed to go to tomorrow morning's press conference but he was not in charge. It worried him; he had a suspicion that his relationship with Brett was taking an alarming turn.

As he drove up to his house, he saw Brett's favourite car parked on the street. Brett was inside and jumped out when he saw Mark arriving, following him up to the house.

'I thought that as from tomorrow I'm going to be you as far the world's concerned, we should celebrate tonight.' He produced a bottle of Cristal from behind his back.

'OK, but we'll have to cook dinner for ourselves. I'm not going out and I don't have a chef.'

'Cool, it'll be fun.'

Cooking involved putting the microwave on high for four minutes and preparing a salad. Brett poured the champagne. They talked about their days. Mark whinged about the Pergone negotiations. Brett made no response, but took a mouthful of Cristal whenever Pergone's name was mentioned.

Mark poked around in the fridge, trying to find the salad dressing. Brett's eyes never left him. As Mark turned to flourish the dressing in mock triumph, Brett steeled himself to bring up the one subject they had never discussed. He could not bear the thought of the weeks of promotional work ahead without knowing something for certain first.

'Mark, there's something we've never talked about.'

Mark realised he had won the charm offensive. Brett might be the most beautiful man in the world, but he had fallen. It was a horrible victory. In the split second as he waited for the next sentence, a terrible sadness destroyed any vainglory Mark might have opted for. He thought of Rae and how contemptuous she would have been of his little scheme and how well deserved she would have thought his current predicament. It was exactly what he had planned, but now all he could see was trouble.

Brett was about to become him in the public eye: the fantastic, redeemed father of a child whose mother had died so beautifully of leukemia. They were to be two incarnations of the same media identity. People would commiserate with Brett on his loss and congratulate Mark on his acting.

'I told you I was gay the other day, but I didn't tell you everything. I didn't tell you how I feel about you. I'm not going to make that mistake again.'

With that, Brett pulled Mark to him. Mark panicked, thinking he was in for a passionate kiss. Instead, Brett hugged him. Mark's relief was physically palpable. His shoulders dropped and he relaxed into Brett's arms. 'He wants to be friends,' he joyfully thought, 'we're doing the male bonding thing.' Brett felt the wave of Mark's relief and knew it meant Mark felt the same as him. He hugged him tighter, let go, looked him in the eyes and kissed him.

Mark was trapped. Having been taken by surprise, he could do nothing. His eyes open, he could see the intensity on Brett's face. The act of kissing was itself not physically unpleasant, it just did not do anything for him: there were no tingly feelings and no bloodrush. A man's kiss felt a lot harder than a woman's and the sensation of stubble, however closely shaved, was a real minus. How did women not have permanent pash rash? His analysis was brought to a sudden halt by a strange poking at his thigh. Perhaps Brett had keys in his pocket. He hadn't noticed them during the hug. Suddenly Mark knew exactly what was causing the poking. Stepping back quickly all he could say was 'Wow.' It was unfortunate that his one word was so open to misinterpretation.

'Wow,' Brett repeated it. 'That was some kiss.'

'Look, I'm just not...It's...'

'I know, it's kinda new for me too...'

'It's not...I'm not...'

'I've never really fallen in love like this before either. I've only had sex with men. I didn't realise it could be so different.'

There was a pause. Mark stood looking at his feet, leaning one hand on the kitchen bench, running the other through his hair, desperately trying not to have to come up with something to say. He had no smile for this situation.

'Perhaps we need time to process what happened here.' Brett retreated to psychobabble.

'I think that's a great idea.'

Brett gave Mark another big hug before leaving.

'Don't worry,' he said, 'between us, we can do anything. I'll see you at the premiere.'

Mark shivered. His fleeting relief at Brett's departure was consumed by the dread of what might come next. Mark cursed himself for his puerile need to prove his beauty. The appalling selfishness of what he had done crashed home. He had deliberately provoked feelings in someone else, purely to exact revenge. He had thought he was conquering America, being a huge success—but right now he felt a failure. He was floundering. He had no connection to the real world, no idea what the plan was, what his direction was to be.

It was this place, he thought, LA did that to you. It was turning him into a local. But he knew he could not really blame the city. Many people lived perfectly sensible lives there, he just had not met them. This situation was of his own making and, whatever the consequences, he could only blame himself. Sex, he thought, always caused problems with people he really liked. It had not caused problems with Pergone, which indicated a problem of a different kind.

He wondered what time it was in Sydney and thought about what Rae might be doing. He needed her grounding influence and felt as if he could drift away completely without her. He picked up the phone, then put it down again. He could not call her now after so long. He promised himself he would re-establish contact. Perhaps an e-mail would be a good first step.

♦

Bart D'Elgaro, producer of *The Mark Boyd Story*, the (final) director, and Brett, the star of the movie, sat on an elevated platform. With any luck, Mark figured, standing at the back of the room, Brett would not be able to get a moment alone with him all day. Then after the premiere, he would be touring the country in a publicity blitz. That would give Mark some breathing space. Pergone was with him. She was represented in the film and wanted to monitor personally any implications for her image. Mark had never been so relieved to have her by his side, and squeezed her hand tightly. She immediately shook him off. She was there as one of the real people portrayed in the film, not as Mark's partner.

The media were still taking their seats. They had drunk their coffee, eaten their pastries and been presented with media packs which included miniature toaster key rings. No great news was expected. The director, producer and star would slap each other on the back, praise the rest of the cast, talk about it being a dream job, say how proud they were, etc. A few photos, a little bit of humour and that would be it. It was not a senior reporter situation.

The film's publicist welcomed Bart, Brett and the director to the stage and the questions began. Brett looked discreetly around the room for Mark, then allowed himself a little smile when he located him. Mark's nerves, which had been calmed by the security of a well-oiled publicity machine in operation, were jarred once again. Brett had a distinct glint in his eye and his words the night before echoed in Mark's head. He tried to reassure himself, this was a media conference. If he was safe anywhere, it was here.

A reporter stood to ask one of the agreed questions. 'I see Mark Boyd is here at the launch. Tell us, Brett, what was it like playing someone who you've clearly got to know quite well?' It was the cue for some of the standard camaraderie, which everyone loved so much.

Brett smiled and paused before answering. 'I can honestly say playing this role has changed my life. Spending time with Mark, I've learned what an amazing guy he is, he's one hundred per cent. He's honest and true to himself. Being with him has made me realise who and what I really am.'

As the media noted the reply, thinking this was going slightly overboard, the colour drained from Mark's face. He heard the plaster on the walls around him crack, the first fissures in the breakdown of his world. Brett continued.

'Something incredible has happened to me, and happened to me last night. With Mark I realised what is truly important in life.'

The sharper journalists were now on the edge of their seats, the photo-flash rate increased slightly. Bart sensed the rising tension in the room and rubbed his finger along the inside of his shirt collar. What the hell was this fruitcake going on about? He did not like it.

'Mark knows exactly what I am talking about and I think he knows what I am going to say. I'm coming out, I'm gay and I'm in love with Mark Boyd. What d'you say Mark, wasn't it Shakespeare who said, "Come live with me and be my love"?'

The press sat motionless for thirty seconds as the cracks in the plaster turned into the deafening rumble of walls collapsing. Mark stared forward in horror, trying to find options and evaluate them. He could pretend to be in love with Brett, appear incredibly romantic and ruin his career, or deny everything, appear a callous, closeted bastard and ruin his career. Or he could walk away silently and ruin his career.

He looked to Pergone for a lifeline. She was staring at Brett in disbelief. A rising panic caused her stomach to rock violently within her and then rose right up to her eyes which twitched and narrowed. Her breathing became short. There was nothing she could do, she was not in charge. Her one overriding promise to herself was never to let anyone control her life again. That promise was being broken for her by the man she was about to contractually bind herself to for life.

Her mind raced to find a suitable clause in one of her agreements with Mark that covered this situation. Her terrified mind could find none.

The silence enveloped Mark and Pergone and Brett, and pulled them in so close they felt they were staring each other directly in the face. Then it exploded, hurling them back to their corners of the room. The media erupted, a hundred questions poured out. The camera operators grew dizzy, unable to decide who to film, Mark and Pergone or Brett. They swung back and forth as nothing was said, settling eventually on Mark. The novices honed in on Mark's face, thinking they had to catch every fleeting emotion that played across his features. The pros pulled back enough to keep Pergone in the shot. Her reaction to what Mark said would be worth a million.

Mark had to say something. Pergone was looking at him, Brett was standing with his arm outstretched, the microphones were closing in.

'I will release a statement in due course having given today's events full consideration. I hope that Pergone's and Brett's privacy, and my own, will be respected, thank you.'

Mark turned to flee. He reached out to take Pergone's hand, desperate for support. She refused it.

'You do not control me,' she hissed, storming ahead of him as the pack pursued them into the lobby. Familiar with the hotel, she sprinted straight for the manager's office where she would be protected from the mob. Mark, trapped in an unfamiliar world, headed outside. Getting his car out of valet parking would take forever, he would be mauled by then. With intense relief he saw a cab pull up. Leaping in, he shut the door as the photographers hit the windows like a hurricane blast.

◆

The controversy reigned supreme across America. Disbelief, horror, shock and jubilation. Homemakers wept, KitchenArt objects were smashed. Several shops ran out of stock as buyers decided KitchenArt appliances might soon be collectors' items. A distraught Claudia Jenkins in Atlanta tried to jam her hand in the rotating blade of her Monet Food-processor. Thankfully the foolproof safety device proved to be just that.

Every sentiment of every cause going was aired on television. Gay rights groups were thrilled with Brett, but divided over Mark. Some condemned his cowardice, others saw him as a victim of homophobic big business attitudes. Sundry reverends in the Midwest declared Sodom was finally collapsing, others claimed the devil's mantra could be heard in the whirring of the Gauguin Breadmaker as it kneaded its dough faster than all other comparable breadmakers. No matter the opinion held, there was a program claiming that Mark, Brett or Pergone had proved it right.

Mark sat at home, flicking from channel to opinionated channel. Within three hours of the media conference, Pergone had found a clause with which to end their relationship. She made a brief doorstop statement to the press, requesting privacy to rebuild her shattered life and wishing Mark and Brett well 'whatever their future may be'. Like the rest of the nation, Mark got the news by watching the statement live on television.

The release of *The Mark Boyd Story* was immediately aborted. Even the premiere was cancelled. For a moment, Bart D'Elgaro hoped that the furore might drive people to the cinema. However, advance notice of the critical drubbing the film was set to receive combined with some very strong pressure from the studio's board of directors ensured the film was canned. The accountants estimated that the amount the studio would receive from an insurance payout (collectible if the film was canned due to circumstances 'beyond the studio's control') was considerably greater than any income its release could possibly generate. The studio lawyers confirmed that the circumstances were watertight. The decision was made. Bart's artistic credibility was ruined, but the studio would make a healthy profit. His job, at least, was safe.

Brett had attempted to call Mark, but only got the over-full message service. Even as he realised that Mark was not going to accept his proposal, the horror of what he had done exhilarated him. It was the most dramatic, the most real moment of his life. Whatever the outcome, it was the one solid thing he could hold on to, a shred of real life. Yet his heart was torn as the nation screamed around him. The promise of love had made international adulation seem a poor second and now he had neither. As Mark walked out, he had seen his per picture fee plummet before his eyes, crashing from the millions down to the hundreds of thousands, and lower. Cameo appearances spoofing himself, and a guest spot on 'Will and Grace', that would be his career. It was not an option—he decided to vanish. A few phone calls and one packed bag later, he was in a cab setting off past the clipped representations of his former career, or at least what remained of them. The taxidriver sensitively swerved to avoid running over Brett's decapitated heads lying in the driveway. It was only three days later, on a Polynesian island with a population of 1000 and virtually no electricity, that he finally removed his baseball cap and sunglasses and allowed himself to think for more than two seconds about what had occurred.

As his therapist would have said, there was some industrial-strength processing to do.

Mark holed himself up in his house. The phone was off the hook. He set up an alternative mobile number and called Felicity, who had been trying frantically to reach him. Pergone was on her other line. Felicity had a decision to make. She could no longer work for both Mark and Pergone. She had never had to handle a crisis like this and, as she put both her clients on hold, she felt a surge of exhilaration. This was what PR was all about, this gorgeous blood and guts. Pergone was the easier option—a nuclear bomb had gone off over Mark's career. Rebuilding his profile would be her greatest challenge; it might even be more than she could handle. It would be a risk, but for all Mark's vanity and her total incomprehension of the weird Californian thinking he had got into, she liked him, she enjoyed working with him and she owed him.

'Pergone, I can't handle you anymore. You don't need me. You are bigger than ever. I'll tell you now, whatever you are offered for your next job, double it on the spot. There is no greater role for the global public than the wounded woman. You're Hillary Clinton without the nasty hair. Keep in touch. Ciao...Mark, I'll come round.'

Felicity devoted herself to Mark's revival. She cleared her books of all other clients. The rest of her team could deal with them. She treated the entire affair with cool professionalism as he explained what had happened with Brett: the kiss, the assumptions, the disaster. Agreeing he should lie low for at least a few weeks, she contacted Glocorp on his behalf. They were a little too willing for Mark to work from home. Felicity decided against releasing an immediate statement. The storm of debate was firing along without Mark's participation.

He had become a completely unfathomable object for the public—and Felicity thought that was the best place to start. They had filed away Brett as a classic Hollywood gay, of the type everyone knew existed, who could not take the pressure anymore. Mark was harder to categorise: a relative newcomer, a megamarketer, a star in a unique category of his own making. Now nothing was certain in the public's eyes. Was he an innocent victim of his looks, a jealous manipulator or a weak homosexual unable to escape the security of his closet?

'Mystery is good, darling,' Felicity soothed him. 'Everyone on Earth knows you're beautiful, that's about all they know and all they need to know right now. They'll decide who and what you are to please themselves. That way we at least engender a level of universal satisfaction. Once that's settled we hit them with our chosen truth.'

The opinion polls supported her. Virtually every TV station was running its own poll on whether Mark was gay, straight or bisexual, victim or monster. The results depended on the demographic of where the poll was taken. In West Hollywood Mark was gay, in Utah he was straight but had been led into evil by Hollywood. In Silverlake they refused to pigeonhole his sexuality and in Roswell, New Mexico, he was an alien invader. The 0100 numbers ran hot and serious money was made as millions of Americans cast their vote on whatever question was being asked about the Boyd affair.

The next wave of the scandal brought the celebrity claims. Every magazine and talk show wheeled out a different wannabe who claimed to have slept with Mark. Weather reporters, minor daytime soap stars, hand models all clambered aboard the publicity bus with their definitive first-hand evidence of his sexuality. Chance encounters, long-term flings, fifteen minutes of passion in an elevator: Mark, it seemed, was a sex maniac. Nothing and nobody seemed able to stop his raging libido, which, if every claim made was true, would have resulted in an average eight sexual encounters a day. *National Enquirer* ran a headline, 'Will the last person to sleep with Mark Boyd please turn ON the light?'

At the heart of the frenzy was one person whose fifteen minutes had finally arrived: Lucy. The moment the news hit Australia, she was on the next plane to the States to discuss her exclusive interview. She negotiated her way to prime time, a considerable payment and a cut of overseas rights. As negotiations went back and forth, Lucy sold all her Telstra shares and invested in a two-week intensive media training course. Her interview was to be the definitive tell all, the story from the woman who had made Mark what he was. The woman who could finally reveal the truth behind the beauty.

The interview was a ratings bonanza. Everything everyone had said was true. Mark was a sex maniac. With a remarkable sensitivity and understanding Mary Marshall, top-rating interviewer, elicited tears and candid detail from poor Lucy. She sobbed in Mary's arms on camera.

'It's just such a relief to finally be able to talk about it. No-one would believe me. The things he made me do! I am so ashamed. I did it all because I loved him more than anything. If he told me to kill myself I would have.'

'Would it help to say what he made you do?'

A tiny voice moused out an answer. The studio audience leaned forward to hear the terrible word.

'Threesomes.'

'Was that with another man or a woman? I'm sorry, that's prying, you don't have to answ——'

'… both and, God forgive me, I did it.' Lucy broke down sobbing and they cut to a commercial break.

At the end of the interview, Lucy got a standing ovation and Mary had a special announcement.

'Lucy is a model for us all. She's learned her lesson and stands before us a strong independent woman. She's too modest to tell you this, but I just have to. Lucy has agreed to host her own program in which she will talk to other women...or men...who have fallen under Mark's or someone else's spell, and see if she can give them some of the strength she has found.'

Lucy blushed and smiled coyly.

'I just want to help,' she mouthed over the screams of support. She was a star.

Felicity watched with Mark in her apartment. She had managed to persuade him out of his house, if only to escape the stench of dirty clothes, stuffy air and despondency. Every time she had been round to his place he had been sitting in front of the television. He could cite the poll results from every talk show, he knew the level of sympathetic support for Pergone and the latest speculation on Brett's whereabouts. Every hour of every day he tortured himself with gossip and innuendo. He was destroying himself. Felicity knew that the Lucy interview would be the one that could send him completely over the edge. She did not want him seeing it alone in the cesspool his house had become.

She also wanted to get her cleaners in there to make it presentable. If a TV crew managed to get in, she did not want the world to see what looked like the lair of a serial killer. She gave the cleaners instructions to throw out all the newspaper articles, all the reports and features Mark had clipped, and to destroy all the tapes he had made of the television coverage.

Felicity had never seen anyone slump so badly. She had always admired Mark's ability to keep on top of a situation as if it was something he had planned precisely. He had not planned this and he was struggling to cope. It was as if his entire insides had been sucked out and a shell continued the daily motions of existence waiting for the substance to return. Watching the Lucy interview, she began to wonder if her strategy was too big a risk. Allowing mystery and speculation to evolve was one thing, but inaction had allowed Mark's self-pity to take hold. Now Lucy, turning herself from a joke to a national heroine, was filling the information void they had deliberately created. Felicity could not believe she had underestimated television's ability to fill in blanks far more quickly than a person's imagination.

As the credits rolled, Felicity had her positive spin ready to stop Mark crumbling completely.

'She'll fall flat. People can't stand a woman who can't let go. In a couple of months she'll be a bitter old cow.'

'But they love her. Look at the crowd going wild.'

'She'll be a bitter old cow.' Felicity repeated the words with determination. 'OK, Mark, it's time to start work. You have till Monday to pull yourself together. I've done everything I can, now you've got to get off your buffed behind and get cracking. We'll make a press statement on Monday. Ridicule all the claims with your charm. Give them the sex every two hours figure——'

'There's no point, I can't do it.'

She ignored him. 'Fine, so you've lost your clean-cut image. The world thinks everyone wants to get in your pants and you've let them, but the flip side is you now have the planet's greatest sex appeal. No-one's safe from your charms. That's good. We can work with it. You can't help it if people find you attractive, you even wish you could turn it off sometimes.'

'Do I look like I've got sex appeal?' Mark's face was

unshaven, a matt glaze flattened the depth of his eyes. Tired rings around them and lack of sleep gave his face a waxy smoothness. He thought he looked dreadful and he did, in the most endearing way. Felicity wished Mary Marshall's TV crew could have been there at that very moment. There was not a mother in the world whose heart would not have gone out to the dejected boy pushing his bottom lip out at her.

There was no point arguing with him. Felicity made up a bed for Mark in the spare room, gave him a sleeping pill and wished him goodnight.

◆

The next day brought the next blow. A phone call from Bob Jervis, Glocorp President, with an ultimatum masquerading as a 'selection of solutions'. Mark had two options. He already owned 30 per cent of KitchenArt. He could buy out the remaining 70 per cent or resign. Given Mark's tattered public image and KitchenArt's total marketing dependence on him, getting funds for a buy-out would be practically impossible. Glocorp wanted to get rid of the cash cow that had suddenly dried up. No-one else was going to take it up. Mark thought resignation was his only option. Perhaps he could disappear like Brett.

Felicity begged him not to give Jervis an answer for one week. 'Just seven days and then you can tell him whatever you want, no arguments from me.'

The idea of another seven days of inactivity appealed to Mark. 'What about the press conference on Monday?'

'Forget that, we're on Plan B. In seven days, you will answer Bob Jervis, Mary Marshall, Lucy and every goddamn television viewer in the world.'

Felicity had to work fast. Plan B needed considerable organising. There were some phone calls to make; it was time to bring reinforcements. Next she sent her team round to the KitchenArt offices to collect all the mail that had arrived there for Mark. They also went to Del Rio Studios. They sifted through every item, all fourteen sacks of mail and pulled out all the positive letters: everything from grannies praying for him to people sending their used underwear. It made a formidable pile of ego boost.

It took three days to collate. Once ready, it was sent to Mark's house. Felicity then turned up herself, armed with the results of the research she had ordered. This was her big pitch. She had the research, she had the fan mail and the necessary support had arrived. If Mark did not turn around right there and then he was lost. It was the presentation of her career. Lose him now and she could soon kiss her other clients goodbye. She might have taken on this task through altruism, but having committed so much to the cause, it was a fight for her own survival now.

'You've got a strong base for a comeback. Look at this lot.' She tipped sack after sack onto the floor, forming a mountain of adoration. Mark picked up a few letters from between the underwear and saw the words 'love' 'sexier' and 'hot love rod'.

'They love you,' Felicity continued, 'they want you so bad. You have got serious sex appeal. I got Attention to US! to do a teensy bit of research. I won't bore you with the stats, but it boils down to this: you were the dream husband for housewives, and that's why you sold your products... apart from them being brilliant innovations, of course. Now you're repositioned, we're beginning to see a new trend and I think it's going to grow... you're the dream lover, the wild boy. You've swapped your Aran sweater for leathers. You're sexier than ever, but not so clean-cut. There are signs of some serious bad boy appeal.'

'You want me to start riding round the country on a Harley in a latex singlet?'

'No darling, we're gonna play it smart.'

'But what for? I can't buy out KitchenArt with used knickers. I need a backer.'

'Fuck, Mark, I can't do everything. I'm here to look after your image and I am doing that. *You're* the business genius, *you* come up with a new scheme. Do you men know how totally, utterly and completely draining you are when you're miserable? You could power the whole of Santa Barbara on the energy you've sucked in recently.'

'But I don't know what to do. I don't even know if I *want* to do anything.' He was about to embark on another bout of self-indulgence when the doorbell rang. He looked round in surprise and fear. Felicity smiled. The cavalry, at last. They had timed it perfectly. 'I'll get it,' she said.

Mark looked up to see the reinforcements enter the room. He tried to speak, but his throat was blocked with an intense pain, as if his muscles had spasmed. His mouth was open and a quiet little 'Oh my God' squeaked out as Rae and JayJo stood before him.

◆

When the news broke in Australia, Rae had wanted to contact Mark immediately. Monica had passed on his numbers, but warned her that Mark had gone very Californian. He had drunk de-ionised, demineralised twenty-dollar bottled water in front of her, so anything was possible. Rae knew he would be hurting. She could not bear the idea of him in pain, even after the years of silence they had given each other. She tried calling but could never get through. She e-mailed his office and was thrilled when she got a reply straightaway. Sadly it was an acknowledgment of receipt: her e-mail was important to Mark and he would be sure to get back to her as soon as he possibly could. Meanwhile, she was to have a great day.

She had received a phone call from Terry. The jubilation in his voice bubbled down the line and made her ear feel extra waxy.

'I knew it—no guy's that pretty without being a fag. He's blown it now. Did you see him at that movie press conference? I think I'll fund a float based on him in the next Mardi Gras parade. Heard from Ms Boyd recently?'

'No...but I'm surprised you're so happy.'

'It's the moment I've been waiting for!'

'Yes, and you had nothing to do with it...'

The slammed phone told her his glee bubble had just burst. After that she heard nothing until JayJo called her. Felicity had contacted her suggesting that the two of them get to the States as fast they could. They were on the next flight.

As she looked at Mark now, gazing up at them from the sofa, unshaven, rough-haired, bleary-eyed and gorgeous, Rae's heart went out to him. She had never loved him more and moved forward to sit next to him. His head keeled over into her lap and he sobbed deeply. She felt his tears on her skirt. JayJo and Felicity decided it was time to go out for coffee.

'We'll be exactly two hours,' Felicity announced.

For the first time since leaving Australia, Mark felt real comfort. Rae ran her fingers through his hair as he tried and failed to get past the pain that blocked his throat. All the words he desperately wanted to say could not get out.

Eventually he sat up, looked at her with his swollen blood-shot eyes and broke into a sheepish grin. 'The most beautiful man in the world eh?'

'You're the best-looking one in the room, that's a start.'

Mark poured out the whole story. All the conversations they hadn't had over the last years were condensed into the next sixty minutes. He told her about his life, about Pergone, about Brett.

'The weird thing is I miss Brett more than I miss Pergone.'

'Oh yes?'

'Not like that. Pergone, well I thought it was a good move and she was certainly fun in bed, but really there was nothing there. Brett, he actually became a friend. I've never had a male friend before and I enjoyed it. I miss him. I seem to spend my life missing the people I like.'

'Did you miss me?'

'God yes.'

Mark grabbed her face between his hands and kissed Rae on the lips. It was his first kiss since Brett's and it was charged with everything that had been missing then. A siren wailing in the distance suddenly became deafening to his ears, his senses burst forward and his mind was dizzy. The kiss grew deeper and harder until Rae pulled away. Mark reeled as he almost lost balance.

'Why stop?' he asked.

'You should try kissing that much stubble.'

'I have,' he said and laughed.

They continued talking. After Mark started to recap his problems for the third time, Rae stopped him.

'Don't you want to know what's happened to me? Aside from having a baby and dying of leukemia.'

Mark realised his selfishness and their remaining time, all five minutes, was dedicated to Rae's life.

When JayJo and Felicity returned, Mark was composed and already looking better. He stood to give JayJo a huge hug. Access was easy as she was not wearing the hooped dress, but the static from the friction of her expertly distressed and voluminous synthetic creation made its dazzling blue colour genuinely electric.

'We're here to help in any way we can. Whatever you need, just say,' JayJo said as Mark slowly worked out where the electric shock had come from.

'You'd better not stand too near your art in that thing, you could send a whole collection up in flames,' Mark teased JayJo. His spirits were returning. Suddenly he sat down and was quiet. The three women looked at him, fearing he was having a confidence relapse. Felicity dreaded the thought of having to pick his spirits up again; she was drained. Just as Rae put her hand on his leg in a comforting way, he was on his feet again. The charge from JayJo's dress had fired up his eyes. They were ablaze.

'Thanks JayJo, your dress, as ever, has been an inspiration. I'm buying out KitchenArt, but I'm going to need you to back me; the banks won't touch me. You said once you could put me at the head of any corporation in Sydney. Well, how about my own one here? I promise you I'll not only double your fortune, I'll make you the biggest name in art since da Vinci.'

'With a pitch like that, how could I say no?'

Mark hugged her again, careful not to rub against her dress, and pressed on.

'Felicity, organise that press briefing you were talking about. I'll need a stylist in beforehand to pep up that new sex appeal. Get hold of William from KitchenArt and tell him to meet me here tomorrow morning and bring my accountant with him. JayJo, I want you there too. We've got some serious number crunching to do. Now, I'm sorry to push you out again, but Rae and I have some far more important business to attend to. The first item of which is a good shave.'

With that, he gave Rae a grin that sent Felicity's raw sex-appeal thermometer racing. She and JayJo beat another tactful retreat. She trusted he could recreate that look at the briefing.

♦

'You know, I've been in this office before.' Stephanie, blonde voluptuous temptress, locked the door to the Vantex MD's office and moved towards the desk. Terry could hear her body desperately trying to escape from her PVC mini-dress.

'Oh yes, who with?'

Stephanie climbed onto the desk and posed on all fours, her face so close to Terry's he was overpowered by the spearmint freshness of her breath.

'Well,' her hand took hold of his tie, 'I can't really say, but he certainly wasn't as good-looking as you.' She unzipped her dress two centimetres and stopped, titillating Terry with a peek of her breasts.

'Go on,' he said.

'He did this KitchenArt thing. Stupid idea, but he really got off on it...everyone else thought he was a big stud.'

'And what did you think?'

Stephanie flexed her breasts. The pressure forced the loosened zip further down and allowed them to pour out, bigger and even more luscious than Terry had imagined. She was incredible. She flipped over to sit on the desk, with a high-heeled shoe resting on each arm of Terry's chair. The view was spectacular.

'I think I'm looking at someone a lot hotter than him... but I guess you're gonna have to prove it. He was pretty good you know.'

Terry stood up. Pushing his chair away with a quick flex of his knees, he caught Stephanie's legs and pushed himself up to her. 'I suppose you want to see some *hard* evidence?' he asked.

She squeezed his bottom through his trousers. 'Let's see if you make the grade, stud.'

Terry grasped the breasts flopping provocatively in front of him. They filled his hands and he squeezed hard. Stephanie hid the yelp she would have let out and moved her hands to the belt of his trousers. She undid it, loosened the pants and they dropped to the floor. Terry looked her in the eye and stepped back. He removed his shirt and tie.

'Wow, let me get my hands on that chest. You kept *that* hidden in your shirt.' Stephanie's hands squeezed Terry's pecs and she scraped her nails over his nipples. 'Mmm, so hard, you must really work out.'

'You want hard, you got it.' Terry dropped his boxer shorts and Stephanie gasped.

'Oh my God, you're gonna have to go slow with that. It's just so... Wow... I don't think I've ever——'

'So it's bigger.'

'Oh boy, is it bigger. I think you're gonna go places no man's been before. I'm just so hot. I have to get out of this dress.' She unzipped the full length of the dress, slipped it off and stood naked in her sky-high heels before Terry.

'Take me, take me now. I can't wait any longer.'

'You want it? You want to feel the whopper?'

'Oh yeah.'

Terry came forward and pushed himself up against Stephanie. He thrust himself right in. She was going to feel what a real man was like.

'Oh Terry, it's so big, it's so...'

She lay back on the desk with her legs up in the air. Terry stood between them. He grabbed her hands and pushed them down above her head. Leaning over her, he licked her ear and spoke into it.

'So who was it you had here?'

'I can't say.'

Terry thrust into her again.

'You don't want me to punish you, do you?'

'Oh it's too much, I just can't stand it. I'll tell you, it was Mark Boyd.'

'Who?'

'Mark Boyd, but he was nothing compared to you. Oh that's so good.' Terry rewarded her with a gentle rhythm from his hot stuff.

'That's so good, give it to me, I want it all.'

'So who's better?'

'Oh, you're so much better. You're a real man. Terry's the best.'

'Say it.'

'Terry's better than Mark. He's so good. Please, stop teasing me and give it to me, I want it all.'

Terry took hold of her hips and began pounding away. Stephanie writhed with the greatest pleasure ever known to woman.

'Oh yes, yes, that's good, give it to me, oh, oh yes, Mark, yes, yes Mark, yeeeees——'

Her writhing was stopped by the back of Terry's hand smashing across her face.

'You stupid bitch!'

'I meant Terry. I'm sorry, you're the best, Terry's the best.'

His hand punched across her other cheek and then gripped her throat hard. She couldn't breathe.

'You fucking whore, you're supposed to be the best and you call out *his* name. You think he's better, you stupid cow?'

He thrust as hard as he could into her, intending to cause pain with his big hard stuff, but she could feel that his erection was already fading.

She looked into his eyes as he realised he was losing it. He withdrew. She hated it when they lost their erections, they always took it out on her.

'You're gonna pay, bitch.' He grabbed her hair and pulled her forward onto the floor in front of him. He held her face to the sharp edge of his desk. All her eyes could see was a smooth polished line that would crunch into her face any moment.

'Now, who's best?'

'You are, Terry, honestly you are, please don't hurt me.'

'And what's Mark Boyd?'

'He's nothing, he's a loser... You're the one, Terry, you are. Please let me back at that big boy. We'll soon get it going again.'

'I wouldn't waste it on a scrubber like you.' He let go and pushed her to the floor. He picked up the PVC dress from his desk and tossed it onto her.

'Get dressed and get the fuck out of here, you useless bitch. Best in the agency, my arse. You're nothing, d'you hear?'

Stephanie pulled on her dress as fast as she could. Her breath was short; she was worried he was going to get really violent. She cursed herself for calling Mark's name aloud and for completely misjudging this guy. She had no idea he was going to be such a weirdo. She had done this kind of trick loads of times: executives who wanted to screw her in their offices, to hear her tell them how much better they were than their bosses. Normally it was easy money; it never took long for them to come. This one was deranged. As if he was anything on Mark Boyd, she thought. It was pretty crazy, but he was not the first guy who had asked to be told that.

'You'll never work in this town again,' Terry shouted at her. She raised an eyebrow as she stood up. Who did this jerk think he was? Terry caught her look of disdain and grabbed her wrist, holding it tight in his hand. As he panted, his face went red and Stephanie saw the violence coming in his eyes. She did not see it often, but she knew it meant get the hell out. With a quick jerk she shook her hand free and ran for the door. It was locked, she had locked it herself. Her fingers grasped the mechanism, but not quickly enough. Terry's left hand gripped her shoulder and spun her round to see his right formed into a fist and flying at her face. The back of her head slammed into the door as pain seared from front and back. His fist was ready again, but this time so was Stephanie. She ducked, far more used to fights than this office boy. His hand slammed into the door hard. Terry winced with pain and Stephanie moved. Grabbing his shoulders in her hands, she crunched her knee at top speed into his crotch. He let out a low windless groan and crumpled to the floor. She unlocked the door and opened it, ready to escape quickly, but paused and looked down at Terry as he gasped for breath. This was one sorry bastard who was not going to get the better of her. She had done bad tricks in her time and taken her share of blows, but being trashed by this wimp? It was not going to happen.

She turned and let six inches of patent-heeled fury fly into his stomach. He deflated completely.

'You loser! I may be a hooker, and yeah, maybe I do have to think of Mark Boyd when I'm doing tricks just to make your filthy flesh bearable, and I might even call his name out by accident, but I'm still better than you.'

She kicked him again.

'And for the record, your dick is a joke. I'll be collecting the "smallest dick of the week" bonus from the agency on Friday. And just so you understand the difference between you and Mark Boyd: I'd pay to have sex with him, but you, you have to pay to have sex with a cheap whore like me. How sad is *that*?'

Terry looked up at her just in time for her to spit in his face. His head dropped back to the floor as he heard her slut heels clatter down the night corridor. He groaned in pain. His rage and agony, bitterness and misery melded into a hammer that slammed again and again into his stomach. The only words he could form in his mind were the hammer's name: Mark Boyd.

◆

Mark had begun to move with an energy and commitment none of them had seen before. At the press briefing he dazzled, he joked, he cajoled and he flirted outrageously. Felicity, watching from the back of the room, thought that if ever she had to resort to teaching, the tape of this media briefing would be the one she'd use to show how to turn around an entire room. Mark took a snide and challenging media, made them smile, made them laugh and then hit them with his news. He was buying out KitchenArt with JayJo's financial support and launching a whole new range within a year. They were desperate to find out what the new products would be, but Mark coyly refused to tell them.

'I've been accused of not being able to hold back on anything; well today I'm proving that wrong. You'll just have to wait.'

He silenced one aggressive reporter trying to establish her hard-hitting credentials by licking his upper lip midway through her challenge. She gulped, stared and hastily sat down, saying he had already answered her question, really. Everyone agreed it was a masterful performance, but the hard business proof was yet to come. They could not deny his sex appeal, but would it really be backed by the greatest transformation of the domestic appliance industry in history?

Felicity's only regret was that she'd had nothing to do with it. Mark had insisted there be no controlled questions, no plants, and he made sure the journalists knew they could ask any questions they wanted. It was an unrehearsed dance on a high wire without a safety net.

The existing KitchenArt range was scraping by in sales terms. The company could keep trading, but it would involve considerable downsizing. Gone were the Glocorp glory days of sitting in an office making a few decisions. It was back to hands-on work and Mark loved it—visiting production plants, discussions with designers, crotchety production managers refusing to implement changes until he charmed them into it. Best of all he was working with Rae. She was brilliant. Her clarity and dedication and her refusal to get bogged down in the process were inspirational—and the sex was fantastic.

The pleasure of seeing Rae again and having her in his life

had also brought pain. Every intense moment, every time they lay in bed looking into each other's eyes, he wanted to talk and could not. Every time he thought of the words he wanted to say his throat seized up and he could barely swallow.

About a month after their reunion, Rae and Mark were lying in bed, or rather lying on the floor with various pieces of bedding scattered around the room. It had been a hot night. Mark lay on his back, breathing hard; his hand felt the damp warmth of their mingled sweat on his chest. He thought of what had occurred, or, more accurately, what had not occurred.

From the moment he and Rae had made love for the first time (they decided a drunk session which they hardly remembered did not count), Mark had stopped being turned on by the pleasure he was giving and became rapt in the pleasure he was sharing. Rae laughed at his sombre announcement of this achievement, but to him it was significant. He loved not searching for signs of how she was feeling, waiting to see her eyes drop and her limp body tense before he could begin to enjoy himself. It was a miraculous experience measured in the noise the two of them made. They felt their love could be heard around the world, and the neighbours agreed.

This time it was Mark's turn to vague out and be observed as Rae sneaked a look at him. This was when she loved him most, the moment he did not know what he was. As she looked down on his face, his eyes opened to greet hers. Tears welled up and he began to feel the usual pain in his throat. But he felt her kisses on his neck, soothing away the blockage. The pain ebbed away and the words at last emerged.

'I love you.'

Rae looked into his eyes and silently moved back on top of him. The words had fired his energy and they made love again. To the relief of the neighbours, poised by their phones, their orgasms this time were of a quiet intensity that shot between their eyes.

◆

On the public profile front, the year leading up to the relaunch was quiet for Mark. There was too much work to be done to maintain a high profile. For once, Felicity had to admit that a quiet approach was the best policy. Fortunately, she had one major piece of business to distract her from her publicity addiction—Lucy. Her program, 'A Girl Needs a Friend', had not died as quickly as Felicity had predicted. Lucy had extended her help to any woman who'd had a rough time with her boyfriend, and on Gay Pride Day had welcomed a lesbian complaining about her girlfriend. The lesbian was the only one counselled to get back together with her partner. The others all received advice along the lines of 'He's a bastard, you're worth ten of him.' Lucy usually managed to relate her guests' situations back to some atrocity Mark had committed at her expense. Her weekly show was occasionally visited by women who claimed to be former partners of Mark, including one who brought her sixteen-year-old daughter with her, supposedly fathered by Mark on a flying visit to the States in his early teens. Mark subsequently had attempted to seduce his own daughter.

True to Felicity's belief that such a one-issue show could not run for long, audiences were beginning to tire of Lucy's bitterness. Even so, Felicity wanted the show off the schedules by the relaunch date. It was an itch for Mark that would not go away, at least not without a little help. As Felicity's goal of easing the itch neared fruition, she insisted that Mark watch a certain episode of 'A Girl Needs a Friend'. With some reluctance, he and Rae joined Felicity in front of a TV screen just in time to see his old friend Nathalia announced as a special guest.

Mark groaned and put his head in his hands.

'Daughter or lover?' Rae queried.

'I dated her twice, she was really sweet and understood there was nothing happening, but now I probably seduced her, her brother and made advances on the dog. Why are we watching this?'

'Let's just listen.' Felicity hushed their doomsaying with a pleasing smugness.

Lucy introduced her guest, an 'old friend' from Australia. She reckoned this would turn her ratings around. They could do the whole bonding thing and show the critics the program was not all negative.

'And guys, guess who ruined her life?'

The studio audience shrieked out the program's catch-phrase as the lights flashed. 'That bastard!'

'Yes, Nathalia is another victim of Mr Mark Boyd. They just keep coming up, don't they?'

'That bastard!' the audience chanted. A cut to the audience saw them looking up at the cue board. A few pointed to themselves on the monitor and the producer quickly cut back to Lucy.

'So, Nathalia, tell us all about it. We've got the sympathy. We've got the support and we've got the Mark Boyd punch-bag. Girl, *you* need a friend.'

Nathalia smiled. Several years of 'Million Dollar Babes' and promotion to hosting 'Pets A Plenty' had fine-tuned her media skills.

'Well, it all started when I met Mark through a mutual friend in advertising...'

Nathalia went on to give accurate details of her encounters with Mark, naming precise dates, times and places. There was no emotional exaggeration, no tears, no complaining, just facts. She detailed their 'thanks but no thanks' conversation without a trace of malice. 'He was a really lovely guy,' she concluded.

'And *then* what happened?' Lucy was ready for a major bitchfest. The sweetness had thrown her, but she thought Nathalia was just establishing her credibility. It was smart.

'Then we became really good friends.'

'But surely you're not saying that bastard...' the lights flashed but only a few audience members echoed the line, 'that bastard is OK after what he did to me and all those other women...and men around the world?'

'I am,' Nathalia turned directly to the camera, 'because I've been checking a few dates. The night you claimed he forced you into a threesome, I have proof he was in Perth and you were in Sydney...they're a four-hour plane ride apart. The time another of your guests claimed he was seducing her daughter while she was watching 'Wheel of Fortune' in the next room, I can prove he was having dinner with me. In fact I have proof, verified by a whole team of lawyers, that Mark Boyd did not perpetrate a single one of the shams that have been paraded on this program.'

The audience gasped and desperately searched the cue board for some clue how to react.

'Now hold on there. I know what I know.'

'Prove it then, Lucy. I know you dumped Mark before he made it big and you've hated yourself for it ever since. You tried to get him back and when you failed you tried to destroy him. I've had enough. He's a friend, he's a great man. Yes, he's sexy as hell. Yes, any woman in her right mind would want to sleep with him and a lucky few, including myself and you, Lucy, have. I have the proof he is not "that bastard", but you, Lucy, you are "that bitch".'

The audience was thrilled at the turnaround. They looked up for a cue and got it.

'You bitch, Lucy,' they cried in unison.

Lucy gasped. It was a set-up. Everyone except her had known this would happen. Her producers, her researchers, they must all have known. She looked to her autocue. It had stopped running. She had no words, no support. She had been betrayed in front of her entire audience and now she was stranded. She stared down the camera that had been so good to her. It had turned, the lights around her formed shadows like teeth. She was being eaten. There was nothing, just silence. They were killing her off: no discussions, no warnings, no mercy. She pressed her earpiece. Surely someone would feed her a line, someone somewhere would help. She waited, still staring into the camera. The audience looked on, glancing up at the monitors, wondering what would happen next. This woman was dying. Eventually Lucy heard a click in her earpiece and she was fed a line. She did not care what it was as long as it got her to the end of the program.

'Well, no-one can claim we don't give both sides of the story. That's it for "A Girl Needs a Friend", goodnight.'

Mark would have howled in triumph at the horror with which Lucy stared out of the television had it not been so familiar to him. No-one deserved the torture she had experienced.

'Well, that's me vindicated. How the hell did that happen?'

'I did the research, got all the facts on Lucy's guests and then I cast around for somebody from Australia with a good word to say for you...and who wanted a break on American TV.'

'But this is prerecorded,' Rae was being the logical analyst, 'why didn't they just cut it out?'

'The ratings were falling, they wanted to axe it. I just gave them a spectacular way of doing it and splashing the station's brand new Australian weather girl across all the papers. Everyone's going to trust her, because she tells the truth.'

'Give me her number. I have to call and thank her.'

Felicity was way ahead. She had already dialled her mobile and passed it over to Mark. Nathalia was happy to hear from him. Her portfolio was doing wonderfully. She had diversified successfully. 'When KitchenArt goes public, you better let me know.'

Mark promised she would be the first to profit from it.

◆

Sheridan Michaels was art critic for the *LA Times*. He was standing holding the usual glass of champagne in the palatial expanse of the Getty Centre. His truculence at being dragged up beyond Brentwood to this vast monstrosity he detested for just ten works of art was modified as he admitted it was an amazing collection of work. Probably the top nine artists in the world along with someone who was apparently big in Australia had all produced a work specifically for this show. That they were almost all present in the same room was itself pretty newsworthy. Only one artist was missing. Mae Dragisovic had sadly been killed in a car accident just a week before.

The works were hung high on the walls with a small podium in front of each one. They were all cordoned off. It seemed slightly pretentious to Sheridan. Normally one could approach new works. The cordon suggested they might be old masters which could be ruined by proximity to art critics' breath. A bit rich, even if it was the most expensive collection of new work ever. Estimates for the ten works ranged up to $30 million.

The works were superb. Each one, Sheridan had to admit, was the finest piece any of the artists had ever created. This Australian curator, JayJo Bonnet, was a force to be reckoned with. At least two of the artists represented were generally considered to be past their best work. Judging by today's offerings, this was not the case. Deep inside, Sheridan felt a certain frisson of delight. It did not happen often and he would never admit to it. But here, ten disparate and talented artists had produced works of powerful individuality which interacted so engagingly. It was as if a higher conversation was going on above them between beings from a greater civilisation. Magnificent, he thought.

'So what d'you think the Dragisovic is worth now?' Sheridan was jolted out of his artistic transport by Vanessa McKillick, his counterpart from the *Washington Post*. Her clipped English tones matched his. Neither was English, but it helped their art world gravitas.

'I'd say at least double what it was worth last week after what Christie's were quoting this morning for that old piece of hers from '96,' he replied.

'Yes, lucky for JayJo, or Boyd or KitchenArt or whoever is running this show.'

'It's the KitchenArt collection, curated by JayJo, launched by Boyd…shame really it's such stunning work I'll be panning.'

'You too? Didn't get a generous phone call from Australia, did you?'

Sheridan turned to her in surprise. '*Peut-être*, my dear. Of course I couldn't possibly compromise my critical integrity and write a deliberately bad review...'

'...for less than six grand?' Vanessa finished his sentence with the figure she had agreed to.

'Eight actually.' It was a lie. Sheridan had agreed to Terry's proposal to slam the launch for a fee of $5000, but he was not going to let Vanessa think he had sold out for less than she had.

'Somebody really hates these people,' Vanessa mused. 'It's only an art launch for God's sake. The most brilliantly innovative collection I've ever seen, admittedly, but just bloody paintings.'

'I think you need to take a harder look at the crowd, my sweet. It's not just art, it's power. There are news reporters, TV crews, a couple of senators, the governor. I suspect we've been conned into a KitchenArt media launch of some kind. I heard some mention of the editor of *Appliance Review* being fawned over.'

'Oh how tacky. I shall enjoy earning my $6000 now, such a pity about the work.'

The lights had dimmed and Mark Boyd, sex symbol of marketing, was standing on a platform in front of the Dragisovic work. As he welcomed the guests, the other artists silently made their way to the podiums by their respective pieces of art. Mark made his usual impression. Even Vanessa and Sheridan hung on his words, watching his lips as a smile formed briefly round his phrases. A glimpse of his tongue made it hard to concentrate on their Australian benefactor's fee. Boyd was supposed to be the particular object of their erudite derision.

'It is a great sadness,' Mark said, 'that the creator of this brilliant piece of work beside me, *My Happy Belgrade*, cannot be with me tonight. However, it is a great honour to be able to carry out personally Mae's final wish regarding this work.'

As he spoke Mark produced a razor-sharp chef's knife and held it above his head. It flashed in the strategically placed spotlight. Turning quickly, he plunged it right into the heart of *My Happy Belgrade* and pulled it down. His lapel microphone picked up the sound and the terrible rip of canvas echoed round the hall.

'Fuck me!' Vanessa's Bronx accent suddenly escaped as the appalling piece of cultural vandalism took place before her eyes. Mae wanting her greatest work destroyed...Her executors allowing it, more to the point! Vanessa's horrible ruminations were disturbed by a crashing sound behind her. She turned in unison with Sheridan and the stunned crowd to see Arthur Taylor smashing his work on the podium where he had been standing. Sheridan was lost for words, turning back to the main stage as if some meaning could be found in this terror. He saw a spotlight appear on his favourite work as its creator, now wearing a motorcycle helmet, removed it from the wall and smashed it over her head to tear her way out of it.

Lights flashed on all the works as their creators began to destroy them. Sheridan let out a sob as he witnessed Nagoya, the artist who refused to be classified by gender and ate only once a fortnight to ensure creative flow, began to eat the delicate watercolour she/he had created. This was hell. Within minutes the greatest collection of new art ever assembled was reduced to canvas scraps, splintered frames and a none too tasty snack.

'Ladies and gentlemen,' Boyd drew their attention to the main platform once more, I present to you a new age, not just the marriage of art and function, but their progeny: the new KitchenArt range.'

Choral music suggesting every angel in heaven had been hired for the gig burst forth. From the ceiling above the artists, the new KitchenArt range descended. The products were based on the artwork that had just been destroyed. The form of each product perfectly complemented and added nuances of meaning to the work. Sheridan gasped with relief as the Nagoya appeared not on but *as* a hand-held blender. The work, which had been a one-dimensional rectangle, was now a full object, the tubular casing revealing that what had been the right- and left-hand sides of the work now merged to form a never-ending piece of beauty. The precise sharpness of the rotating blade perfectly represented the cruel surgical incisions made on children born with both genders. It was what Nagoya had always been trying to say about gender fluidity. Thanks to KitchenArt she/he had finally succeeded in expressing him/herself.

A wave of relieved joy swept the hall as if lost children had been found alive and well and cured of all ailments. Vanessa had tears in her eyes. If she had not been present here she would never have believed appliances could be so powerfully moving.

Boyd continued: 'As you can see, the new KitchenArt range does not recreate art—it *is* the art. From now on each KitchenArt product will reflect a partnership between artist and scientist, coming together to create a new work of art.

The only form in which anyone will be able to purchase or view that art will be as KitchenArt.'

The small man standing next to Sheridan and Vanessa with a grubby notepad in his hand was talking furiously to anyone around who would listen to him. 'This is spectacular, it's the most amazing thing that's happened in appliances since the blender was invented. Look at the forms, and the tech specs are out of this world. This is art.'

Sheridan and Vanessa turned to look at the little man. He realised he had been babbling, and extended his hand.

'Sorry, Fred Schmidt, *Appliance Review*. We were expecting some smart rehash of his old stuff, but this is incredible. If you knew appliances you'd see this is total—I mean *total*—innovation.'

There was another surprise in store. The Dragisovic work which Mark had so lovingly destroyed did not have an appliance in front of it. As the crowd started to come to terms with what had happened, Mark hit them again.

'Now, having revealed our new range of small appliance art, I would like to present the centrepiece of our revolution.'

The host of angels returned, the lights dimmed and a searchlight ran round the room looking for the grand finale, then struck it along with three other intense spotlights. Descending to the central stage was a large, elegantly curved and exquisitely proportioned object which pushed *My Happy Belgrade* into the third dimension.

'Ladies and gentlemen, I present to you the RW 3000. Frost-free, intelligent temperature control, infinite shelf height adjustment, CFC free, chill zone, salad crisper, and built in ice-cream maker. I present *My Happy Belgrade* as Fridge–Freezer.'

Fred Schmidt was awestruck. 'Oh my God, he wouldn't dare.'

Sheridan, still drinking in the astonishingly powerful statement that had been lowered before him, could only agree. 'Yes, to transform a work of art on hunger deprivation and destruction into food storage for the American people, that's just so... it's an internalised juxtaposition. It says, it says...'

'It says fuck you to Glocorp, that's what it says.' Fred had less artistic preoccupations. 'He's taking on the big boys at their own game. This is a declaration of war.'

'How exquisite, how apt!' Sheridan was in raptures. Fred was surrounded by appliance industry types. They marvelled at Mark's audacity at moving into stand alones and taking on the might of Glocorp. Fred led the push forward as appliance aficionados and art critics moved to see KitchenArt's bold move up close. Art and appliance, two forms were merged and two tribes were united in ecstatic appreciation.

Sheridan and Vanessa looked at each other in amazement and realised they were about to lose out on thousands of dollars.

'We can't pan this. We'd be laughed out of the country.' Vanessa stated the obvious.

'Bugger the Australian. He can't buy our integrity.' Sheridan leaped for the moral high ground. Spotting an ABC news crew, he realised his best option now was to reveal the scheme and show that America's top critics were beyond corruption—and able to star in their own news story. Vanessa came to the same realisation.

'Can you remember what the guy was called?' Sheridan asked her.

'Terry something, he was head of some Glocorp subsidiary in Australia. We need the facts.'

'Nonsense my dear, that's what journalists are for. We'll give them the lead, do the interview and they can fill in the blanks. Let's go.'

◆

Mark and Rae got home from the launch at around three in the morning. Mark was as energised as if he had just got up and drunk a very strong espresso. His eyes were bright, wide open, and he could not keep still, physically or mentally. Each moment of the launch had to be subjected to a post-mortem: each reaction, every comment was scrutinised. Mark was not just savouring success, he was digesting it. He played and replayed the video of proceedings, commenting on the effect of each light change, every hand movement, any slight variation in his appearance.

'Does that look like a wrinkle to you?' Mark had freeze-framed himself mid sentence and was minutely examining the screen.

Rae could not believe that he might think the evening had been anything other than astonishing. He had generated so much electricity—and was worried about a wrinkle. She had watched him at the launch as he worked the vast room filled with the rich and powerful. They had arrived with raised eyebrows and whispered jokes and were transformed into sex-starved groupies. Mark had smiled, flirted and stood suggestively that bit too close to people while he enthused about his products. He had achieved what no other person on the planet could. He had combined high art and sheer sex appeal and injected it into a sandwich toaster with additional pie-making plates. Just by touching the object he gave it some of his own allure. Suddenly, the revolutionary reverse-cycle rice-steamer and fruit-dehydrator became an object of desire. Something about its surface, graced by Arthur Taylor's confusion of a thousand exquisite shades of black, drew hands and lips inexorably to it. Rae caught California's longest serving senator kissing his hand then touching the espresso maker with built-in self-frothing cappuccino function which moments before Mark had held aloft.

The night belonged to Mark and he knew it. He exalted in the discovery that a comeback triumph was even sweeter than new success. It had a familiarity. There was no shock as the wave of public attention hit. He knew what to expect, knew he loved it and knew he had brought it back by himself.

That night Mark made love with an incredible intensity. Rae, whose energy levels were more in tune with the hour showing on the clock, could barely keep up. He had energy for both of them and Rae let herself be carried away by his excitement. His intense high exploded spectacularly and he collapsed into sleep. Rae lay on her side looking at him. As pleasurable as the sex was, she had been a passenger. She remembered how hard it had been to be part of Mark's life when KitchenArt first hit. They had both put it down to conflicting schedules. This time round, living together and working together, there would not be that excuse. Perhaps their schedules had not been the real reason. Something about his brilliance that night set Mark apart. He was on a stage once more, enthralling the world. She was proud of him and happy for him, but there was a distance. Mark's beauty isolated him. There was only room for one person inside it and everyone else, including herself, was left outside. She might be closer to him than anyone else, but she was still part of the outside world. It was only when his looks were not in play, when he was dejected or working towards his success, that Rae felt she was part of him. A thought insidiously worming in the back of her weary mind told her his beauty would always be a barrier.

◆

Terry lasted another day at the MD's office at Vantex. He knew as soon as he read the rave art reviews in the internet editions of the *LA Times* and the *Washington Post* that his bribery attempts had failed. Unfortunately he had bypassed the news sections and so completely missed the bribery scandal lead stories. They gave Mark's launch even greater publicity and elicited yet more sympathy for him. The public perception was sealed: Mark was a victim of beauty, the object of intense love, jealousy and professional hatred. Buying the *My Happy Belgrade* fridge–freezer was a blow for the people's hero against the bitter hatred of big business. The papers were especially thrilled that their thundering editorials could claim their own reporters as bastions of incorruptibility in a shoddy world. Glocorp was in crisis.

Had he read the news stories, Terry would have realised the media calls plaguing his office were not from hacks wanting glib comments on Mark's comeback, but from leading journalists seeking to confirm the bribery allegations.

He did take one call—from Bob Jervis, President of Glocorp—but only at Francine's insistence.

'This discussion will be held on the basis you are acquainted with the full situation. The call is being recorded and any verbal contribution on your part will constitute an agreement to said recording. Naturally, your current position is incompatible with a successful image impact limitation exercise.'

'Excuse me?'

'You're fired.' The ever-helpful Tom Petrillo chipped in on the conference phone.

'A statement has been prepared for you, accepting sole responsibility, confirming you acted alone against the express policy of the company, apologising for all emotional and commercial damage and sincerely regretting your shameful action. Your security card is being revoked. You have a maximum period of thirty minutes to finally and completely vacate the offices. Any purposeful or accidental media communication will result in the immediate invocation of clause 12 subsection viii of your employment contract and immediate induction of legal proceedings.'

'Get out now, and don't speak to the press or we'll sue your ass off,' Tom translated.

They hung up.

Terry did not achieve his objectives target that day. It took a three-hour refocus and self-nurturing analysis session to find the positive in the situation. Without a company to run and with the assets he had accrued over the last two years, he was now free to concentrate entirely on his key objective: the ruin of Mark Boyd.

'It's only when the door is closed that you realise the window of opportunity is open,' he wrote in large capitals on his realisations pad at home. He was empowered by this understanding. The apparent disaster was really the greatest opportunity for him. With $900 000 in realisable assets, and an iron determination to succeed, his goal was clearer and closer than ever. The world had to be made safe from Boyd's pervasive beauty. How many lives had already been ruined? How many people had lost their rightful positions thanks to his disgusting charm? The time had come to act. Terry felt a surge of energy course through his body, and ran to the window to roar so loudly Boyd himself would tremble.

He had effected such a complete refocusing that when Mark—'the Comeback King'—appeared on the television in a replay of his latest interview, Terry could not tell if he hurled his goat-slaughtering knife through the screen in fury or exultation. 'Frustration is the first step to action,' he joyfully intoned to the Qantas operator as he booked his flight to LA.

◆

In New York, Monica was watching the same television interview as Terry. She also felt levels of frustration, not from being robbed by Mark, but being robbed of hearing Mark's comments by the children screaming around her. Greg had extended his pride to four children. George, the lipstick prodigy, and the twins had been joined by Julius, another orphan, a victim of East Timor's troubles. Mark's interview had coincided with Monica's designated quality time as mother. George read quietly while the other three screamed to make themselves heard over the television. Monica turned up the volume to hear Mark over their screams. Greg attempted to ignore the noise as he researched bone-strengthening foods on the internet.

From the little she could hear, Monica realised that this relaunch was special. Such a stunning comeback would put Mark in the big league permanently. There was something even sexier about him now, she mused. The way he moved had a naughtiness to it. She watched as he casually patted his thigh or touched his chest. She could barely hear his words, but his body language was saying 'Undress me now'. A finger on the lips followed by a slight pursing sent out a kiss to the women of America. Her mind drifted back to the time she had seen a lot more of his body and she decided that the new improved version of Mark would be even tastier. A particularly loud yelp from Julius, trapped in a pincer movement by the Kosovar twins, brought her back to reality.

'Christ,' she thought, 'three screaming kids, no sound and he's still setting me off. The man has no limits.' She pulled the Timorese one from the grip of the twins, whom she was beginning to suspect were Serbian not Kosovar. They had an alarming habit of taking over everyone else's territory.

◆

The launch of Pout in America had gone well. It seemed George was as much in tune with the make-up tastes of American women as he had been with Australian. It had been Greg who suggested that Monica herself head up the American operation. It was the major market and would soon dictate all production. Besides, he wanted the children to be exposed to a variety of cultures and become true citizens of the world. Monica agreed it would be best for the children.

She had missed the KitchenArt product launch because of a crisis in New York, where they were now based. George had been presented with twenty-four new shades of eyeliner and had refused to touch a single one. Monica was due to make her final decision on which should go into production the next morning and the brat would not play. She had tried luring him with sweets, drawing on paper, even drawing on herself, but to no avail. When Greg walked in, having bathed the young ones and put them to bed, he was touched by Monica's commitment to her son. He thought how charming she looked sitting on the floor with squiggles on her face and lines up her arms. He wanted to make another baby right there and then, but had to take a very bored George off to bed.

Returning, he offered to give Monica a bath. An exhausted and frustrated chief executive agreed. Greg joined her in the tub, gently scrubbing away the eyeliner shades and then smoothing her skin with his kisses. His hand reached round to her erect nipples, he nuzzled his nose into her neck and they made happy uninterrupted love. Since their marriage Monica had been pleasantly surprised by their love life. Now that sex was no longer a career move, she enjoyed relaxing into it and not having to prove she was the dominant partner. She had learned the joys of receiving as well as taking. It had set a few alarm bells ringing that she might be losing her touch professionally, so she had toughened up at work, just in case.

For Greg, any sex that did not involve the exacting rigours of their first encounters on Hayman Island was great. The idea of seeking casual sex elsewhere did not occur to him and he looked back on his previous life as the misguided antics of youth. The Greg of today led a life of rich importance and relevance to humanity.

In the morning Monica rejected the entire range of eye-liners, bawled out her designers for being out of touch and demanded a new set of options within a week. Tears all round from the designers, distraught at rejection, reassured Monica that she was not going soft after all.

George was much happier with the new shades and played for several hours with a vibrant set of four strong colours.

Monica tried them. They were certainly different. Her staff would scream, but the expert had made his choice. The range would be called Gorgeous George.

◆

There was a Vantex reunion in New York shortly after the KitchenArt launch. Mark was starring at a charity auction at the Guggenheim and took the opportunity to seal a deal whereby all KitchenArt products would be held at the museum as genuine artworks, with a retrospective planned for the tenth anniversary of the relaunch. Serious art credentials were essential to KitchenArt's image and those could only be bought in New York. Rae was able to catch up with some production plant reps at the same time and so Monica, Greg, Rae and Mark finally had dinner together for the first time.

'So, Greg, what's happened to the lion then? Seems to be more of a mother hen now,' Mark could not resist teasing. After all the lectures Greg had given him at Vantex about oomph, drive and determination, Greg himself had dropped out big time. To other diners at the restaurant, Greg appeared the opposite. His mobile rang incessantly. He was in constant contact with the temporary infant development supervisor ('That's the baby-sitter,' Monica clarified), the kindergarten counsellor, the baby's inter-cultural rehabilitation worker, the twins' war trauma recovery psychologist and members of AMPCGA (American Male Primary Care Givers Association). The AGM was due in three weeks and Greg was shoring up support for his presidential bid.

'Does this look like a man who's dropped out?' interceded Monica. No-one was going to accuse her life partner of wimping out of anything, especially while he was arm-twisting the AMPCGA Minnesota branch secretary to recruit an extra thirty members in time for the AGM.

'So what if their wives haven't even conceived yet, sign 'em up, we're not prejudiced…no, fourteen is not too young. There are kids out there screwing around at twelve, they can be parenting at fourteen, sign 'em up. Get the votes in.'

'Don't suppose he spent any time in the NSW Labor Party, did he?' Rae was impressed by Greg's political skills.

'Greg, enough. Switch the phone off.' Monica asserted herself before the dinner was completely ruined.

'I take it all back, Greg, you're as ruthless as ever,' Mark conceded.

'So you haven't quite got the same sales for the new KitchenArt as for the old.' Greg had just read an article in the *New York Times* saying that sales had only been 70 per cent of those following the initial KitchenArt release. It was his turn to tease. 'Bit disappointing?'

'Not at all. The new range retails at more than double the price of the previous range, production costs are only 10 per cent higher, and, thanks to Rae, falling all the time. Profitability is way ahead of budget. And this time round, *we* get to keep it.' Mark was just as defensively proud of his babies. 'The RW 3000 accounted for 35 per cent of all fridges sold in America last week.'

As if to prove the point, a table of diners leaving the restaurant stopped to congratulate Mark on both revitalising the art world and bringing real art to the average home. It was the kind of restaurant where diners thought the average home could happily afford over $250 for a toaster. Mark switched immediately to dazzling form. Monica managed to pull herself away from gazing at him to notice Rae looking down and playing with her food. She was distracted by a waiter cooing over Mark and asking him to autograph the chef's hat. The chef herself could not leave the kitchen. She never appeared in public. That was her speciality: no-one knew what she looked like.

three years later

Felicity stood at the entrance of the vast lobby of the Attention to US!! offices in SoHo. Mark and Rae were late yet again. She had been on the phone to Mark all day, begging, pleading, cajoling him to be on time. Arriving fashionably late was one thing, getting a reputation for holding things up was another. She called Rae on her mobile.

'We're about four blocks away, traffic's quite clear, we'll be there any moment.'

'He does know this is a major honour, even for him.'

'That's why we had to spend so long getting ready.'

Felicity could hear the teeth clenching down the phone. She hung up and went inside to alert the *Megahome* editor to their imminent arrival. The launch of the most eagerly awaited new publication in the States for over a year had been held up forty-five minutes for the arrival of the star guest, Mark Boyd. The event manager had started breathing into a paper

bag after thirty minutes. He had subjected the food to precise time-engineering in order to surround and complement
the speeches. Mark had thrown out the timetable. The truf-
fle dumplings would have to be brought forward and there
was only enough champagne to last one extra hour. Felicity
was talking him through the crisis while the editor searched
for a fresh paper bag to replace the breath-sodden one currently being used to prevent hyperventilation.

Felicity's phone rang. It was Rae. They had run into traffic, they were walking now, and two blocks away. The event
manager heard 'walking' and passed out.

Megahome's editor, Janice Jarrow-Healey, smiled grimly at
Felicity.

'I'm losing my advertisers. I've practically had to lock the
doors to keep them here.'

'Any second. You know what he's like, two minutes at the
microphone and they'll double their spend with you.'

'We've invested heavily, I left a very serious publication
for this magazine, my event manager is lying at our feet with
a damp paper bag and the person on whom the whole launch
feature is centred is too busy combing his hair to turn up.
He'd better show and fast.'

Down the street, Rae was pounding the pavement, ten
metres ahead of Mark.

'You could at least hurry. It's your fault we're so late.
Come on.'

'I'm not turning up all sweaty and flustered. I've got to
look good.'

'I don't think anyone cares at this stage,' Rae shouted over
her shoulder. 'Come on.'

Mark knew differently. He had to appear perfect. It was
what he did. There was nowhere for him to change or freshen

up at Attention to US!! Once he was through the door, that was it. Arriving panting, beaded with sweat, was not an option. He stopped to check how he looked in a window. He knew the right amount of exertion would give his face a fresh glow; too much and he would look flustered. Panicking did his appearance no good.

Rae stormed on, infuriated by his complete calm. She was panicking for both of them, willing him to walk faster, and feeling the dampness under her arms that Mark was so studiously avoiding. This launch was supposed to be as much about her as him. It was their home that was featured in the first issue of *Megahome*—an at home story with America's first couple of marketing, successful co-presidents of Boyd–Whyte Enterprises (BWE), best friends and husband and wife.

Megahome had broken through their tight security by offering them complete editorial control of the feature. Every photo, every word of text had been approved by Rae or Mark. Mark looked after the pictures, Rae the text. Rae had been happy with the words. They were honest, they were refreshing, they avoided the usual sycophancy. The magazine was also running a piece on homes around the world featuring KitchenArt products and how different cultures treated their beloved works of functional art. It was the best publicity money could buy. Rae did not want to piss off the magazine and Mark was falling further and further behind. She ran back to him and grabbed his hand.

'Please Mark, it's not far, at least look like you care.'

'It's because I care that I can't hurry.'

Gripping his hand, Rae stepped up the pace. If she had to drag him there, she would. It was always such hard work nowadays.

. Inside the building, the event manager came to. Janice Jarrow-Healy was guarding the door to prevent any advertiser escapes. They had all been there over an hour and not a glimpse of the magazine. Restless was not the word. Everything was geared to go as soon as Mark walked through the door. She had cameras poised ready to flash, the stage microphone primed and staff hidden behind a screen with stacks of the first issue of *Megahome* to distribute.

The door opened and Rae fell through, panting, sweating and dishevelled. Her dress stuck to her back from the rigours of forcing Mark along. Mark swept in, looking as fresh and relaxed as if he had been dropped off by a mobile beauty salon. Janice beamed. Felicity sighed with relief.

Rae pulled the material of her dress off her back and flapped it slightly in an attempt to cool down. She was interrupted by a flash. The cameras were documenting the arrival of New York's glamour couple, or more accurately, New York's glamour man and his sweaty wife. Rae's shoulders sank. Mark had been right not to hurry. The extra ten minutes were worth it for him. She looked and felt dreadful as he beamed, safe in the assurance of his perfection. To have him dawdle, increase her stress levels and still be right was infuriating. She excused herself quickly and made for the toilets. She thought there might be a few moments before they had to climb onto the platform and officially launch the magazine. As she rinsed her face, a round of applause went up. They were starting without her. She heard Mark's voice. He was doing the usual. In two minutes they would have forgotten about having to wait.

Rae relaxed. There was no hurry now. She breathed out and looked at her flushed face. She was an attractive woman, she knew that. It was just that next to Mark, anyone paled by comparison. She had once had a set of pictures taken of herself by one of the top photographers used by BWE. With lighting, make-up, posing, and on her own, she had looked sensational. Even the photographer had commented on how well they had come out, but of course she was an influential client. Rae had been going to give them to Mark, but changed her mind. They would be for her, to remind herself of her own beauty. Her secret emergency ego-repair kit. She always carried one little print of herself in her bag. She pulled it out and held it up by the mirror. The difference was not that great really, now her flush was dying down.

Even the birth of their son, just five months ago, had not seriously affected her physical appeal. They were rich enough to ensure that her pregnancy was as painless as possible, and Mark had been most supportive in helping her regain her figure. She had been impressed with herself for producing such a miracle as little Brett, running a company and still keeping her shape. You could not get much nearer the head of the herd than that.

Even so, next to Mark was a difficult place to stand, especially as it did not seem to matter whether she stood there or not. This was supposed to be a joint launch, but they had sailed ahead without her. Part of her said it did not matter. They would soon be smarming over her. As BWE co-president, everyone knew she wielded considerable power.

KitchenArt had become a division of BWE. The new range, launched so dramatically at the Getty Centre, had maintained its cutting art edge and the bold move into the stand alones continued. KitchenArt had grabbed 25 per cent of the refrigerator market, 19 per cent of washing machines, 27 per cent of dishwashers and had broken out of the kitchen with a superb range of wall-mounted reverse-cycle air conditioning units. These took pride of place on the wealthier living room walls of the world, often fitted with their own halogen spotlight to emphasis their role as artistic centrepiece. A launch of 35 per cent of the stock in BWE funded further expansions into different markets. Success on shining success. Rae was a business force to be reckoned with, but was always considered a behind the scenes person. Occasionally she would have liked to be part of the spotlight, rather than be asked to make a critical assessment of it for her husband when they got home.

She looked up again at the mirror. Everything was calm. A quick retouch of make-up and she was ready to go. Back at the launch a copy of the magazine was thrust into her hand. She looked at the cover. It was a shot of Mark on their sofa. She had expected to see the two of them there, but Mark *was* the star.

A lot of effort had gone into creating the perfect photos. Mark had personally selected the photographer. They'd had a stylist to the house before the shoot. Naturally, she had spent longer with Mark, but Rae had been groomed too. She flicked through the pages of their article. A great shot of the garden, their bedroom, Mark working the food-processor in the kitchen, Mark in the hall, Mark with their son, Brett, in the nursery. Brett in his nappy on the living room floor, Mark in the bathroom, Mark in the dining room placing a glass on a perfectly set table. Rae went back through the pages, thinking she must have missed something. She counted the page numbers to see if her copy had been mis-collated. All the pages were there, all had wonderful shots of their home, none featured her. She looked up to find Mark, but the milling crowd obscured him.

The magazine was already a hit with the launch crowd. The style was modern, dignified without being staid. The photographs were exciting. Fresh, innovative photographers were used and every attempt made to avoid people blandly showing off an idealised version of their homes. The feature on KitchenArt was a great insight into different homes around the world. Everyone loved it. They were pointing out their favourite shots to one other. Rae wondered how many were commenting on her absence.

'Hi Rae.' She was interrupted by Felicity.

'Oh, hi.'

'I'm sure it's a mistake.' Felicity's eagle eye did not miss a trick. As dedicated as she was to Mark's public image, she was not blinded by it. Rae smiled and shrugged her shoulders.

'Are you OK?'

'Sure, Mark's the celebrity, you know.'

'I'm furious. I'm speaking to Janice, they guaranteed approval and no subsequent changes or omissions. They're in breach of contract. It's outrageous. They're all about total subject control and they do this in the first issue.'

'Perhaps. I'm off to find a drink, excuse me.' Rae appreciated the gesture but sympathy only deepened the humiliation.

Soon everyone would notice her pictures were missing. There would be whispering, pointing, giggling. She retreated to a discreet corner, wishing she was as invisible there as she was in the magazine. She bit her lip to hold back tears and shook her head slightly trying to stay in control. She could not make another dash for the toilets without being seen. Toughing it out was the only option. She glanced through the magazine again, pretending to be engrossed, and to check that her picture was not hidden somewhere else within its pages. It was not. Rae thought of the photo in her bag. At least her image was somewhere.

'I do exist. I am important,' she repeated to herself, and almost laughed at someone as successful and happy as she was having to repeat these lines. She looked at Mark, impressing, flirting, doing what he did best. He noticed her and looked quickly away. A smile would have been nice.

Felicity was not impressed. From her perspective there was no greater humiliation to be had. She knew the integral role Rae had played in Mark's success. She knew Rae never pushed her own publicity agenda, but this was a slap in the face that could not go unanswered. She pulled Janice rather forcefully aside and waved the magazine in front of her.

'This is outrageous. How could you be so cruel?' Janice knew immediately what she was talking about. It was a sensitive topic. She was not sure how much to say.

'All the photos were approved by Mark.'

'Yes, and you just happened to drop a few from his selection.'

Janice looked at her awkwardly.

'Felicity, this really is difficult——'

'Tell that to Rae!'

'I'll take the blame with her if you want me to, but *you* have to know we published all the photos Mark selected... *all* the photos.'

There was silence in the taxi as Mark and Rae went home. Rae assumed he was too embarrassed by the photo selection to talk. She longed for him to offer some words of comfort. For all the respect, all the business kudos and all her protestations of it being unimportant, she had wanted her photo in the magazine. She wanted people to know she was a presence in her own home. Nursing her hurt, she felt childish and silly. She should rise above such concerns. She had a fabulous business, a dream home, a gorgeous baby, and the world's most desired man (topping *Woman* magazine's poll for three years in a row) as a husband. What did a stupid photo in a magazine matter? She wanted not to cry, but she could feel the tears welling regardless. The silence grew. Surely he was going to say something before she screamed? He did.

'Rae, I think you could at least apologise.'

Rae turned to him, stunned.

'What?'

'I read the text, Rae—thanks a lot. You were supposed to make sure it was all OK.'

Rae had not even glanced at the text during the launch. She felt a wave of relief; perhaps they had both been duped. If something had gone into the text without her approval, it might not have been Mark's decision to exclude her from the photos.

'What do you mean? I haven't read it. I didn't get past the pictures.'

'I'll read it, shall I? "This great house is a place to cherish for Mark and Rae as they grow old together and look forward to little Brett's future".'

Rae could not see what was wrong. She thought it was a nice summation of how they felt about the house. Mark clarified the problem.

'*As they grow old*? You know we're not supposed to say that kind of stuff. People don't want to think of me as ageing. I'm supposed to be above all that. How do you think I feel? All that hard work to look good for the shoot and you let them say I'm getting older.'

'But you're happy with the shots, you look good there?'

'They're fine. Look, I suppose it's not a big deal really, you were probably really busy, didn't have the time.' Mark could see Rae was upset. It had not been a good evening for her. He did not want to give her a hard time. 'It's not a big issue, honestly, but a teensy little apology might be nice.' He held his fingers close together and screwed his eyes up as much as he dared to be cute and conciliatory.

Rae wanted something cleared up before she contemplated rejecting the notion of apology. 'Apart from that, you were happy with it all? Happy with the pictures?'

'Yeah, little Brett looks so cute doesn't he?'

'You don't think they missed anything out.'

'No, all the best angles of the home are there. The one in the bathroom might make me look a bit vain, but I thought allowing that shot had a nice element of self-deprecation.'

'It's so humiliating, Mark. Not one shot of me, not my arm, not the back of my head, nothing.'

Mark stopped. He knew she was not in the pictures, it had been a deliberate choice.

'But you don't like that sort of stuff. You always say *I'm* the public face, you want to preserve your anonymity.'

'But Mark, our home and I'm not in it, I'm not there.'

'You should have said——'

'I shouldn't have to. My home, my family and I'm not there. Everyone's wondering why. What d'you think that does for our image?'

'But everyone respects your determination for privacy. It's a skill in this town. People comment on it...with admiration.'

'You might have at least consulted me, otherwise why bother having me photographed?'

'OK, but you have to say these things Rae, communicate with me.'

There were other reasons, which Mark did not go into. Since their wedding, photos of Rae with Mark always caused adverse public reaction. The woman who had snared him was not popular. Every magazine shot of her with him resulted in a barrage of hate mail.

In the week leading up to the wedding, Rae had received over three hundred hate letters and four death threats. She had been placed under 24-hour protection. No attacks eventuated, but that did not stop the fear. There were abusive phone calls and dog turds in boxes addressed to her. She had always known her relationship with Mark would cause jealousy, but she had not been prepared for so much hatred.

Their wedding day—final and conclusive proof that Mark Boyd was off the market—had been a day of bitter disappointment for many women around the world. They would have to wait at least a few years until Mark and Rae drifted apart. Then Mark would walk into the Starbucks coffee store where they worked, be transfixed by their double moccaccino, realise only they could fire the wild passion his virility demanded and begin divorce proceedings.

Church groups were happy that such a potent temptation had been brought safely into the sanctity of marriage. The Catholic Church gained an additional benefit when years of declining novice numbers were reversed by women marrying themselves to Christ as a second-best option.

Mark had found it amusing. He'd kept a collection of the funniest abusive letters. They were hilariously inventive in their accounts of the evils that would befall Rae if the nuptials went ahead. Michelle of Miami had suggested that a pound of cocaine would be found in Rae's handbag and she would be carted off to prison 'to become a lesbian'. An anonymous letter suggested Buffy the Vampire Slayer had been informed Rae was one of the undead and was on her way to put a stake through her heart. Mark made light of them. In his view they were harmless, and the sheer scale of the upset was flattering to him. He did not think they had unsettled Rae until she burst out crying as he regaled Monica with the vampire story.

'It's not about you,' he tried to reassure her, 'it would happen to any woman I married.'

'Thanks.'

'You mustn't take it personally.'

'It's hard not to take a death threat personally.'

'I know, but you've got to shrug it off. It's flattering to both of us in a way. It happens to all celebrities.'

'I know, but do you have to read them out all the time?'

'I'm trying to trivialise them.'

Mark had felt for Rae. She was not as used to this as he was. He remembered some of the hate mail he had received. It was certainly not pleasant and engendered a sense of bewilderment that there were people he did not even know existed who hated him with a passion. It seemed so unfair, so one-sided. From that time he had decided that the less Rae was exposed to this sort of thing, the better. It would be best for both of them if all publicity focused on him. Anyway, she was not a creature of the spotlight and did not have a natural ease in front of the camera, as he had. Perhaps he should have made an exception for *Megahome*, but they certainly had used all the best shots. The ones with Rae all had something wrong with them: a bit of movement, strange lighting, a shadow on his face. It had been best for all concerned to edit them out.

◆

When she read of Mark's marriage, Lucy felt she had dealt with her issues, taken them on board, processed them, achieved closure and was comfortable. She just felt sorry for

Raelene, tying herself to a complete bastard who had ruined so many lives. She wished wholeheartedly for that poor woman's sake that she would see sense and escape the torturous depravity she faced.

After the spectacular end to her fifteen minutes of fame, Lucy had flirted briefly with being born again. She had turned to Jesus and accepted him into her life live on television. Over $50 000 in pledges was generated of which she received 10 per cent. However, the Reverend Bob Patton's obsession with going over the lurid intimate details of her former life with Mark 'just one more time' and his offer to exorcise her demon by making love to her while reciting the Lord's Prayer soon ended that potential revenue source.

It was shortly after Lucy's brush with Christianity when her agent first appeared on the scene. He was just what Lucy needed: some guidance, some advice and above all someone on her side. For days she had been sitting in her tiny one-bedroom apartment staring at the television. It was switched off, but she could see that final 'A Girl Needs a Friend' show as if it had been playing. She saw herself staring into the camera, her look of desperation. The memory still hurt. Each time she played it over in her mind, each time she saw her dwindling bank account and read yet another story of Mark's success, it hurt more. She was just at the point where going through the agony another time would destroy her when she heard her phone ring. The voice on the other end said he wanted to be her agent. She readily agreed and he soon became much more.

He immediately advised her to write an autobiography. She still had enough residual fame to make it a sizzling bestseller—a titillating exposé that was sure to sell. In a passion that exorcised all her bitter memories, she dashed the story off in less than a month. Writing was easy when you had an agent. They had both been disappointed when it was rejected by every major publishing house. One rejection letter suggested she move on from her bitter hatred; a story about dealing with her obsession, confessing her lies and exposing the hypocrisy of the media might be more commercially viable. Her agent agreed and they reworked the book into *With Friends like These*, a bitter story of how she was trapped into lying about Mark by the TV station to launch 'A Girl Needs a Friend'. The rejection letter for this treatment suggested she engage a ghost writer and concluded, 'If you intend to write fiction you may be better off submitting a novel rather than an autobiography.' The woman from the apartment next door, who had been with Lucy as she read the letter, suggested she should 'just tell the truth, darlin', you've got a story there. All you need's a publicity hook and it's made—you know, like if he died or something.'

This was the inspiration Lucy needed. She immediately contacted her agent. He was thrilled. If Mark died, any book on him would sell a million, especially if it was already written and ready to roll out as soon as the coffin lid was closed. He wondered how much more Lucy would make if she killed Mark herself. The work was retitled again, this time as *Murderous Obsession: Confessions of a Lunatic Psychopath*. Lucy was worried about going to gaol. Murder was not treated lightly, and wouldn't she lose the money if convicted of a crime? Her agent laughed, reeled off a list of his former clients who had got away with murder and told her she could too.

Lucy smiled neatly in the mirror.

◆

'Look,' said Mark, 'it's there, it's obvious. It screams out OLD.'

'Mark, I can't see it. This light is blinding me.'

Rae and Mark were peering into the bowl of dazzling light that was Mark's Double Day Illuminated Bathroom Face Mirror. It was, the manufacturers claimed, 'twice as bright as daylight'.

This was a regular event: Mark insisting he could see time damage, Rae reassuring him in his perfection. At first Rae had tried not to give in to his vanity. However, she'd learned that the quickest way to deal with it was to move straight into reassurance. That way, he might be ready on time. It did not always work. The Double Day mirror was usually the reason.

There had been a time when a quick shower, a bit of hair gel, a dob of moisturiser and he was out of the door, looking fresh, sharp and utterly seductive. Not anymore.

'My triceps have gone saggy, look.' Mark flicked the underside of his upper arm and the muscle swayed. Rae grabbed his arm, pulled it straight and prodded the now rock-solid muscle with her finger.

'Look, I've fixed it. Now please get your clothes on, Monica and Greg will be waiting for us...as usual.'

'Be honest, do I look the most gorgeous you've ever seen me?'

Rae thought back to the moments when she had seen him crumpled and crying, lying back in total post-coital unconscious bliss.

'That's not fair, I've told you when I find you most attractive.'

'So the answer's no. I'm not going out.'

'Mark, for fuck's sake, it's dinner with friends not a *Mega* photo shoot.'

'It's a public event, Rae. I don't need to tell you how much we depend on this face.' He pointed to the offending item.

'Do we Mark? Do we really? You could be horribly disfigured tomorrow and we'd have a successful business, a great home and a beautiful son.'

'He is gorgeous.' Mark managed to tear his thoughts away from his own physical decay to smile about their baby.

'Mark, we are all getting older—and older is sexy. There's a huge market out there that finds the 30-plus age group really attractive.'

'But look at my eyes, I've got bags. It's not an age thing today. I'm just not feeling well.'

'Christ, will you forget about your damn looks.'

Rae had been storming in and out of the bathroom and changing dresses to see which one looked best. Mark had not noticed.

'I am leaving here in five minutes either with or without you. You look great, you always do. I just hope I don't show you up.'

'Rae, you look great. I love that dress.' Mark was looking in the mirror as he spoke these convincing words.

'Yeah? What colour is it?' Rae did not wait for the answer. The door slammed.

Five minutes later Mark emerged from the bathroom. He was not dressed.

'Rae, I'm sorry. I can't go out. I know it's wrong. I know I shouldn't feel like this. But I have to be perfect. I'll stay home and look after little Brett. Celia can have the night off.'

Rae looked at the stunning man before her. He was right, he did look a little older, more lived in. She loved it. She loved the changes that growing older together wrought, but Mark was too fixated on the 'older' to appreciate the 'growing'.

'Mark,' she said softly, 'this is a real problem. We have to do something. You have to do something.'

'I know, but not tonight, OK?'

She kissed him and left.

◆

Rae, already delayed, was even later than she expected. She had not been to the restaurant before and did not know that the two giant unmarked doors she had walked past five times since her cab had set her off were the entrance to the venue. There was no sign, no plaque. Those who knew, knew. On the verge of telephoning for help, she saw Monica step out of a cab.

'Thank God. Have you any idea where this place is?'

'Apparently it's unmarked, just two giant doors. I've been told to brace myself before I enter.'

Between them, they located the doors and managed to pull one of them open. Light burst into the street's night. It was blinding, like stepping inside Mark's Double Day mirror. A disembodied voice spoke.

'This is Lux.' There was no welcome. 'Reservation?'

'Mark Boyd,' Rae answered, unable to see who had spoken or where from. Given the intense light, she understood Mark's reluctance. Everyone already inside was probably watching her and Monica squinting and trying to shade their eyes.

Making a reservation was no guarantee of securing a table. A silence ensued while the invisible manager decided whether to let them in. Given Mark's social standing, they were a safe bet.

'Here,' the voice spoke, and sunglasses were placed over Rae's and Monica's eyes. They could see, but there was not much to look at. Everything was white: floors, ceilings, tables, uniforms. The diners looked like dismembered torsos as only their top halves were visible above the white tablecloths. It was impossible to tell how large the place was. Perspective was lost in the uniform whiteness. The seated diners all seemed to be looking at Rae and Monica as if they were on a stage. A slim waitperson took them elegantly to a table and placed them without a word. Monica and Rae did not break the silence. They were aware of muted conversations going on around them. Occasionally a word would echo round the restaurant, or a solitary peal of laughter. It was as if everyone was listening to everyone else.

Drinks were brought without being ordered. Lux did not have a menu. Meal and drink selections were made on the diners' behalf. Other than 'Reservation?', no questions were asked of the guests. The diners' needs were to be totally anticipated. Should a diner have to ask for something, their server would lose their job. Questions and choices were distractions from the purity of the eating experience. Knowing what you were eating or drinking was irrelevant to the stimulation of the tastebuds, which Lux sought to isolate from other senses and heighten to an almost unbearable intensity. Not only were the other senses irrelevant they also informed the tastebuds with self-fulfilling expectations. Lux sought to eliminate these.

'So where's Mark?' Monica whispered, not daring to turn round.

'At home. He was too ugly to come out.'

'Must have known about this place. Greg's not coming either.'

'Look, someone's just come in. They look terrible, so garish, all that colour, that squinting.' Monica cringed at the thought of how she had walked forward with her arms outstretched for fear of bumping into something. Everyone would have seen her.

They downed their drinks, which tasted like neat gin.

'No men. I say we eat, run and find a decent bar to get drunk in.'

'Great idea.' Rae spoke through clenched teeth, trying to smile.

The food came. It looked very colourful given the surroundings.

They ate in silence. When the meal was finished, a dilemma arose.

'I'd say let's go, but how do we leave? We can't ask for the bill.' Rae was afraid of being trapped all night.

'I've been watching. People just get up and walk out. Do they have credit card details or something?'

'Don't know. William, Mark's PA, booked.'

'Sack him.'

They decided to go for it. Getting up, they tried to walk slowly towards the white space they presumed was the door. They kept walking, unsure if and when the whiteness in front of them would prove to be their destination. Suddenly a face appeared from behind what must have been a white screen in front of a white wall. Their sunglasses were removed. The light dazzled them again, a black hole appeared in front of them and they walked towards it. It was the street. After a few minutes of standing still in the pitch black, leaning against the wall for security, their eyes adjusted to the evening light.

'Shit,' Monica said, 'I've left my handbag in there.' Rae shrieked with laughter. 'I'm not going back in.'

Fortunately, she did not have to. Her need had been anticipated, the door opened and a white-clad arm emerged from the light holding the bag. If an arm could express disdain, that one dripped with it. Monica grabbed the bag and they walked off quickly.

'Follow me, I know a decent bar. It's great—colour, sound, everything.'

◆

From across the road Terry watched them trying to adjust to the dark night. For the last three years he had been single-minded in his pursuit of Mark. He had recently spent a month in Malaysia, lurking near KitchenArt's production plant, meeting with Alfred Lau, one of the chief machine operators. Dinners, gifts for his family and significant incentives in sealed envelopes had weakened the operator's resistance to sabotage.

Together they had created an innovative malfunction for the latest KitchenArt rice-steamer. A minor adjustment to the electronics, and the twelfth time anyone put the steamer on the rapid setting, the heater would start five minutes late and at a temperature 10 per cent higher than normal. The buzzer would sound at the regular time. Whoever removed the steamer lid would get a scalding jet of steam in the face. The law suits would be enough to destroy BWE. This sort of sabotage had worked for Big Fucker, Terry thought; he was just as capable of pulling it off.

The day Terry was due to leave Malaysia, Alfred had given him the prototype. Terry's flight was not until the evening, so he took the steamer to a small restaurant to trial.

'We think it is the best steamer in the world and we want to test it at the best restaurants. Will you use it for us?' He offered an additional cash incentive on the spot and left.

Settling down in a bar across the street, he ordered a beer and waited. Within two hours of the midday rush, Terry heard screams of agony coming from the restaurant.

'Perfect,' he beamed and hurried to his hotel before anyone from the restaurant could find him. Alfred came to visit him after he'd finished his shift. Two thousand of the modified steamers had been produced.

'It works perfectly. You are to be congratulated,' Terry announced, handing over Alfred's final payment. 'When will they reach the States?'

'Two, maybe three weeks.'

It seemed like an eternity. Terry wanted to hear those screams again, as soon as possible. Alfred left the hotel. With this final payment, he could get his son to a university in Australia. He knew no real harm could come of the accidents. Terry had explained everything.

'So people get hurt a little. They'll complain, sue for millions and be set up for life. They'll thank you for giving them such good fortune.'

Alfred gripped the money tightly and headed to his brother's restaurant where his son was working in the kitchen to help pay for his local tuition. Alfred wanted to give him the great news. When he arrived, the restaurant was closed. There had been an accident in the kitchen; his son had been rushed to hospital with terrible burns. By the time Alfred got back to Terry's hotel, he had already left for the airport.

◆

Terry had been very satisfied with his work. Things were finally going his way. In his mind's eye, he had seen the lethal cargo heading to the States. He had almost heard the fearful screams. His satisfaction had been shattered a few hours before he stood outside Lux. He'd checked his e-mails in an internet cafe. There was a message from Alfred. The weak bastard had told his superiors there was a faulty batch. They had all been recalled and destroyed. KitchenArt had agreed to pay Alfred's son's medical bills and to send him to university in Australia. They were generous employers who built up great employee loyalty. Terry was disgusted at the niceness of it all. It was no way to do business.

He had learned of the planned dinner at Lux, and had booked a table for himself too. The dazzling light might provide the perfect chance to strike a blow against Mark. He would not know what hit him; he would simply crumple to the floor, hit by invisible forces. It was perfect. Just the fillip to cheer him up after Alfred's depressing news. Terry congratulated himself on the foresight of having a Plan B ready. Arriving at Lux just before Rae and Monica, he had endured the silence and the wait to see if he was acceptable. The voice had spoken.

'The only free table is reserved for Mark Boyd, you will leave.' With that, he had been turned around and pushed back onto the street. He hammered on the huge doors to no avail. As Rae stepped out of her cab, he stumbled across the street, tripping on the curb in the darkness. He waited. Another opportunity might arise.

Rae looked good, he thought; motherhood agreed with her. She was cute, apart from her fatal affliction. How could she stand being with him? Having all those women fawn over him. Knowing that people were continually throwing themselves at him. How could she bear the knowledge that every day physically incredible women were seducing him? It had to happen. He was a man after all. He could not resist all the time. He was probably porking some million dollar babe right then instead of turning up with his wife.

The frustration welled up. His every attempt to cause havoc with Mark's business had failed. What was wrong with the world? How the hell was anyone going to make a living if bribery and corruption did not work? It was as if Mark had put a spell on everyone except him. He alone had been singled out for special torment and it had gone on and on. Part of him wanted to give in, be mesmerised and view Mark like the rest of the world. But how could he? Everywhere he went there was a billboard, a magazine cover, a housewife cooing over Mark's products. His views, his comments, his social life, his clothes, his baby, his wife, his universe. There was no escape. The anguish produced tears. The guy had been nothing, you could have spent half an hour in a room with him and not notice. Now he was God, he controlled everything. He had totally cocked up with the film star business and still he came out bigger than ever. The hot tears fuelled Terry's rage. 'I'm not letting that bastard make me cry, I won't,' he shouted across the road at Lux. For locals it was a familiar sight: people got very upset when New York's most exclusive restaurant turned them down.

Terry decided then and there that Mark had to go in public. It would not be a quiet anonymous execution. Mark would look his killer in the face and see the revenge seep from his body. And not just Mark; Terry wanted the world to watch and to know why. With that happy thought he saw Rae and Monica stumble out of the light and followed them.

◆

The bar Monica selected was suitably dark. She and Rae sat in a corner and the drinks came at regular intervals.

'So, how's Greg? Is he OK? Is one of the children ill?'

'Not one of ours… actually it's all a bit of a worry.'

It was not like Monica, ball breaker extraordinaire, to admit to being worried about anything.

'Normally I'm just not interested in how he raises the kids. As long as George keeps picking winners, then Greg's doing a good job. But it's all getting too serious.' Monica took another gulp of vodka and embarked upon an account of the 'school play incident'. George's school for gifted tots was putting on an end of semester play—*The Lion King*. It was the usual opportunity for the kiddies to dress up in impossibly cute, very expensive and very bulky costumes. George had been cast as a non-speaking giraffe. Greg was furious and complained to the principal of cultural discrimination, claiming George was excluded from the speaking parts because of his Australian accent. After the full weight of the AMPCGA was brought to bear, the principal had agreed to have George play Pumbaa. Greg was still not satisfied. The heir to the Haddrick Pride could play no part less than Simba—so Greg took matters into his own hands.

The entire cast had been invited to a post-rehearsal party at Greg and Monica's apartment. In the pandemonium of thirty children, no-one noticed Greg ushering a neighbour's child through the crowd, ensuring she drank from every glass, stuck her fingers in the honey-sweetened tofu and generally distributed her germs as best she could. As she did not attend George's school, none of the parents present knew she had measles. George had been carefully kept in his room. Greg had said he was being punished for downloading a poisoner's handbook from the internet. So it was that George was the only child who did not come down with measles four days before the big night.

What had started as a cast-of-thousands extravaganza ended up as a one-man show. George, clambering in and out of costumes, narrated the story and put on a variety of hilarious animal voices. He was a huge hit and saved the day, even doing a special performance for his fellow cast members in their hospital ward.

Rae did not know whether to be appalled by or proud of Greg's true-blue Aussie determination.

'God help anyone who beats the twins into a cheer-leading squad,' was all she could say.

'I know,' Monica replied. 'Part of me thinks it's just playing hard ball, but two of the kids are still in intensive care. He always says there's nothing he won't do for the kids and I'm beginning to take that literally. At least at Vantex he had a sense of perspective, however determined he was, but when his business skills are combined with his great love, the results are…well, scary. I think he needs some focus beyond the kids before he loses it completely.'

'At least he's thinking about something other than himself.'

'Unlike Mark, I take it.'

'I know I don't understand the pressure of his looks, but he's getting worse. The tiniest wrinkle sets him off on this obsessive trip.'

'I hate to say it, this city must be getting to me, but should he get some therapy?'

'We've tried, but he always charms the shrink into believing he's right and that his whole life depends on his looks… I sometimes wish he could go back to how he was before. He's got the respect and the prestige he wanted.'

'It's his drug, Rae. He doesn't believe he can live without

looking totally gorgeous and until his looks are gone he'll never realise he doesn't need them. He needs to go cold turkey. Can't you just rip his face off?'

'Look at us. Successful women, happy marriages, sitting in a New York bar complaining about our men.'

'Cheers!'

As they clinked glasses, Monica noticed a man approaching their table. 'It could be worse, we could be married to *him*.' She indicated Terry.

'Well, if it isn't the Mark Boyd Fan Club General Meeting.'

'We were waiting for you to turn up.' Monica's lip curled. 'After all, you're the one with the strongest feelings for him.'

Terry smiled. 'But at least I managed to keep my knickers on. You know about that Rae... don't you?'

'Yes I do. What do you want, Terry?'

'Just being friendly, you know, Aussies together in the Big Apple. Thought we could get pissed on Fosters and sing "Waltzing Matilda".' The waiter brought him a drink; he was planning to stay. Monica was not impressed.

'Terry, sweetheart, shouldn't you be looking for a job? Last I heard you were fired. Bet that wasn't on your list of daily objectives.'

'All part of the plan.'

'What plan? First person to run a company then be a loser nobody by the age of thirty-two? Face it Terry, you're a jumped-up product manager who gets lost when he's looking after more than bun-making attachments. Go home little boy, this city's for the big players.'

'Monica, you're not intimidating your little make-up nancies now. I've moved on. I'm a man of independent means.'

Rae could not resist joining in. 'So you're over Mark then?'

Terry nodded, smiled and drank. 'I admire him, I honestly do.' He would not let them rile him.

'What do you admire most about him?' Rae was extracting revenge for that kiss.

'His choice in women of course.' The line came out more genuinely than Terry intended. Rae looked into her drink. Terry tried to cover himself.

'He seems to pick good kissers. With the possible exception of you, Monica—I suppose kissing's too soft for you.'

'The only thing that's too soft for me, lover boy, is your dick. Now bugger off, will you.'

'Sure, you two can get back to your cooing. Say hi to Greg—remember him, the one you married 'cause Mark turned you down…Look after yourself Rae—nice feature in *Megahome*, thought you looked great!' He downed his drink and sauntered off.

'Below the belt, even for him. I'd say he had a bit of a soft spot for you, though,' Monica noted.

Rae told her the story of the kiss. Monica squirmed.

'Ugh, I had no idea you'd sunk so low.'

Rae hastily changed the subject. 'You got your tickets for the premiere, didn't you?'

'You mean *KitchenArt, the Musical!* You can tell me, it's a product launch, isn't it? It's not for real.'

'It *is* for real, I've even seen a rehearsal, it was a love scene between a toaster and a breadmaker. Quite a good song really, "Love is Rising".'

'Will Mark never learn? It'll get hooted off the stage.'

'Apparently not. He got several critics to look at the concept, the songs, the costume designs and they all agreed it's a really good musical.'

'No such thing!'

'It's already a hit. Felicity has negotiated the initial reviews—they're glowing... "The *Cats* of the New Millennium". Everyone's desperate to be in it. Debbie Reynolds is appearing as a hand-held blender. It could run for years.'

'In that case, how could we miss? Perhaps George could perform it single-handedly when Greg releases Ebola virus on the cast.'

They laughed and then stopped, realising it was not that far-fetched.

◆

Mark spent the evening with Little Brett. Rae's pregnancy and the birth had been a challenging time for him. Initially he had freaked. It was hard evidence that time was running out, he was no longer the youngest generation. The birth had changed that; the baby was just so beautiful. And besides, the father–son publicity shots were sensational. Black and white, Mark in just his jeans, holding this perfect naked bundle. The world had issued a collective coo. It was a great hook for BWE to break into nursery objects.

It was Rae who had decided to call him Brett. She had always liked the name and knew that Mark wanted to make up for what had happened with Brett Josco. Felicity at first baulked at the idea, but then thought it could be turned to Rae and Mark's advantage. Picking a name that would set tongues wagging—just because they liked it and thought it was the right thing to do—could work. It suggested Rae and Mark had concerns greater than public opinion. Besides, Brett Josco had not been seen or heard of for three years beyond a big question mark in *Mega* magazine's 'Where are They Now?' specials.

When he was alone with his little boy, Mark could forget about the Double Day mirror for a few moments. Every little gurgle, movement of his hand, roll of his head, or kick of his leg was a fascinating stage in Brett's development that would have been a shame to miss. His skin was the really magical substance. Nothing in the world could be softer, smoother, warmer, more perfect. If only skin could stay like that forever, Mark thought.

Although Mark had heard nothing from the big Brett, he still thought of him from time to time. As he sat watching his sleeping son, he reflected on Rae's anger that evening. Brett would have understood why he could not go out tonight. He had known the loneliness of perfection too.

As that very thought passed through his mind, Celia, the nanny, came into the nursery. There was someone at the front door claiming to be Brett Josco. Mark ran downstairs.

The guy looked similar to Brett Josco, but more like a real person. His hair was short, not particularly well styled and his clothes very ordinary. He did not have the preened, moisturised, filtered-water-drinking, eyebrow-shaped perfection of before and he had grown older. Mark spotted wrinkles. Brett looked well, but a little nervous. Mark hugged him to let Brett know he was not uncomfortable with the gay thing. Brett responded enough to let Mark think he appreciated the gesture. It was all very modern.

'Where the hell have you been?' Mark asked.

Brett smiled. 'Everywhere, nowhere.'

They went to the living room.

'I brought you a present,' Brett said, and produced a Digital Video Disk. 'It's the only known copy of *The Mark*

Boyd Story.' Mark gasped. He had never seen it. After the launch fiasco, he thought all copies had been destroyed.

'I got a copy before the…press conference. I've never watched it. I couldn't.'

'Brett, I never got a chance to say sorry. I am so sorry.'

'Yeah I know, I was really hurt, but it wasn't your fault, or mine. If we'd just been two guys working at the office, I'd have made a pass, you'd have said no, I'd have cried, got drunk, got laid and forgotten you. That would have been that. Instead, we had to do that whole Hollywood game bullshit. I'm glad you're not living there anymore.'

'Right, New York. Different game…'

'…Same bullshit, just less of a tan.'

'So d'you want to watch the movie?' Mark smiled.

Brett hesitated.

'I really didn't know when I came over whether I would. Chance said I should, something about closure.'

'Chance?'

'Yeah, remember that guy from that soap I worked on years back? After I left, he was the one person who came to find me. It took him three months, but he did it. I couldn't believe it. He just walked up to me on a beach and that was that. We've been together ever since.'

'That's fantastic,' Mark tried and failed to hide the relief in his voice.

They decided to watch the DVD. It was more comfortable than plunging straight into personal conversation. Within thirty minutes they were convulsed with hysterical laughter. Brett's Australian accent was spectacularly bad. The plot, which Mark had forgotten, was that weird mix that could only come from market-researched, committee-driven, multiple-director-altered, star-tantrum-influenced ludicrousness.

'Mark, kiss me for the last time. Kiss me so I can remember through eternity until we are together once more.' Rae was dying.

'Raelene, moi luv, oi need youse,' Mark/Brett replied.

They screamed on the sofa and played the line again.

'I hope you won't find the real event this amusing,' the real Rae said behind them. She had returned from the dinner.

Mark stopped the DVD and they both leaped up like two boys caught by their mother watching porn.

'This must be *The Mark Boyd Story* and you must be the star,' she said to Brett.

'I said she was smart,' Mark smiled. She shook Brett's hand. This was not what she had expected to come home to.

'How's Brett?' she asked. Brett looked bemused and said, 'OK.'

'Not you, the other one.'

'I hadn't got round to that,' Mark intervened with an awkward grimace. 'We sort of named our son after you.' Big Brett looked surprised. This was not what he had expected either.

'Can I see him?'

Mark took Brett up to the nursery. As he looked down on his namesake, an unremovable smile appeared on his face.

'I *so* did not expect this. I thought you must have hated me. I remember the look in your eyes at that press conference. It's all I ever saw when I thought of you. I can't believe I was so crazy. I did love you.'

'Yeah, I'm sorry, I guess I sort of led you on.'

'You won the contest. Besides, it was the best thing that ever happened. And this...' he pointed to the sleeping baby, 'this guy's the sweetest thing ever. I can't wait to tell Chance. He loves kids.'

He gently stroked the baby's hair.

'Since Chance came I've really learned to be happy. It's great living without all that star crap. Look...wrinkles. Aren't they great?' Mark looked at him in disbelief.

'I was thinking of you when you turned up,' he said. 'Rae and I had a row. I couldn't go out tonight. I looked a serious mess. I know it's wrong. I know it's not supposed to bother me, but I just can't help it. The thought of hearing someone say, "Boyd's looking a bit rough" or, "he's past his prime" brings me out in a cold sweat.'

'Mark, you gotta drop that shit. It'll destroy you and your marriage. You gotta escape your looks.'

They went back downstairs and joined Rae.

'It's late, I'd better let you two get your beauty sleep... one of you seems to need it.' Brett was about to go, but he hesitated. 'There's something I have to ask. It's about *KitchenArt, the Musical!* They want me to do a cameo, as a fruit-juicer. I get my own number, 'Squeeze Me Baby', where I seduce a dozen oranges, suck 'em dry and spit them out. I'd like to do it, but I wanted to talk to you first.'

'Great idea, the press'll go wild.'

'We're not publicising it. I won't get any billing. I'm doing it for fun, not making a comeback. I'll see you.'

'Wait.' Rae followed him to the door, out of Mark's hearing. 'Don't disappear again. He really needs a friend.'

'Disappear? With my little buddy sleeping upstairs, no way. Just try and keep me and Chance away!'

Back inside, Rae and Mark looked at each other. The anger of the row had been wiped out by the most bizarre evening Rae had experienced in some time.

'What a night and what a restaurant. Remind me to kill William.'

'Tell me about it in bed.'

'And who or what is Chance?'

'Brett's partner. They met on a soap years ago.'

'That figures... Chance! I guess he liked the name of his character so much, he took it with him.'

◆

KitchenArt, the Musical! had hit written all over it. It was rumoured that so many celebrities wanted to appear in it, different guests had to appear as different appliances every night just to accommodate them. The buzz on Broadway was hot. The day tickets went on sale saw the biggest box office queue in memory. Those at the head of the queue had camped out for a week. Their progress had been webcast live over the internet. KitchenArt had offered random appliance prizes for those who bought tickets on the first day. Somebody in that weary line would soon have the first of the new singing irons that played hits from the musical and incorporated a revolutionary anti-scorching device. 'Sing don't singe!' the box declared. The queuers had established a friendly rapport with each other, swapping their Mark Boyd stories: how sexy he was, how nice he had been to their grandmother, how wonderful it was he had insisted that 50 per cent of the opening night tickets go to the general public.

Lucy, dressed in a puce schoolgirl pinafore, green slacks and an ill-fitting corn yellow wig, stood in the queue. She sang to herself as if listening to very loud, very bad music on a personal stereo—except there was none. Her agent had suggested this would make a suitably mad impression. To further make her point she deliberately stared at people in the queue until they became uncomfortable. The plan was to establish herself as totally loopy with potential witnesses to the assassination of her book subject. The book was complete, except for the final chapter of course. It detailed her descent into lunacy, her hallucinations, psychotic episodes, black-outs, schizophrenia, claustrophobia, agoraphobia, Boydophobia, multiple-personality disorder, post-coital depression and manic depression. Her dictionary of psychiatry had been most useful.

On joining the queue she had been immediately exposed to a test of nerve. Would the counselling and support her agent had given her sustain her as she heard the words 'Didn't she used to be...?' Once it would have reduced her to anguished tears. She paused, waiting to feel the pain and see the jaw-like camera prowling towards her, but nothing happened. She was cured! Just as her agent had recommended, she used the situation to help establish her alibi.

'I still am, you know,' she screamed, looking the unfortunate questioner so close in the eyes she could feel their breath on her nose.

It was all working. The man in front of her was getting extremely irritated. He was not accustomed to theatre queues. The camaraderie evident between those eager to secure first-night tickets repulsed him. These people were competing with each other. Why pretend to be nice? Eventually the maniacal singing behind him became too much.

'For Christ's sake will you stop your squawking!'

Lucy recognised the accent immediately. 'You're an Aussie! Where are you from?'

Terry groaned. The less people knew about him the better, but he did not want to arouse any suspicions, even with this fruitcake.

'Sydney, what about you?' He resigned himself to an expat conversation.

'Sydney too. Here to support our great leader in the States?'

Lucy decided it was best not to reveal her hand to this man too much. He did not seem to recognise her from TV. The show had not been shown in Australia, apart from a 3 am cable spot. She would play the fan. Everyone in the queue was bound to be a big Mark Boyd fan. She did not want this man spoiling the last chapter of her book by defending the man he worshipped.

'You mean Boyd, Mark Boyd.' Terry grinned, trying to say the name as calmly as possible.

'Aw yeah, who else?' Lucy chewed her gum a little faster to hide her agitation.

'He's a remarkable person.'

'Isn't it heaps cool how he did that comeback after all that sex stuff?'

'Yes. Got much KitchenArt?' Terry decided to play along in the big fan routine.

'Only the whole range. Everything,' Lucy lied. 'What's your favourite?'

Terry thought back to the many times he had been into department stores and casually knocked a KitchenArt bench top item to the floor or scratched one of the stand alones. For the past few years, it had been his way of cheering himself up, knowing that every unpurchased item he damaged was less profit for Boyd. He reckoned he had got away with $120 000 worth of lost profit. A slim but vital scrap of comfort.

'I don't know, I've had such pleasure with so many of them,' he answered, almost truthfully.

Lucy thought there was something spooky about his eyes. He seemed to be trying really hard to keep himself under control. A lot of anger issues, she decided, and thought it would be good to replicate that look as he seemed genuinely to be a bit crazy.

'So, you one of his gay fans? You know he's straight.'

Terry clenched his hands and smiled hard. This was really difficult. This stupid woman knew every nerve to touch.

'No...I'm straight.'

'It's fine you know, I just thought, coming from Sydney...'

'No.'

It was a great relief to both of them when the queue suddenly surged forward as the theatre doors opened and tickets went on sale. Terry was happy to see that the crowd camaraderie suddenly dropped away. Places were guarded jealously and anyone needing a toilet break now would just have to wait. Conversation ceased as the queue inched slowly forward.

◆

It took forever as everyone seemed to require a detailed description of every seat in the auditorium, but eventually Terry got to the front. There were two single seats left in the stalls, one three rows from the front, the other four rows behind.

'How far is the nearest one from the stage?'

'Real close,' came the indifferent answer.

'I need to know exactly how far.'

'Christ, OK, I'll look it up...It's twelve yards exactly, OK?'

'And Boyd will definitely be on stage?'

'Read the sign.' Lloyd, Terry's friendly ticketing consultant, pointed wearily to a hastily written note stuck on the window with tape: 'On opening night, Mark Boyd will appear on stage after the show, but not on subsequent nights.' Terry was not the first person to ask. The seat was perfect,

Terry decided, close enough for Boyd to recognise his nemesis from the stage. He paid cash.

'And please,' he added to Lloyd, pushing a ten-dollar note
forward, 'make sure that loony bitch behind me is miles away.'
He did not want some crazy person drawing attention to the
area in which he was sitting. He left with his ticket, grimaced
at Lucy and wished her luck.

'I want a seat in the stalls, and nowhere near that weird
guy,' Lucy said to the friendly ticketing consultant. 'I think
he's trying to kill me, you know. I'm not mad, honestly I think
he really hates me.'

'There's one seat left in the stalls, it's nowhere near
that guy.'

'Super,' Lucy said and slipped Lloyd an extra ten dollars.
Locating the nearest public phone she called her agent to
report on progress. He congratulated her and told her to head
to Bloomingdales and start kissing the windows. She asked
why, but he just barked at her to do it. She should have known
better than to question his authority. She set off immediately,
sure that he would be watching her somehow, from wherever
he was.

Terry scurried away to Central Park. He made his way to
his daytime training spot. It was wooded and not many people
turned up during office hours. He found his tree with its
familiar stab wounds, paced out twelve yards, turned quickly
and hurled his knife. It landed high in the trunk of the tree,
just where he figured Boyd's chest would be, if he were on
stage and Terry was in the stalls. Terry retrieved his lovely
weapon. Something rustled in one of the other trees. It was
on a branch, moving slowly. He threw silently. There was a
squeal and then a thud as a dead squirrel hit the ground.

'Yes!' Terry shouted. His reflexes were hot and his aim had never been better. The next blood on the knife would be Boyd's.

◆

Mark was at his ad agency going over the shots that had been taken of him to promote the latest reverse-cycle air-conditioners. The new remote control was the big breakthrough. The artist had designed an amusing piece that indulged in an aesthetically provocative dialogue with the wall-mounted unit.

Mark's face filled the computer screen. He had got the operator to zoom in close. It looked fantastic. They had used a new photographer, Juanita. An ex-prostitute from Queens, she had risen to fame taking snaps of her colleagues with disposable cameras stolen from the corner store. She had done a great job, Mark thought. She always found the sex in her subjects. It had not been hard to find in Mark, but these photos had the raw energy of a candid snap taken while desperate for a trick to turn up.

Even Mark could honestly say he looked great. It was reassuring after all his concern about his looks. Sleepless nights worrying about not looking good only made him look worse. Tonight would be different.

'Can I look at the trannies?' he asked. 'I want to see which other shots we might be able to use elsewhere.'

The operator looked up at the account director hovering nervously next to Mark. They could not afford a moment's delay on production. Final approval was needed within the hour.

'I think Juanita's still got them,' she said. 'She's getting dupes for her portfolio.'

Mark had heard this one before. 'I want to see the shots.'

The operator and the director smiled to hide their discomfort. They had agreed that under no circumstances should Boyd take a look at the original shots. Mark saw the operator glance at a cardboard-backed envelope sitting on the desk. He picked it up.

'What a surprise, they were here all along—don't suppose you've got a light box?'

The director gave in. The disaster was going to happen like it or not. She took Mark to the light box and switched it on.

She handed Mark a little magnifying glass to better view the shots. He looked at those which had been circled by Juanita and found the one that had been chosen for this job. He examined it carefully, then walked back to the computer screen. The operator had clicked over to another image. Mark looked at him without a smile and he clicked back to the shot. Mark stared at it and returned to the light box.

'You've done an excellent job. Juanita's shot was great, but obviously a little too raw. We don't want wrinkles to show on our pics, now do we?'

The director and operator laughed with relief. When the shot was scanned and put on the screen, they had noticed some slight lines around Mark's eyes and just a hint of a shadow. They both agreed it was a fantastic image. Mark looked hot, but it was standard practice in the industry to remove any 'time references'. They only felt nervous about doing it because it had never been necessary before. This was the first time that the legendary Mark Boyd had needed computer enhancement. It was only to be expected, they thought, the guy had to be over thirty now. Even he could not stop time. Nevertheless, they did not like being the first to do it. It was Mark's first tiny step down to everyone else's level.

. Mark surprised them with his composure. He accepted the fact he had aged, that a slight correction was needed. A business professional, he looked at the shot as if it were just another model. He quickly approved the selection and asked to keep the trannies and a print-out of the screen image for a few days.

'Rae likes to see them. She has a good eye,' he said. He went straight home from the agency, calling Rae on the way, asking her to meet him there.

He was sitting in their living room when she arrived home.

'It's over... I'm over. It's done.' Rae thought there must have been a share price collapse, an exploding rice-steamer injuring hundreds.

'Look.' He thrust the shots into her hands and lolled back on the sofa, exhausted with worry. She held them up to the window to look at them.

'They're great shots. These are the Juanita ones? Fantastic.'

'Yeah sure, now look at what the agency's using.'

Rae looked at the colour print. 'Looks excellent, where's the problem?'

'Look closer, for God's sake, it's obvious.'

'Mark, it's not obvious. I can't see anything.'

'Perhaps you need more light,' he growled, and jumped up, thrusting back curtains, switching on lights and turning up dimmer switches.

'See anything now?' He stood with his hands on his hips, jutted his head towards her and screwed his face up. 'Don't you recognise the old wrinkly Mr Crowsfeet?'

It had to do with ageing, Rae realised. She looked again and saw it. His photo had been retouched.

'And don't tell me this happens all the time. Not to me. It's never happened to me.'

He was looking at her with complete desperation. He was scared.

'What am I going to do?'

Rae stood on the borderline between anger and pity. He was hurting, she understood that, but this vanity was overwhelming. Pity would not solve anything. Before she could respond, he continued.

'I can't explain it... it's like, you know when you go gooey over something because it's just so smooth and so perfect, like a surface that's blemish-free so you just want to kiss it and then you see this tiny scratch. It's heartbreaking.'

'Mark...'

'Let me finish. It's devastating because even though it looks great it's not perfect anymore and that makes the difference.'

'Christ, you sound like Big Fucker and his damn desk. Mark, you are gorgeous!'

'Yes, but I'm not perfect and that's what counts.'

That was it. Rae consciously decided to be angry.

'Mark, get some therapy—some serious therapy, not an ego massage. These shots are fantastic. They're real, they're sexy. So you're a human being, you're ageing. Tell them to scrap the retouch. This is far better.' She brandished the transparencies.

'Yes, but——'

'Yes but I'm not as beautiful as you. I don't know what it's like. I've heard all this bleating before, Mark. *It's so hard being almost perfect. I'm so miserable, poor me.* Try living with perfection. Trying going out and being photographed next to the world's greatest sex object, that's if you even make it into the photo spread. Try being the plain thing no-one knows what he sees in. Try knowing you look even older, even more haggard than you really are because the person next to you is a dazzling beacon of perfection.'

'Rae, this isn't about you.'

Angry tears were rolling down her face.

'No, it's about you, it's always about you. Come here.' She grabbed his arm and marched him upstairs to the nursery. Celia had just finished changing Brett. She heard the row approaching and quickly ducked into the bathroom to hide from the storm. Rae picked up the baby.

'This is what it's supposed to be about now, our child. You've had your turn, your years at the centre. It's his turn now.'

Brett started crying. Rae paused for a moment, letting his sobs build. Then she cradled him in her arms, kissing his forehead and soothing his tears.

'Mark,' she continued more gently, 'we are all growing old, all three of us. If you don't, then Brett can't. Yes you look older, but I love that. It means we've grown. It means we're living life, we're sharing important things. You've got to let go of the beauty thing, Mark. OK, it allowed you to achieve what you wanted, but now it's holding you back and it's ruining us.'

'Oh bullshit, Rae, you're jealous, that's understandable, but you need to get some perspective.'

'What?'

'You're overreacting because it's touching on your own esteem issues.'

Rae's mouth dropped open and it was a moment before she could speak again.

'Overreacting? Me? And when was the last time we did anything, had a conversation, eat a meal that wasn't totally dominated by your looks?'

'Rae, it's my job, it's who I am, we can't change that.'

'It's not *who* you are, it's *what* you are.'

'Yeah and what's that?' he challenged, scowling at her

briefly before remembering the damage it might do to his face. Rae did not respond. She looked at him determinedly and breathed slowly. She did not want this argument yet again. She kissed Little Brett's head.

'Do something or I will.'

They stood for a moment holding their baby. His new-found calm spread to them, but they were filled with their own thoughts. Mark was wondering how he could get cosmetic surgery without Rae knowing. Rae was thinking that drastic measures were needed. Her family and the happiness of the man she loved were at stake.

◆

Lucy skipped into the domestic appliances department of Macy's. It was the middle of a Tuesday afternoon. Her agent figured it would be a quiet day and so anything out of the ordinary she might do would be noticed by the store staff. Gambolling up and down the aisles had failed so far to rouse their attention. She decided to move on with her plan—that would bring them running. Waiting for the security camera to turn in her direction she suddenly screamed.

'That bastard, I'll kill him...it's coming for me, it's coming for me.' She picked up the display fruit-juicer with durable micromesh tungsten filter and hurled it to the floor. She leaped onto it.

'Die, you're not going to juice me, die!'

It worked. Within seconds she felt herself being knocked to the floor by a large man in a blue polyester shirt. He was heavy and she felt crushed under his weight. She had not expected such a vigorous attack. A crowd of staff gathered around her. She looked up at her assailant.

'Ma'am, calm down. I'm going to release you and I want you to lie very still,' he said.

He released her and she screamed again, closed her eyes and fell back.

No-one moved.

'Oh my God, is she dead?' Lucy heard muttering.

'Drugs,' another voice said.

'Wasn't she on that show...you know.'

She decided it was time to come to.

'Where am I...what's going on?' she said hazily.

'Just lie still ma'am, you've had an attack of some sort.'

'Oh no, not again, what did I do?' Lucy was speaking in her sweetest tone. 'I didn't hurt anyone, did I?'

'No ma'am, only this KitchenArt fruit-juicer.'

Lucy sat up as the people around her looked wary.

'I must apologise, this has happened before. I blank out, and next thing I wake up and something's destroyed. I'm terrified that one day I might kill someone.'

'We're gonna have to charge you for the juicer.' An assistant was clearing away the debris which Lucy had created. The tungsten micromesh filter had been stomped past the limit of its durability.

'Of course. I'm so sorry.' She paid for the juicer and the security guard escorted her to the door, suggesting she see a doctor. He knew a great herbalist who specialised in mental disorders, and gave Lucy his card. Lucy walked down the street. Her agent would be thrilled, the diminished responsibility plea was as good as sealed.

◆

Rae had not encountered such toxic odours since leaving her high school chemistry class. She severely doubted that the laboratory she was standing in was capable of producing anything. It was chaotic: a sink full of discarded test-tubes; a Bunsen burner flaming away for no apparent reason. Tube attached to plastic tube passed through globes full of liquid hanging open over the bench. It looked like a thousand experiments had been started and not finished.

Rae had inquired about a lab that could be relied upon for absolute discretion. She had claimed to be looking into a secret new product departure for BWE and so needed cast-iron guarantees of confidentiality. She had imagined a state-of-the-art research facility—eye-scan security codes and pristine white uniforms walking down immaculate corridors with clipboards. That, she had been informed, was too risky. The greater the number of staff, the greater the chance of a leak. For total secrecy, this lab and the brilliant Dr Lobos were required.

'Dr Lobos, are you there?' She called out to the chaos of tubes.

'Yes, here,' a voice spoke behind her.

Rae turned to find a neat little woman. A school chemistry teacher if ever she had seen one, Rae thought—black-rimmed glasses and tight bun of hair from which not a single strand could escape, skin that looked scrubbed clean, a lab coat that could not possibly have spent any time in this disgusting lab and, Rae was relieved to see, a clipboard.

'You must be Ms Black.'

'Yes.' Rae was embarrassed by her miserable attempt at a false name.

'I'm Dr Lobos, how can I help you?'

'It's a bit tricky. I've been told you guarantee confidentiality. Is that absolutely true?'

'Yes, you sign a disclaimer taking all responsibility for what we make for you. We do not divulge anything about what we produce.'

'Good. I need two…substances,' Rae tried to remember her HSC science, 'which on their own are benign, nothing dangerous, but when brought together…'

'…produce a large explosion. We get such requests all the time.'

'No, I just want some sort of acid to be produced, that can burn things, but not too much. I wouldn't want to kill anyone and it would have to act slowly.'

'Interesting. It's certainly possible, we'd have to blend them in some sort of retardant. Mmm, I wonder…'

Dr Lobos darted off into her warren of a lab and disappeared.

'Would it help to know what it was for?' called Rae.

The good doctor was brought back from her pursuit of exciting possibilities. She reappeared several benches away from Rae.

'If you think it would help, yes.'

Rae explained exactly what she needed.

'Mmm, deliciously Jacobean, if I might say, Ms Black. Most inventive. One in a moisturiser and one in a lipstick… yes, I think that could work. Yes, come back in one week. Goodbye.'

Dr Lobos had spoken.

As she walked down the corridor, Rae heard a scurrying noise behind her.

'I'll need the lipstick and the moisturiser tomorrow. Three lots of each, any brand. I find the supermarket ones are just as effective as the high-priced ones. I should know, I created half of them.'

The doctor tittered and ran back to her nest of smells. Rae watched her shiny black court shoes clack towards the lab. There was no need for her to make any drastic decision at this stage. She had gone there simply to explore options for resolving the hell that their homelife was becoming. Mark's looks were consuming them as rapidly as his moisturisers were filling the bathroom. It was all he seemed to talk about—the business, little Brett, her own feelings were all linked to how he looked. Mark's mood set the tone in the house and the Double Day mirror set Mark's mood. Rae needed to liberate them all from the mirror, and no option, no matter how drastic, could be discarded.

◆

Greg was having an exhausting day. All the children were on holiday from school, kindergarten or trauma therapy and he had a major paper to prepare as part of the AMPCGA submission to Congress on the child punishment bill currently being considered. George had been playing up. Bored with reading *Moby Dick*, he had conquered the Nintendo Star Wars Racer in thirty minutes. The problem with child geniuses was trying to keep them entertained. In the end Greg succumbed and let George loose on the internet. He was a bit worried about the information George might consume there, but his previous attempts at censorship had failed completely. He had tried all the parental locks and net-nanny programs but always needed George's help to set them up. The prodigy then had no problem disabling them.

The other offspring were in a state of war. The twins were

both having an 'I hate being a twin' day and were not speaking to each other. They fought over everything; currently it was for little Julius's attention. They had each tried luring him with crayons, compulsory cuddles, and screaming 'I love you more' at the tops of their powerful voices.

Monica was at work. Greg still had several hours before she got home. Not that she would then share the burden. She would try to relax and demand he keep the children quiet while she unwound. He was in need of unwinding himself. He loved the children, he loved his life but there was the occasional day when he wished he could just scream, run out the door and go for some beers with the lads from the office. This longing was normally cured by remembering just what the lads from Vantex were like. Beers with the mates was no group bonding, but a desperate bid for advancement while the women's backs were turned.

Julius unleashed his most piercing scream, which indicated actual danger rather than need for attention. He had received all the attention he could take. The twins each had hold of his arms and were trying to pull him apart. He had foolishly attempted to pay attention to both of them rather than submitting to one's will and then moving aside while they slugged it out for possession. Greg settled the dispute by tossing a coin. The winner got to play with Julius, the loser got to be minded by George as he scanned the world for information.

George was a child-minding godsend. His younger siblings obeyed his every word. It was as if they were an alien invasion force and George was the leader. While they paid enough attention to their father's requests to get what they wanted, George was obeyed without hesitation or argument. George was avidly scanning some papers on dormant Icelandic volcanoes, posted by a research team from the

University of Colorado. He did not want to be interrupted and so held a hand up to his siblings. They sat in quiet obedience staring at it. Greg glanced at the words on the screen. He almost wished it was live Busty Betsy-cam taking a shower—that would have been more normal.

He considered the four of them. He did not like relying on George's natural authority, but right now he needed some calm. After hours of torment and noise the children were peaceful. Exhausted and stretched as he was, his heart filled with pride. Here were four functioning, well-adjusted young people and it was he who was shepherding them through the world. It was he who would make sure they triumphed, that they were blessed with success at every turn. He was determined they would never know disappointment, would never feel they could not achieve. They would rule the world. Actually, he knew only George would rule the world; his siblings would be his generals with the twins in charge of war. He was awed at the vast potential of his children and was determined they would not go down the path of ever-diminishing opportunity that constituted growing up for most people.

He loved all the children, but in his heart the genius who was part of him, who had DNA strains based on his genes, brought feelings greater than pride and love. He was going to be so remarkable. He was already remarkable and it was all due to Greg, and Monica. It seemed all the more satisfying that the most important thing he had ever done—creating George—was one of the easiest and simplest. At such moments he glossed over the sexual torture of Monica's fertility window.

He left the children and went to the study to find some research material on the effects of loud verbal abuse on children, which he needed for his submission. He had filed it away so long ago he could barely remember where it was. Looking at the filing cabinets, he was ashamed at his total lack of organisation. Time lost looking for poorly filed material was time that could be spent on revenue generation. That was what he had said at Vantex. He did not follow that maxim now. He had not really followed it at Vantex; he had someone else do his filing while he did the revenue generating. Consequently, the filing cabinets were in chaos. The move to America, then the moves around New York, had failed to prompt any proper culling or filing of information. It had always seemed easier to have everything moved and to promise to sort it out later.

Personal files were jumbled in the same drawers as research material. Monica's were mixed up with his. He had two choices—either go through everything logically from the front to the back of each drawer or make random stabs at various files in the hope he would find what he wanted. He chose the latter, darting here and there at bits of paper that looked promising. He found George's inoculation certificates, the twins' adoption papers, his address to the AMPCGA on first becoming president and Monica's paternity test result. He was about to put it back, when he realised that he had never seen it before. He had joyfully asked for it when Monica told him the greatest news of his life, but there had been some excuse. After that he had completely forgotten about it. He looked at it again and thought about getting it framed. It would look great, he thought, a proud piece of history. But it might make the other children feel second-best. Holding it with warm satisfaction, he proudly read it out to himself— until he came to the word 'negative.' It took a couple of seconds for him to realise what it meant. Negative: the test had shown he was not George's father. Monica had lied. He sat back on his knees. Negative. The word said everything. Negative was not what he thought he was. Being George's father was the linchpin of Greg's life. It was the reason for everything. Without that it fell apart. Negative: Greg's genes were not running through the complex brilliant strains of George's DNA. He was not the font of genius, he was the nanny. He had been drafted in because the real father had more important things to do, and Greg knew exactly who the real father was.

'Of course, he'd produce a genius,' Greg thought. 'His sperm could do in one session what mine failed to do in all that time. He's perfect, he does nothing wrong. How could I be so stupid as to believe I could beat the Golden Boy.'

Greg stood up, took another look at the word 'negative' and tossed the piece of paper on the ground. He had given up everything to rear his son. Abandoned his career, stood aside so Monica and Mark could sweep to the top and for what? So they could have their child raised and not sacrifice a thing. Charge ahead with their corporate lives while he washed nappies, played with crayons and had the majority of his conversations in pre-school monosyllables. This was the ultimate carve-up and he had not even seen it coming. He'd been roasted, sliced, drenched in gravy and served with potatoes. He had to get out, escape while there was still something left of himself. He walked into the hall. 'Look after them till Monica gets back,' he said to George, and walked out of the door, down to the street and away.

When Monica came home, she found the front door to the apartment open. She reached into her briefcase for her capsicum spray. This was New York and an open apartment door could only mean one thing. She quietly put her briefcase down and walked slowly into the apartment holding the spray in front of her. She paused, wondering whether she should call out as a person normally might on returning home. This would let any invader know she was there without letting them know she knew they were there. The invader could then prepare themselves and have a blade held at someone's throat. She decided not to call and to do a room by room search with the spray. She heard a squeal coming from George's room. It was one of the children. Perhaps she should check there first. Leaping into the doorway she positioned herself with the spray held out in front of her body. George looked up from his computer.

'Hello Monica.' He always talked to her like a colleague, which in a way he was. 'Daddy went out. There are no burglars.'

Monica put the spray away, but something was still wrong. Greg would never leave the children.

'Did Daddy leave me a message?'

'No. He was in the study and then he left.'

'Right, look after the others, George.' Monica left them and grabbed the phone. She called Greg's mobile. It rang from the living room table. She went into the study, saw a piece of paper on the ground and picked it up.

'Oh shit.'

At eleven o'clock that night, she called Mark and Rae. Rae answered and immediately heard a scream followed by Monica shouting, 'Put him down, put him down. George, tell them to behave.'

'Monica,' she asked, 'what's going on? It sounds like a riot.'

'It is, Greg's disappeared. He walked out before I came home and hasn't been back.'

'Greg left the kids? No!'

'Yes, and now they've gone mad. I think he must have

been giving them some form of good behaviour pills and they've missed a dose. They've gone mad. It's George, he's engineered it. He's staging a revolution.'

'We'll come round now.'

'Don't bring Mark. I'll explain later.'

When Rae arrived, the twins and Julius were chasing each other round a table in the living room: falling over, bumping into each other and screaming. George sat reading a book. Monica looked dazed.

'It's midnight, and they're not tired at all. The cordial hasn't done a thing.'

'Cordial!' Rae gasped in horror, noticing the half-empty bottle of raspberry flavouring on the kitchen bench top.

'George said it's what they always have before bedtime. I couldn't find any so I got some delivered from the store, but it's done nothing. I keep giving them more, thinking it must start working sometime, but they get worse.'

The children started a screaming competition: who could jump highest on the sofa and scream the loudest.

'I'm not surprised, this stuff's like speed for toddlers. Monica, you know what Greg's like. He'd never let them have this. It's their first time, they'll be wired for ages.'

'It's George, he's evil. He's doing this deliberately. George, come here.'

George obediently walked to his mother.

'Does your daddy really give you cordial?'

'No, it's an experiment, I wanted to see what would happen.'

'We'll discuss this tomorrow. Go to bed now.'

George put himself to bed while the others giggled themselves into exhaustion. Their bodies could hardly move but their minds were still charging round the room.

Fearing it would be an all-night vigil, Monica resorted to her own supply of pills. She gave half a tablet to each of the wired children. In fifteen minutes they were fast asleep on the sofa.

'Thank God for Rohypnol.'

Rae put the unconscious children to bed, deciding a lecture on the ills of feeding children drugs was not appropriate at this stage. Monica had two large whiskies poured when she returned.

'What the hell has happened? Why couldn't Mark come round?' It was late and Rae wanted to get straight to the point.

'Look, I'm sorry to drag you into this and I know it's the *KitchenArt!* premiere tomorrow. But you're kind of involved anyway.'

'How?' Rae was surprised.

'Well, I'll be frank. You know I fucked Mark when I was trying to get pregnant.'

'Yes.'

'I had to do paternity tests to find out who the father was. Mark and Greg both agreed to it.'

None of this was news to Rae. She could not see how she was involved.

'Tonight I came home and the door was open. Greg had walked out, left the place unlocked, left his wallet, his phone, everything. Then I found this on the study floor. He'd obviously found it too.' She handed Rae Greg's test result.

'Shit! Greg's not the father...oh my God.' The colour drained from Rae's face.

'I think Greg came to the same conclusion.'

'How could you not tell anyone? How could you not tell Mark? He had a right.'

'Calm down. If Greg had bothered to look at the piece of

paper sitting right behind this result instead of firing off on a virility ego trip, he'd have seen Mark's results as well.' She handed it to Rae, realising that her words alone would not be proof enough. 'It's negative too.'

'Oh my God, not Terry.'

'Gross! Give me some credit. It was this courier with fantastic legs who just happened to be there at the right time.'

'But Greg doesn't know, so he thinks Mark's the father and now he's disappeared.'

'That's about it really.'

'Wow, nice one Monica. Why didn't you just tell the truth?'

'I was scared. I knew I couldn't do the child-rearing thing. You've seen me in action. George would have been dead of an overdose by now if it had been left to me. I need Greg and I'd do it again. He's been fantastic and well, I...'

Rae looked at Monica in disbelief as her voice cracked and tears welled up in her eyes.

'It all worked out so perfectly. I love our life and I can't do this without him, and fuck it, I can't stand the thought of him out there in pain. He'll be absolutely devastated. George is everything to him. God knows what he'll do.'

'Have you reported him missing?'

'Apparently you have to wait twenty-four hours. But who knows what he could've done by then? You know what he's like, he's capable of anything.'

Rae understood why Monica had not wanted Mark to come round. If Greg had returned home to find him there, it would have been the final straw. She went to the kitchen to grab a paper towel so Monica could wipe her eyes. When she returned, George had beaten her to it. He was standing next to Monica with some toilet paper which he gently pressed into her hand. He hugged her. This made her cry even more.

'Don't worry, Monica, he'll be back,' he said and went back to bed.

Monica could not speak. She had assumed George had absolutely no feelings for her. How could he have any? She had shown none to him, other than a well-done kiss on picking some top-selling cosmetic shades. She looked at the sodden piece of toilet paper in amazement. It did not make sense. How could someone who had been gleefully torturing her a few minutes before, suddenly make this beautiful gesture? She dried a couple more tears and hoped Greg would not do anything stupid.

Greg had not done anything more stupid, as yet, than walk the streets of New York at night with no money, no ID and no idea where he was going. The steady pacing helped to meld his random bits of emotion into coherent thought. He thought of Terry and his hatred for Mark, the obsessive anger that Mark had stolen his life. He understood it now. Mark had stolen his life too, and given him a pretend one to live instead. If Terry felt a fraction of the anger and desolation that Greg felt now, no wonder he had kept it churning for so long. Mark's beauty was a vacuum, sucking up everything around him. It was as if no-one else was allowed to be a man. No other man could run a company, could be desired, could father a child. Mark stopped other men around him being successful men. Even that actor could not stay a heartthrob with Mark around. Mark destroyed careers and made the competition disappear. He was utterly ruthless without even trying. He lived life as if it was a marketing campaign and every other man was the competition. Even now, Greg realised, Mark had stolen his thoughts. He should have been thinking about George and Monica. It should not matter who the real father was, and yet that was what consumed him.

He focused his mind on George, Julius and the twins. Whether he was their real father or not, they needed him and he wanted them. He had briefly thought of going straight to the airport, booking the next flight to Sydney and starting his career again. He had missed out on a few years, but his time in New York could be dressed up to look good on a résumé. He could be back in his old life before Monica and Mark knew where he was. He aborted the plan due to his lack of money and passport. And the children, whoever their fathers were, were what really mattered. He could divorce Monica, get good alimony and continue to raise them. Raise Mark's little genius. But then, Mark would take that away from him somehow. Mark would deny him even that second-best pleasure. It was back to Mark. It was always back to him. He could have coped if only it had been someone else.

He thought about going home, imagining the chaos Monica would be presiding over. George would have unleashed his sisters' worst behaviour just for kicks. Greg smiled. Monica should stew for a while, recognise the significance of his role. He would not return, he would confront Mark. There would be no peace until Mark had been stopped. He could not be allowed to carry on removing the masculinity of all the men he ever met. As president of AMPCGA, Greg was fully versed in the literature of men's power. Mark could have had a whole thesis written on him. The inability of the modern man to love and accept his fellow men. The instinctive competitive urge taken to dysfunctional extremes. He would confront Mark, man to man, and do whatever it took to preserve his own manhood. Greg stepped up the pace; there was a large island to cover before dawn.

It was a sleepless night all round. Rae had told Mark of the events at Monica's apartment on her return. He had been shocked and momentarily terrified at the thought of being George's father. The truth, whatever the fine-legged man's name, was a huge relief. Rae was worried about Greg and what he might do. Mark did not share her concern, or at least it played second fiddle to the main one staring at him from the Double Day mirror.

'Get a grip,' Rae said, switching off the mirror. 'There's a man in the city hating you right now for shattering everything he held dear, a man prepared to make an entire school ill with measles just to help further the chances of the boy he now thinks is your son. And you're worried about a few wrinkles for the opening night of a bloody musical?'

'Greg's a good man. Sure he's angry, but he won't do anything stupid. He'll get home, find out the truth and everything will be OK.'

'But your face...' Rae returned sarcastically.

'Exactly. Let's just hope everything looks good tomorrow.'

Rae breathed deeply. Following her visit to Dr Lobos, she still had not decided whether to go ahead with her plan. When a package was delivered from the Lobos laboratory, her heart had raced. She'd had to consciously control her breathing as she looked at the products the package contained. She had reasoned that a decision need not be made until the last moment. Tonight's conversation made the decision for her. Mark's sense of what was truly important had been lost. A potentially violent man focusing his anger at Mark was less of a worry than a wrinkle.

She knew the wonderful, funny and caring man she loved was still there behind the face, locked in by maturing perfection. She had to liberate him for everyone's sake. His beauty had become a cancer. It had to be removed. It was a huge risk, but right now she, little Brett and Mark himself had nothing to lose. If she went ahead, their family would be either saved or destroyed. If she did not, a slow and painful disintegration was all she could see. She decided to act.

'I know you're worried about how you'll look tomorrow. I think it's wrong, and I don't encourage it——'

'Rae, you've got to understand——'

'I'll make a deal. I'll support you through tomorrow. We'll indulge your vanity in any way that gets you through, but after tomorrow night we get serious about getting over this. We do anything, and I mean anything, to get your life back in perspective.'

'Rae, you're wonderful. I promise, after tomorrow night, it'll be therapy, hypnotism, acupuncture, spiritual healing, whatever you say.'

'You may not think me wonderful after tomorrow night, but just to show I mean what I say, I got you a present. It's the absolute latest in face care technology. God knows how long you could feed a family on what I paid for it, but it's supposed to be miraculous.' She showed him Dr Lobos's moisturiser.

'Fantastic, I should put it on now.'

'No, it's instant, but temporary. Plumps up the skin, injects moisture, smooths wrinkles, takes years off—but only for about four hours. After that you return to the shrivelled prune you normally are.'

'Rae I love you, we'll try it tomorrow. It's going to be a great night. Everyone's so excited. And Brett was fantastic at the run-through, he'll steal the show.'

They went to bed. Mark fell asleep quickly, reassured by

Rae's wonderful gift. Rae lay awake, explaining to herself why this was the only option.

Elsewhere, more Australians were proving New York was the city that never sleeps. Terry sat on the bed in his hotel room, meditating on his knife. He realised why he had always failed to beat Mark at every turn before. He had never used his knife. This was the real source of his power. The one that had seen off that goat and had put him at the Head of the Herd. The knife was the only way he could defeat Mark. His disappointment at not having made this realisation years ago was tempered in his meditative state by joy that the realisation had been made at all. He would win in the end and that was the one place it counted.

The discipline of years of setting and meeting objectives had served him well. His time in America had been tough. Keeping his vision on his ultimate goal, he had trained, practised, sweated and meditated himself to a physical peak. He had ruthlessly committed himself to fitness targets, and never once had he failed to meet any objective that he set. He was rightly proud and knew with confidence he could not be better prepared.

Within the calm of his lotus position, his ears picked up a sound. A fly had got into the room. Buzzing around, it touched on the banana in Terry's complimentary bowl of fruit. Without opening his eyes, he picked up the knife, hurled it at the bowl and pinned the fly to the banana. He did not even need to look to know he had succeeded. He breathed with satisfaction. He was ready.

In a much cheaper hotel that did not give away complimentary anything except for a sachet of soap, Lucy was lying on her bed, holding her gun in front of her, with the phone resting by her ear, listening to her agent. He told her to focus on the pistol, hold it out as if it was an extension of her arm. He wanted her to sleep with it in her hand. She had to feel naked without it.

She had practised shooting at a firing range and reckoned she had got close enough to her target. She was no Olympic sharp-shooter, but she would hit the mark. At the range, she had been equally pleased with her howls and screams. The supervisor had eventually asked her to leave and questioned whether she should be carrying a gun. Lucy had simply replied, 'My agent said he wanted me to. He said, "Lucy, get your gun, you know what you have to do".'

At the gun shop, she had decided it would be best not to act mad for once. She reckoned there had to be some provision for not selling firearms to someone who was not of sound mind. After the man beside her in the store warned her that the entire population of Greenland was on its way to New York to stage a mass invasion and would make Buddhism and whale-eating compulsory for all, she realised it had been an unnecessary precaution. Her agent had been angry when she told him. It was a missed opportunity. He was scary when he was angry. She was terrified of letting him down. Something about him chilled her, but she needed him, relied on his authority and the fact he always knew exactly what to do. Tomorrow was her big test. She would be on her own, he had said. He could not come to the theatre and she was not to call him. He would be with her in spirit. He went quiet and she eventually fell asleep, her unloaded gun in one hand and the phone nestled to her head, just in case he came back.

◆

'Have you sent the flowers from me and Rae?' Mark was on the phone to William.

'Sure, although I felt kinda stupid sending them to "the Fruit-Juicer". Can't you tell me who it is?'

'It's an old friend.'

'Oh my God! It's Brett Josco. He's making a comeback,' William shouted. 'I can't believe you didn't tell me.'

'I still haven't. I've said nothing. Is everything set for the strategy meeting tomorrow?'

'Yes.'

'OK, I'll see you at the theatre, and not a word.'

'I can't believe it!'

'Then don't, not a word.'

'I know nothing.'

Mark hung up. He was at home beginning his preparations for the opening night. It took some time. There was no way you could rush having two hours of rest to ensure a relaxed and clear skin tone. The alarm went. It was time to remove the face mask.

'So William knows, then?' Rae inquired. Mark gave a massive smile and cracked the dried face pack as he padded into the bathroom.

'I swear he must be psychic sometimes. Still, he'd have spotted him tonight, Juicer outfit or no. Excited?' His skin felt moist and soft as he washed off the mask. The mud had been shipped in fresh from Japanese volcanic pools that very day. Just twenty hours ago the goo washing down his skin had been happily bubbling away in a hot spring. He dried it carefully and moved to the Double Day mirror.

'I'm fine,' Rae answered as she got out four dresses and held each up against herself. She had not been able to sit still since she had got home.

'Look, you can mention the film…' It was pluck time. Any hairs to be plucked had be done now, to give the skin ample opportunity to calm down. '… I'm scared too, but I've got a good feeling about tonight. It's going to lay old ghosts to rest.'

Mark checked his eyebrows. Each hair was perfect. He removed the one hair that grew blond. It was a quirk which Rae said gave him character. Tonight it had to go: he wanted perfection, not character. Then he turned to the few hairs at the top of his cheek-bones. They were fine and could have been shaved, but he did not want to risk causing his regular shave line to move higher. Plucking smoothed out the cheeks and was the better long-term option.

'Besides,' Mark continued, 'tonight's not about me.'

'Everything is about you, Mark,' Rae countered, feeling awful that she was selecting a dress that would match Dr Lobos's lipstick, 'but I'm sure it'll be a hit. I'm just a bit nervy I suppose. Monica called. She still hasn't heard anything from Greg. She's going to file a missing person's report after tonight.'

'That's Monica, won't let a missing husband get in the way of a theatre premiere.' It was time to scruff. Gently across the forehead and around his nose and over his cheeks.

'Actually she's really upset. She thinks he might turn up there for some strange reason. She's bringing the pride.' Rae did not mention that both she and Monica were concerned that Greg would try to confront Mark at the theatre. Monica was taking the children with her, in the hope that the sight of them might stop him doing something foolish. She would also be armed with Mark's paternity test results.

'I'm shaving now.' That was the signal that conversation had to end. Mark could not afford any distractions when he shaved. Nothing could be allowed to go wrong with the riskiest part of grooming. It never had gone wrong, but there was always a first time for a rash or nicks.

It went superbly, a gloriously smooth shave with the blades gliding effortlessly, no scraping sounds, no need for double swipes. Every skin cell felt like it was lined up perfectly, no loose bits, no irritation and absolutely no nicks. He barely needed the fresh aloe vera pulp he had taken from their plant earlier, but he applied it anyway. It felt great.

He let it soak in as he did his two-minute work-out: flexing muscles, squeezing his hands across his chest to beef it up and generally getting the blood pumping round. There were no nude appearances planned, but he had to be perfect to feel perfect. He looked at his pubic hair in the wall-to-ceiling mirror and then checked to see that Rae was out of the bedroom. With electric clippers he trimmed the sides to give his hair the perfect shape and then trimmed the tops of the hairs, so they were not too bushy. Rae was the only one outside the gym changing room who saw the results. A minor improvement, but one that made him feel better. He had just managed to sweep up the bits of hair and wash them down the sink when Rae came back into the room.

She looked at him, her eyes drawn downwards. His naked body looked as gorgeous as ever, even if he had taken to trimming his pubic hair. She would have loved to have pushed him into the shower there and then and made wild love with him. There was a time Mark would have pulled her into the shower himself, happy in the knowledge that whatever he did, he would still look great. For Rae, all the plucking, masks and treatments did not improve him—he just looked a bit too clean.

Mark entered the shower and began his body scrub, a gentle menthol-based exfoliant with bristle brush—stimulating, cleansing, refreshing. Post shower, it was the full body moisturiser and then back to the Double Day mirror for the final stretch on the face.

An astringent was applied with an organic unbleached cotton ball, preparing the ground for the new moisturiser. Mark was touched that Rae, feeling as she did, was helping him this way. Perhaps she was beginning to see past her own ego to how important this really was.

'Do I apply this on top of or underneath my regular moisturiser?'

'Instead of, you only need one.'

'I dunno Rae, I'd feel a bit naked.'

'The senior dermatological consultant who briefed me was most adamant, only this one.'

'OK.' Rae had made a concession to him by buying this, Mark was going to make one back. He smoothed it on. It felt good and absorbed rapidly, leaving a smoother, fresher texture. It had a faintly chemical smell but that went quickly. It was probably the active ingredients that plumped and rejuvenated.

'How much do I use?'

'Slap it on, apparently.'

He applied a second layer. The area round his eyes felt fresh without any greasiness. The visible signs of ageing just smoothed away.

'This is fantastic, Rae. How do I look?' He turned with a flourish, dazzled her with a smile and bound up to her, pressing his body to hers.

'You turned on?' he asked.

'You turned on by me being turned on?'

'I'm turned on by you.'

'So do something about it.' Rae could see in his eyes and

feel between her legs that he wanted to. She writhed suggestively in his arms. Perhaps this time he could forget the
preparations, let his beauty be overcome with the need to
make love. Rae held him, praying for some small gesture that
said he *could* regain control, and that she could choose a different lipstick. He kissed her and her heart rose at the thought
of not having to go through with her plan. Then it sank.

'Sorry darling, have to torture you a bit longer, but when
we get home tonight, I promise you, it'll be pure pleasure.'

Rae smiled weakly. 'If you've finished in the bathroom
could I pop in for a moment?'

She did not apply her lipstick until the last moment. It
looked perfectly normal. A harmless attractive shade of red
as selected by George for dynamic women going places. It
was her turn to look in the mirror and be nervous about
everything having to go right. Her hand trembled as she raised
the stick. She stopped, breathed, looked at the vast array of
Mark's potions and treatments that filled their bathroom and
steeled her nerve. She smoothed on a layer of red, bit on a
tissue and applied a second layer. Thick, rich and deadly. She
flushed the marked tissue down the toilet, and took both the
lipstick and its companion moisturiser with her. She would
dispose of them later.

◆

There was to be a reception in the dress circle bar of the theatre before the performance. Mark was the guest of honour.
Thanks to the early start to his preparations and their smooth
progress, the two of them arrived on time for once. Rae concentrated hard on polite conversation, desperate for the show

to start so she could stop talking and sit silently with her dreadful thoughts.

A vast crowd of people thronged in the foyer, pushing their way up the stairs, forcing their way to the toilets for last-minute relief. It looked impossible that such a sea of people could fit inside the theatre. Terry liked it. The huge crowd was too excited, too bent on seeing the right people and catching their eye for a smile and a finger wave to notice him. The more anonymous he was at this stage the better. He felt the knife pressed to his inner thigh. He'd strapped it there in case of security. It meant he had to walk with a slight limp to avoid stabbing himself. He had already caused one small nick and repaired himself with a bandaid. There was no sign of Boyd. He, no doubt, would be in the finest seats in the house. Terry could have worked his way through the crowd, found his target and slipped the knife in while no-one noticed, but that would not have been satisfying enough. He wanted Boyd on stage, where everyone could see him fall.

Monica was pushing her way through the crowd with the Haddrick pride, or more precisely she was pushing the twins through the crowd, carrying Julius and noticing that George was missing. She sighed with exhausted frustration. She had to find George, but did not want to drag the others back through the throng. The children were there as a means of protecting Greg from himself, but Monica also wanted him to see how well she was coping. Losing one of them within minutes of arriving was not coping well.

'Hold onto my dress,' she instructed the twins and waited for two firm little hands to clamp onto the silky fabric.

'We're scared,' they announced to anyone who looked at them. There were a few tuts of disapproval as people were pushed out of the way. Monica tried to get back through the crowd to the entrance, but it was just too hard with her entourage. Julius started crying and the twins announced they needed pee-pee. She needed help. Swinging Julius onto one arm, she fished with the other in her handbag for her mobile and dialled Rae. It went straight to her message bank. Monica slammed the phone shut and threw it back into the bag. The situation was hopeless. Now she just hoped that Greg would miraculously turn up with George, regardless of how badly she was coping. She decided to take the twins to the toilets and get that distraction out of the way. Turning once again she fought back through the crowd with a renewed determination and made it to the powder room.

'Emergency!' she cried and moved past the head of the queue and into the first available toilet. She put Julius down on the floor.

'Right, go,' she instructed the twins.

'Too high,' they replied. She helped each of them in turn onto the seat, but only after they had argued as to who needed to pee-pee more. As she finished with them, a voice from two cubicles along shouted, 'Whose is this child?'

Julius had crawled under the partition, across a whole cubicle and into the next one. Monica crouched down on the floor and saw her youngest crawling for freedom.

'Julius, come back.'

He shrieked joyfully and continued to the end cubicle and from there into the general area. Monica stood up, opened the door and instructed the twins to stay put. Holding out one hand, she stopped the woman she had queue-jumped from entering the cubicle, and started to chase Julius, now on two feet, to the delight of the women around him. Julius captured, she returned to the cubicle and locked the door again.

'Now, I've got to find George. You want George, don't you?'

'Yes,' they all nodded, missing their leader.

'Good, now stay here, stay very still until I come back. Make sure Julius does not climb under the wall again, OK?'

'OK, Monica.'

With those words, Monica dropped to the floor and slid herself under the cubicle door, hoping the floor was both dry and clean. She stood up as the queue looked on in amazement. She brushed the dust off her dress. The woman she had pushed past had still not made it to a cubicle. She sneered at Monica contemptuously. Monica scowled back.

'You're far too pale for that foundation. I should know, my company designed it for *youthful healthy skin types*.' She turned and shouted, 'Be good, I'll be back,' towards the cubicle door and charged out of the toilets to locate George.

◆

Lucy had decided it was best to arrive as late as possible. The less time she spent at the theatre, the less chance of being discovered before her big moment. It was scary without her agent, knowing she had to go through this all alone. She had toyed with the idea of staying away until near the end of the show, but she had paid a fortune for the ticket, and besides, if her seat was empty, someone might try to take it. Her small handbag felt incredibly heavy with the gun inside.

The first person she spotted when she arrived was the guy who had been in front of her in the ticket queue. He appeared to be limping through the melee. She decided not to speak to him. Buying a program, Lucy moved to a quiet corner and opened it up in front of her face. She was immediately greeted by a smiling full-page shot of Mark wishing the cast and crew all the best for the show. She jumped, as if confronted by the real thing. Then she paused for a moment, caught by his eyes, and remembered when he had been hers alone. It seemed so long ago and so far away.

'Where did we go wrong?' she murmured to the picture and indulged in a moment's fantasy of Rae being knocked down by a bus and herself consoling Mark out of his grief.

As the first bell rang to announce the imminent start of the show, Rae felt a second of relief that the polite chatting was over. Then an even greater dread filled her. The evening was progressing so fast that her moment would too soon arrive.

Rae and Mark headed to the stairs to the lobby. As they stood at the top, a voice knocked Lucy out of her reverie, shouting, 'There's Mark Boyd.' A round of applause rippled through the excited foyer. Lucy looked from her picture to the real Mark, smiling, warm, friendly and totally oblivious to her existence. There was no turning back the clock and no going back on her plan. He was the reason she was reduced to hiding in corners behind programs. He had made her dump him and had used every opportunity to humiliate her since. She spat on his face in her program and tossed it into the potted palm that was shielding her.

Monica's search for George failed. She went out to the street and asked the security staff if they had seen a small boy. She walked into the men's toilet and called for him. She ran into the auditorium to see if he had made his way to their seats. It was the sensible sort of thing he would do. He was not there. Just as the bells rang and everyone else was making their way into the theatre, Monica was forcing her way back to the foyer. She quizzed the program sellers, the bar staff, everyone whose eyes met hers. In a crowd that big, someone of George's size could disappear easily.

She returned to the toilets, now deserted except for two locked cubicles. Monica knocked on the door of her personal nursery.

'Girls, open the door, it's Mummy.'

'Monica said not to open door.'

'This is Monica,' she tried to sound patient, 'Monica is Mummy.'

'Busy, Jool in bath.'

Monica groaned. There was no end to their innovative ways of torturing her. Back on the floor, she put her head under the door to see Julius naked and splashing in the toilet bowl, squealing every time his foot slipped down the u-bend. Sliding back into the cubicle, Monica fished him out of the toilet, opened up the door and carried him to the hot-air hand-drier to dry him off. She put him down to fetch his clothes and he immediately started running around the floor. The twins took up the chase and they were all dodgem cars, bumping into each other and bouncing off the walls. Monica decided the cordial from last night could not possibly have kicked in again. They had slept for fourteen blissful Rohypnol hours.

The door of the cubicle next to theirs opened and an explanation came from the inhabitant, still seated on the toilet.

'I gave them some sweeties to keep them happy. They seemed a bit worried.'

'JayJo Bonnet?' Monica asked in amazement. After the last twenty-four hours, she felt she should learn to accept even the most strange coincidence.

'Yes, you're Monica, aren't you? Used to work with Mark?'

'Yes. Why are you sitting there? The show's starting any moment.'

'I thought someone better stay with the little ones.'

'They were fine,' Monica started defensively and then gave up. 'But I've lost George, the eldest. I needed to keep them somewhere while I looked for him.'

'Oh well, seeing as it's true confessions, I've actually got the back of my dress caught on the toilet seat and I can't move.'

The dress was a magnificent creation made up of cords of gold material, each around half a metre long.

'It looks marvellous when I'm standing,' JayJo explained, 'but it jams in things went I sit. I think one cord is caught under the toilet seat. Perhaps you could...'

While the children decided to imitate a three-car pile up in the corner of the room, Monica squeezed behind JayJo. Brushing aside the bulk of the dress, she located the trapped cord and tried to pull it. It was stuck.

'I'm going to have to cut it,' Monica said, 'got any nail scissors?'

'I did bring some just in case. I didn't want to start cutting randomly or the whole dress might have been snipped off.'

Monica cut the restricted cord and JayJo was released.

'Right, let's go and see Mark's little play. I should be there, I'm one of the backers. Want some help with the children?'

'Here are our tickets, could you sit with them? I've got to find the missing one. And we need to make sure these ones don't run off.'

The party emerged from the women's toilet: three children fully dressed and all with one wrist tied securely to a cord on America's top art dealer's $6000 dress.

'Come along now.' She mothered them towards the stalls.

'Thanks,' said Monica. 'I'll join you when I can.'

'No worries. Besides, it's marvellous. I feel like an installation.'

Monica watched the doors shut behind them as they shuffled into the auditorium. Sitting on the steps that led to the dress circle bar, she paused for a moment to wonder again where George might be.

◆

Rae's lips were itching furiously. They felt dry and cracked as if she had attempted to eat a whole box of doughnuts without licking her lips. They were burning. She had to stop thinking about them. They were only irritating because she knew what the lipstick could do. As the overture finished, Mark leaned over to her.

'You haven't kissed me for good luck yet. How about now?'

'I don't know if this lipstick smudges or not. Don't want you appearing at interval with a big red mark.'

'OK, but I'll want extra ones later.'

Why was he suddenly so concerned with being kissed, Rae wondered. Every moment she felt as if she was having to avoid a kiss. Did he know? Was he deliberately baiting her, seeing if she would go through with it? She calmed herself. He could not possibly know. If he did, there was no way he would have put on the face cream. He could have switched face creams, she thought.

'Don't be so stupid,' she told herself, 'he doesn't know and...he will understand.'

She swallowed and wished she loved musicals. At least that way she would be transfixed by the giant RW 3000 now opening to reveal fifty crisply chilled and tap-dancing lettuce leaves on the stage in front of her. She should at least have felt some measure of pride that the best-selling fridge in America which she had masterminded and which was named for her was being immortalised on stage.

◆

Terry squirmed with discomfort as Mark's stupid marketing idea was paraded in front of him like a piece of world history. He nearly whipped his knife out as the breadmaker, based, he knew, on the technical specs of the Doughmatic he had nurtured at Vantex, performed a solo, 'I've Got a Bun in the Oven' and gave birth on stage to three baby breadmakers. It was an insult. A bastardisation of the fine industry of domestic appliances, and one man alone was responsible for this sham. Terry's only comfort was that the audience would be turned off in droves. He waited for the embarrassing silence at the end of the breadmaker's solo. His hands were poised for a slow clap, but instead his ears were deafened by roars of delight from the audience. They adored it. Mark Boyd was not even on the stage and they loved it. Terry focused and repeated his mantra for the day to steady himself: remove Mark Boyd from my world, remove Mark Boyd from my world. The breadmaker ushered in the interval. As the audience filed out excitedly, working out which celebrities they had spotted, Terry remained in his seat, too disgusted to stand in a crowd that adored this offensive rubbish.

◆

By interval, Monica had searched every bar and every lobby at every level of the theatre. She had consulted the manager, and a search had been carried out backstage. George was not to be found. She felt sick. Greg would appear, if not today then another day, and her complete incompetence would be exposed. He would deride and spurn her before she could explain that she had lied to him, but not the lie he thought. Her actual lie had been better than the one he believed was her lie. If only she could explain everything her life would come back and, she hoped, bring George with it.

'Monica, where are the kids?' It was Mark.

'The twins and Julius are tied to JayJo's dress, George is missing. Greg hasn't appeared.'

'George missing! Surely someone has seen him.'

'No-one, I've tried everything. Another round after the interval and then it's the police. How's the show?'

'They love it.'

'I'd better check on the others.'

'I'll come with you. I should see JayJo. Rae went to the toilets, she'll be the whole interval.'

They went into the stalls, with Monica fully expecting some new hell to reveal itself. JayJo and the kids were still in their seats. The children were working their way round JayJo's dress, plaiting all the cords.

'I thought it best to stay here. Any luck? Hello Mark, my dear.'

She attempted to stand up, but a quick jerk from the twins' hands and she was back in her seat. They giggled, enjoying the power.

Monica glanced around as if looking for inspiration as to where George could be. The auditorium was empty apart from one person sitting in his seat, three rows from the front. Monica stared at him.

'Isn't that...no it can't be...it is Mark, it's Terry!'

Terry was aware that they had entered. Now might be an opportunity. He looked forward, determined not to let them know he knew they were there. He slid down in his seat, to straighten his legs and hips and so draw the knife out without stabbing himself.

'Look,' Monica said, 'he's trying to hide from us.' She enjoyed the distraction. 'Yoohoo Terry.'

He ignored her and unzipped his fly. Reaching in with his hand he tried to pull out the knife, but he could not straighten his leg enough to draw it out.

'Don't look children.' JayJo had no idea who this Terry was, but she knew what a man playing with himself looked like.

'I think we better get the children outside,' Mark said. It certainly looked like Terry was fiddling with his fly, but would he flash at Monica's children? It was better to be safe than sorry, Mark supposed. They crept out as quietly as three children tied to a plaited gold cord dress could.

However hard Terry pushed out his legs to straighten his hips, he cut himself whenever he tried to move the knife. In the end he had to stand up and pull it out. He turned with it, ready to throw, only to see empty seats. The bastard had evaded him. Obviously it was not the right time. Terry would never have escaped through the mob in the foyer and there would have been no crowd to witness his triumph. He thanked the universe for guiding him and opened himself to receiving the patience to wait for the right moment.

In the toilets Rae rushed into the first available cubicle; she had to do something about her lips. She took a double piece of paper and pressed it to them. The relief was wonderful. She decided to remove the lipstick she had on and apply it afresh. She carefully wiped her lips. It was so good to touch them again, even through toilet paper. She flushed the paper, opened the door and made her way to the mirror.

Lifting up the lipstick, the woman next to her cried, 'Oh same shade, hon, it's great isn't it?'

Rae, startled by the sudden comment, dropped her own stick and knocked her neighbour's out of her hand. Both fell into the basin in front of her and clattered to the plughole. Rae looked down at them, unable to work out which was which.

'Oh shit.'

'No matter, hon, they're both the same shade. Both pretty new, and you look kinda germ-free to me.'

'But mine was special.'

'Relax hon, chances are you'll pick up yours. No-one will know.' They looked down at the two identical lipsticks resting in the basin.

'You don't understand.' Rae could not believe her foolishness. If only she had stuck out the irritation, everything would have been fine. The woman picked up a lipstick and was about to start re-applying.

'No,' Rae grabbed her hand and then looked around. She mouthed the word, 'Herpes.'

'Oh I see.' The woman examined the stick and sniffed it. She looked again.

'This one's mine, I know it,' she announced happily. 'See, I was in a hurry and tried to put it on while my nails were still wet. I smudged a bit on the tube and had to redo my nails. Look, varnish mark.'

Rae smiled with relief and picked up the other one. 'Thanks.'

'No, thank you, most girls woulda just spread it around if you know what I mean.' Rae's neighbour left her staring at herself in the mirror. She breathed deeply and put on another rich thick layer.

◆

Lucy was standing outside the theatre, trying to calm herself. The moment was coming. She had started shaking during the first half. It felt as if her whole body was convulsing and she was afraid of drawing attention to herself. As soon as the curtain went down, she had pushed past the other people on her row and run outside. Holding out her arms, she saw her hands were shaking. She began to doubt her ability to go through with it. Spotting a payphone, she could not resist going to it. She knew she was not supposed to call. This was her task to accomplish alone, but she could not stand the silence. It was the longest she had gone without his calm authority and it was driving her nuts. The woman on the phone hung up and left. Lucy dashed in quickly, forcing her way past a man who had been waiting nearby. She picked up the receiver and instantly felt a wave of relief as she heard his voice. She poured out her concerns. 'What if they don't believe I'm mad, what if I miss, what if they won't publish?' .

Her agent was furious at her weakness and her disobedience, but his anger soothed her. He was in control. The harsh tones sent a shiver through her body that quelled her nerves and she relaxed. 'I'm sorry…yes…if you say so… but what if…'

She knew it was a mistake to question him further. He fell silent. She called to him and cried out 'Sorry,' but heard nothing.

'Hey lady, first you push in, now you hold it up!' The guy she had pushed in front of hammered on the door. He turned to the person behind him. 'She hasn't even put any money in, the fruitcake's talking to herself…hey lady, go be a loony someplace else.'

Lucy turned and looked at the guy in wonder. She dropped the receiver and walked out of the booth.

'What did you say?'

'You're nuts, let people who really want to use the phone in.'

'Thank you,' she whispered to the sky. It was the sign her agent had just promised her. He was angry, but he had not abandoned her. She grabbed the guy and kissed him.

'Yes, you're absolutely right!'

Lucy beamed. Her hands stopped shaking. It was a sign. It was exactly what she needed to hear. Nothing could possibly go wrong. Her agent was in control.

◆

After the interval, the lobby returned to muted tranquillity, disturbed only by the muffled joy of the theatre full of people enjoying the show. Monica resumed her search, phoned the police, who had no record of any children fitting George's description being found, and rechecked with all the theatre staff. If George turned up now there was not a staff member who did not know to grab him and call Monica's mobile. She decided to take to the streets, unable to sit still in the place she had already searched so thoroughly. As she walked to the door, it opened before her. Standing there was a gleeful George and a dishevelled Greg. Monica let out an unidentifiable noise, grabbed George and hugged him.

This threw Greg completely. He had meant to drag her out of her seat and demand an explanation for her appalling neglect of the children. He had expected indifference and professional calm; instead she looked distraught and had shown affection towards her son. He was astounded, but still mustered some anger.

'Your son was wandering alone on the streets of one of the most dangerous cities in the world.'

'I looked everywhere.'

Greg raised a contemptuous eyebrow. After his all-night walk through the streets, he had spent most of the day trying to sleep in Central Park. Every time he nodded off, he would wake with a start, panicking that he might be robbed. Then he would relax as he remembered he had nothing to steal. He had been determined to keep away from home, storm the theatre and confront Mark, but it had not been easy. He was exhausted, absolutely starving and aching to see his children. He was appalled at his own lack of resolve, disappointed that the furious anger he'd felt pacing the streets seemed to fade away as his discomfort grew. Hunger was supposed to make people angrier.

He had tried to enter the theatre before the show, but given his dreadful appearance, lack of ticket and strong aroma, security had intercepted him. He had crossed the road to watch everyone arrive. George had seen him, turning around as Monica and the others entered the theatre. He had looked directly at Greg as if a sixth sense had told him he was there. He carefully crossed the road and joined his father.

It was that look that persuaded the near-delirious Greg that he was George's father, whoever had porked Monica. Instinctively knowing where he was could not be mere coincidence; it was their carefully nurtured bond. After much hugging and kissing Greg asked George if he had the twenty-dollar note he was supposed to have pinned in his pocket in case of emergency. Naturally he had and so took his father off for something to eat. George told his father everything that had happened the night before. The cordial, Rae's visit and Monica's tears. He did not raise the issue of his own paternity. They had intended to return to the theatre for the interval, but missed it by a few minutes. Instead, they arrived in perfect time to meet Monica.

She decided it was best to get straight to the point.

'Greg, if you're going to go poking around in my files, you should at least do a thorough job.' She pulled out Mark's test result from her handbag. He read it and his weary shoulders dropped even further.

'Neither of you is the birth father. But one of you raised him, loved him and made this wonderful young man.'

They looked down at their son.

'So who . . . not Terry?'

'Why does everyone think so little of me? I don't know his name, but he had great legs.'

'Dad, I think you should explain to me now how you aren't my birth father and Monica made me with someone else. You should tell me you both love me and that's what counts.'

They looked at each other and shook their heads. Was there nothing they could teach this boy? Did they always have to learn from him?

'We still need to talk.' Greg did not want this brushed over, for their sakes and George's. He did not want it bursting out as drug-crazed adolescent rebellion in a few years time.

'At home?' Monica suggested. Greg agreed. He practically drooled at the thought of their apartment, a hot shower, a bed and the warm nurturing atmosphere which he had created.

'Any idea where the other kids are?' he asked.

Monica smiled smugly. 'Everything is under control.' She went back into the theatre and proudly brought out the twins and Julius, all intact. JayJo had to come with them to be released. The twins protested, they were enjoying the bondage. However, when they saw their father, JayJo was forgotten and practically pulled over as they rushed to hug him. Rather than attempt to keep them still long enough to untie the now very tight knots, JayJo brandished her nail scissors and cut herself free. The dress was ruined but it had served its purpose. She went back to watch the show that was making her richer with every cheer and left Greg's pride to go home.

◆

In the second half Brett caused a sensation with his song, the sexiest number of the show. Everyone whooped as he ground his hips and made the central juicer part of him rotate. The audience, most of whom did not have a clue who he was, were wondering who the sensational new talent could be, until a man screamed out, 'It's Brett Josco!' and a gasp went through the crowd. Mark looked down and shook his head. He would have words with William in the morning.

'I can't believe it,' Terry cried. That was the final proof. Everyone had been given a love-and-forgive-Mark-Boyd pill, except him. Even that talentless actor, his career ruined, his life in tatters, was back in the fan club appearing in this drivel. It was too much. Terry could not control his rage. He had to do something immediately. His hands clenched, he breathed hard through his teeth. He wanted to scream. Without even looking to see if anyone was watching, he grasped the knife which he had placed on the seat underneath his leg. He had to use it, he had to kill something. The frustration was overpowering. With a grunt and a clenched jaw, he plunged the knife between his legs into the edge of his seat. The relief was enormous. The sensation of the blade ripping through the material and deep into the firm padding was bliss. It brought his anger back into the controllable range. He reached deep inside, calling on even greater reserves of self-control. He could do it and achieve the maximum one-day point score. Surely his moment would come soon!

The people next to Terry had been too transfixed by Brett's performance to notice the random act of violence occurring next to them. The woman to his left had heard his exclamation and turned to beam at him.

'I know, isn't it marvellous after all these years . . . that Mark Boyd, you have to give it to him.'

◆

Hearts were pounding as *KitchenArt, the Musical!* came to its spectacular conclusion. Sixty appliances moved in perfect unison. The near impossibility of such shapes moving with such grace and athleticism made it seem like a computer generation come to life. The audience leaped to its feet. Cheers and more cheers rang out.

As soon as the number finished, Mark and Rae quietly moved from their seats and were escorted backstage, ready to walk on to congratulate the cast and present bouquets to the writers and directors. They waited in the wings as endless curtain calls rang down. The audience did not want to let the cast off the stage. Eventually the stage manager cued Mark and Rae to go out anyway. Any more delays and they would be into overtime for the crew and front-of-house staff. She was not going to let that happen.

The audience hushed as a microphone was brought out for Mark. Rae, standing by his side, now had no difficulty controlling her lips. They controlled her. In the glare of the stage lights, they seemed to take over her whole face. Her lips were huge, they were all she was aware of. She tried to distract herself by looking out at the audience. All she could see were the first three rows and then nothing. It was like looking into a fog-bound night.

Mark praised the fine performers and thanked all the celebrities who had appeared. He went on to pay tribute to the show's subject. 'I guess it's no secret that this musical is on a topic dear to my heart. Over the years it has been a privilege to share my vision for domestic appliances with the world, and to find that the world felt the same as I did. We have elevated objects which were once taken for granted and given them their due. Our toasters, our blenders, our popcorn makers, these are not just things, not just objects to collect dust...'

Just within vision of the stage, Terry gripped the knife and removed it from the murdered seat. He looked from side to side; he was just two seats from the centre aisle and he could easily leap there and be out of the theatre as his blow brought confusion raining down. His heart pounded, calculating the right moment. He needed Mark to see him. It could not be anonymous. Boyd had to see who had decreed his destiny. Terry moved his head, coughed, leaned forward, laughed out loud when everyone else was silent, anything to attract Mark's attention. It did not work. The bastard was talking as if he was invisible, as if Terry was the nobody no-one noticed was in the room. 'He's not doing that to me,' Terry said under his breath, and hurled every passionate hateful feeling silently at the stage.

'They help us provide for our families, they make us feel good about ourselves, they make our lives more interesting and now, thanks to your support, they make our homes more beautiful. They embody the spirit that makes a house a home. They show we care about ourselves and others. They are our household gods. Tonight we finally celebrate them and acknowledge their beneficent power.'

Lucy knew the moment had come. Her hand lay in her lap, the gun nestled in the folds of her skirt. Her mind was willing her hand to keep still, but it was shaking. The gun was an extension of her arm, she reminded herself. She thought of the message from her agent: people would believe she was mad. This was the right thing to do. The moment of truth. She rose. The whole audience stood with her. Everybody leaped to their feet, worshipping their household gods. The appliances on the stage took another bow.

Terry stood up seconds after everyone else. He had not expected this perfect cover. As he rose, his eyes met Mark's for the first time in years. There was a strange familiarity. Terry was momentarily transfixed, drawn into their blue spotlit depths. He snapped out of it. Finally Mark knew his nemesis was before him. He saw Terry's wild eyes in the crowd of clapping people. He was not clapping. Rae, too, saw the hatred burning up gloriously from the third row. They both stood motionless, unable in the tumult to do anything other than acknowledge what was about to happen. I should have known, thought Rae, as in a split second every conversation she had ever had with Terry became hard evidence that this moment had been approaching.

Four rows back Lucy held her gun in both hands, hidden between her legs. She imagined her agent standing beside her, talking in her ear, his hands pressed to her elbows, ready to help lift her arms. She just had to raise the pistol and pull.

Terry wondered if his heart would explode before he could do what he was there for. He was encased by inertia.

Something was stopping him. He could feel the blood vessels pumping on his temples and his shirt lifting with each powerful beat of his heart. He could only trust that his knife was guiding him to the absolutely perfect second. Mark had seen him, Rae knew why he was there, he just needed the brain–body connection to make it all happen. Beating faster and louder until it felt he would be the one to die, Terry's heart finally broke through. The knife flew.

A shot fired. Rae, Mark, Terry and Lucy all stood, frozen for an enduring fraction of a second. The audience erupted around them as if moving in a completely different time scale. Rae turned to Mark. She waited for him to crumple. He looked at Terry in disbelief. Terry's eyes were wide, waiting for the impact. Mark's mind lifted off. They said it sometimes took a while to realise you had been struck a fatal blow, he thought. He felt nothing but a lightness, a blissful knowledge. He turned to Rae, horrified at leaving her. Still no pain. Lucy gripped the chair in front of her. Invisible in the stage lights, she waited for a spot of red to appear. It came and screams, panic, noise and time all crashed back.

Holding each other, Rae and Mark looked at Terry. He smiled, leaned forward and slumped over the now empty seat in front of him as the bullet burst out from his right shoulder, splattering blood as it arched its way to the floor.

Rae turned back to Mark. He was not falling, not collapsing in her arms. She let go and looked at him. There were no holes and no blood. To Mark's right a bewildered breadmaker stumbled and screamed, shocked to see the handle of a knife sticking out of her casing. Still in character, she smiled when she realised only her outfit and not her flesh had been penetrated.

Rae and Mark grasped each other in thankful relief.

'Oh thank God,' Rae cried, kissing Mark hard on the lips and then the cheeks, his forehead, his chin. She had to feel every part of his beautiful living skin on her lips.

'To hell with lipstick marks,' he whispered and kissed Rae on the lips again. The words made her pull back in horror.

'Oh no, I forgot. You must understand. I thought it was for the best.'

Mark looked puzzled. Rae was talking as if she herself had fired the shot.

'Please, we're evacuating the building.' The stage manager attempted to move Mark and Rae off the stage. The house lights were up, the theatre was deserted apart from Terry lying over the second row seat and Lucy standing, still trying to work out what had happened.

'Mark, you must wash your face. Wash it now!' Rae sounded desperate.

'Rae, it's OK, I don't care if I've got lipstick. Shit, I nearly died.' It was hot under those lights. Mark's face was feeling itchy. He rubbed it.

'My face, it's…I think I'm having an allergic reaction.' The itch was beginning to really hurt. He rubbed his face again but felt no relief. It was burning, becoming more intense. It was agony.

Dr Lobos had done her work brilliantly. The substance in Mark's moisturiser had reacted with Rae's lipstick, and acid was now burning into his face. He screamed and fell to his knees. The crew left backstage turned and gasped as Mark cried out in pain. Blood was pouring onto the floor.

'Someone, a doctor, quick,' Rae shouted. 'Quick!' she shrieked, torn apart by the agonising screams of the man next to her. Screams which she had caused.

Mark slumped to the ground. He looked up at Rae, confused by the searing pain. Perhaps he had been shot, perhaps this was his entry into hell. He saw the wild panic on Rae's eyes. Then blood ran into his eyes and he could just hear screaming, unsure if it was his or Rae's. The red blur turned to black as the screaming retreated further and further away.

When Mark came to, he was sitting in complete darkness.
'I'm blind,' he thought and then a winged Van Gogh toaster
flew into view. He saw it clearly and he realised he could smell
something. It was familiar, an acrid smoke he had smelled
before. It was the smoke from the teepee on *Assertion: the Path
to the Head of the Herd.* Brian, the course facilitator, popped
up out of the toaster.

'Where am I?' Mark asked.

'That you know. It's more a question of what are you?'

'The most beautiful man in the world.'

'Really, after acid has burned into your face?'

Mark was stumped. The pain had been acid? An RW 3000
fell and landed with a thud. The freezer door opened and a
blob of ice-cream was hurled towards him, and formed itself
into Rae. She fell to her knees.

'Mark, I'm sorry. I wanted you to escape your looks. They
were destroying us, they were destroying you. I did it.'

Having experienced this sort of thing before, Mark calmly accepted the absurdity around him, but what was Rae saying? He remembered the pain and suddenly he was back at the theatre. Rae's lips bounced off his face as she kissed him. Each time they touched his skin there was an explosion.

'Your lipstick?'

'It combined with your moisturiser to form an acid to burn into your skin.'

Mark was incredulous. The woman he loved had tried to ruin his greatest asset, the thing that had created their wonderful life.

'Mark, look inside yourself. See your real beauty. Then, perhaps, you can understand and... forgive.' The final word faded into silence as the ice-cream Rae melted into a pool of milky pink liquid and dribbled away.

Everything was black once more. How could Rae do something so crazy? How could she hurt him like that? He fumbled for some form of understanding, some clue. Why had she not said something? Suddenly, he was surrounded with images of Rae: shouting, storming, crying, begging, cajoling. The faces multiplied and moved closer to him. Each one replayed a conversation he and Rae had gone through. He felt a peevish annoyance at having his rhetorical question answered so forcefully.

He brought his hand up to his face. It felt strange: rough bits, wet bits, blisters. Some skin came off in his hand. He dared not ask what he looked like. He dared not even think it for fear of being answered.

He sat still, emptying his mind. Once calmed, he tried to think logically. He was disfigured, but he was in the teepee. This was where he had created his face. He could fix it here too. As the thought entered his mind his face appeared before him. There were burn marks on his cheeks, forehead, nose and chin. His lips seemed to be intact, but he remembered Rae kissing him. The head before him shook itself and answered his unspoken question. 'Thank God for lipsalve or we'd be in real trouble.'

Mark set to work on his face. As before, his fingers moved the skin, trying to smooth over the scars. It was hard work. It had been difficult before, but this time he was exhausted. He pushed and scraped at the scars, blending them until the perfect skin underneath began to reappear. If he stopped for just a second, the scarring would return and he had to start over. Every time he moved to a new area of his face, the previous one regressed. It was a never-ending task. His mind wandered to thoughts of Rae. She must have been desperate to do this. He went over their rows and recognised the pain that had been in her voice. He had mistaken her agony for whining. He saw her holding out little Brett and her remembered words, 'It's his turn now.' He looked at little Brett who grew fast and became Brett Josco. 'Mark, you must drop this beauty shit. You gotta escape.'

The word 'beauty' brought his mind back to the task in hand. He looked at his face again. He had lost concentration for a moment and all his hard work had vanished. He started again with renewed force, but it seemed tougher than ever. The face was becoming stone. He pushed himself, but there was something lacking. He was too drained. There was not the willpower to carry it through. In desperation he gripped the head under his arm and used all his might to try to move the skin, knowing he would fail. It was like granite. He stopped.

The head moved itself in front of him as he sat panting with exhaustion. It turned from side to side, looking at Mark all the while as if admiring itself in a mirror. It smiled, pleased and satisfied.

'Healing nicely,' it said.

'You're scarred for life,' Mark answered.

'That's right, scarred...for life.'

'I can get surgery, it will heal.'

'It's not the outside that needs healing,' the head said, 'the truth is...'

The head waited for Mark to fill in the blank.

'The truth is...' the head tried again.

'The truth is my beauty was everything.'

The head laughed, 'In that case, you've got nothing... unless you take a look inside.'

It lunged at his face and forced a kiss. Mark was repulsed. The blistered wet flesh was sucking away at his lips. He felt its tongue force its way into his mouth and grab his tongue. It pulled back, taking his tongue and his whole body right into its mouth. It swallowed him. Inside he saw a frame: it was the reverse side of the Double Day mirror. He saw himself standing in his bathroom looking into it. He was scarred, but the scars had healed. His features were still strong but nothing more than a reminder of his former glory.

In the mirror Rae came up and smiled through the glass. Then she picked up little Brett and put him in his father's arms. His face lit up as soon as his skin touched his father's and he chuckled with delight. The three of them looked through the mirror at Mark, all touching each other, running their fingers over each other's faces, enjoying the sensation. They were joined by Big Brett; he kissed them all and looked through the mirror at Mark. Felicity came up and waved a piece of paper. It wafted through the mirror to him. He grabbed it. It was a piece of market research saying that

85 per cent of respondents thought market research merited further research to see if it was actually worthwhile. JayJo appeared, dressed in jeans and a T-shirt. Monica, Greg, George, Julius, the twins were there. Pergone walked in, raised her eyebrow and shook her head gently. She moved over to let Nathalia look in. Soon everyone he had ever known was crowded into his bathroom. Bob Jervis from Glocorp, the old Vantex CEO, Lorraine from the course, Nigel from the Sydney ad agency, William. The whole world was on the other side of the mirror, waiting for him. He suddenly felt very lonely; he longed to join them. He stretched out a hand to the mirror.

'What about me?' a voice cried from behind him. It was the head with his old perfect face, all wounds vanished, all wrinkles gone. His heart leaped and he picked up the head. He really had been astonishing, he thought. He knew at that moment just how much he had been in love with this perfect vision. He felt pride in having created it. He alone had made the face which had transformed the world. He smiled, thrilled to see its familiar beauty. He looked back at the mirror. Everyone was still there but they were getting bored. The children were restless. Monica was looking at her watch. He raised the head to his lips, kissed it gently on the forehead and dropped it on the ground.

The sound of it smashing woke him up.

When he opened his eyes, Rae was sitting by the bed, holding his hand. She saw his eyes move and leaped up.

'Mark, I'm sorry.' It was obviously not the first time she had said that to him at the bedside. He said nothing, just looked at her, the woman who had scarred him for life. She was crushed by the intensity of his glare.

'Oh God, I'm sorry,' she sobbed again and ran from the

room. Mark lay alone in the flower-festooned private ward. He manoeuvred himself to sit upright. Tulip petals surrounded the base of the vase next to his bed, dusted with lumpy pollen from the stamens. The water was murky. Picking up one of the petals, he rolled it between his fingers, unsure what he should be doing or thinking. He could not tell if this was part of the plan. It had been a while since he had even thought of the plan. For the last few years, everything had gone so well there did not seem to be the need for one anymore. Perhaps the plan was complete and he needed a new one. The petal between his fingers became moist and crushed. He let it roll open.

'Rae,' he croaked and then cleared his throat.

'Rae,' he said again, as loudly as his bandaged head would permit, 'we need to talk.' She edged sheepishly into the room. She had been standing in the door.

'What is it with you and ruining men in public?'

Rae looked puzzled.

'First Big Fucker at the conference and now me.'

'That's not the same.'

'Isn't it? We both stood between you and what you thought was right and you went for total public annihilation.'

'Mark I did it for you...'

'... Thanks.'

'For all of us. Our lives, our home—they were falling apart.'

'So it was better that my face should?'

Beneath his bandages, his jaw was set hard. Rae was horrified—had what she had done changed nothing? Despite all that had happened it was still about his face. His looks were still everything. It was not as if she did not have valid reasons. There had been no other way. Her frustration turned to anger. He should thank her for having had the guts to go through with it, for doing what was necessary. She answered honestly.

'Yes Mark, it was. I was losing you and you were certainly losing me. I had a choice—us, or your looks. We couldn't have both. I chose us.'

Mark closed his eyes. He remembered the vision he'd had of all the times they had talked and argued about his obsession. He recalled the looks of frustration and desperation that increasingly shone in her eyes, but he had never seen resignation. She had never shrugged her shoulders and turned away. Rae had never given up. He could not deny she had tried a more rational way. He opened his eyes.

'I just feel so ordinary. You've taken away the one thing that made me special.'

'That is so untrue! I'll show you how special you are.'

She left the room and came back with a pair of scissors. Cutting a bandage, she began to remove the covering from Mark's face, winding it round and round until eventually he could feel the fresh hospital air on his skin. She took a mirror from beside the bed and held it in front of him. Mark closed his eyes, too haunted by the image of the ravaged face to look.

'Open your eyes, Mark, open your eyes to the truth.'

He opened them and looked at the vision in front of him. His face was scarred, there was no denying it, but the scars had already healed. They were not angry red blemishes, but distinguished marks. He looked into his eyes—crystal clear, they drew him in. They were the eyes he had always seen and recognised, the ones that had always told him he was the same person. He saw tears forming. He had never seen tears well up in his own eyes before. It made him smile, a beautiful smile. It was him and he loved it.

'Guess I've done it again.' He turned his dazzling smile to Rae and returned to the mirror for a closer inspection. The acid had done nothing to get rid of the wrinkles round his eyes, but they were the evidence of countless carefree smiles, and he quite liked them. His irises were still clear, not a cloud in the sky of his deep blue beauties. His cheeks retained their firm clear definition, the scars just seemed to accentuate their shapeliness. The marks across his forehead seemed random, but on one he could just make out the shape of Rae's upper lip.

'At least,' he said, pointing at it, 'I'll always have a reminder of your tough love.'

Over the course of the day, Rae explained to Mark what had happened in the theatre.

'Terry and Lucy both tried to kill you—and foiled each other. Terry threw a knife, but Lucy misfired her gun and hit Terry's shoulder. His knife missed its aim and plunged into the breadmaker's costume. They've both been arrested, but it looks like they're going to be committed to psychiatric care. Monica and Greg are fine. He's still processing not being George's blood father, but they seem to be happy together. Monica's making more of a parental effort. She's even allowed the kids to call her Mom.

'The rest of the world is still in shock. You're up there with Princess Di in the flower stakes. Every patient in this hospital and three other hospitals in New York has serious bouquets by the bed thanks to you. Sales are up again—sympathy buying. *KitchenArt, the Musical!* is sold out for the next three years. Three people have been rushed to hospital with burns to their faces. One claimed it happened spontaneously—a psychic connection because you're long-lost twins;

the other two did it to themselves out of sympathy...Are you sure you're OK? Oh God, I smeared acid on your face.'

'I'm working on it. You'll have to put up with a few bitter and twisted lines for a while.'

'That's fine.'

'Does anyone know what you did?'

'No-one could work it out. They were too busy concentrating on your face to notice what I was doing.'

'As per...the evidence: the cream, the lipstick?'

'Safely disposed of...how did you know?'

'I was back in the *Assertion* teepee. I saw everything,' he smiled.

'Did Brian pay you a visit?'

'And a few others. I got to see what I was doing to us. I don't think I ever would have noticed, if not for you. Still, your solution was a bit drastic.'

'I was desperate, it seemed logical at the time. So are you out for revenge?'

'You will have to submit to my kisses whenever and wherever I demand—and you'll just have to hope they don't burn.'

She submitted to a few on the spot.

This tender scene was interrupted by Felicity. She had heard Mark had woken and was ready with press releases.

'Mark, good to have you back, you look...amazing.' She had intended to talk PR furiously to distract herself from his ravaged face. Instead she was taken aback. He looked so distinguished, like a war hero. Professional to her pedicured toes, she came up with an improved pitch on the spot.

'This is marvellous. It's a whole new image. I see statesman, solid gold opinions, deference. I'll tee up an honorary doctorate from Harvard. Now, a few shots so we can do a teensy bit of research on what your new face says to people. Smile.'

She whipped out a camera before anyone could stop her. As well as being good for research, the snaps would fetch a good price from *Mega*. The thrill of seeing Mark alive and well put her at her creative best.

'The Democrats phoned, wanted to see if you were an American citizen; the Republicans want your position on abortion. Of course you have to be born here to be President, but I think we should go global, maybe the UN.'

'Stop!' shouted Mark. 'We're not doing politics, we're going to do some good in this world. Turn our backs on superficiality. Felicity, come back tomorrow at nine. Rae, get hold of William, please. He'll be camped outside Brett and Chance's home. Monica and Greg may want to give some input and...see if Pergone happens to be available.' His beautiful eyes were ablaze once more. 'I've got a new idea.'

◆

Sheridan Michaels and Vanessa McKillick stomped their feet and pushed their way closer to the gas-fired heaters. New York in February was cold at the best of times, but standing on top of the Boyd–Whyte Enterprises building was even colder. The wind-chill factor did not bear considering.

'He really does push it with these damn launches.' Sheridan felt he was too old to be traipsing up skyscrapers for media events. 'As usual, not a clue as to what it's about. It better be pretty exciting.'

Vanessa was bored with his whining. A Boyd media call was a major event and Sheridan knew it. He was just trying to hide his own excitement. 'Look, there's Fred Schmidt.' She waved at him and dragged Sheridan over with her to chat. As the editor of *Appliance Review*, Fred was now a major media player. Thanks to KitchenArt, the once humble trade journal was now a large-circulation general-interest magazine and required reading in art circles.

'Quite a reunion isn't it?' Schmidt said.

'Come on Fred, what do you know?'

'Nothing, I swear, other than a new departure. I pestered Felicity, but all she would say was everything would be "made clear" today.'

The cloudless blue sky and low sun made the city sparkle but drove everyone closer to the heaters. Mark did not keep them waiting. His new distinguished face and his bold refusal to have reconstructive surgery were considered an inspiration. (Fifty-two per cent of those polled backed an amendment to the Constitution allowing Mark to stand for president.) A panicked Institute of Cosmetic Surgeons had offered him unlimited free operations. His insistence on not altering his face had caused a slump in business. Facelifts, even in LA, were being cancelled every week.

Mark tapped the microphone confidently and began his speech.

'It's freezing so I'll be brief. As you may realise we're here so I can launch an exciting new departure for Boyd–Whyte Enterprises. It's no secret that my face has been altered. The word disfigured has been used, but I reject those negative connotations. My changed face has liberated me. I was trapped more than anyone can imagine in the prison of looks, judging myself, my worth and value entirely on appearance because that's what the world expected. I don't blame the world, I led by example. My looks got me where I wanted to go and then trapped me there.'

Sheridan raised his eyebrow at Vanessa. 'I didn't trek up here just so Mark Boyd could share. Where's the goods?'

Mark continued.

'I want everyone to experience that liberation. We are all trapped by appearances. Every year we spend millions on cosmetic surgery because some people think we should look younger or more beautiful. It's time to end all that. It's time we concentrated on what is inside. Things need to *be* good rather than look good.'

Not only Sheridan was getting restless now. This was all very lovely, but they wanted a new product. Instead, they were getting a political speech. They were worried that they might be in for a campaign launch.

'I'd like to introduce someone who knows as well as I do that beauty can be a trap. Please welcome the official spokesperson for our new enterprise, Pergone.'

Pergone stepped out from the warm cover of the building and strode to the platform. She kissed Mark on the cheek and smiled. It was Fred's turn to look surprised now.

'Are they back on—what about Raelene?'

'Don't you read anything other than appliance manuals,' Vanessa tutted. 'Pergone's renounced relationships. She loves being single, having close ties with her friends, and she has three legally contracted sex providers…that's according to *Mega* of course.'

Pergone began her speech.

'Our love of appearance has gone too far. Look at our world. Our girls starve themselves and make themselves sick because they believe they should look thinner. Our boys pump themselves with poisonous chemicals because they think they must have big muscles. It is time we spent as much money on making people feel good as we do on making people look good.

'To that end, I am thrilled to announce the opening of the Mark Boyd Centres for Inner Beauty. These will be clinics, the first one opening right here in New York, where people go to address self-esteem issues. They are centres dedicated to nurturing inner beauty, where anyone can learn to love themself. The centres are non-profit making and will offer counselling programs and some residential care.'

Pergone's speech had become difficult to hear. A helicopter hovering in the distance had moved gradually closer. To the crowd it seemed a strange piece of event mismanagement. They applauded Pergone politely. It was all worthy and every media representative there would enthuse about the fantastic initiative to turn the nation around, but it was a bit dull. Sheridan wanted to feel again that thrill he had experienced at the Getty Centre. He wanted something new, innovative. He wanted appliances.

Mark returned to the microphone. The noise was still getting louder. The helicopter kept coming nearer. Suddenly it appeared behind Mark like a monster rising from a swamp. Vanessa and Fred pushed forward. This was better. This could lead to something. Mark ignored the noise and the gale-force wind which had blown up behind him. The helicopter rose higher to reveal it was lifting something, a huge object covered in a white cloth. This was more like it: bugger inner beauty, the crowd wanted product.

Suddenly Mark's voice boomed out louder than before drowning even the sound of the blades whirring above him. The whole of Manhattan would be able to hear him.

'To ensure funding for these important centres, I am pleased to announce the latest range of KitchenArt. Profits will fund the centres. Ladies and gentlemen, I give you "Inner Beauty".'

Mark reached to one side and pulled the cord that was hanging from the giant object suspended from the helicopter. The white cloth fell neatly to his feet. Vanessa gasped. Sheridan's hands dropped in awe and Fred swore softly as they gazed up transfixed at what had been revealed. A giant crystal-clear food-processor sparkled in the winter sun. Every part was transparent: blades, casing, bowl, cogs—everything picked up the watery light and refracted it across the winter sky. It was dazzling. At its core, completely visible, was the motor, beautiful as a beating heart. So pure, so clear, so simple it made everyone think of their first beloved toy, of the unaffected joy of childhood.

'"Inner Beauty"—the most innovative range of domestic appliances ever. Every component is transparent. The electrics are made of a revolutionary clear ceramic. As you can see, it really is what's inside that counts.'

The crowd gazed up in awe as the giant processor turned and spun, catching the sun. Every angle revealed different light patterns and spectrum displays. They watched longingly as the helicopter set off to present its astonishing cargo to the city. They followed it, walking to the edge of the building, unable to tear their eyes from the beauty. Their hearts reached out as it flew to the Chrysler building, did a lap of honour, and set off to liberate the world from the tyranny of appearances.

'Boy, will this sell!' said Fred Schmidt, and he was right.

one year later

'Now come along everyone, behave, it'll only take a teensy while.' Felicity had been on some troublesome shoots in her time, but this one was impossible. The models were running around screaming. The two girls who were supposed to stand on either side of the group were refusing to separate and instead were holding hands, trying to capture the other models in their powerful arms and hold them fast. The others squealed at the new game. Julius, used to these antics, was hiding behind the nearest pair of adult legs. Little Brett had already been captured and was being bounced from arm to arm. Elizabeth, exposed to the twins for the first time, clutched her fathers' hands and screamed that she wanted to go home.

Felicity smiled weakly at the photographer. She had promised it would be a quick easy shot, but the children were simply uncontrollable. It had seemed a great idea. Get the magazine *Terrific Tots* to pay for Little Brett's second birthday party in return for exclusive pics and, of course, a feature on the new range of children's games being launched by BWE. She looked at the group of adults sitting around watching, none of them lifting a finger to help her. She looked pleadingly at Mark.

'Sorry Felicity, this is your gig. Nothing to do with me.'

Rae beamed and clung to Mark's side. 'I'm just the wee wifey, I do as he says.'

Mark roared with laughter.

Brett and Chance managed to persuade Elizabeth to stay and have fun. It was a tricky time for them. She had been with them for just three months, following a considerable battle for them to adopt. It had only been when the formidable forces of Greg Haddrick and the AMPCGA had been brought into play that Elizabeth became legally theirs. Brett had thought Little Brett's birthday would be a good way to introduce her to other children. They had not counted on the twins.

Julius had now been captured and dragged by the twins to join Brett in prison. They set their eyes on Elizabeth. As one guarded the captives, the other dashed over and grabbed Elizabeth by the legs. She screamed again. Things were getting out of hand.

'Stop!' a weary voice commanded. The twins stood still and the other children fell silent. George looked at his mother, shrugged his shoulders then jumped down off her knee to organise everything, as usual.

Within a minute, Brett was sitting happily smiling at the camera, Elizabeth and the twins were forming a trio of charming innocence and Julius was gurgling happily. The group shot was taken.

George then directed them in individual poses, pair shots

and impromptu play shots. Each time the children obeyed his instructions. The photographer was impressed and wondered if the boy could be hired for other shoots. He had a great eye for composition. It was all over in twenty minutes. Felicity breathed a sigh of relief, tinged with the slight concern that a child as young as George had easily controlled the rabble she could not. His father, however, was not so impressed. Greg had noticed the high levels of excitement and giggling, the excess of energy. It could only mean one thing. He had personally vetted the menu for the party. He knew there were no sugars and no additives. Someone had smuggled them in.

'George, have you been giving out cordial again?'

'No,' he replied, irritated by the false accusation. He nodded at JayJo who was quietly sitting in a corner, trying to look inconspicuous. She looked up as everyone turned to her.

'What, my darlings?'

'Sweets,' Mark replied with a stern look.

'I've no idea…perhaps…oh dear, my dress.' The fringe of JayJo's dress had been made of licorice allsorts to complement the garment's broad stripes of colour. A bright little confection had been attached to each strand. JayJo stood up to demonstrate how wonderfully they swirled as she moved, but sadly they did not. They were all missing.

'I'm so sorry my dears, it won't happen again.'

The parents collectively dreaded handling their children for the next hour. Punishment for the transgression had to be meted out immediately.

'George,' Monica nodded to her son.

'OK, go!' he shouted and a small army ran, toddled and crawled its way to JayJo, pouncing on her and smothering her in kisses of sugar-charged attention. Elizabeth loved it.

'This is fun,' she shouted to her dads. They smiled in proud relief that she was doing so well.

Mark and Rae looked at each other. She kissed him exactly where her lip had once left an imprint on his forehead.

'Tough love,' he whispered and kissed her back. He stopped suddenly. 'I've one more present for the boy. How could I have forgotten?'

He dashed out and came back with a small wrapped box.

'Brett, one more present.'

The torturing of JayJo stopped and the posse made its way to Mark. The twins naturally got there first. They had decided Brett was too little to open his own presents, and so it had been their self-appointed duty to do it for him. They snatched the box and ripped off the paper. Inside the box was a small jar. They were about to open it, but glanced round to check if George was watching. Spotting him looking at them, they handed the jar to Little Brett, who was too young to know what to do with it.

Rae, curious to see this present she knew nothing about, picked Brett up as he held onto the jar. Her expression quickly changed.

'Mark, how could you? He's only a baby...moisturiser, honestly.' Everyone looked aghast. This was a little close to the bone and very peculiar. Perhaps Mark was not quite as well adjusted after his accident as they had thought.

'Just wait...Rae, why don't you open it.'

Rae unscrewed the top while Little Brett held the base. A bright yellow flash streamed out with a screaming noise. They all jumped and Brett squealed with delight.

'Again!' he shouted, demanding a repeat performance. The springy yellow snake was squashed back into the jar and this time Brett opened it himself, waiting until the adults pretended to be off guard. He let it rip and they all shrieked.

'Again.' The snake was brought back for another go.

Rae turned to her husband as the snake shot between them.

'I'm beginning to wish it was moisturiser.'

On the fifth burst of the yellow snake, the phone rang. Celia answered and called for Mark. He returned a few moments later.

'Who was that?' Rae asked.

'Oh,' Mark said vaguely, 'just the director of the Connecticut Centre for Inner Beauty. He had some good news to pass on. I'll tell you later.'

After several minutes of everyone pretending to be taken by surprise by the whistling snake yet again, the twins grabbed it and started playing tug of war. The adults were relieved and no-one moved to stop them. Little Brett sat alone on the floor with the lid of the joke moisturiser. Inside was a mirrored surface. He held it up to his face, looked at his eyes and smiled. He pouted, then smiled again, tilting his head to one side. No-one noticed except George, who watched him intently. Brett realised he had been caught out. He tried his smile on George who stared at him, transfixed for a second, and then moved over and took the lid from him.

'Careful, you could hurt yourself.'

◆

The director of the Connecticut Mark Boyd Centre for Inner Beauty put the phone down and nodded to himself in satisfaction. He buzzed reception and asked them to bring in the new patient. The majority of the long-term patients at the centre were in need of serious therapy. All suffered from what had been termed Boyd Obsessionism, a condition in which people became so obsessed with Mark Boyd they claimed to be his relative or his lover and managed to construct detailed and seemingly accurate memories of the time they had spent with the object of their worship. Mark felt it only fair they should be treated for free in one of his centres. This centre was dedicated to that end.

Treatment was difficult. The patients often became violent in the belief that they were being kept away deliberately from their loved one, or that he was in danger. Others concluded that Mark had rejected them. Their obsession curdled into violent hatred. Often sedation was required before a careful rehabilitation program could begin.

This new patient was an interesting case. The director turned his chair to look out of the window as he waited for her. The gardens were stunning. Vast lawns, immaculate flowerbeds, a long drive, peace and tranquillity. He felt simply being there was therapy in itself. The door opened and he swung round to greet the new arrival, quickly checking her name on her file sitting on his desk.

'Lucy, welcome to our centre. My name is David Mygrave and I'm the director. I want you to know straightaway that no-one here is perfect. We are all learning to deal with life. I myself have overcome drug addiction and studied for and received my psychology degree in prison. I tell you this because there's a lot of hard work ahead of you, and I want you to know everyone here has been through that work and wants to help you.'

David explained to Lucy that hers was a very common dysfunction.

'Many people genuinely believe Mark Boyd has been an integral part of their lives. It's understandable, he's one of the most remarkable figures of our age. Soon, we hope, you'll see this is not true for these people, nor for you.'

Lucy nodded vaguely. All her memories seemed so blurry since she started on the tablets, but she was sure of one thing.

'I did know him. I loved him.'

'Yes, I'm sure that seems totally real to you. And that's why we're here to help.' He walked around the table, beaming, and patted Lucy on the shoulder.

'Now, we're getting straight to work. I've assigned you to a therapy group. It's important to see you're not alone.'

'But my agent...' Lucy sounded hesitant. Mygrave recognised this from her notes. She invented some sort of agent who was selling the book of her imagined life with Mark Boyd. She was going to be a tough one, he thought. He buzzed staff to take her immediately to her group. As soon as she left, he picked up her folder and filed it away. He hated anything cluttering the gorgeously smooth surface of his desk.

Lucy introduced herself to the group and told her Mark Boyd story. It was supposed to help the patients realise that not all their stories could be true. Lucy struggled to work out the order of events. Did he dump her before she became a big star or after? Had he been angry at her book and dropped her? She was sure the book had been published, but she could not remember seeing any copies. It must be a bestseller by now. And her agent, try as she might, she could not remember what he looked like. She did remember Australia, they were together in Australia, she was sure of that.

'Rubbish,' a woman in the circle of listeners screamed, 'lies. You bitch. That's impossible—we were married for twelve years. I'd have known.' The woman leaped from her chair and forced her hands around Lucy's throat. Her body shook under the force of the maniacal fingers. Orderlies rushed forward to pull the assailant off, but she was too strong. Lucy's face began to turn blue. A hypodermic was jabbed into the woman's bottom. She dropped and released Lucy. Falling blissfully into the arms of the guards, she was removed for more medication.

Terry smiled to himself as the newcomer told her tale. These crazy people, he thought. He knew the real story, but (a gossamer net of bliss wafted over him) it really did not matter. It was all so unimportant, it was better to go along with their charade, let them believe you had lost the faith. But he had known Mark, he had been friends with him before he was famous. They had worked together, he and his friend, Mark Boyd.

The facilitator, Lorraine, guided Lucy to a seat. She sat bewildered, still choking, the word 'bitch' ringing in her ears: she'd been called that before but there had been more voices.

'Now, Lucy, everyone, pay attention.' Lorraine tried to bring her back to the present. 'I have some dead good news.' She showed them a copy of the latest *Mega* magazine, with Mark scarred, happy and magnificent on the cover. 'Look, Mark Boyd has been named as the all-time most beautiful man in the world. Isn't that brilliant?'

'Just what he would've wanted,' Terry smiled to himself and nodded. A little dribble of happiness fell through the corner of his mouth.